HEMLOCK HALL

SILVERTHORNE LANE

WISTERIA WAY

Waverly Green

lesser demons
ice dragons

THE SEVEN CIRCLES

THE SHADOW REALMS

IRONWOOD KINGDOM
The Shifting Isles

House Vengeance

Sundry

Waverly Green

MALICE ISLE

THE FALLEN

THRONE OF THE FALLEN

ALSO BY KERRI MANISCALCO

STALKING JACK THE RIPPER

Stalking Jack the Ripper

Hunting Prince Dracula

Escaping from Houdini

Becoming the Dark Prince

Capturing the Devil

KINGDOM OF THE WICKED

Kingdom of the Wicked

Kingdom of the Cursed

Kingdom of the Feared

THRONE OF THE FALLEN

KERRI MANISCALCO

LITTLE, BROWN AND COMPANY
New York | Boston | London

Little, Brown and Company
Hachette Book Group
1290 Avenue of the Americas,
New York, NY 10104

littlebrown.com

First Edition: October 2023

Print book interior design by Taylor Navis
Map by Virginia Allyn
Sword and snake art in Barnes & Noble exclusive edition (ISBN 9780316568920) ©Shutterstock

ISBN 9780316557290 (HC); 9780316571524 (HC signed edition); 9780316572538 (international tpb); 9780316568920 (HC Barnes & Noble exclusive edition); 9780316571494 (HC Barnes & Noble Black Friday signed edition); 9780316571500 (HC Barnes & Noble regular signed edition)

LCCN is available at the Library of Congress

Printing 1, 2023

LSC-C

Printed in the United States of America

For those who can't help falling for the villain and love a sinfully wicked fairy tale, this one is for you.

Gentlemen of virtue are not nearly as nice
As the wickedly sinful men of vice.

Poems for the Wicked, Volume One

THRONE OF THE FALLEN

In a small city called Waverly Green, which is somewhat similar to Regency London but not quite, *a few mortals have seen strange occurrences that cannot be explained. Some with secrets of their own—like Miss Camilla Antonius—have heard whispers of a shadowy nether realm full of vice, where seven demon princes rule over seven deadly courts full of sin. Magic isn't immediately laughed off in Waverly Green, though it's never openly spoken about either. Unless of course one ventures into the illegal dark market, where it's said that the stolen art and artifacts are imbued with mystical powers and the dealers might not actually be human…*

Unbeknownst to Camilla, or anyone in the Green, a curse in that devious realm recently broke, setting one sinfully handsome prince free.

Unlike in a fairy tale, the prince who's now coming for Camilla isn't at all charming. But like all storybook villains, if Camilla isn't careful, this dark prince just might end up capturing her heart.

Unless she succeeds in the impossible and steals his wicked one first…

PROLOGUE
House Envy

SEVERAL DECADES BEFORE

"GODS-DAMNED FAE BASTARD."

The Prince of Envy stared at the emerald feather that had just fallen from the unfolded parchment in his hand, heart thundering from the taunt. The area between his shoulders suddenly burned, the need to summon his wings almost painful.

That prick certainly knew where to hit Envy the hardest.

The spell tattooed across the feather glowed in invitation.

Be ready.

—L.

He took a steadying breath and glanced up, searching his reflection in the gilded mirror across the room, studying himself with the eye of someone who appreciated art, including the fine art of deception.

Outwardly his expression was calm, bored even. The portrait of royal indolence. His nearly black hair was combed perfectly, his cool, arrogant features set into that troublesome half smirk that easily won lovers to his bedchamber.

It was just another pretty deception.

Inside he raged, that emotion blazing so wildly that his brother Wrath, the king of demons, would sense the disturbance from his circle and eventually come sniffing around.

Envy had gotten good at pretending over the years; a necessity to save his court.

He knew what others saw when they looked at him, the mask he'd crafted of a handsome, devil-may-care prince who liked games and riddles. He understood that the well-dressed exterior and disarming dimples he rarely flashed were simply two more weapons in his arsenal. Clever ways to hide the dangerous demon lurking beneath his chiseled façade, the ruthless prince who'd long since lost any sense of morality when it came to accomplishing his goals.

Envy picked up the feather, his thumb brushing the emerald plumage almost in reverence, until that feeling gave way to something darker.

The feather was a reminder of the time his own edges had been more soft than hard, and the note itself was a warning that a new game was beginning.

Be ready. That at least was a challenge Envy intended to win. He'd been waiting for this game to start for more than half a century now, watching his court slide closer toward ruin every year. In being soft, in making that one mistake, Envy had damned them all.

That was a secret that wouldn't remain hidden from his brothers for long, especially if things continued as they were.

Already the signs were clear enough, should anyone look closely. It was apparent in the way Envy's courtiers grew foggy, or that constant half-second delay amid conversation. As if they couldn't recall where they were or who they were speaking with.

Thus far it only lasted for a heartbeat, but it would worsen. Time would see to that.

And Envy knew that the Fae bastard would draw the game out, wait as long as possible to start, just to weaken Envy as much as he could. Envy, like all his brothers, drew his power from provoking his sin. And a court in peril was the envy of no one.

His court's falling would toss their realm into chaos, leave an opening for others—like this devious game master—to try to infiltrate.

If Envy's brothers knew how dire the situation was...well, he'd make sure they'd never find out. Let them think he was playing one more frivolous game, with nothing driving him other than his need to win to inspire envy, to stoke his sin.

They'd expect nothing less after all his careful maneuvering.

Envy stared at his face in the mirror one last time, ensuring that there were no cracks showing, no hint of his true feelings bleeding through his favorite mask, then tucked the feather into his waistcoat and crumpled the note in his fist.

When the time came, Envy would play the game. He'd reclaim what was his, restore his court, and he'd never endanger his circle by becoming intrigued by a mortal again.

Envy tossed the parchment into the fireplace, watching the flames destroy the letter from that cursed prick, vowing to one day see the game master reduced to ash too.

And just like the fire contained within his private study, inside Envy burned.

SEVERAL DECADES LATER

"Oi! Wanna ride the famed one-eyed monster that's painted on my ceiling, darling?"

As Lord Nilar Rhanes stumbled up the dais to the throne, mocking the Prince of Envy's legendary bedchamber art, he became dimly aware that something—aside from the obvious treason he was committing—was very wrong with him.

And yet, try as he might, he didn't exactly care enough to stop his unseemly antics.

"Who wants to see if life truly imitates art?"

Rhanes pointed to the buxom brunette standing nearest.

For the life of him he couldn't recall her name, which also struck him as rather odd. Deep down he felt as if he'd known her for ages and had never leered at her like some degenerate from House Lust, one of their rival courts.

Any peculiarity he felt swiftly vanished.

"You, there!" he shouted, voice booming.

Knees high, he pranced before the glittering throne like a proper fool, his legs seeming to move of their own accord.

"Come sit on my lap, love. I've got a mighty gift for you."

Rhanes grabbed his limp cock, sending the ladies into titters.

"You're a dead man if His Highness finds you up there!" Lord... whoever... called out to him.

Rhanes shook his head, attempting to clear it. He must have had much more demonberry wine than he recalled. Even in his younger years he'd never gotten so pissed that he'd forgotten the names of his friends.

They are his friends, aren't they?

He glanced at the semifamiliar faces of the lords and ladies gathered—a drunken group of twelve, thirteen including himself. Aside from Rhanes, who wore red, they were all dressed in a deep hunter green. The colors and numbers both felt significant somehow and a bit foreboding as he noticed that the hour was nearing twelve.

Midnight.

Flashes from earlier that evening crossed his mind. He was almost certain he hadn't started the night wearing the red suit—it wasn't one of Envy's House colors.

His pulse pounded as words emerged in his fog.

"Same lie Lilac." The phrase was bizarre. He couldn't recall whether he'd heard it before; he must have, though.

Everything in his head was jumbled and wrong. Except...

Something was happening in their court. Something spoken only in whispers, in shadows, then forgotten...but something was missing. Something vital.

Rhanes disregarded his worry almost as quickly as it had appeared, compelled to keep up his mockery as if he were a puppet whose strings were controlled by some unseen force.

"Come here, you little minx." Rhanes thrust his hips, pretending he'd bent the giggling brunette over. "Forget the bedchamber, let's make everyone jealous as you suck me off right here!"

"She can't suck what she can't find, now can she?" someone else heckled.

Rhanes squinted, unsure whether this foggy haze was real or only his imagination. A tall blond male with a razor-sharp smile cut through the crowd.

Recognition slowly filtered in. Alexei. The prince's second-in-command.

If the vampire was here, His Highness was likely nearby...

A flutter of panic stirred in Rhanes's belly before his attention was yanked to the sudden tolling of the clock tower's bells. The witching hour was upon them.

Voices, hundreds of them, began whispering as each stroke of the second hand brought the top of the hour ever closer.

Are those memories? Are they purging at last?

Why had he thought such a ridiculous thing? He struggled to recall the last time he'd drunk from the chalice. Perhaps that would make this end. Whatever *this* was.

Rhanes covered his ears and squeezed his eyes shut as the cacophony grew.

The voices unified and that same odd phrase broke free, loud and clear.

Same lie Lilac. Same lie Lilac. Same lie Lilac. Same lie Lilac.

"Shut up!" he yelled, earning a few more jeers.

Rhanes cracked an eye. Bloody hell. He was drunk as sin. No one else was speaking now.

He staggered up toward the throne, willing to take his chances with angering his prince in favor of stopping the room from spinning. He just needed one moment of stillness, one beat to breathe, to think. If he could only remember…

Everything screeched to a halt the moment he sat.

Each lord and lady crumpled to an unmoving heap on the checkered floor, like chess pieces knocked astray.

A game. That had to be what was happening. The prince would know for certain. And Alexei would find the prince.

Rhanes stiffened, searching for the vampire, but Alexei was nowhere to be seen.

"What the—"

The bells stopped ringing. Midnight had finally come.

Dark smoke suddenly twisted up and around the throne, forcing Rhanes to hold his sleeve to his nose, eyes stinging. He searched out the source and caught sight of himself in a mirror across the chamber, his mouth falling open in horror.

Half the throne was untouched and the other half, the part where he sat, now chained by magic, was engulfed in flames.

He was burning.

Whatever fog had been hovering vanished and reality hit Rhanes hard and fast. He screamed as the very real flames whipped him like a sadistic lover, melting his flesh.

He wanted to save himself, run far from the deadly flames, but for some reason, all he could scream was "SAME LIE LILAC!"

As the blessed darkness of unconsciousness slowly descended, Rhanes could have sworn the prince finally emerged from the shadows, emerald eyes glittering.

A tiny spark of hope lit within him. The prince was stronger, he'd resist the madness before they were all damned. He had to.

"Same lie. Lilac," Rhanes whimpered.

Same lie Lilac. Same lie Lilac. Same lie. Lilac.

The prince stood over him, merely surveying the scene, as if committing it to memory.

With Death hovering seconds away, Rhanes finally gathered the last of his will. "What...does...it...mean?"

"It means the game has finally begun."

Anger flickered in the prince's face before he strode from the chamber.

Soon Rhanes was alone. Or maybe he wasn't...

He closed his eyes, his mind growing dark. Still.

Maybe Prince Envy had never truly been there and maybe he wasn't burning on the Hexed Throne at all.

PART I

The Game Begins

Rules of Conduct

1. No magical persuasion will be used to influence nonplayers who directly relate to your clues.
2. Each player will have three chances to move to the next clue. Failure after the third means disqualification.
3. The punishment for disqualification will be determined by the game master, including but not limited to death.
4. The prize will be tailored to the individual winner. Everyone has something at stake.
5. Players have been personally selected by the game master.

By agreeing to participate in the Game, you hereby bind yourself to its will until a winner is chosen.

Mark the below line with a drop of blood to activate the bonding spell.

Once activated, the Game will keep track of your progress, reporting directly to the King of Chaos.

Good luck.

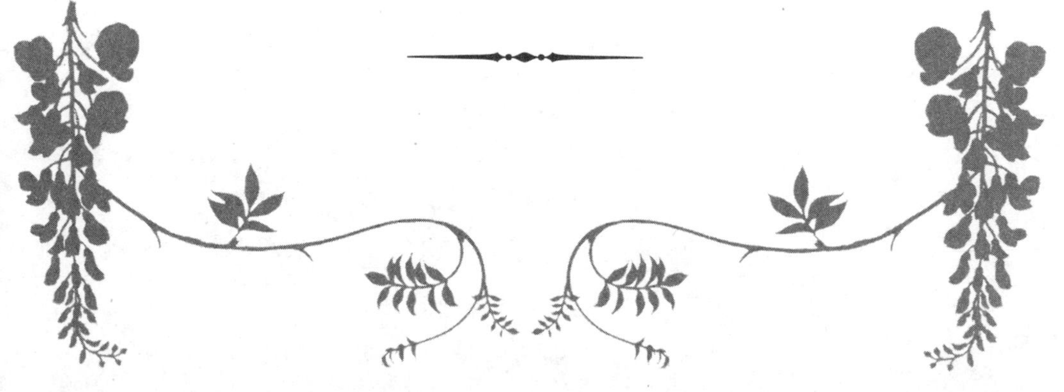

ONE

Miss Camilla Antonius had very little patience for fools, even handsome ones.

And Lord Philip Atticus Vexley—with his golden hair, tanned skin, and roguish grin—was among the finer specimens in both areas. Especially if he thought she'd create *another* forgery for him.

Which, as he swept into the art gallery just as the sun was setting—in his buffed riding boots, burgundy swallowtail jacket, and close-fitting camel breeches—Camilla knew was precisely the reason he'd come.

It was almost closing time, and the secretive glint in Vexley's eyes was most unwelcome; they were not friends or confidants. Nor were they lovers. In fact, if Camilla never saw him again, she'd host a soirée fit for the crown to celebrate her good fortune.

"Working on anything intriguing, Miss Antonius?"

"Just a landscape, Lord Vexley."

It was not the truth, but Vexley didn't deserve to know that. Camilla's art was deeply personal to her, drawn from her mother's warnings, her father's stories, and her own loneliness, which helped her see the world as it truly was.

Her art was often her soul laid bare, a part of her she hesitated to share with just anyone.

Thankfully the easel faced away from the door and Vexley would need to walk around to view it. He rarely put such great effort into anything but his own scandalous reputation.

Camilla pushed the stool back from her easel and quickly abandoned her painting as she moved to the old oak desk that acted as the register *and* a wonderful partition to keep the irksome lord at bay.

"Was there anything I could assist you with, or are you simply admiring the art this evening?"

His attention dipped to her paint-splattered smock. She hadn't removed it upon his arrival, and the slight pressing of his lips indicated that he wished she would.

"Don't play coy, darling. You know why I've come."

"As we've previously discussed, my lord, the debt has been paid. I've even secured a memory stone for you. All you have to do is feed that particular memory to it."

Or so Camilla had been told by the dark-market dealer she'd purchased the alleged magical stone from. She hadn't felt any buzz of magic, though that wasn't exactly a surprise, all things considered. Still, Vexley refused to accept the stone.

He gave Camilla a bemused look as if her denying him something he wanted were more outrageous than a magical stone that could withdraw any memory he chose to give it.

Lord Vexley wasn't quite a dandy, but he certainly spent money like one. He was the firstborn son of a viscount and as such had indulged in only the finest things for the whole of his spoiled thirty years.

Four years prior, after a rather scandalous theater incident that involved not one but two stage actresses and a very public display of drunken affection during what was now called "the intermission of infamy," his father had cut him off from his inheritance and named his brother the heir instead, a bold move that should have shocked all of Waverly Green's elite.

But much to his family's surprise, Vexley's antics hadn't disgraced him in the slightest. If anything, he'd become something of a rapscallion legend around the Green.

Society praised incorruptible morals above all, especially for women. But virtues never held the same appeal as sin. They weren't as thrilling to gossip about over tea, and no matter how prim and proper high society claimed to be, they all loved a good scandal, the more salacious, the better. Nothing in Waverly Green was ever as entertaining as watching someone's fall from grace.

Satire-sheet columnists often followed close on Vexley's heels now, desperate to be the first to report on his next potential scandal. Everyone knew he'd been disinherited, so the source of his income was a growing mystery most of the city wished to solve.

Vexley laughed it off, claiming he was a smart gambler and made wise investments, but people still whispered more nefarious stories about his growing fortune.

Some rumors claimed he'd made a deal with the devil, while others whispered about a bargain he'd struck with the Fae. Camilla alone knew the full truth.

Due to what she called the Great Mistake, *she* now unwittingly funded his extravagant lifestyle and placed herself in danger of being caught by the press.

The last painting Camilla had created and sold for him had almost been discovered as the fraud it was, and if the collector hadn't imbibed too many glasses of claret, then promptly relieved himself on a priceless sculpture, in front of the entire party of lords, ladies, and even a duke, thus causing *quite* the stir as the duchess fainted right onto the foul mess, Camilla's reputation would have been ruined.

A scandal of that magnitude would destroy her hard-won standing as Waverly Green's most sought-after art dealer. And the selfish scoundrel standing before her—with his damnably charming smile and freshly pressed suit—knew it and clearly couldn't care less.

"Honestly, Camilla darling—"

"Miss Antonius," she corrected primly.

Camilla's smile was nearly as tight as the grip on her paintbrush.

Vexley, or Vex the Hex, as she'd taken to calling him in her head, had been blackmailing her for that one horrid mistake she'd made eons ago, and—after they'd struck a bargain for his silence—he was *supposed* to have purged the memory into the rare magical stone after she completed three forgeries to sell for him.

The trouble with scoundrels and blackguards was, they hadn't a modicum of honor.

They were now approaching *six* forgeries, and Camilla needed this to end.

No matter how talented she was, if anyone found out what she'd done, aside from possible arrest and facing the gallows, she'd never sell another painting in Waverly Green. Or any of the surrounding towns or villages in Ironwood Kingdom, for that matter. Not that she ventured outside Waverly Green often.

Ironwood Kingdom was a small island nation that could be traversed by carriage in a handful of days, but everything she knew was in her city and at the country estate two hours north of it. If she were forced to leave Waverly Green, all Camilla's hopes and dreams of having her gallery flourish to keep her father's memory alive would wither and die.

Men like Vexley could thrive on scandal and ending up in the satire sheets, but women—especially of her station—weren't afforded the same status. Camilla needed to walk a fine line, showcasing the art she curated in scandalous ways but never becoming the subject of scrutiny herself.

Through personal experience with her father's most famous painting, Camilla had learned early on that high society loved a bit of drama and a good show—as was evidenced by the soaring popularity of satire sheets and caricatures.

Luckily, for now, society couldn't stop talking about her unique exhibitions. Short of committing a heinous act of violence upon Vexley's person, Camilla would do nearly anything to keep her gallery and name free from the more vicious gossipmongers, who loved nothing more than to tear others down for a passing bit of drawing room entertainment.

She often read the gossip sheets just to remind herself what was at stake, to serve as a constant warning of how carefully she needed to tread as she fought to maintain her glittering reputation in society while also garnering respect as a gallery owner. They'd tolerated her taking over her father's gallery because they'd loved Pierre and his unconventional nature. But she knew the gossips were waiting like carrion vultures, hoping to swoop in and feast.

Camilla's true hope was to one day win people to her gallery through her own paintings alone, and that would never happen if her reputation was in any way sullied.

She stole a quick glance out the window, relieved that no columnists were lurking, waiting to report on Vexley's current whereabouts. She could already imagine the unflattering headlines if they found the Angel of Art and the Devilish Deviant cavorting alone.

"I can no longer help you with that other matter," Camilla said quietly. "If you'd like to commission a custom work," she added before Vexley could continue any paltry attempts at charming her, "I'm more than happy to—"

"*Cannot* and *will not* are extremely different things, Miss Antonius."

She seethed at his arrogant, dismissive tone. As if she were unaware of the difference between the two and he'd just shared earth-shattering news with her.

Vexley raked his ice-blue gaze over her face, taking liberties to admire her lips a bit longer than was considered polite. His attention shifted to her cool silver curls, her delicately upturned nose, and naturally golden skin.

Camilla's deep silver eyes were always what drew a suitor in, though, and at the moment, Lord Vexley was seemingly transfixed by them.

She'd heard rumors that that half-lidded, come-hither look he was giving her now had worked in seducing several widows and even some women who weren't lacking a husband.

Lord Philip Vexley was an unrepentant rake, and rumor had it that his troublesome mouth was quite pleasing when he got someone between his silken sheets. He hadn't visited Camilla's bedchamber, nor would she ever invite him there.

Blackmail, she found, dampened any thoughts of passion.

"Correct me if I'm wrong," he drawled, ignoring the steam Camilla was almost certain billowed out from her ears whenever he adopted that condescending tone. "You aren't *exactly* in a position to turn down the work, are you? What with the information I have about that one little famous painting you sold me. You remember the one, don't you? I still have it."

"Vexley," Camilla warned, glancing around the quiet room.

No columnist had showed up, and since it was the middle of the week and it was near closing, the gallery was blessedly empty. Due to her limited funds, she'd had to dismiss her assistant this morning, a choice that broke her heart. And was now proving even more terrible as the opportunistic scoundrel closed in on her.

"In fact, it's such a fine painting I had to hide it from view," he continued, pressing a hip against the large desk as if leaning in to share a secret. "Lest anyone try to steal it from me."

The famous painting was a forgery, the first and the last she'd ever wanted to create. Two years prior—and nearly eight years to the day after Camilla's mother abandoned them—her father had abruptly taken ill with a mysterious affliction and could no longer work.

Camilla had emptied their coffers in a desperate attempt to save him, and she would do it again. She'd had several physicians visit their home, had even ventured into the forbidden dark market in search of a magical elixir, convinced his illness was not of this realm.

All attempts to battle Death had been in vain.

It had hurt terribly when her mother disappeared, one bright morning the spring before Camilla came of age, but her father's death had truly broken her heart.

Pierre had been fearless, as an artist sharing every part of his soul with his audience, as a father raising Camilla on his favorite tales of magic and adventure, of dark realms far beyond Ironwood Kingdom's shores. Camilla still worried she wasn't living up to all he'd taught her.

After his death, she'd painted the forgery only to raise funds. She'd hated being dishonest, had considered trying anything else, but both their town house and the gallery were set to be wrenched away by debt collectors, even after she'd pawned all her jewels, and the silver, and rented their country estate for barely enough coin to maintain the staff and groundskeeper's salaries. Camilla had had nothing left to sell. Save her art or her body.

Or the one thing she hadn't the heart to pawn. And that sentimentality had come back to haunt her. In more ways than one.

Somehow, though not utterly surprisingly, Vexley had been both cunning and sober enough to spot a minute difference between the forgery and the real painting, and instead of being enraged that she'd attempted to cheat him, had immediately come up with a scheme to profit from her talent. It wasn't honest work he was requesting now.

Nor would he be paying for her services.

Camilla smothered the urge to knee him in the groin and plastered on another smile.

"A gentleman of your breeding is known to stick to his word, sir. We had a bargain and I've more than paid in full. Shall I fetch the memory stone?"

Vexley tossed his head back and laughed, the sound genuine yet somehow grating for that very reason. He found her amusing. Wonderful.

"My darling, what if I were to propose marriage? Would you be more inclined to please your husband then? Surely you'd wish to ensure that we had a comfortable life with a roof over our heads and fine foods in our bellies."

Now it was Camilla's turn to laugh. Marriage. To Vex the Hex. And with it a lifetime of servitude and forever being a cheat and liar. Along with the string of lovers he'd not be discreet about and the whole *ton* thinking she was a plumb fool.

He eyed her speculatively, brows raised, and she realized he hadn't been jesting.

Camilla cleared her throat, searching for the most diplomatic response to soften the blow. The privileged men in their world did not take well to their whims and fancies being denied, and while she might loathe him, she needed to remain in his good graces until he purged that damning memory and set her free.

"Unfortunately, I am not in the market for a husband, my lord. My gallery keeps me quite thoroughly busy and—"

"You'd continue with your gallery, my dear. With your talent and my connections, we could make more gold annually than the Crown."

"We were almost discovered!" she hissed. "There will be no money if we're hanged."

"You worry too much."

Vexley waved off that most important detail as if it were nothing at all.

"And there won't be another scare like that. I hadn't heard that Harrington already possessed that piece. It was easy enough to convince him that his original was the fraud and Walters's was the original, wasn't it? He handed it over to me just as I said he would. And anyway," Vexley went on, "do you really believe anyone would question my wife? If they did, all we'd need to do is update your wardrobe with some low-cut gowns and they'd hardly care what you were saying or selling after that, my dear. I assure you their attention would be thoroughly diverted. Your bosom is quite impressive for someone of your stature. We can certainly work with that, use it to our advantage."

"I—"

Camilla was at a loss. Vexley seemed entirely certain that she'd be pleased to have her mind ignored in favor of her body being ogled to further their scheme.

A scheme she wanted no part in.

If he pressed the issue of marriage, it could become a true problem.

In fact, since they were alone and he was encroaching on her personal space, they were teetering near scandal now.

Camilla wasn't exactly middle-class, even if she operated a business. Her father, eccentric though he might have been, had been high-born and titled. She'd spent nearly all her inheritance trying to save him, so her earnings were critical for maintaining her home and staff. Her father used to say how proud he was of taking care of generations of staff. She did not want to let anyone else down by having to let them go.

All Vexley would need to do was come around to her side of the desk and give the impression that something untoward was happening; then if one columnist spied the action through the window and reported on it, Camilla's life and all she'd worked hard to achieve would be in total ruin.

An icy finger of dread trailed down her spine.

The lord standing before her had no qualms about blackmail and might very well be desperate enough to trap her in marriage. Then she would be his pawn for the rest of her days.

Vexley suddenly reached for her bare hand and brushed a chaste kiss across her knuckles, his cool lips causing a slight shudder of revulsion that he mistook for pleasure. His pupils dilated, mouth quirking upward. He thought *much* too highly of his ability to seduce.

"I see you're overcome by my charms. Let's continue this discussion another time. I'm hosting a lavish dinner party in two nights to show off my most recently acquired treasure; expect an invitation shortly."

Before she could find a reasonable excuse to decline, Vexley turned on his buffed heel and exited the gallery.

The bell tinkling overhead was the only indication he'd truly been there and it hadn't been a wretched nightmare.

He wished to make her Lady Camilla Vexley. God save her.

She pushed that horror from her mind and glanced at the clock. Thankfully it was almost time for her weekly dinner with her best friend, Lady Katherine Edwards, and Camilla's own beloved cat, Bunny, whom Katherine watched while Camilla worked at the gallery.

Kitty had been there during Camilla's darkest hours, a guiding light and advocate for Camilla's place in society who ensured that Camilla attended all the balls and social gatherings, regardless of her financial difficulties. She not only acted as Camilla's chaperone when necessary, she was the truest friend Camilla had ever known, and Camilla was grateful for her in many ways. Without Kitty, Camilla wasn't sure what would have become of her.

To pass the last half hour before closing, Camilla returned to her painting. Getting lost in creation was precisely what she needed to do to forget Vexley's absurd proposal.

She'd been trying to paint a world she saw repeatedly in her dreams, one where winter reigned in all its stark, lethal beauty.

Camilla had just returned to her easel, plucked up her paintbrush, and sat when the bell over the door sounded again. This time she nearly snapped her brush in two.

How dare he come back and coerce her again.

She closed her eyes and prayed for some hidden well of strength to appear and save her from committing murder. At eight and twenty, she was far too young to be either locked in a cell or beheaded for strangling that scheming, arrogant rake right then and there.

"Apologies for any insult it causes," she said without peering out from around her easel, "but I am *not* in the market for a husband, my lord. Please just go."

A beat of silence passed. With any luck, Vexley would be insulted by the bite in her tone and would turn right back around and leave for some faraway city at the edge of the world.

"Well, that's quite a relief, considering I'm in want of a painting, not a wife."

The deep, rumbling voice had Camilla immediately standing up from her stool to see who it belonged to, her lips parting in surprise.

The man who stood just inside the doorway was most decidedly *not* Vexley.

For a moment, Camilla somehow lost the ability to speak as her attention roved over the dark stranger.

This man was tall, his hair black with the slightest hint of brown in the flickering candlelight, and while his frame was lean, she noticed the hardness of his body as he moved farther into the gallery, his clothes tailored to show off the definition.

Not moved but *prowled*.

Camilla innately sensed that she was in the presence of a jaguar—a sleek apex predator one couldn't help but be fascinated by even as it drew close enough to bite.

His eyes, a unique, lovely shade of emerald, glittered as if he knew where her thoughts had traveled and he rather enjoyed the idea of sinking his teeth into her flesh.

Whether he would do so for pleasure or to cause a bit of pain, Camilla couldn't immediately discern. Though if the wicked gleam flaring to life was anything to go by, she'd choose the latter. Which indicated he was *quite* dangerous, yet her heart wasn't pounding from fear as he stalked closer, his gaze lazily taking her in as if he had every right to do so.

This man owned every inch of space around him, including her attention. Camilla found she couldn't have looked away if she'd tried. Not that she was trying very hard.

He wasn't simply handsome, he was *striking*, his face a study of fine contradictions that made her fingers twitch with the urge to paint the hard, chiseled angles of his face, the soft curves of his lips, and those jewel-toned eyes that stood out against his bronze skin, forever capturing that devilish glint on canvas.

His beauty was cold ruthlessness with a regal edge. A polished blade meant to be admired even as it cut you down. He'd make a fine portrait, one Camilla imagined would cause quite the stir among noblewomen.

Her cheeks pinked at what she'd said about marriage, and she hoped it was too dim in the room for him to notice.

A hint of mirth curled the edge of his sensual mouth, indicating that he had indeed picked up on her embarrassment.

If he was a gentleman, he'd let it pass without comment.

"You are Miss Camilla Elise Antonius, I presume."

His knowing her middle name struck her as odd, but when he studied her appearance with quiet intensity once again, she could barely form a clear thought.

No one had ever looked at her with such singular focus before—like she was both the most glorious answer and an exceptionally troubling riddle tied into one.

"Correct, sir. How may I help you?" she asked, finally regaining her wits.

"I came to discuss details of a piece I'd like to commission," he began, his voice like warmed honey melting over her, "but I'm intrigued by you now, Miss Antonius. Is that how you welcome all patrons or just the ones you find incredibly handsome?"

Only the ones I find insufferable, she thought crossly as the spell she'd initially felt broke.

Camilla bit her tongue to prevent herself from outwardly commenting on his arrogance.

She'd been wrong. He was no jaguar, he was a wolf.

Which meant he was just one more cocky aristocratic dog she'd need to rid herself of this evening.

"Are those the specifications?" she asked, nodding to a crisp piece of hunter-green parchment he held.

Her tone was as cool as the autumn air outside, but the gentleman didn't seem at all put off. If anything, a flicker of intrigue ignited in those impenetrable, jewel-like eyes.

He silently held the parchment up for her, not moving from where he stood near her desk.

Camilla hesitated. He was making her come to *him*.

It was either a subtle show that he could be trusted, or a calculated move to exert his will upon her. Given the dangerous curve of his mouth and the cold calculation in his eyes, it had everything to do with power.

Here stood a man who wanted to be in control. Camilla considered kicking him out to put him in his place and his wolfish smile grew wider, his gaze quietly mocking.

"Unlike asking for your hand, you'll find it's a rather simple request." His attention never wavered from hers. "Come. Look for yourself."

Said the wolf pretending to be a sheep.

Camilla highly doubted that *anything* this man wanted would be simple but made her way to him nonetheless. The faster she knew what he desired, the faster she could send his dark, mysterious arse on its way and be rid of him—and his wicked grin—for good.

TWO

Few things pleased the Prince of Envy more than making a strategic move.

Fortunately, as he placed the parchment down and slid it across the old desk, careful to avoid snagging the paper on the scarred wood, today was one such glorious day. He was one step closer to unlocking his second clue.

From what he'd briefly observed of Waverly Green, the females in this realm were taught to please males. He had little doubt that Miss Antonius would have the painting completed by week's end. All he'd need to do was walk in, command the room, and she'd do his bidding.

The woman who now stood across from him narrowed her silver eyes, her full lips turning down as she read. Her embarrassment had quickly given way to annoyance.

The feeling prickled over his skin, not quite the stabbing sensation of fury, but with enough effort, he was certain she'd get there. And as that was his brother Wrath's sin of choice, Envy wanted nothing to do with stoking Camilla's anger.

"See?" he asked, his tone deceptively casual, though internally he was feeling anything but. His heart thudded against his ribs the longer the artist stared at his note. She wasn't reacting the way he'd imagined.

When she finally glanced up, he offered her one of his most sinful smiles.

She arched a brow, less than impressed.

Well, then. He'd get straight to the point.

"As promised, it's a rather simple request, Miss Antonius. I want a painting of a throne. Pristine and dazzling on one side and blazing with flames on the other. If you succeed in this piece, I'll commission another."

The petite artist carefully handed the slip of paper back, then brushed her hands down the front of her work smock as if the paper had grossly offended her.

His gaze sharpened at the unexpected movement, his hand simultaneously flexing toward the emerald-studded dagger he always wore strapped beneath his jacket.

Wrath was the general of war, but Envy could wield a weapon just as easily, and any sudden movements had the warrior in him on high alert, no matter how mundane a potential adversary might seem.

Miss Antonius repeated the motion, and Envy forced himself to relax and really take her in, realizing that—with her shimmering silver hair and unique eyes—there wasn't anything mundane about Camilla's appearance after all.

In fact, as he studied her further, he couldn't help but note that her mouth looked like a heart, and if he'd had a mind to paint her, that was precisely the shape he'd use to capture it on canvas. The gentle sweeps and curves of both the upper and lower lips were wonderfully balanced, her Cupid's bow a study in perfection.

Unaware that she'd caught his attention, Camilla dragged her teeth across her lower lip as she fussed with her clothing.

Those lips were plump, tempting things that caused his gaze to linger and his mind to spin with all sorts of wicked ideas. He'd been so focused on his weakening court, on the game, and on the curse before that, that he hadn't thought of much else.

Temptation and sin fueled him, and he'd neglected both for far too long, it seemed.

His brother Lust would be pleased.

Envy immediately stopped his mind from wandering down roads he refused to travel and watched Camilla cringe slightly at the rough-spun work garment, then untie the strings at her waist, promptly removing the paint-smeared apron and shoving it under the desk.

He gave her a cool look.

"When can you begin work? This is rather time-sensitive, Miss Antonius."

"Apologies, but I must have missed your name, Lord..."

Clever woman, her interrogation was subtle. Based on his fine suit and the elegant, cultured manner in which he spoke, she already knew he was a blueblood.

Little did she know he wasn't human, and he was no mere lord; he was one of the seven ruling Princes of Hell.

In some mortal realms they were known as the Wicked—a name they'd earned after centuries of perfecting that moniker through sinful games and debauchery.

He was playing one such game now—except these stakes were the highest he'd ever played for.

"Lord Ashford Synton. But those who know me best simply call me Syn."

It was a lie, naturally, but it would be the first of many now that he could do so.

"Well, Lord Synton," she said, using his full surname to clearly remind him she was not one of his acquaintances, "I must decline this commission but am happy to consider another."

"Pardon?"

Envy's eyes narrowed. Of all the ways he'd considered this meeting might go, he hadn't once imagined her declining his patronage.

He needed that painting to unlock the next clue.

And, according to the previous clue, which had played out in his throne room, she needed to be the one to create it. *Same lie Lilac* deciphered was *Camilla Elise*. He still hadn't quite figured out why it had to be her, but he'd have an answer to that particular mystery soon enough.

Envy's spies were currently unearthing all they could find on the artist, and whatever secrets she had wouldn't stay hidden from him for long.

By week's end, Envy would know every sin, vice, or virtue she held dear, and then he'd exploit that knowledge for all it was worth. Everyone wanted something, and he'd happily pay Miss Antonius whatever price she required.

Camilla nodded to the paper.

"You'll need to find someone else to paint that for you, my lord."

"That won't do. You're the best, hence my coming to this... establishment."

He glanced around the gallery. The wooden sign outside swinging pleasantly in the breeze proclaimed WISTERIA WAY. It was hand-painted, yet elegant, and utterly charming.

The exterior was a simple stone cottage with lush vines of wisteria hanging over the entry. Something quaint one would imagine in any provincial countryside, if one had brought the countryside into the heart of the vibrant art district and wedged it between two larger, less welcoming buildings.

Inside, it felt more like a darkened chamber where secrets were whispered and clandestine meetings were held.

Dark carpets were layered over broad floorboards, and the walls were papered with a deep hunter-green brocade. Paintings and sketches in every medium hung in gilded frames, while sculptures and statuary stood guard over dark corners.

On a tiny round table in the alcove where she'd been painting by candlelight, multiple cups of used paintbrushes were collected in every size and shape imaginable, the water a swampy array of discarded colors.

Her canvas faced away from the door, leaving him to wonder what she'd been working on. Everything else in the gallery had been meticulously set up, showing the art to its best potential. It was all most intriguing. And not entirely what he'd expected.

Much like the woman standing before him, who, he realized, was studying him as closely as he'd just examined her gallery.

"I've not seen you at any society function nor heard any mention of you before, Lord Synton. Are you visiting?"

A tinge of annoyance hit him. He'd been in this mundane city for nearly two weeks, slowly restoring an old estate that overlooked the whole damned town. Surely she'd heard *some* whispers of his arrival. He managed a tight smile.

"For the time being, I'm staying indefinitely, Miss Antonius."

It was close to the truth. Envy was prepared for anything—perhaps Miss Antonius would take longer than expected to paint the Hexed Throne, or the following clue might keep him here.

Of course, he'd also wanted a base from which he could keep watch—if the game had led him here, other players might soon follow. Or worse, had already arrived.

"Well, then, welcome. I can happily direct you to someone else who can help you."

Envy noticed that her emotions had changed slightly. While he still sensed her annoyance bright and clear as day, he also felt a rising tide: impatience.

He could not fathom anyone feeling put off by his company.

Perhaps he should have listened to his brother's ridiculous scheme to woo Camilla. If he flirted with her, she couldn't possibly dismiss him so thoroughly.

Envy quietly seethed. Most humans had *quite* a different reaction to his kind. Demon princes had a certain dark charisma that attracted lovers; some believed it was due to their power to wield sins. He'd been certain she'd be taken in with little to no effort on his part.

He tried to keep the contempt from his voice.

"Is it a matter of payment?" he asked. "Name your price."

"I assure you it has nothing to do with money, my lord."

Her chin notched up defiantly. Envy knew damn well that she wasn't in any position to turn down work that would pay so handsomely.

"Is there anything else I may help you with, or will you be on your way?" she asked. "I'm afraid you've come at an unfortunate time, as the gallery is closing."

"Perhaps."

Envy debated whether to use a bit of his sin to influence her agitated mood but decided against it. Fae games were tricky. Players couldn't use magic to win. It kept the playing field level, reducing immortals to mere humans. Envy would burn before he'd admit how exciting he usually found that challenge. But these weren't usual circumstances.

For him to move forward in this game, Camilla needed to freely choose to paint the piece.

And she'd need to do so soon.

"Might I inquire as to why you'd turn down my work?" he asked, mindful to keep his tone pleasant.

"Of course." Her smile was as sharp as the dagger hidden on his hip. "I refuse to paint any hexed object. And correct me if I'm wrong, my lord, but the Hexed Throne is one of the most powerful."

Envy appraised her in a new light. "What does a woman of your standing know of hexed objects?"

"Enough to decline getting involved with one."

At last, Miss Antonius came out from behind her desk, sweeping past him toward the door, where she placed her ungloved hand on the crystal knob. Paint speckled her skin like a colorful constellation of freckles.

"Perhaps you should visit the dark market on Silverthorne Lane. They'll know much more about that particular realm of art than I do."

With that she tugged the door open, the bell ringing in finality. The Prince of Envy was being summarily dismissed.

He blinked down at the little hell beast before him, and she smiled even more sweetly back up.

"You may wish to hurry, my lord." She glanced out at the darkening sky, her silver irises like strikes of lightning against the storm clouds. A beautiful portent of doom. "It looks about ready to rain."

A clap of thunder punctuated her warning, and before he knew it, Envy was standing outside and the quaint door was being slammed and locked in his face.

Two beats later, the candles went out, plunging the gallery into complete darkness.

Envy cursed every saint he could think of under his breath as the first plump drops of rain freckled his shoulders. Then he heard the scrape of a boot, only seconds before his companion stepped from the shadows, chuckling darkly.

"You'll just walk right in, was it?" the Prince of Pride asked, his eyes an annoyingly bright silver against the night. His chestnut-brown hair was mussed, giving the impression that a lover had run their hands through it. "Simple as that."

Envy gave his brother a murderous look. "I thought you were waiting at the pub."

"Changed my mind." Pride shrugged. "I wanted entertainment. How does it feel to have your balls handed to you?"

"Not now."

Envy headed across the street toward the nearest awning, wanting to escape the impending storm and his damned brother. His cavalier mask was slipping.

"Now is the perfect time to point out it was a dismal plan," Pride said, strolling beside him, hands shoved deep in his pockets. "Even Lust's idea was better."

"It's Lust's only idea."

"Point? It always works."

Envy gritted his teeth.

"So, Lord Syn." Pride still drawled, but there was a sharper edge to his voice now. "Care to explain how the fuck it's possible for you to lie?"

"Not particularly." Envy wasn't in a giving mood. "Aren't you supposed to be searching for clues to Lucia's whereabouts?" he asked instead. "Perhaps you aren't as heartbroken as you'd like everyone to believe."

It was a low blow, but Envy needed to be left alone before Pride noticed the cracks in his armor. If he could have risked the power needed to summon his wings, he'd have catapulted into the heavens, leaving his brother behind. As it stood, Envy had to remain grounded until he won the gods-damned game and fully restored his magic.

All levity vanished from his brother's face at the mention of his missing consort. Pride's lips pressed together tightly, revealing the ancient scar that still carved a path across his lower lip. For most, Pride pretended to be a drunken rake, obsessed with all that glittered. Frivolous, egotistical. Unconcerned with anything aside from pretty lovers, parties, and baubles.

But Envy, king of masks, knew these were false identities his brother wore. Pride was much more calculating than he let on. His secrets were so vast, even Envy's best spies hadn't unearthed them all yet.

"Don't get pissy because I was right," Pride snapped icily. "I told you to court her first, then ask her to paint the throne for you. Why else would she help a stranger do something so dangerous? Put yourself in her position—would you risk yourself?"

Envy grunted, and Pride studied him more closely.

"Wrath said you're abysmal at strategy, and you're proving him correct."

Envy swallowed a retort. Wrath and Emilia had visited his House of Sin a month or so previously, and he'd narrowly avoided them discovering the slow decline of his court. Thankfully the worst symptoms had been held at bay by a curse that was recently broken.

Pride mistook his silence for quiet contemplation.

"If you're that repulsed by Camilla, perhaps one of our brothers might seduce her in your stead. I'm sure Lust or Gluttony would be willing to help," he said. "Perhaps they'd even team up if she asked them nicely."

"You're not offering," Envy pointed out, watching his brother's face carefully.

Pride glared at him but finally shut up.

Envy glanced back at the gallery, annoyance rocketing through him.

Even in the dreary storm there was something otherworldly about the building, something enchanting. Much like the vexing woman who owned it.

Pretending to court her wouldn't be a hardship. But he had enough to focus on without adding another distraction, and mortal courtship was rife with inane rules and tiresome ballroom dances. He had no patience for promenading around for others to gossip about.

He had a game to win. And he'd wasted enough time.

"I'm quite through with your ego for one night." Envy yanked his House dagger from its sheath, the emerald in its ornate hilt winking in the growing darkness. Princes of Hell couldn't be killed by one another's daggers, but they could be sent right back to their circle of the Underworld, whether the prince wished to travel or not.

"Go home, Pride. Unless you'd like a matching scar on the other side of your face."

"Stubborn prick." Pride held up his hands and stepped back. "Why won't you just ask for help?"

Envy pressed his lips together, remaining silent.

His brother gave him a disgusted look.

"With Camilla's first refusal, you've now got two chances left to unlock the next clue, right?" When Envy still refused to speak, he added, "I hope you know what the hell you're doing."

THREE

"HONESTLY, HAVE YOU considered selling the gallery and moving to the country?" Lady Katherine Edwards asked, handing Camilla a glass of sherry. "Vexley would surely lose interest with time, especially if a buxom theater singer caught his fancy. Again."

"Mm. If only I could be so lucky."

Camilla sipped her drink as she warmed her slippered feet by the crackling fire in Lady Edwards's finely appointed drawing room. A beautiful redhead with dark brown skin who didn't believe in holding her tongue, but who could certainly hold her own in society, Katherine had been Camilla's dearest friend since they both debuted ten years prior.

Katherine had been new to Waverly Green herself then, and she'd bonded with Camilla immediately over their both being outsiders of a sort. Even after she'd married, Katherine had kept their weekly dinner plans, becoming like a sister over the years, someone Camilla confided almost all her fears in.

With a few exceptions…

While Katherine might be Camilla's dearest friend, even she didn't know the full truth behind Vexley's proposal.

"Well, if he's hell-bent on courting you, why not consider his offer?" Katherine asked, settling back into her velvet chair as Camilla took a generous sip of her sherry to drown out the absurd idea. "He is the son of a viscount. Grandson to an earl."

The door creaked open as a large gray-and-white feline nosed its way in.

"Bunny!" Camilla immediately brightened, and Katherine snorted.

"I had a carriage sent for her earlier. I know how lonely she gets when you're working."

"You're looking as regal as ever," Camilla said lovingly to her cat, who gave her a once-over, then sat and began washing her long, beautiful fur.

"Anyway," Kitty said, "back to the matter at hand. Why not Vexley? He's from good stock."

"He is the *disgraced* son and a notorious scoundrel. Satire sheets have now dubbed him 'the Golden-Tongued Deviant,' for heaven's sake, Kitty. Did you not see that last caricature of him? *Lewd* would be too mild a term for it. It was so explicit I heard that three carriages collided outside the storefront where the illustration was displayed last week."

"And *I* heard that seven new lovers visited his bedchamber because of that very satire sheet," Katherine volleyed back. "I also have it on good authority that the moniker is *quite* fitting. And it has nothing to do with his scintillating conversational skills or lack thereof."

Outside, the light rain that had begun earlier turned into a menacing storm, the howling winds now whipping tree branches against the windows like great demonic beasts as the two women cozied up to the fire with their glasses of sherry.

Like clockwork, after dinner Lord Edwards had gone off to his gentlemen's club, affording the women time to drink and laugh like they used to before he and Katherine married three Seasons prior. Rumor had it that he went often to stave off frustrations over not yet producing an heir.

It was a subject Kitty didn't like to speak about, though Camilla knew why and kept her secret, just as Kitty had kept so many of Camilla's.

"I cannot even fathom Vexley seriously considering marriage," Camilla mused. "Seven new lovers in as many nights is appalling, even for Vexley."

"Now, darling, I never said seven nights. Rumor has it he took part in his very own bacchanal and not one lady went away disappointed."

"Of course." Camilla exhaled loudly. "A gentleman ought to only indulge in vice when purchasing art—as to spend copious amounts of coin on it, most especially in *my* gallery—and then be virtuous in his marriage. On that principle alone I'd never marry Vexley."

Her friend snorted. "Oh, darling, no. There's a reason people say reformed rakes make the very best husbands. You want a wicked man in the bedroom. The wickeder the better, in fact. If anything, you ought to thank Vexley for his recent escapades. At least you know he's well seasoned and has stamina."

"'Well seasoned,'" Camilla repeated with a smile and a slight shake of her head. "It's hard to tell whether you're describing a man or the perfect cut of meat."

"Some would argue that that's precisely what rakes are. If you're lucky, you'll find yourself a prime piece of filet to sink your teeth into."

Katherine pretended to take a big bite.

"Kitty!" Camilla laughed. "That's horrid."

"Teasing aside, if you recall, William had quite the reputation before we wed, and I have no complaints."

She sipped her sherry, eyeing Camilla over the glass.

Camilla stayed mulishly silent.

"Vexley might be crass and vulgar, but I know several women who've complained that their husbands are selfish lovers, never concerned with ensuring that their wives are equally satisfied. Is that not a virtue?"

"Katherine," Camilla sighed. "Be serious. Virtue and Vexley are as compatible as oil and water."

"You just need to find yourself a virile man with questionable morals and bed him whenever the mood strikes you."

As if anything could be that simple for a woman in this world.

"Since Vexley is clearly not to your liking," Katherine finally continued, "have you come across any other potential prospects for a loyal companion?"

Camilla cringed. *A loyal companion* was what Kitty insisted upon calling the object of her search for a discreet lover for Camilla, an endeavor Camilla heartily disapproved of.

Aside from a few heated kisses, some heavy petting, and a clandestine meeting with an infamous hunter that introduced her to her first orgasm, Camilla had little real-world experience, living off the details told to her by her married friend. After seeing the pain of her father's heartbreak when her mother left, Camilla rejected the idea of marriage.

She'd never seriously considered Kitty's idea, though she still desired a man's touch. Katherine not only knew this but often tried to play matchmaker, much to Camilla's amusement and horror. Once her mind was set, Katherine wouldn't be deterred.

Had Katherine been in the gallery tonight, she would have thought Lord Synton would do just fine for Camilla's *loyal companion,* thanks to the sheer dominance that seemed to radiate in the space around him. He was a man who knew what he wanted and went after it.

Synton had walked in and practically laid claim to the gallery with just one arrogant glance, owning everything, including Camilla's good sense.

Irksome though that trait might have been during the day, Katherine would claim it was a desirable attribute at night in the bedchamber, especially if he'd made it his mission to own Camilla's body with that same level of authority.

"Your silence leads me to believe you *have* found someone interesting."

"No," Camilla lied. "Not at all."

Unbidden, and not for the first time that evening, her thoughts turned to a mesmerizing pair of emerald eyes and a sensual mouth that had boasted a *very* devilish grin earlier.

On the carriage ride to her friend's house, while the rain lazily drummed its fingers over the roof, Camilla had rested her head against the cushioned wall, closed her eyes, and somehow found herself imagining Lord Synton sitting next to her on the bench, slowly tugging her close, his fingers drifting along her arms, exploring the tiny swath of skin exposed where her gloves and gown diverged as if it held the answer to each mystery in the universe.

He'd lock those emerald eyes on her, watching as he leaned in slowly, affording her time to stop his pursuit, before gently running his lips along the sensitive skin of her neck in a whisper-soft kiss. When her breath hitched from the sensation, he'd work his way along the curve of her shoulder, then down along her décolletage.

His mouth becoming bolder as each expert flicking of his tongue or gentle scrape of his teeth caused a bolt of heat to sear through her.

When she was practically panting, only then would his singular focus fix on her bodice, as he carefully pulled at each lace, undoing them with maddening precision. And then he'd discover one of the most scandalous secrets for a spinster: her love for lingerie, garments that made her feel beautiful, pieces that she acquired quietly from the modiste that were delicate and soft and feminine as they hugged her curves.

Camilla had trailed her own fingers from the bench to her lap, drawing her skirts up, the rustle of the silk its own forbidden music against the rumble of the carriage's wheels. Slowly she'd begun stroking the sensitive skin above her lace-edged stocking, inching ever closer to the growing heat between her legs.

She had touched herself in the carriage while envisioning *his* fingers between her thighs, working her body until the coachman rapped at the door, startling her back to her senses and—frustratingly enough—preventing her from achieving her release.

Lord *Syn*ton indeed. He was just a rake she needed to stop fantasizing about. *Especially* after he requested the one thing she would never paint. Anyone interested in a hexed object was to be avoided at all costs. Both her mother and her father had warned her against them—it had been a rare time they'd both been insistent.

Hexed objects weren't quite sentient, but they weren't entirely without thought, either. Camilla knew that the witch who'd created them had done so out of hatred, and through dark magic, granting the objects leave to become more twisted and chaotic as the centuries went on.

According to her father's stories, this meant they could even shift forms—what was once a throne might take on the appearance of a book, or a dagger, or a feather, allowing it to prick or sting or kill for amusement. It might even decide to take over a living creature, inhabiting their form until it grew bored and abandoned the shell of the host.

"Camilla?" Katherine's concerned face came into view. "Darling, should we open a window? You look a bit flushed."

"No, please. It's that last sip of sherry, I think."

Camilla internally cursed Lord Ashford Synton and his seductive, arrogant mouth for distracting her all over again. It was entirely infuriating to at once dislike a man and be attracted to him. She couldn't believe she'd thought of him in that manner.

Though the same couldn't be said about some *other* men she despised. She'd never almost brought herself to climax in the back of a carriage while imagining Vexley.

And Camilla silently vowed never to think of Synton in that way again either.

"Vexley mentioned hosting a party, have you received an invitation?" she asked.

Katherine regarded her for another long moment before finally nodding.

"It was delivered right before you arrived. Please say you're going," she pleaded. "I cannot bear the thought of being there without you."

If Vexley had sent an invitation, Camilla would need to say yes to avoid his ire, no matter how much she wished not to.

Though an idea was beginning to take shape.

If she went to Vexley's home during what would certainly turn into a raucous event, she might be able to locate that first forgery.

Vexley had said he'd hidden it—which meant he was keeping it in a private room no guests would visit during the festivities, giving her an excellent starting point.

While the party was fully underway, Camilla would search until she located it, then set it in the nearest fire before Vex the Hex ever knew what she'd done, thus saving herself from any further attempts at blackmail.

It was risky, but should the plan work, the reward was too great for her to miss taking the opportunity.

There had been desperation in the troublesome lord's words earlier, and Camilla knew that one day soon he'd find a way to force her hand.

"Of course I'll attend." Camilla held up her glass to her friend's and clinked it against hers. "I cannot think of a better way to spend the evening."

"Liar." Katherine laughed and shook her head. "But I'm glad you'll be there. You know how delightfully boisterous those affairs get, especially when Vexley's been drinking."

Camilla did know, and she prayed Vex the Hex wouldn't let her down.

Katherine's face brightened. "Speaking of interesting affairs, have you heard about that new lord who's recently arrived? A Lord Ashford something. Everyone's talking about him."

Camilla swallowed the sudden lump in her throat.

"Oh? I hadn't heard. At least people aren't still whispering about my mother."

Katherine gave her a sad smile. She'd tried to shelter Camilla from the worst of the gossip over the last decade, especially as ruthless mammas did their best to ensure that their daughters married the best men of their Season.

"From what you've told me, Lady Fleur was never a shrinking violet, which is why they still speak of her ten years later," Kitty said, sensing where Camilla's mind wandered. "And she was right that all those doltish mothers just envied your talent. Do you remember what you told me she said?"

Camilla huffed a laugh. "They didn't envy my talent, Kitty. They thought me odd and didn't wish for their sons to court me."

Kitty's smile turned devious. "She said, *They are all fools who seek only to divert attention from their idiotic heirs and their undeniably tiny members.*"

"You must have remembered that story wrong," Camilla said, amused.

"Perhaps I might have embellished. But I think they were worried you'd paint unflattering but horridly accurate nude portraits of their flaccid noble cocks."

Camilla covered her face with her hands, trying to get that imagery from her head.

Before she'd left, her mother—Fleur—used to smile mischievously and tell Camilla she'd send an army of fleas into the bedchambers of the nastiest nobles, ensuring that the insects bit their bottoms so they'd incessantly feel the need to scratch their rumps at the next ball.

The idea of the prim and proper lords and ladies struggling to maintain decorum with rashy backsides gave Camilla a perverse glee. For all her faults, Fleur knew how to make Camilla smile with her wicked sense of humor.

"Has she written?" Katherine asked, her voice quiet now.

Camilla shook her head.

"No. I imagine she's exploring the world the way she always wished to."

Katherine sipped her sherry, giving Camilla a private moment to collect her thoughts. She always felt conflicted when conversations turned to her mother, though it was easiest to recall the confusion and abandonment she'd felt when Fleur left.

Yet, when Camilla was a child, Fleur had been the one to start telling stories almost too fantastical to be real. She'd speak of shadow realms filled with curious creatures. Goddesses, demons, vampires, and shape-shifters. Seven demon princes, each wickeder than the last.

Camilla would curl up on the settee beside her, close her eyes, and dream.

Pierre had listened intently to each story too, and Camilla suspected it was the magical way her mother spoke that had inspired her painter father to turn his brush to the scenes she'd depicted.

At first, Fleur had been enchanted with his art, encouraging him not to worry about his title, to pursue his passion and open the gallery. But as he'd become obsessed with capturing the elusive fables she retold, he'd begun demanding more stories, more descriptions. Fleur grew annoyed, then bored, and then withdrawn.

Looking back, Camilla should have seen the signs. Fleur had become restless, leaving the house nearly every day, never settling when she finally was home.

She'd never told a soul, but her mother had left her one thing: a locket, one last secret she shared with her daughter.

Camilla didn't want to dwell on the past. She felt the loneliness creeping back in, an ache that never fully went away, only quieted with the passage of time.

Nervously, she toyed with the locket, which she still wore every day.

Katherine noticed her friend's familiar gesture. "You're hiding something."

"I met him earlier," she said, drawing the conversation back to less treacherously emotional grounds. "The mysterious new lord."

"You rotten bore!" Kitty's eyes rounded. "Why wasn't that the first bit of news you shared? Was he handsome? Or did his eyes look as if he could burn your soul from your body?"

"Who on earth do you speak to?"

"Live a little, darling. He's either handsome or homely. Though beauty is rather subjective, isn't it?"

Camilla lifted a shoulder casually, then dropped it, not committing to revealing anything.

"There's not much to tell," she said.

"Humor me, then. What were your first impressions?"

"You're impossible," Camilla said teasingly.

"Curious, not impossible. You do know how much I adore learning secrets first."

"Very well. He's tall, arrogant, and probably has a tiny member. I can't imagine why else he'd behave so boorishly. You should have seen the way he walked in, demanding a commission. Men like him are abhorrent. I wouldn't be surprised if he's convinced the sun rises and sets because he wills it to. Forget laws of nature. Lord Synton is God the Creator and don't you dare forget it, peasant."

Kitty's eyes sparkled with barely suppressed mirth.

"I see there's *nothing* to tell at all. Except you're going to fall madly in love with him. Or maybe he would be the perfect *loyal companion*!"

Camilla was going to do no such thing and he would absolutely *not* be her anything. She held her glass up when her friend offered a refill, keeping her convictions to herself.

With luck, the troublesome Lord Synton would never darken her doorstep again.

FOUR

"If you go around biting everyone you fuck here," Envy said between clenched teeth, "rumors are bound to begin, Alexei. Do you think terrorizing the entire city of Waverly Green is conducive to winning the game?"

"No, Your Highness."

The blond vampire delicately dabbed at the corner of his mouth with a black neckerchief, removing the last bit of evidence before the human staff at Envy's newly acquired manor spied the blood. The move was civilized, wildly at odds with the blood dripping down his chin.

"For what it's worth, I didn't *intend* to bite him. I only planned to give him what he'd asked for. A night of passion."

"All the same, keep your fangs and cock to yourself. If you need a snack or a tumble, leave Hemlock Hall. The last thing we need is for any overwrought human to associate our arrival with vampire attacks. Have I made myself clear?"

His second-in-command inclined his head, wisely keeping his mouth shut.

Envy had returned to his manor house to plan his next approach to Miss Antonius, only to find the vampire in the middle of the main corridor, fangs deep in a femoral artery. His human lover's trousers were around his ankles, and he was moaning loudly as Alexei alternated between drinking from his leg and stroking his erection.

Vampire venom was intoxicating for humans, enhancing pleasure tenfold and causing most mortals to quickly lose all sense of reason.

The more powerful the vampire, the more potent their venom. And Alexei—once mortal—had been reborn into the vampire kingdom with the frosty blue eyes of royalty. As such his bite was wildly potent. In fact, a mere lick of his tongue or brush of his fingers could drive a lover mad before they even experienced his venom.

It had been a horrid day and Envy was ready to retire alone to his studio, where he could take out his frustration on a fresh canvas.

Instead, he found himself reprimanding his second as if he were a nursemaid punishing a child.

If they'd been in the Seven Circles, this wouldn't have been an issue. The very realm itself thrived on seduction. Alexei could fuck—and often did—any willing lord, lady, or member of the house.

Even a certain goddess, Alexei's most recent tryst. Envy had to admit the affair had its uses, no matter how much Envy disliked the female involved.

Alexei retreated to the other side of the room, giving Envy time and space to think. That was one good thing about a vampire: they could remain silent and motionless for hours, almost making you forget they were there.

Envy glanced out the tall window to the thick blanket of fog curling around the limestone manor, brooding along with the abysmal weather. Rain thudded against the glass, growing in intensity with his darkening mood.

Pride and Lust had a point—seducing Camilla seemed the clearest route to success. But if he took Miss Antonius to his bed, she would likely want more, crave it—most mortals who found themselves tangled in his sheets were tainted with his sin. They envied anyone who came before and anyone who'd come after. It was why he'd created his cardinal rule—he would spend only one night, ever, with a lover. Never more. His one-night rule had become legendary, along with the hunger of his lovers.

Often this was part of the fun, but with Camilla, it seemed too complicated to begin. Granted, Envy drew his power from provoking envy in others, and fueling his sin was critical now. He needed to store as much power as he could to win the game.

But he hadn't allowed a mortal into his bed in decades, not since the last time had gone so very wrong, and felt reluctant to start again.

If a night of passion was Camilla's price, perhaps he could leave the task to Alexei. It would be less complicated... but surely there was another way.

Envy abruptly flipped open the journal before him, staring down at the lines he'd written, the two clues he'd received over the last month with accompanying notes on how he'd solved them.

The first clue still made his blood boil—a taunt wrapped within a riddle, it had arrived while he'd been visiting House Greed a week after Wrath's queen had taken the throne, nearly a month ago now.

He didn't typically gamble in his brother's House but was feeling petty. When Envy had turned over his cards, he'd realized the game was on. Twelve hunter-green cards, with one lone red card, all blank save for the solid colors.

Envy had been waiting decades and had almost given up hope of the game ever starting. Pulse speeding, his attention had shot to the clock, noting the hour that was almost upon them.

Midnight.

Hunter green. House Envy.

Red: a bull's-eye target, he'd guessed.

Without delay, he'd rushed home to his throne room, arriving right before midnight. And there it had really begun, as his throne burst into flames on one side.

Just as in the painting he now needed Camilla to create.

It took two weeks to track the correct artist down based on the clue. Then he'd spent nearly two more weeks setting up his base in Waverly Green. He wanted to move on to the next clue quickly.

Previous games had anywhere from four to six clues, although none of those games had stakes anywhere close to the ones he faced now. But

that meant Envy could be halfway through already, as long as Camilla agreed to paint the gods-damned throne.

He glanced down at the clues again.

12 green, 1 red = midnight, House Envy, target/next clue
The Hexed Throne
Same Lie Lilac. Anagram
Anagram solved: Camilla Elise

A raven landed outside the window, its beady ebony eyes fixed on him before it shot into the storm drenched sky. It could be a simple bird, or a spy. He did not need a reminder that he wasn't the only player in this game, though he knew each player would have different clues leading to the prize.

That Fae bastard Lennox often chose those he'd wronged at some point to play his games, allowing them a chance to win back whatever he'd taken. The clues, the prize, everything would be tailored to the individual, though clues often overlapped. For example, if another player was in Waverly Green, they might need Camilla to paint them something as well.

Envy slammed the journal shut.

He was in the right place. Now he just needed to convince Camilla to help. He cleared his mind of all but his surroundings, needing to let a new strategy form on its own.

Hemlock Hall was a sprawling manor house located at the top of a rather large hill that overlooked the twinkling city below. In that respect it reminded Envy of his own House of Sin. But that was where the similarities ended.

This study was all dark wood and leather-bound books, with an oversized desk and comfortable high-backed chairs. No vibrant art, no elegant sculptures. Only bland mortal maps, inaccurate and odious in their design.

A slight odor of cigar smoke lingered in the damp air, seeping into the wood after years of indulgence, a hint of the previous owner's favorite

vices, of which it seemed he'd had many. In fact, the lord had recently had to abandon Hemlock Hall altogether after falling on hard times, and had struggled to secure a buyer due to rumors that his lands were cursed. It was the sort of terrible news Envy had been all too happy to hear.

And perhaps those rumors might have been planted by Envy himself in the weeks leading up to his grand offer.

Not that money was a concern for Envy. But the crumbling estate had held so much potential, and he knew the rumors only added to his mystery, ensuring that locals would accept any invitation to come tour the property.

And personal distaste aside, there was no better way for the Prince of Envy to enter mortal society than by hosting a masquerade ball, the likes of which he was certain they'd never seen before.

Envy reached across his desk to pull a bottle of dark whiskey closer, uncorking it and splashing a little into a cut-crystal glass. He swirled it slowly as he considered the game again.

A Fae overlord never went out of his way, and knowing Lennox, Envy suspected the other players would also be drawn to Waverly Green after their first clues. A masquerade might give Envy a chance to discover who the players were, and how many. And if they were all charged to commission Camilla, then Envy needed to be ahead of the pack.

He already had his spies watching her gallery day and night, but he needed to consider other ways he could keep her close.

He finally glanced at Alexei. "Have there been any updates on Camilla's vices? Any temptations we can exploit?"

"No, Your Highness."

A knock sounded at the freshly polished mahogany door, interrupting them.

"Enter," he commanded.

Goodfellow, his butler, swept into the room, bowing politely at the waist. "My lord."

It was sad, really, how easily mortals believed lies. Money, fine clothing, arrogance—with only Envy's word, his solicitor's backing, and

Alexei's agreement, it was far too easy to create a story for the humans here. Envy was a lord who hailed from the southern region of Ironwood Kingdom; his arrival heralded his family's desire to expand their territory and wealth through marriage.

"Did you need something, Goodfellow?"

Goodfellow shot a nervous look toward the vampire.

"Alexei," Envy said, "tend to that matter."

His second inclined his head, then left.

To Envy's knowledge, humans in this realm didn't necessarily believe in vampires but could certainly sense they were prey when near one.

Fear heightened mortal senses, bringing them closer to the animal world before they reasoned their natural survival instincts away as silly.

Whether due to hubris or ego, man was the only creature who often ignored what no other prey did: trust your instincts or suffer the consequences.

"Yes?" Envy asked, drawing Goodfellow's attention away from the vampire as he exited.

"Invitations have all been sent, my lord. No noble family in Waverly Green will want to miss it. Cook has been—"

"Did you send one to Miss Antonius?"

"The artist?" Goodfellow asked.

Envy offered a slight nod.

"Not yet, my lord. But I suppose she's become a society darling despite her rather tragic past, so I'll add her to the list. As I was saying, Cook has—"

"Explain."

"Er, about Cook or..." Goodfellow trailed off at Envy's hard look. "Oh, Miss Antonius. Her mother left right before she debuted, poor thing. Made things proper difficult for the young miss with all those nasty rumors. No mamma wanted their son to court her. She's as good as a spinster now, though the *ton* love her gallery, which has kept her current, I suppose."

Envy considered that a moment. Camilla's mother was gone, she had no marriage prospects...so why had she so thoroughly dismissed him? Envy had made it clear he was titled, and he was obviously handsome. Camilla should have at least attempted to flirt. Unless she'd been waiting for him to do so...

Why was Lust's gods-damned scheme always the correct path to take? Maybe Envy *should* attempt to seduce her next. It was worth trying.

Goodfellow took Envy's quiet pondering as an invitation to continue his report.

"Cook has been given the market requirements, and I've sent the footman out to secure the masks you requested. The gardener has also been instructed on the floral arrangements. Ballroom renovations are underway and should conclude at least two days prior, allowing time for any adjustments Your Lordship might desire."

"What about the blackberries and brown sugar?"

"Taken care of, my lord. Along with the finest bourbon in Waverly Green."

Envy nodded. "Progress on the gallery in the north wing?"

"The portraits have all been unveiled and the sculptures are being cleaned now."

"I trust the hedge maze is also under control."

"Of course. The groundskeeper has the images you rendered and is tending to it."

A bit of the tension Envy had been feeling since Camilla's refusal released. At least something was going his way tonight.

Goodfellow cleared his throat, and Envy fought a sigh.

"Was there something else?"

With a bit more theatrics than was entirely needed, Goodfellow produced an envelope. Crisp, decent ivory stock. Bland and uninspired.

"An invitation has arrived, my lord. From Gretna House."

Envy stared blankly at the butler.

"Pardon me, my lord. Gretna House is Lord Philip Vexley's home. He's a favorite of society, though a bit notorious, if I may speak freely."

For all his pomp, Goodfellow was also a horrible gossip, only too happy to help Envy learn the ins and outs of Waverly Green.

"What makes him notorious?" Envy sipped at his whiskey, curious.

Goodfellow's ruddy face flushed a brighter crimson, signaling that licentiousness must be involved.

"It's rumored he hosts…er, debauched parties, for a select circle of friends, my lord."

Envy schooled his features. *How predictable, and so very human,* he thought.

He might as well have some fun and watch Goodfellow flounder.

"Do guests engage in lewd behavior?"

Goodfellow drew in a sharp breath, then nodded. His eyes sparkled with the need to share this delightful scandal.

"And?" Envy encouraged.

"Oh, well, I've heard that some guests sneak off to the gardens to"—he glanced around as if to make sure no one else had snuck up on them—"kiss."

"Kiss." Envy mentally counted until the urge to stab himself—repeatedly—passed. "Does anyone actually witness this…lewd behavior?"

"Well, I imagine so. Though I haven't heard any specifics."

Envy must not have hidden his annoyance as well as he'd thought; Goodfellow quickly continued.

"That's not saying anything of the art he's collected. Most of it isn't fit for polite company. Not that Lord Vexley concerns himself with that. He's rumored to have an entire private collection of virile-member-shaped implements. He keeps those hidden, else the ladies would faint at dinner. Society looks the other way with Vexley up until a point."

"That point being virile-member-shaped art," Envy deadpanned.

"Indeed, my lord. This one is unsubstantiated, but there's another rumor, that he hosts…demonstrations…once the gentlewomen retire after dinner."

Goodfellow would have an embolism if he ever visited House Lust.

Demons playing with *virile-member-shaped implements* was the daily standard there.

However, at the mention of art, Envy's interest was finally piqued.

"This Vexley is an avid art collector, is he?" Envy asked. Goodfellow nodded. "Is his collection as large as the one here?"

Goodfellow opened his mouth, then snapped it shut, reconsidering.

"I personally haven't seen it, my lord, so I can't speak with any authority on that. But I have heard he visits Silverthorne Lane. And you know what they say about the dark market."

"Enlighten me."

"Well, my lord, almost everyone in the Green believes the dealers aren't exactly... human."

Envy's brows rose a fraction. He hadn't heard this. But his spies would certainly hear from him about missing this detail.

"And what, pray tell, are they instead?"

"They say the dealers there are exiled Fae. Mind you, most who enter are also deep in their cups. Personally, I don't believe in such fairy tales."

Envy stilled. This was very interesting news indeed.

"You're certain this notorious lord visits these... Fae?"

"Aye. His footman told me himself, my lord. Once per week, like clockwork."

"Accept his invitation," Envy said, dismissing the butler with a crisp nod. Maybe he'd found another player after all.

If Goodfellow disapproved of his master's decision, he wisely didn't let it show.

Envy wanted to get a feel for this rake who dealt with Fae, see if his theory was correct.

Goodfellow left to do Envy's bidding.

If there was one truth that ought to be universally accepted, it was this: when sin was involved, no gentleman in this realm or any other could ever hope to compete with a demon.

Most especially a Prince of Hell.

FIVE

CAMILLA FUSSED WITH her skirts as the carriage rattled over the cobbled street and, next to her, Lord Edwards prattled on about a rooster named Peter.

Apparently, Edwards was having newfound trouble with his cock.

Something Camilla prayed wasn't a euphemism.

She met her friend's gaze across the carriage, noting that Lady Katherine had pressed the back of her gloved hand to her lips, likely stifling a giggle. A fact that didn't surprise Camilla in the least. Camilla and Kitty were made of the same twisted material; they simply hid that fact well. Most of the time.

"...which is why, dearest," Edwards said to his wife, "we ought to go to Winterset to oversee the estate as soon as possible. We simply cannot permit Peter to run amok."

If only society felt the same way about Vexley.

"Darling," Katherine soothed, impressively without any hint of mirth in her tone, "we aren't due back to our country house for months. I'm sure the chickens will be fine until summer." She flicked her attention to Camilla. "You will join us again, at least part of the time?"

"Of course."

Warmth suffused Camilla along with gratitude. When she'd had to rent out her family's country estate the past summer, Kitty had made sure Camilla stayed for nearly the entire season with them. And Camilla had never said so aloud, but even if she hadn't been forced to rent out her father's country home, going there after he'd died would have been torturous. She worried she would feel the ghost of his presence wandering the halls, smell the piping-hot chocolate he always made for them to sip despite the summer heat while he painted and told stories of Fae-kissed humans, beholden to the mysterious fairy king.

In some stories the king was cruel, in others he was godlike and benevolent. As she got older Camilla understood that it was all nonsense, but she adored how Pierre loved his legends, even if, by the end, he clung to them too desperately as his grip on reality loosened.

"Perhaps Miss Antonius can paint Peter's likeness."

Kitty heaved a sigh.

Camilla was saved from any further mention of the fowl's foul behavior when the carriage rolled to a stop. She swallowed the sudden lump in her throat, her nerves tingling as the driver came around to open the door and help her down.

They'd arrived at Gretna House, Vexley's home.

A town house on Greenbriar Park, in one of the most exclusive neighborhoods on the east side of the Green.

The building—an off-white stone accented with wrought iron terraces and flowering trees and bushes, which cascaded along its front—was perfectly maintained, matching all the other town houses on the street. A beautiful stone fence separated the tiny front yard from the cobbled avenue.

Camilla exited the carriage with her head held high and stared at the town house, at the lights inside glowing warmly, the merry partygoers unaware of what all this had cost her. It was her illegal dealings that had helped Vexley purchase this house. Here stood a physical manifestation of her crimes, taunting her with its decadence.

Much was at stake for her over these next few hours. Tonight, she'd either steal back her freedom, or she'd be forever trapped in Vex the Hex's web of deceit.

Much too quickly their trio ascended the grand stairs, were divested of their coats and stoles, and were seen to the drawing room to mingle with the guests who'd already arrived.

Someone called out to Lord Edwards, but Camilla was so nervous she barely noticed when he and Katherine shifted course to say their hellos, leaving her to seek punch on her own.

She scanned the small group for Vexley. In the corner, the idiotic but wealthy Lords Walters and Harrington were attempting to entertain the Carrol sisters, two pretty honey-haired women tarnished by rumors that their father's title had been purchased by the success of his gaming hell. She smiled politely at them and a few others but caught no glimpse of Vexley.

Camilla reached the punch and claimed a cup, sipping from it as she scanned the room again. Katherine and William were now speaking with William's best friend, Lord Garrey. A man of thirty who—like most here—was known to grace the satire sheets from time to time.

Garrey remained one of the most eligible men Season after Season, thanks to the fact that he'd one day inherit a dukedom. His wicked smile and boyish charm didn't hurt, though his gambling was hard to overlook, as Camilla reminded Kitty regularly.

Miss Young and Miss Linus were also in attendance. Though Camilla doubted either of their parents knew they'd snuck off to visit Vexley's home. Both women were nearing spinster status but weren't fully on the shelf yet.

Their chaperone, Widow Janelle Badde, raised her glass to Camilla in hello. Camilla had always admired Janelle. She'd married a man three times her age and he'd died shortly after, leaving her a young, happy widow who took full advantage of her status, taking lovers and volunteering to play chaperone for her unmarried friends when the occasion called for it.

Society didn't approve outwardly, but they couldn't disapprove, either. Camilla had just turned back to survey the other half of the room when her gaze landed on *him*.

Lord Ashford Synton in all his commanding, irksome glory.

He stood alone, admiring a painting on the far side of the room, and hadn't noticed her yet, so she took a moment to study him, feeling vaguely annoyed to realize she wasn't the only one doing so. Widow Janelle was practically wetting her lips as her gaze raked over him.

Camilla understood her reaction. The man cut a severe figure, even from across the room, candlelight gilding the sharp planes of his face. With a jolt, Camilla saw what was holding his attention. He was stepping closer to her favorite painting in Vexley's home.

It was a watercolor of a field holding one rustic barn—something she'd imagined in the north, or even in one of her father's tales. It was rich in shades of green and cream, from the mountains in the background, which were a dark hunter, to the long grass in the foreground, a glowing, pale sage.

The painting evoked a sense of peace. The idea of simplicity, of a life lived without secrets, without a societal cage.

What would it be like to run barefoot through that soft grass? To hike her skirts to her knees and not give a damn about whether it was ladylike? Camilla longed to feel the dirt under her feet, to dance in her nightgown under the stars. To live without the rules of others binding her. She was a wild, untamed thing under all the pomp and circumstance.

She wondered what Synton saw, what he felt as he raised his hand, tracing the barn almost in reverence. "He is . . . something, isn't he?"

Camilla started at Widow Janelle's voice. Although she wasn't even looking at Camilla. The woman's gaze practically burned the clothes off Synton's back.

"Do you know his name?" the widow asked hungrily.

Camilla bristled at the question, though her reaction made little sense.

"No, sorry." She quickly diverted her own attention back to the party. "I'm parched. Would you like more punch?"

Widow Janelle made a noncommittal sound. Camilla returned to the nearby refreshments, leaving Janelle to her ogling. Vexley hadn't graced them with his presence yet, indicating he was either already drunk or hoping to make a dramatic entrance. Either way, she might have a few extra moments to explore while everyone was otherwise occupied.

Excited, Camilla stepped away from the table quickly and bumped into someone who'd come to collect a glass of punch too.

"I'm—" Her words faltered as she glanced up. Two piercing emerald eyes stared down at her.

It took another second for her to realize that Lord Synton's two strong hands had steadied her, preventing her from spilling her drink. The coldness in his gaze was at odds with the burning she felt where he gripped her tightly, his long fingers easily fitting around her upper arms.

"How did you get over here so quickly?" she asked.

His mouth quirked up on one side, his expression slowly thawing.

"You saw me but didn't say hello? I'm wounded, Miss Antonius."

Synton's voice was like a deep rumble of thunder in her ear as he finally dropped his hands but didn't step back.

"Perhaps I was getting the lay of the land. A lady must know where it's safe to step," she quipped.

"Yet you're stepping all over my ego."

"Forgive me, my lord. I had no idea you'd be so easily damaged."

He looked her over slowly, one brow arched.

"You attend gatherings here often?"

"I do."

Camilla realized two things simultaneously as the handsome lord's expression shifted from indifference to curiosity—first, that he was as sinfully arresting as she'd pictured earlier when she'd almost given herself an orgasm in a moving conveyance, and second, that Synton must already have heard the rumors about these parties.

Heat flooded her cheeks.

Nothing untoward usually happened here, at least not while she was in attendance. Though couples did sneak off for trysts more than usual, and Vexley was in possession of a few fertility statues that were probably used for the exact purpose people speculated.

She quickly motioned to the still life paintings on the walls, tame by comparison.

"Lord Vexley is an admirer of fine art. I help curate his collection."

"Interesting." He said the word like he meant *repugnant* instead.

Synton's gaze turned shrewd as he looked her over again.

"What brings you here?" she asked to divert his attention. If he assumed she was here for a wild tryst, then she was very intrigued by what he would have to say for himself.

"So you're responsible for most of his pieces? He doesn't...work with anyone else?" Synton asked stiffly, ignoring her question entirely. There was an edge in his tone now, subtle but there. She'd think it hinted at envy, but of what, Vexley's art?

Camilla hid her annoyance.

Answering a question with another question was an excellent diversionary tactic.

She wondered if he was really asking about the dark market, which often intrigued newcomers, but it was neither the time nor the place to discuss that scandalous enterprise.

Silverthorne Lane was an area most in high society pretended didn't exist. She avoided it herself, after her father's obsession with it had grown so intense in his final months.

She hadn't wanted to fuel any of the rumors they'd faced toward the end—society had whispered that her father had fallen in love with a Fae dealer there and had become addicted to the dark magic that could offer a few hours of oblivion.

Camilla knew neither was true.

Her father was obsessed with something far more dangerous.

"Vexley does purchase through me quite often, though I'm only one of many dealers."

An arm slipped around her waist.

"Now, darling, you're much more than an art dealer to me."

"Lord Vexley."

Camilla's spine stiffened at the most unwelcome weight of Vexley's arm on her person.

When she thought it couldn't get worse, the rake's palm shifted lower, cupping her backside.

Camilla seethed from both the uninvited touch and Vex the Hex's bold insinuation that there was more to their relationship. If she needed further proof that she must act tonight and win back her freedom, *this* was her sign. In fact, she prayed she wasn't too late.

She quickly sidestepped, dislodging herself from the embrace without anyone—aside from Synton—noticing the lapse in propriety.

But Synton wasn't looking at her at all. He was coolly staring Vexley down. His expression had turned so frosty with displeasure, for a moment she swore she could see her breath in the air.

"Do you always lay claim to things that don't belong to you, Vexley?"

Camilla's lips parted in shock. Did Synton sound...jealous?

Luckily, Vexley snorted like Synton had told a clever joke, signaling that he'd already helped himself to a few glasses of spirits.

"You must be the newly arrived Synton. I've heard you're quite the collector yourself. Though I doubt yours is as large as mine."

Synton ignored the insinuation, his attention landing squarely on Camilla once again. "I'd love a private tour of your gallery, Miss Antonius, to see your taste. I'm in the market for several pieces for my own gallery at Hemlock Hall."

"Hemlock Hall?" Vexley interrupted, realizing he was being slighted. "That place is a wreck."

"Miss Antonius?" Synton pressed, still not deigning to acknowledge their host.

Camilla understood immediately what Synton was offering. In his own bullheaded, arrogant way. She had no desire to be alone with him in Wisteria Way again, but that circumstance was far preferable to being within pinching distance of Vex the Hex.

"I can make time later this evening or tomorrow at first light."

"Tonight, then."

"Very well, my lord."

Camilla wasn't sure she should be grateful for Synton's interference. It felt a little like hopping from a cast-iron skillet into a blazing fire.

Synton had an agenda of his own, but at least she was choosing which devil to get into bed with. Proverbially speaking, of course.

An image of Synton lying sprawled across dark sheets, bronze skin gleaming, arms folded behind his head, flashed in her mind before she banished it.

"Come now, Synny." Vexley either missed or ignored the anger flickering in Synton's eyes at the nickname. "Camilla shouldn't be traipsing around the art district at indecent hours."

"Miss Antonius has made her decision, and I don't recall inquiring after your uninformed and, frankly, rather dull opinion, Vexley."

Camilla sank her teeth into her lower lip to keep from drawing attention by either gasping or laughing. Synton had well and truly dressed the disgraced lord down in his own home.

A beat later, Vexley's face flushed scarlet, the tips of his ears turning the brightest shade of pink she'd ever seen as his mind caught up with the insult.

Objectively, Vexley was a physically attractive man, but the way his face contorted now made him look demonic.

"How dare—"

A knock came at the drawing room door, quickly followed by the butler.

"Dinner is ready, my lord."

Called to duty, Vexley immediately returned his demeanor to that of the unruffled rake, his mouth hitching high on one side in a lopsided smirk.

"The time to feast has arrived!" he announced, then twisted on his heel, wavering only slightly before offering his arm to Camilla. "Miss Antonius. Friends. Shall we?"

Camilla felt Synton's heavy gaze land on her once again, weighted with disapproval, but she didn't dare to look at him, nor to publicly reject Vexley's theatrical chivalry.

All she had to do was make it through this dinner.

Then, after the more polite crowd had departed and the drinking began in earnest, she'd sneak off to find that forgery and set it ablaze, incinerating Vexley's hold over her once and for all.

SIX

THE PRINCE OF Envy watched Camilla slowly place her hand in the crook of Vexley's arm.

The very arm Envy had just fantasized about bodily removing. The splatter of blood would look rather arresting against the pale wallpaper, but he tamped his more violent instincts down.

Vexley was walking Camilla around like a prize. One he'd stolen, not won.

Envy was firmly of the thinking in the Seven Circles: when it came to the game of courtship, each person should *want* to play.

Vexley hadn't given Camilla a choice—and from what Envy knew of the mortal customs, if she denied him, it would cause a scene.

And Miss Antonius didn't appear to want to draw anyone's eye for long tonight, for some reason. Though the deep hunter green of her silk gown matched Envy's cravat and that kept holding *his* attention. Amid the sea of pastel-colored dresses skirting his peripheral vision, Camilla was a bold splash of darkness, intense and rich.

Despite his best effort not to notice, Camilla was beautiful.

Her silver hair had been curled delicately and clipped back from her face, showing off her pointed chin, her slender neck, and the simple yet stunning silver locket she wore that matched her eyes.

There was an elegance in the way she carried herself—her body made of the sort of delicate angles and swooping curves that begged to be captured on canvas. The way she moved now indicated that she wished to be as far from their host as possible.

Player or not—Envy still hadn't decided—Vexley was making himself a complication in more ways than one. And Envy had no time to waste on fools.

Every day, his court weakened, a fault that was his alone.

Which was why he'd decided to go the more trusted route for this second attempt and seduce Camilla. It was purely a practical decision: it had nothing to do with how the candlelight was reflecting off her silver curls up ahead.

Envy offered his arm to the nearest woman—a vibrant redhead he briefly recalled had arrived with Camilla—and followed the procession down the corridor to the dining room.

"You're the mysterious Lord Synton, I presume?" the redhead immediately asked.

"Is that what people are saying about me, Lady...?"

"Lady Katherine Edwards."

He felt her gaze on him but kept his own locked on the procession of lords and ladies parading slowly toward the dining room. Envy fantasized about jabbing magical pokers at their asses to prod them along. Dinner hadn't even started, and he was ready to leave.

"You've certainly made an impression," she continued.

Envy glanced sidelong at Lady Edwards. "I do have that effect."

She laughed, full and deep, drawing the attention of a dark-haired woman in front of them. The woman glanced back, surprising Envy with the open lust shining in her eyes.

Her focus shifted to Lady Edwards, and the dark-haired woman's jealousy flared. He flashed a smile meant to intimidate and she averted her gaze.

"I see what my friend meant. You are trouble."

His attention went to Camilla's silver head at the front of the line. Lady Edwards was baiting him. And having entirely too much fun doing it.

But perhaps befriending her would put Camilla at ease. He allowed himself to don the mask of a charming but aloof noble.

"Tonight, I'd say I'm only slightly wicked, Lady Edwards."

Envy was rather put off when he realized it was the truth.

He'd kept his flirting to a minimum, had only asked pointed questions that could help him with the game. And once Camilla had stepped into the room, he'd given her all his attention. Not wanting to appear too forward, he'd admired the most intriguing painting in the room, giving her five minutes before seeking her out. *A perfect fucking gentleman,* he thought with annoyance.

And yet she'd been completely, infuriatingly, unimpressed that he'd swooped in to catch her cup and save her from ruining her gown. No matter that he'd been the one to cause her unsteadiness in the first place. Prince Gluttony had claimed that that move always worked to woo a mortal. According to his brother, mortal women loved a dark hero. As if heroics were determined by an unsullied cup of punch.

But, as usual, Envy was discovering that Gluttony was a moron when it came to courtship. Camilla's tongue had been as silver as her hair, lashing him with her quick dismissal.

If he was going to try seduction as his second attempt at securing her help, he'd have to tease out what aroused her. Surely she had some fantasy he could toy with.

The parade finally entered the dining chamber, and Envy schooled his features to hide his distaste.

The long cloth-covered table had been dressed in candelabras and an ungodly number of crystal vases. Wisteria—that must have come from a hot house and cost a small fortune—was the flower of choice, and he knew from the way Camilla's eyes squeezed shut for a moment that the detail hadn't been lost on her, either, and it didn't please her.

Intriguing.

"Where is your family from, Lord Synton?" Lady Edwards asked, her voice cordial as she brought Envy's attention to her. "Is Synton a western surname?"

"Southern," he said evasively.

She gave him a once-over as she unfolded her napkin in her lap. He had the distinct impression that she was mentally flaying him, in search of his deepest secrets.

"I saw you speaking with my friend earlier. How do you know Miss Antonius?"

"I'm an art collector and her gallery came highly recommended."

"Mm."

Lady Katherine sipped her water.

Envy didn't need to use his supernatural ability to sense emotions to know she was skeptical of him.

"Many gentlemen find themselves very intrigued by her... art."

His sin ignited before he smothered the sensation.

Lady Katherine turned those shrewd eyes on Camilla and Vexley, who were now seated directly across from them. A man named Harrington took his seat on Camilla's other side, causing her to stiffen ever so slightly. Envy made a mental note to look into him, too.

"She's quite talented, and much more modest than her father."

Envy tore his gaze away from the artist in question. "Her father also painted?"

Of course, he knew Pierre had painted, but acting as if he didn't would garner much more information.

"Pierre Antonius became famous for *The Seduction of Evelyn Gray,* among many others. Surely you've heard of it, even in the southern region? It's his most famous portrait. The woman who posed was nude, except for a veil, hiding her identity. Of course, she also had great, raven-like wings. Pierre's work often depicted the fantastical, especially what he called halflings."

"Humans who have unique parentage," Envy supplied.

"You could say that." Lady Katherine smiled demurely. "Women with wings, men with horns or devilish tails. Others certainly seemed to share his obsession. Through his art, society could indulge in their own fantasies, display pieces that would otherwise be considered unholy."

Envy listened to Lady Katherine's unsolicited but much-appreciated art history lesson as the wine was poured. His spies hadn't found much on the man, aside from the fact that Pierre had opened the gallery two decades prior, and died two years back, leaving Camilla alone in the world. She had no maternal or paternal grandparents that he'd found, no aunts or uncles or cousins.

Strange, he thought, given how humans bred like rabbits.

"What of his family?" Envy asked, sipping his wine.

"Pierre? He had a tragic origin. His mother and father were killed in a carriage accident when he was a boy, and he'd been brought up by a family friend. Both of his parents had been only children and their parents had also met violent ends."

"Some might say their family is cursed."

Lady Katherine gave him a sharp look.

"Some have said that, and they are quite obviously fools."

He smiled faintly. She'd very delicately suggested he might be one too.

"What of her mother's family?"

Lady Katherine's expression shuttered. "That's a sensitive subject I'd rather avoid."

Envy smiled pleasantly, though inside he churned with curiosity. "No need to sharpen your claws, Lady Edwards. I meant no harm. What else intrigues Waverly Green's finest?"

Lady Katherine went on to tell him about Pierre's fondness for riddles and mysteries. If he hadn't been dead, Envy would have thought he was a player in the game too. But it was clear that this fondness was shared by many in Waverly Green. *How dull the games of humans*, he thought while nodding along.

The butler appeared again, solemnly chiming a bell to announce that dinner was to be served. It was presented *a la française,* so guests began serving themselves from the wide array of entrées and side dishes a barrage of servants had placed along the table.

Platters of roasted beef tenderloin with a rosemary *jus;* whipped potatoes topped with chives and dotted with pads of melting butter; glazed carrots; stuffed whole fish with dull eyes; steamed asparagus; oversized prawns with their tails still attached; and tenderized chicken breasts with a rich lemon cream sauce made their way around the table.

Envy could have done without the accusing stare of the fish, or the manual labor involved in cleaning the prawns, but kept his thoughts from his face. The food was otherwise decent and the company of Lady Edwards surprisingly tolerable.

Once they'd all sampled the first round, the second was brought out. Dishes inspired by the southern region of a nearby realm took center stage.

A salad made of oranges, diced onion, and pine nuts tossed with a tangy dressing made of salt, pepper, oregano, and oil and vinegar.

A second fish course came out, bringing a genuine smile to his face. It reminded him of his sister-in-law's family restaurant and a dish served there. But in no other way did this feast compare to the luxury of dinner parties back home. Though he didn't like to admit it, Envy's brother Gluttony had recently impressed him, fashioning candles from bacon lard that, once they'd been lit and melted, created a rich, decadent sauce for the shaved Brussels sprouts.

Of course, his brother was highly motivated to have the best, most talked-about parties—he was locked in a feud with a reporter whose dismissals of him proved quite inspiring.

On and on the dishes came, and so did the wine. Blessedly.

He downed one glass and called for another, earning no admonishments. In fact, several other guests did the same.

Apparently, Waverly Green's high society grew bored with their pompous, holier-than-thou ways too. Given the fact that Vexley was supposed to be a scoundrel, this dinner party was boring as sin. Envy's masquerade next week would certainly stir things up nicely.

Across the table, the dark-haired woman from earlier, a widow named Janelle, kept trying to catch his eye. She pressed her breasts against the table as she leaned over, fully aware that the position combined with her low-cut bodice offered a tantalizing view.

Envy kept his attention on her face, where her lips were pouting ever so slightly.

"Fine wine, my lady, am I right?"

Her focus slid to his hand. He'd been absently stroking the stem of his wineglass, thinking of how to engage Camilla in conversation and draw her away from Vexley.

"Do you sculpt, Lord Synton?" she asked.

"Why do you ask, Lady Janelle?"

A pleasant flush rose in her cheeks.

"You have the hands of an artist, my lord. I can't help but picture them molding objects to perfection. If you ever need a model, I'd be happy to pose."

A flicker of annoyance surprised him, beckoning from Camilla's side. But when he stole a glance at her, she wasn't looking at him at all. Instead, she was fixated on Vexley, who was leaning toward her, eyes glassy from the fifth glass of wine he'd finished.

"Lord Synton?" Lady Janelle ventured, her breasts near to spilling out as she leaned farther forward.

Envy was saved from having to respond when the man to her left finally pulled his head out of his rear end to take an interest in the woman. And her generous cleavage.

Luckily, Janelle seemed very pleased by this turn of events as if that had been her goal all along. Games within games.

Vexley's dinner party had quickly departed from the polite as harder spirits began to circulate alongside the wine, ensuring that the guests—both the ladies and the gentlemen—were getting as intoxicated as they desired.

"Sweet manna from heaven," Envy whispered, swiping a whiskey cocktail from a tray, for the first time in his life regretting that his demon blood kept him from getting as soused on mortal liquor as all the rest.

Hours later, after the last dessert was brought out and cleared away, the host snatched a chalice from the table and lifted it high, spilling half its contents down his coat sleeve and splattering the remaining red liquor onto the table linen, as if re-creating a murder scene.

Envy kept his face impassive, though annoyance raged within. He despised messy displays. It showed a lack of control.

Surely this inebriated fool couldn't be his competition.

"Ladies, please see yourselves to the drawing room while the gentlemen smoke our cigars. We shall all take a few moments to gather ourselves before I show off my newest treasure. Afterward, how about we all play some... games? If you dare."

Without looking in her direction, Envy tapped into Camilla's emotions, noticing a drastic spike in her nerves. All the while Vexley spoke, her discomfort wound around Envy's insides, as if her growing anxiety were his own.

Miss Camilla Antonius was either up to something nefarious or was nervous about what Vexley had in store for everyone. Or perhaps she was excited by the prospect of his games.

Envy recalled what Goodfellow had said. He fought the urge to look at her.

It was entirely possible that Envy had read Camilla's emotions wrong earlier—perhaps she'd only been upset with Vexley for his public display and not his unwelcome touch.

Anticipation and nervousness were nearly identical at their core, so it was impossible to discern which emotion the artist was currently experiencing. It was rare that his supernatural senses couldn't aid him, and Envy didn't care much for this uncertainty.

But perhaps it was another opportunity. If he could determine what Camilla was up to tonight, then he could devise a way to make himself indispensable to her, thus ensuring that she'd help him in return. No seduction required.

"All right, then," Vexley said finally. "Let's be on our way."

Out of the corner of his eye, Envy watched Camilla bolt for the door. Without drawing attention to himself, Envy quickly stood, but just as he pushed back his chair, he was stopped by Lady Katherine.

"Do be a dear and escort me to the drawing room, my lord," she said, blocking his path.

He glanced from the meddlesome woman to the door, debating whether using his magic now would in any way count against him. It was small as far as risks went, but Envy couldn't chance breaking any rules of conduct.

"It will be but a moment," she added.

A moment was all Camilla had needed to slip away, a fact that her friend either seemed to know or had surmised just as he had.

Outmaneuvered by propriety, of all cursed things, Envy pasted on a pleasant smile and offered his arm.

"Of course, Lady Katherine. Lead the way."

SEVEN

AFTER A QUICK scan of the corridor to ensure that she was alone, Camilla all but ran toward the staircase leading to the rooms on the upper level, the sound of the dinner party growing louder as everyone moved toward the door she'd just exited through.

Hopefully most of the guests were too inebriated to notice her hasty exit and would be focused on the naughty games Vexley had not so subtly hinted at.

It never ceased to amaze her that even the most level-headed man could become so simpleminded with the promise of sin. During her first few Seasons, she'd secretly watched couples sneaking off during balls, rushing to the gardens to give in to their desires. Men were clapped on their backs, deemed rakes and rascals, if they were discovered. Yet the women were tossed aside as harlots, condemned for acting on what was natural to both parties. It was unfair and rankled Camilla more than she ever let on.

Men had the luxury of remaining eligible bachelors while still feeding their sexual appetites, yet women were warned to remain saintly should they refuse the noose of wedded bliss. And Camilla played that game too, loathing it but unwilling to forsake her reputation, her highest bargaining chip in this realm.

Thinking of desire, she thought again of Lord Synton, then quickly shook that away. With any luck, he would become distracted by one of the many ladies who'd openly admired him during dinner.

Annoyance overtook her nervousness for a moment, though Camilla had no right to feel that way. It was just that the idea of Synton sneaking off for a clandestine affair rather than seeking out her company irked her. In her fantasy he'd been consumed only with her, focusing on her pleasure the same intense way she studied a subject she painted.

It was that intensity she'd loved imagining, that feeling of being wholly consumed by another person.

Just once she wanted someone to want her. Not her art. Not her talent. Her.

Sometimes she felt so alone. Her father was gone, so was her mother. The fantasy of Synton had reminded her of all she didn't have but wanted. But in truth Synton hadn't looked in Camilla's direction or sought her conversation during dinner at all.

Which was precisely why she would never confuse fantasy with reality again.

Shoving those distracting thoughts away, Camilla focused solely on the task at hand: find the forgery and destroy it.

Wide oak planks creaked noisily beneath her slippered feet, causing her pulse to speed as she grabbed a fistful of her skirts and leapt onto the first step, ascending out of view right as the dining room door crashed open against the wall and the sound of voices spilled into the corridor like uncorked bottles of wine.

"Oi!" Vexley yelled. "Watch it, Walters. Or you'll cause a bigger scandal than Harrington did when he pissed on that statue."

Camilla didn't dare stop as the boisterous laughter grew closer. She'd overseen the installation of almost every piece of art in Vexley's home, giving her an intimate knowledge of its layout. The first door on her left contained a reading room with a few shelves of books, two comfortable chairs, and a decent fireplace. It was much smaller than the main library downstairs and remained mostly unused by the lord.

She tiptoed inside, closing the door with a quiet snick, relieved to see the fire burning gently. Vexley might not pick up a book as often as he picked up a hand mirror, but he was vain enough to want to give the appearance

of being well-read, should anyone secret themselves away to steal kisses in this chamber.

"Right, then. The painting."

Camilla got to work straightaway.

She rushed to feel along the bookshelves for any hidden latches. When she'd scoured each, she stepped on each floor plank, listening for the most minute difference in sound that would indicate a compartment below the floor.

She pushed against the paneled wall, growing more frantic as the minutes ticked by. There was no closet, no door, no candelabra that opened a secret room. No other place to hide the painting.

Before turning to go, Camilla glanced behind the canvas hanging above the mantel, making sure there was nothing secreted behind the portrait.

Though *portrait* was a stretch. It was a nude man who looked startlingly like Vex the Hex, sprawled across a cloud. His hand was wrapped around his engorged member, paused midstroke, his gaze fixed presumably on whoever had caught his fancy.

By polite society's standards it was rather lewd, but as someone who studied art, Camilla was unfazed by the male form.

She fought the urge to flick his cursed bollocks, and, satisfied that the room was not harboring the forgery, she cracked the door and listened for a few beats before exiting.

Voices carried up the stairs like ghosts of lovers past, but this floor was still otherwise unoccupied by the living.

No couple had sought it out, at least for the moment, but as this was one of Vexley's parties, it was only a matter of time.

Camilla crept down the corridor and quickly slipped into the next room—the bathing chamber. She conducted the same search as before, tapping the walls, pushing at panels, and looking behind other artwork. She dropped to the floor and peered under the claw-foot tub, running her hands over the underside and the floor just in case.

Nothing.

Camilla pushed herself up to her knees, surveying the room from a different angle.

Her father had always told her to pay attention to the details of a room—that sometimes looking at the negative space revealed more than staring at an object directly.

It was a trick that worked wonders in the woods of their country estate. Camilla once spied a heron standing tall among the trees by spotting its legs in the space between the tree trunks.

Unfortunately, there was nothing out of the ordinary here.

Camilla investigated a linen closet that she prayed held her salvation, but she saw nothing more than neatly folded towels, a silk robe, and extra bars of soap.

Her next two searches, of the guest rooms, provided the same frustrating results, except with the added tingle of trepidation when she swore she was being watched.

She waited in the shadows, back pressed to the wall, heart pounding, for whoever it was to reveal themselves, but of course no one was there.

At last, she paused outside Vexley's personal bedroom suite, certain there was no way he'd actually have hidden the forgery there. Vexley had said it was away from public view, and knowing what she did of his nighttime activities, his bedchamber entertained more guests than his receiving room.

Still, she refused to leave any nook or cranny unsearched.

With a prayer that luck would be on her side, Camilla entered the one chamber she'd sworn she'd never visit. The overwhelming scent of Vexley's cologne almost sent her running back in the direction she'd come, but unless he had some secret tunnel that led from his parlor to his bedchamber, Vexley wasn't waiting for her inside.

This was it, then. She stepped fully into the expansive bedroom, leaving the door cracked to alert her to the sound of anyone approaching.

Camilla wasn't sure what she'd expected to find—an oversized bed with messy sheets, a few naked women pleasing themselves or each other while they waited—but a standard-sized bed with pristine coverings, handsome yet plain bedroom furnishings, a well-tended fire on the far wall, and the very painting she'd been looking for proudly displayed above the headboard was not it.

"Vexley, you plumb fool."

Of course he wouldn't be able to resist showing off the forgery to his lovers.

Without delay, Camilla hiked up her gown and climbed onto the bed.

Her fingers had just closed around the gilded frame when she heard a sound that sent ice shooting through her veins: the creak of the floorboard directly behind her.

She froze, debating her next move. But one thing was certain: with the painting fully in her grasp, she couldn't let go now.

The fireplace was at the opposite end of the room, but if she moved swiftly, she might manage to toss the painting in before Vexley could snatch it away. It wouldn't be fully destroyed, but it should be tainted enough that he'd no longer display it or use it against her.

She waited for Vexley to demand she drop the forgery at once, but no cocky or snide remarks came.

Perhaps the noise wasn't from someone who had followed her into the room. Everyone had been drinking quite heavily—she didn't think they'd be able to sneak up the stairs, let alone slip undetected into this chamber. Maybe it was just a creaky old house.

But Camilla knew that wasn't the case; the heat traveling along her neck indicated that someone was indeed in the chamber with her. She steeled her nerves and slowly turned, ready to toss the canvas out the window or throttle Vexley with it if need be.

"Please. Don't stop on my account."

EIGHT

SYNTON CASUALLY LEANED against the wall, arms folded across his chest, an amused upward tilt to his lips. He had somehow managed to enter the room *and* close the door behind him without making a sound.

A feat that should have been impossible for a man of his size.

"I'm rather interested to see what comes next, Miss Antonius."

Instead of allowing him to have the upper hand, Camilla decided to turn this around. False bravado could work wonders.

She let the painting go long enough to place her hands on her hips and leveled her best haughty glare at Synton.

"What are you doing here?"

"We had an agreement. Remember?" Synton's gaze left hers to take in the painting. "I came to intercept you before you disrobed for your tryst."

"My tryst? With Vexley?" Her voice notched up an octave.

Synton cocked a brow, waiting.

"I assure you I would rather attend a Crown ball in the nude than become Vexley's plaything."

Synton's gaze darkened. He nodded toward the painting. "Instead of undressing, imagine my surprise to find you stealing the famed *Seduction of Evelyn Gray*. That's rather naughty for an artist."

"I'm not stealing anything, my lord."

Lying was not something Camilla normally condoned, but she needed to get rid of him before he ruined her best chance to destroy the forgery.

Silence stretched between them. He didn't believe her.

Rightfully so, but still.

"Vexley asked me to have this cleaned earlier this week. I was simply fetching it before we left for the gallery." Before she could stop herself, she added, "You seemed quite enchanted by Vexley's mention of games. I figured you'd be occupied for a while."

Amusement ghosted across his features.

"Is that why you ducked in and out of every chamber on this floor? You were coming to fetch the painting while also considerately ensuring that I had time to woo a lover? How utterly magnanimous."

Camilla's eyes narrowed.

"Do you make a habit of spying on ladies, my lord?"

"Only the ones who declare they'd never marry me without a proper hello, then get jealous over the idea of me having a tryst with someone else."

"I am not jealous. And if you must know, I thought you were someone else that day," she said. "Tonight, I'd been looking for the water closet. If you were a gentleman, you would have announced yourself and offered me assistance instead of lurking in the shadows."

The wry amusement vanished from his face. He cocked his head to one side, his attention languidly sliding over every inch of her as if each dip and curve were for his viewing pleasure alone.

By the time he brought his gaze back up to hers, there was no mistaking the raw hunger that flashed in those emerald eyes. She wished she hated his heated stare, but it made her feel breathless, like a fire crackling to life.

"Do you believe I'm a gentleman, Miss Antonius? I'd wager your heart is beating so wildly because deep down you hope I'm not."

Camilla wasn't sure how he knew her heart was suddenly pounding, but she certainly wasn't going to own up to the fact that he affected her.

"You're mistaken. I don't think of you at all, Lord Synton."

The smile that had been teasing the edges of Synton's mouth turned into a full grin, showing off a pair of dimples she hadn't noticed before.

"Another bold and interesting lie."

He moved closer to the bed, a hunter sighting his prey, and the thought of being caught by him caused her pulse to race harder in anticipation.

With one languid, effortless movement, Synton stepped up, pressed a hand to the wall to settle in, and now stood on the mattress beside her, leaning in close.

As he stared down at her, Camilla briefly forgot about the forgery.

No one had ever looked at her so boldly. So intensely. Like he could see through all her carefully erected walls to who she was at her very core.

Or maybe he simply looked at her like he knew the depth of her desire and it affected him in turn. More than either of them wanted it to.

She'd only wanted to keep up her normal life here. Had fought hard to become what people expected. But now, she could admit, for only a second, that maybe she'd wanted something else, too. Something that called to a secret part of her.

"You ought to know, if I had taken a lover, I would have needed hours, Miss Antonius."

His gaze dropped to her neck a second before he reached out, slowly stroking along her quivering pulse.

A bolt of heat lashed through her from the brief contact of his bare skin, and his hand fell away as if he, too, had felt the burn.

She expected him to draw back entirely, but instead he looked at her curiously and then surprised her by raising that same hand to run his thumb against the seam of her lips, applying steady pressure until they parted and allowed him entry.

An ember of desire ignited in his eyes, locked on hers, when she submitted to his unspoken command, drawing his thumb into her mouth.

He tasted of sin and decadence. A heady mix that heated her core.

"The tongue may lie, but other parts of the body always tell the truth, Miss Antonius. If one looks closely enough."

With what appeared to be great effort, he withdrew his thumb and dropped his hand once again, though he didn't step away.

Camilla wasn't sure what it was about him. Perhaps that he was largely unknown to her, unlike other members of society. Or maybe it was the

quiet intensity with which he studied his surroundings. Whatever it was, she couldn't bring herself to move away, ensnared by curiosity, wondering what he'd do next.

Synton stood entirely too close and not close enough, his intoxicating scent now overtaking Vexley's in the air. There was something dark and utterly masculine about it. Bourbon and spice with only a hint of sweet berries.

Suddenly, Camilla wanted to run her tongue along the seam of his lips, tasting the sweetness of sin she was certain she'd find there.

Instead, he brought that tempting mouth to her ear, lightly brushing it against the lobe. Her eyelids fluttered shut from the sensation.

"Why are you after that painting, Miss Antonius? Did Vexley steal it from you?"

The forgery.

Vexley.

It was as if Synton had dumped a bucket of ice water over her, bringing her back to her senses. The scoundrel hadn't been trying to kiss her at all, he'd been after information. Likely to blackmail her too.

Camilla went to push herself away from the lord of temptation, but he suddenly stepped aside on his own, causing her to lose her footing as the mattress heaved.

She went tumbling forward.

Camilla tensed for what would certainly be a painful collision with the hardwood, but Synton moved faster than should have been possible, leaping forward to enclose her in his arms and break her fall with his body, which thumped heavily to the floor.

Air whooshed out of him upon impact, their knees and hips and chests crashing together, accompanied by the sound of silk ripping. For a moment, both lay still, dazed. But then Camilla stirred.

"Damn," she cursed softly.

She pushed herself up, quickly taking stock of things.

Synton looked all right—not a hair out of place or wrinkle in his suit.

Camilla's full skirts were twisted but were otherwise unscathed. But the seam along the left side of her dress wasn't as fortunate.

She glanced at the exposed stays, cursing like the worst sailor ever to visit Waverly Green's shores. The black lace of her stays, her secret indulgence, was clearly visible, clinging to the outline of her breasts, displayed in all its decadence.

A deep chuckle below her—and its subsequent rumble that vibrated along a *very* sensitive area of her body—drew her attention to more pressing issues: she was straddling Synton in another man's bedroom, her gown half torn as if they'd been in the throes of passion, her hands braced on his chest.

His hard chest.

Lord help her. Synton felt like a marble statue crafted by one of the greats.

Camilla became intimately aware of just how large he was as he shifted between her thighs, how toned and powerful.

She also realized she rather liked the feeling of him beneath her—it was as if she'd conquered some great beast and for a moment, he belonged only to her.

At least until he pounced in turn.

He gave her a lazy sort of smile.

"If you're unharmed, Miss Antonius, you may wish to stand up. Quickly."

"Are you hurt?" Camilla looked him over more carefully, then scooted down his hips before he could stop her. "Should I…oh. *Oh.*"

Something hard pressed against her backside.

At once she understood what he'd been too polite to say.

Synton was as far from hurt as a man could be.

Her mouth went dry, her pulse speeding.

For a breath they both remained frozen, staring into each other's eyes.

Camilla didn't know why he'd paused, but she was suddenly battling a fierce internal war. She should get up immediately, and probably make a small fuss, but her body tingled where they touched, and her pulse pounded a tempting beat.

Any sense of reason was quickly being replaced by physical desire.

And even he couldn't scoff his way out of this one: his body was responding beneath hers.

Camilla glanced down to where his hands now grasped her hips, his strong fingers buried in the silk of her twisted skirts. She had raised her head to meet his eyes again when he abruptly shifted, pushing her up onto her feet, then slowly rose to his own.

"Apologies, Miss Antonius. I assure you I didn't intend for that—"

"No, no," Camilla interrupted, looking anywhere but at the lord and his fierce arousal. "There's no need to apologize or explain. I should have—"

"Hello? Who's up there?"

Vexley. His voice came from what sounded like the top of the stairs.

Dread washed over Camilla, erasing all feelings of awkwardness.

"Oh, God, no. Hide! We mustn't be seen together. Especially like this." She pulled uselessly at the torn edges of her bodice, but the curve of her breast remained stubbornly free.

Indeed, Vexley sounded intoxicated enough to cause a scene. He stumbled along the corridor, cursing as he smacked into things, drawing slowly closer.

Synton, having restored his own cool, didn't seem concerned. He merely straightened his jacket and arched a brow.

"Why?"

"Because I'll be ruined!" Camilla tidied her hair and smoothed her skirts, but the gaping seam couldn't be hidden. "Fuck, fuck, fuck. This is a nightmare."

She glanced up at Synton, who, if anything, was growing more amused by her foul language.

"Why in the name of the Crown are you just standing there, my lord? Do you want us to be discovered?"

"I couldn't care less if that inbreed found us."

"You should!" She couldn't help but drop her gaze. "If you cannot get *that* situation under control, we'll definitely look guilty, my lord."

"That situation, Miss Antonius?" Synton's voice was amused. "Have you never seen a situation before? I suppose propriety would have me offer to marry you immediately?"

She gave him a withering look. Her lack of virginity, such as it was, was none of his damned business.

"I'm not marrying."

"Hullo?" Vexley called out from the room next door, his voice slurred. "Come out, come out, wherever you are! No fornicating up here, least not without me!"

"We could pretend," Synton went on thoughtfully as if Vexley weren't coming to destroy everything she'd worked so hard for over the last two years.

"Pretend?" She must be having a nightmare. "Are you mad?"

"I don't see how that would be a terrible thing," Synton said calmly. "He'd stop ogling you if he thought you were involved with someone else. Unless you actually enjoy his advances?"

Camilla shot him an incredulous look.

"It's not just about Vexley finding us," she hissed. "If I'm found in a compromising position, society will either demand we marry—not pretend, my lord, but actually marry—or I will be forever ruined. My gallery. My life. I'll never be accepted again. Surely you know this!"

"Rules are made to be broken."

"For you, perhaps. But women here do not get that same grace. You have a duty to do the honorable thing!"

Camilla ran to the window, looking down into the dark garden below. There were no guests or, worse, columnists lurking that she could tell, at least.

If only they weren't two stories up, she'd toss herself out. She cast her eyes around the shadowy corners of the room, but wherever Vexley kept his wardrobe, it didn't seem to be here, as each wall gleamed closet-free.

"The forgery!" she cried as her attention landed again above the bed.

"Forgery..."

Before Synton could say more about it, she rushed past him, leaping back up on the bed to snatch the painting off the wall.

But this time it didn't move an inch, catching her off guard. How the hell had Vexley attached the thing? What had changed?

Camilla worked her fingers underneath the frame and heaved her weight away from the wall, doing her best to pry the painting free. But it didn't have the common decency to even pretend to budge.

She stared at the cursed thing, wondering how on earth she'd managed to move it not ten minutes prior. She couldn't have imagined she'd nudged it before Synton interrupted her. Could she?

"Hellloooo."

The bedroom doorknob rattled, chilling her blood. Any second Vexley would charge into the room and find them alone, and disheveled. And knowing Vexley, he'd embellish the tale until they were both nude and caught midact. Or worse: Vexley would claim he'd ruined her dress and say Synton had found the two of them together. It would be his word against Synton's, and Synton was a newcomer.

Camilla yanked at the painting one last time, swearing as it remained stubbornly fixed to the wall. Vexley pounded against the door violently now.

"I'm no longer amused. Open the damned door!"

The knob jangled again but held firm.

Softening her grip on the painting, Camilla looked back at Synton. He held up an ornate skeleton key that apparently locked any door as well as opened it, flashing a devious grin.

"That should slow him down for a moment. Maybe two," he whispered, his voice enticingly smooth. "But we must hurry."

He pocketed the unique key and moved to the window, scanning the garden below. Seeming satisfied, he pushed open the window, then held out his hand to Camilla.

"Are we making our grand escape, or not?"

Camilla glanced between the lord and the forgery. Freedom was so close she could taste it. How could she willingly leave it behind? Synton made an annoyed noise, drawing her attention back to him.

Grinding her teeth, she climbed down from the bed, keeping her voice low. "My lord, you can simply walk out the door unscathed. Why are you helping me?"

"Trust me, I'm as far removed from a saint as one can get." He flashed his teeth. "What I am is someone completely uninterested in society games or playing the role of a besotted fool, Miss Antonius. I do not desire the complication. If you're ruined, it will negatively impact *my* plan. If you're attached to that drunkard, it will also complicate matters for me. I'm helping myself first, which has a trickle-down effect of assisting you."

"How very noble," she murmured. Of all the men in Waverly Green, how had she ended up stuck with him?

Without another word, Synton nimbly hoisted himself out the window, finding purchase on the edge of the iron roof, then poked his head back inside. Shadows carved his face into dangerous lines, and for a moment, his eyes became ebony pools. Then he blinked and whatever hidden depths she thought she'd seen vanished.

Who is this man? She paused halfway to the window, indecision warring inside her. To be so close to her goal and to walk away was unfathomable. To climb out the window with this stranger seemed insanity. Yet if she stayed, she'd find herself in worse circumstances.

"Camilla." Synton's voice rang with authority. "Vexley will break through that door soon. Unless you wish to become his bride, I'd hurry."

With one final look at the forgery, Camilla made her choice and prayed she would live to regret it.

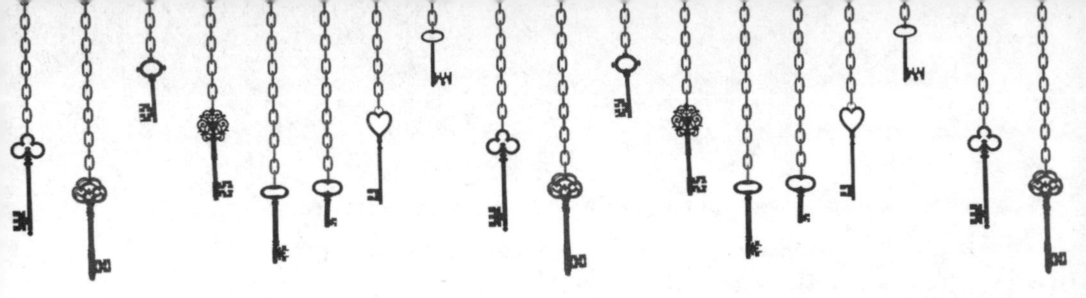

NINE

ENVY HELPED CAMILLA onto the metal roof, more concerned by the way she squeezed her eyes shut and teetered across the steep incline than by the loud banging still coming from the door inside.

He'd have them down in the garden and off to his waiting carriage before Vexley could find them, but only if Camilla didn't have a stroke first.

"Open your eyes," he demanded quietly.

Having her break her neck would be inconvenient, to say the least. He had no idea what her death might mean for the game, but it certainly wouldn't be good.

Camilla shook her head, her face pale in the moonlight.

For the first time since their tumble, Envy tuned in to her emotions, feeling the iciness of her fear travel down his own spine. If he'd been mortal, he'd have shuddered from the coldness of it.

Camilla wasn't simply afraid, she was petrified.

"Is it the height or the fear of being caught?"

"Both," she gritted out, keeping her eyes shut tight.

His magic detected a lie, but he couldn't dwell on it.

Her teeth chattered loudly, and soon her whole body would start shaking. Her slippered foot slid across the roof.

Envy didn't wish to reveal any hint that he was more than human, but Camilla needed to be on solid ground before she did something reckless, like faint.

He slipped one arm under her legs, then banded the other around her middle, tucking her small frame tight against him.

Surprisingly, she curled into his body without resistance, shivering like someone who'd been pulled from frigid waters. Her reaction was extreme, even for human fear, but he had no time to puzzle it out now.

"Relax," he commanded. "This will be over in a second."

"What do you—"

"Quiet."

She squirmed and he stepped off the roof, landing effortlessly with a quiet thunk in the dewy grass before she could cry out.

Instead of being relieved, Camilla latched onto him harder, practically crawling up his body as she pressed her face into his chest, her breathing quick and uneven.

He swept a hand over her forehead. Sweat beaded across her brow and the back of her neck. He glanced up at the roof, brows tugged close.

"Camilla. Breathe. We're on solid ground."

"We... we could have died."

"Death isn't in my plan, pet."

A beat of silence passed.

"Do not call me pet."

"Noted, kitten."

She uttered a filthy name under her breath, her trembling easing as she shifted from fear back to annoyance.

He smiled. Good. She was feeling feisty enough to work through whatever beginning stages of shock she'd been experiencing.

Perhaps he also smiled because he realized he *liked* annoying her. Despite the strict rules of this society that tried to tame women, she bit back. He enjoyed seeing her teeth.

Envy was so focused on Camilla that he didn't notice they had company until a pointed object cut through the night, jabbing him sharply between his shoulder blades as a shadowy arm lashed out from the shrubbery.

A hiss escaped his lips—more from surprise than pain—as he spun around, keeping Camilla out of harm's reach.

"What—"

"Unhand my friend at once, you scoundrel!"

Lady Katherine leapt from the nearest bush, lifting her weapon again—her heeled shoe—and waving it threateningly.

Envy closed his eyes, wondering whether the game was truly worth this cost. If his brothers could see him now. Being assaulted by women's footwear.

"I swear, if you ruin her—"

"Does it look like I'm ravishing her?" he growled, keeping his voice low.

Lady Katherine still brandished her shoe, but she craned her neck and hobbled awkwardly on one shoeless foot to get a better look at Camilla.

Just then Vexley's voice bellowed out from above, drawing their attention to the open window and the shadowy figure stumbling past it. With luck the idiot would fall out.

Envy turned back to Lady Katherine, his patience gone.

"Unless you'd like to be the cause of her ruination, move out of my way. Now."

Lady Katherine kept her cool gaze locked on Envy.

"Her dress is torn."

"You're very astute," he deadpanned, earning a fierce glare.

"You can leave her here in the garden with me and go, my lord. Scandal avoided."

"Please, Kitty." Camilla's voice startled them both. "I wish to leave now."

"You're certain this *gentleman* hasn't accosted you?" she asked, still glaring at Envy as if he were the lowest form of life and cradling the heel of her shoe as if to jab him again. The way she said *gentleman* indicated she meant *vile deviant*. An accusation that was fitting enough.

"Yes. Please. We need to leave before someone spies us. You know columnists always sneak onto the property."

Katherine's expression suddenly shifted. "Oh! Is he a potential loyal companion?"

"Kitty!"

Camilla's strength at last returned, and she practically shoved herself out of Envy's arms to stand on her own, teetering only slightly.

That reaction certainly piqued his interest, but before he could gather any more information, they heard an approach.

Lady Katherine, the shoe-wielding bandit, pressed her lips together but hobbled back, allowing them finally to pass without any more interference.

As Camilla passed by, she reached out to squeeze her friend's hand.

Envy wasted no time. He strode toward the side alley, where he'd instructed his driver to wait, pleased that Camilla hurried along after him without prompting.

Hushed voices and a giggle carried across the garden, sounding suspiciously like Widow Janelle—followed by a soft moan, which spurred Envy to grab Camilla's hand and lead her the rest of the way to his carriage as swiftly as possible.

This villain would play the role of gentleman only so long before he struck back. The next clue was practically in his grasp, and Envy would be damned—more than he and his court already were—if he allowed one more person to stand in the way of his securing that painting before time ran out.

TEN

All Camilla wanted to do was crawl into a hot bath and forget that this cursed night had ever happened. To have had the forgery *in her hands* and to be unable to grab it felt like unjust cruelty. If only she'd had a few more minutes alone or if Vexley hadn't come drunkenly knocking, maybe she'd be soaring high on her newfound freedom.

Instead, she felt leaden with despair.

She'd not only lost the greatest opportunity she'd had, but she'd also nearly died on that godforsaken roof and would have to answer Kitty's questions regarding Synton and the unfortunate lack of anything untoward occurring between them.

She wondered if he felt that strange allure with everyone—she certainly had never become enraptured by physical desire quite like that. Except for maybe that one time with her hunter. Even then things had been different.

Camilla had wanted Wolf, had thoroughly enjoyed their night of passion and being completely free to act however she pleased; he'd been a tireless lover who matched her in so many ways, even if he'd reminded her of how lonely she was, how much she yearned for someone like her, and tempted her to live as he had.

It was wonderful while it lasted, but it wasn't the same urge she felt around Synton. He made her want to shed her own civility and indulge her passions.

Which was dangerous for her life here.

"Dreaming of strangulation, Miss Antonius?"

Synton's deep, rich voice drew her attention to where he sat across from her in the carriage, his face half hidden in shadow as they rolled down the cobbled street toward her town house.

"Pardon?" she asked.

Synton leaned forward and she followed his gaze to her lap.

She'd been flexing her hands in a way that *did* look rather threatening.

"Your tone sounds far too intrigued by that thought, Lord Synton. It leads one to believe you're a secret deviant."

"And your tone sounds far too intrigued by *that* revelation, Miss Antonius."

A smile twitched at her lips.

When they'd first gotten into the carriage, they'd only spoken twice. Once for Camilla to give her address and the second for Lord Synton to insist upon draping his overcoat around her.

It was a slow sort of torture to be surrounded by his intoxicating scent and feel the warmth of his body that had lingered in the fine material when he'd shrugged the coat off and immediately placed it around her shoulders.

She'd been relieved when he hadn't pushed to visit the gallery—after her night, she was far too drained to show any paintings at this late hour.

Plus, Camilla wanted to put some much-needed space between herself and the lord after their awkward encounter in Vexley's bedchamber.

Largely because she couldn't sort out whether she was more relieved or embarrassed that Synton hadn't wished to touch her. Obviously, he'd been physically attracted to her—his arousal had been plain as day. Which made her wonder if he was attached to someone else, or if he'd been repulsed by the idea of touching her.

He'd said he was worried about being trapped in marriage, which might be the biggest reason behind his refusal to even kiss her.

At least he hadn't mentioned the forgery.

Camilla was more upset with herself for that slip than for anything else. Synton didn't seem like the sort to spread news, but she really didn't know him. It would be quite the salacious bit of gossip to share at the next party or ball—the gallery owner and artist who led a secret life selling forgeries and deceiving society.

As if he'd plucked the very worry from her head, Synton said casually, "I won't tell anyone. About the forgery."

Relief flooded her system until he added, "As long as you answer two questions truthfully."

Camilla felt her agitation rising again and fought the urge to roll her eyes as he continued.

"If you lie, I'll know. Do we have a deal?"

He watched her closely, his emerald gaze intense, until she reluctantly nodded, her silver gaze holding his with as much defiance as she could muster.

"Is Vexley using that forgery against you?"

She blinked, surprised by his intuition. And she wasn't certain why, but she believed he was telling the truth about knowing if she lied.

"Yes."

"Has he asked you to paint anything else?"

"Yes."

Camilla tensed, waiting for him to press for more information.

A beat of silence passed while he studied her features, his own expression impossible to read. Synton now knew one of her darkest secrets. As if the threat of scandal weren't enough, he now held the same power over her as Vexley.

"I am *nothing* like him, Miss Antonius."

Something dangerous flared in his gaze.

Did he just read my mind?

"Of course not. Control your expressions. They betray your thoughts as clearly as speech."

Without uttering another word, Synton sat back, his face half hidden as he turned to look out the window once again.

Camilla realized it had been a purposeful action—that he did not want her to glean anything from him in return. It felt like a small victory, all things considered.

They traveled the rest of the way in silence, Camilla practically on the edge of her seat, vibrating with nerves as her home finally came into view. Greenbriar Park, where Vexley lived, was only two streets away, but they were long avenues and took ages to traverse at night because of the street cleaners and the market carts making their creaking way home.

She inwardly sighed when the carriage stopped one door down, just as she'd instructed. Home. A bath. Her bed. Blessed distance from this man who was starting to know too much and, she suspected, had quite a past of his own.

"Thank you for—"

One moment Camilla's hand clasped the door handle, the next she was on Synton's lap, his iron-like arm banded around her waist to hold her still. The curtains that had been tied back from the window were swinging shut.

"What—"

"There is a man outside your home, Miss Antonius."

Synton flicked the edge of the curtain back just enough for her to peer out, scanning the street. It looked empty to her.

"On the west side, over there. He's watching your door and he's highly agitated. I need to know why."

"How do you know he's agitated with me?" Camilla felt exhausted.

"Is there a jealous lover I should know about?" Synton pressed.

"Oh, for heaven's sake. I don't see... Oh."

There, in the darkest part of the shadows, Camilla caught a minuscule flicker of movement. How Synton had noticed it was beyond her.

She swore under her breath when another figure moved next to the first.

"Satire-sheet columnists. With all the excitement tonight, I forgot they sometimes watch the homes of Vexley's party guests. They report on who left with whom so they can fuel more gossip. We should be all..."

Camilla closed her eyes, remembering the glaring reason why she couldn't pretend it was Lady Katherine dropping her off.

Even in the dark alley where Synton's carriage had been waiting, she'd noticed SYN painted across the doors in silver ink. The lord didn't have to come inside for the columnists to run wild with their headlines:

ANGEL OF ART SUCCUMBS TO SYN

Beyond the danger of the scandal, Camilla also did not need Vexley to discover that Synton had taken her home—if Vexley believed another man was a threat to their arrangement, she had no doubt he'd do something rash to secure her forever.

"There's a place we can go to avoid them," she said at last. "Have your driver pull onto the next road."

Camilla would be forced to reveal one more secret to Synton tonight, it seemed.

He pounded a fist against the roof and the driver rolled on.

As they bounced over the cobbled street, Camilla realized she was still on Synton's lap, his firm thighs bulging beneath her. She shifted, but he made no move to release her.

"Have him turn here."

Synton did as she instructed, and within moments they'd pulled in front of a seemingly ordinary house.

Each time Camilla saw its cheery exterior, her heart ached.

Her father had purchased the building on the street behind their town house ten years prior—within a week of her mother's abandonment. Some had called it grief, or madness, and they weren't wrong. He'd renovated it into a house filled with secrets over the last few years of his life.

To anyone passing by, it appeared to be a normal home. But the front door and windows were only excellent sculptures, secured to the walls. The true entrance was located around the private, gated alley beside it. After the gate was manually opened, by tugging the hidden latch, it revealed a secret door in the building's side, tall and wide enough to drive a carriage through.

There were no neighbors to the right, only a stone wall too tall to climb over. And the three-story town house itself successfully blocked any other prying eyes.

It was her father's favorite creation. He'd always loved secret entryways but had become especially obsessed with them toward the end. Camilla never quite knew what to make of this. She suspected it related to his love of the old stories, and perhaps a little to her mother, as if one magical door might unlock all her secrets and reveal where she'd gone when she left him.

No matter the reason, in that final decade, doors, portals, entryways, and passages all became Pierre's greatest source of inspiration. He'd painted them, sculpted them, and made this whole house as an ode to whatever world it was he desperately wished to find.

Camilla had never shown any of this last phase of his work before. It was better that no one knew who he'd become. And while her father might not have understood, she did: some doors were not meant to be opened.

After she had instructed the coachman how to open the gate, they pulled up in front of the massive door. "Have your driver pull the lantern on the right toward him," Camilla said.

If Synton was curious about the odd request, he didn't let it show.

A moment later, the door opened wide, and they drove the carriage into the dark space beyond. They waited for the door to close behind them before Camilla exited the coach.

Synton followed her out, his attention sweeping across the cavernous room, only dimly lit by a few flickering gas lanterns. He quickly took in every bridle, saddle, and stack of hay before looking her over anew.

"What a lovely barn. And how do you plan on sneaking past the columnists?"

"You confound me, my lord. Of all the questions you could ask, *that* is the most burning one? No matter where you're from, a secret door cannot be common."

He raised a brow.

"I've heard of your father's eccentricities, Miss Antonius. I'm assuming this was his doing. A fine workspace, I'm sure, but at present, I am more concerned with getting you home than delving into your unusual family history."

Camilla could hardly believe Synton had gleaned so much from that cursory glance. When her father had been alive, he had used the space as his studio. He'd claimed he needed the space, and the quiet, to truly work. In the back was a staircase that led to a washroom and two bedrooms on the second floor that contained all his art supplies. The third floor had remained an open expanse dedicated solely to showcasing his work.

No one except Camilla had had access to this studio, and until this moment, no one but her and her father had ever set foot inside.

"What I cannot piece together," Synton went on, "is the reason we're here. Are you planning on waltzing down the street on foot, as if you'd been out for a stroll?"

"Of course not. I'm going through the secret tunnel, naturally."

She pointed to a pile of what appeared to be broken wheels in the corner.

It was another of her father's creations. When she turned the topmost wheel, it would release the trapdoor hidden beneath.

"Thank you for your help this evening. I'm capable of traveling the rest of the way on my own. If you press against the haystack, it will open the side door again. Good night, my lord."

Synton appraised her with cool calculation.

"I will not be so easily dismissed this time, Miss Antonius."

He brushed past her and strode into the tunnel after releasing the trapdoor. His steps were sure and steady.

"Come. I'll escort you home. We still have business to tend to anyway."

ELEVEN

ENVY SPLIT HIS focus between the annoyed woman striding ahead of him—now sans his overcoat, as she'd promptly tossed it in his face—and the secret, arched tunnel.

When he'd been informed at dinner tonight that Camilla's father was a bit eccentric, he hadn't gotten the impression he'd been the sort to build secret art studios and subterranean tunnels, filled with doors that seemingly led nowhere.

Yet there they were, walking through a hidden passage that connected one side of the block to the other. He could have sworn he'd sensed a ward outside, too. One that gently encouraged passersby to move on, not to be interested in the house of riddles.

It explained why Envy's spies wouldn't have known about the studio. They would have simply gone by it, focused instead on Camilla's town house, never the wiser.

It was an impressive feat for a mortal. One Envy imagined was due to the time the man had spent on the mysterious Silverthorne Lane.

Thankfully the old man had had gas lanterns installed at even intervals, ensuring that the space was well lit and easily passable.

Not that Envy needed the light to see. It was something Lord Antonius had clearly done for his daughter's benefit.

An odd charge filled the air that had nothing to do with Camilla's darkening mood or the way his gaze kept sliding to her torn bodice and the tantalizing lingerie that peeked out with each of her movements.

The design of the lace was beautiful, and he'd almost convinced himself that *that* was why he kept being drawn to it. Envy appreciated art, and the material was finely crafted.

Surely it didn't have anything to do with the woman wearing the lovely garment, or the flashes of her smooth, golden skin under the black lace.

Camilla was a walking contradiction—he sensed that she was surprised by her attraction to him earlier, yet she also wanted to throttle him.

It would make an interesting combination in the bedroom.

The artist stopped near the middle of the passage and spun to face him, silver eyes flashing like blades in the dark.

A wiser male would take it for the warning it was.

But Envy preferred walking the knife's edge of danger.

"Well?" Camilla's voice was as frosty as the look she leveled at him. "What business is so important that it cannot wait until morning?"

No one would ever accuse her of not being passionate.

"I need you to begin work on the Hexed Throne immediately."

She stared at him as if he'd lost his mind.

"No."

"Why are so you opposed?" For the first time that evening, he felt genuine frustration bubbling up. And then it hit him. "Has anyone else asked you to paint a hexed object?"

She gave him an exasperated look. "We've been over this, Lord Synton. I'm not painting a hexed object. For you or anyone. Why on earth would you think I'd changed my mind?"

"I did you a favor tonight. I expect one in return."

"I see." Camilla's tone was suddenly clipped. "How foolish of me to think you were simply being a decent human. Thank you for showing me who you truly are, my lord."

If she knew who Envy truly was, she'd run away screaming and never look back.

In his experience, women like Camilla denied wanting romance, only to end up offering their hearts for bastards like him to eventually break. Lust was so often confused with love.

Envy gave her a slow, cruel smile that made her take an uneasy step away from him.

He was not good, and he was not mortal.

The sooner she realized that, the better it would be for her. If Camilla was sunshine, he was the darkest of nights. And if she wasn't careful, his shadows would snuff out her light, if only for the fleeting chance to possess her warmth before destroying it.

Love was not for him, but he did rather enjoy one night of lust.

"I warned you. I'm no saint, Miss Antonius."

He closed the distance between them, caging her between himself and the wall.

"Nor am I a gentleman. I didn't help you out of the goodness of my heart. You have a rare talent—one that I am willing to pay an extraordinary amount of coin for."

Anger flashed across her features, and she lifted her chin to meet his gaze.

"Find. Someone. Else."

"No."

"You want the painting. Why? Why must it be of *that*?"

"I desire it for my private gallery," he lied. "Your talent is well known."

Sensing the spike in her nerves—and desire—at his proximity, he brought his mouth to her ear. Seduction, he reminded himself, was the path to his second attempt. He needed her to *want* him badly enough to give in to her desires.

When he spoke, his lips whispered across her smooth skin, the touch barely there but potent in its effect. She shivered in his arms.

"Therefore, I want you. And only you."

He shifted to see her face.

At first glance, Camilla gave no indication of being affected by their nearness; her expression was cool indifference; but then her gaze betrayed her by falling to his mouth.

He knew what she would see—lovers had always praised the fullness of his bottom lip, the crooked arc to his devilish grin that would free the dimples in his cheeks if he chose to show them off.

But he didn't expect his own reaction. The heat in her look awakened something in him, something possessive.

Her breaths were coming faster, shorter, her pulse visibly pounding in her throat.

Camilla wanted him.

And he, in turn, now knew her secret, that this little minx desired the demon, excited by all the wickedly tempting things he would make her feel.

"Name your price, Miss Antonius."

Envy dropped one hand to tuck her loose curls behind her ear, easing his body between her legs, forcing her thighs to spread as he pressed closer.

Her breath hitched as his knee settled at the junction of her body, anticipation thickening the air between them.

Camilla's tongue darted out to wet her lips.

Earlier thoughts of that tantalizing mouth and all the carnal ideas it had inspired returned with a vengeance. He hardened and saw the exact moment Camilla felt it.

She shivered against the cool stone wall at her back.

"I think I know what you'd like in return." His hand ghosted down her silhouette, coming to rest on her hip. "Shall I fuck you against this wall?"

Her desire for him flared as he gripped her harder, bunching her silken skirts between his fingers, igniting his own need. His mouth hovered against the skin of her cheek; his focus narrowed to each point of contact between them. Camilla's chest heaved against his, teasing him with its uneven rhythm.

"First with my fingers, then my cock."

His body strained to feel hers, soft where he was hard. In this battle of seduction, he was slowly winning. He felt her resolve dissipating, felt her slowly arch into his touch.

"Surely there's some arrangement we can come to?"

Camilla's desire evaporated at once.

In its place, he was hit by the familiar prickling of anger.

She shoved at his chest and Envy stepped back, giving her space, surprised at how immediately he felt his own sense of loss.

"There will be no arrangement of any sort between us, my lord. I'd sooner make a deal with the king of demons himself."

Irrational jealousy barreled through him at the thought of Camilla striking a deal with his brother Wrath, but he bit the iciness of his sin back.

"That can happily be arranged. Shall we leave for his residence now? Once you're good and sated, perhaps you'll be more agreeable."

A low, soft laugh escaped her lips, the sound sending a bolt of awareness through him, one he did not care for as he found his gaze ensnared by her.

"Go home, Lord Synton."

Camilla grabbed the hem of her skirts and marched down the tunnel toward her house, leaving him where he still stood.

"I've had quite of enough of your charms for one night," she called back over her shoulder.

And yet he could not say the same regarding her.

Envy would do well to remember that Miss Antonius—with her pretty smile, soft curves, and lilting laugh—was not for him, though as her words replayed in his mind, his sin ignited once again. *I'd sooner make a deal with the king of demons himself.*

Like hell she would.

Camilla was *his* until the game ended, and he was not known to share.

TWELVE

Camilla set her paintbrush down, looking her canvas over with a critical eye.

An act that was more difficult than it should have been.

Normally she could see exactly what a painting needed, where to shade, where to highlight, where to add more depth or color. But today, it just wouldn't come. She was still too damn exhausted to think clearly. After a night spent tossing and turning, kicking off her sheets, then getting tangled up in them, frustrated beyond measure, she'd been so tired she'd forgotten her ritual—her mother's locket still hung around her neck. Yet this painting had demanded her attention from the moment she opened her eyes.

So here she was, in her gallery before sunrise, apron cinched at her waist, skin already speckled with paint she prayed hadn't made its way onto the necklace after all.

Before her wasn't quite a self-portrait, but a scene heavily inspired by her bath the previous night.

Despite her agitation, Camilla thought it was already rather lovely; it captured her as all the things she wished she could openly be. Soft, feminine, boldly powerful. Someone who owned her desire without apology, without pretending to humble herself for a world that oppressed.

She'd captured herself submerged in a claw-foot tub, one hand draped across her lower belly, knees bent, golden legs jutting up from the water. Flower petals floated on the water, hiding that secret place between her legs, which had throbbed with every sinful word that came from Synton's lips the night before. In the painting, one foot was propped against the lip of the white tub, revealing flowers stuck to the silky skin of her exposed thighs.

Camilla's mind flashed back to that bath. As she'd washed away the wretchedness of her evening, she'd understood that there was one thing the water could not cleanse—her memories of the filthy things Synton had said in his deep, velvety voice that had made her burn not with anger, but scorching desire.

And his own arousal...

God, he had been pressed against her, hard and wanting.

When he'd moved his hips, slightly grinding against her, she'd nearly seen stars.

Honestly, she ought to call upon a physician and inquire about a tonic—something was clearly amiss. Surely she ought to be traumatized by his bold and abhorrent behavior.

Also by the fact that he'd lied about why he wanted the hexed painting. He was clearly hiding something. Then when he'd demanded to know if anyone else had asked for a hexed object, she'd gone cold.

She'd forgotten about the note.

A request from a mysterious collector had come earlier that week, asking after an illustrated book of spells. The note was unsigned, had no return address, so Camilla had tossed it aside, not thinking about it again until now. What could Synton know?

Shall I fuck you against this wall?

He certainly knew more about that. Camilla ran the slick bar of soap down the side of her body, mimicking his featherlight touch. If she closed her eyes and drew up the memory, the heat of him still lingered.

Along with annoyance.

Camilla had been wrong when she'd thought Vexley was the most aggravating man she'd ever known. Synton now proudly claimed that honor, except—most maddeningly of all—she couldn't stop thinking of him.

Shall I fuck you against this wall? First with my fingers, then my cock.

Camilla had been rendered speechless. Not by his crude words, but by her immediate internal reaction to them.

Yes. God, yes. She'd never wanted anything more.

In public Synton had been the perfect gentleman, seeming offended by Vexley's crass behavior. How different he was when no prying eyes were near, how wondrously sinful.

His whispers felt like their own dark secret. And Camilla was certainly fond of those.

Then he'd gone and ruined everything by negotiating it as payment for her services. As if he could not simply desire her without a price being attached!

His stupid proposition made her feel lonely all over again.

When Camilla had debuted, just after her mother's disappearance, she'd almost been like any other young woman of her station—charmed by the idea of some prince waltzing her across a ballroom, declaring his love.

In truth, everything had been horrid.

Her father's eccentric behavior and her mother's absence had made her a wallflower, standing in the shadows while her friends danced and flirted. It got worse her second and third Seasons, until she stopped believing in her fairy tale.

It had been a foolish dream anyway, one her mother had warned her against.

From the moment Synton strode into her gallery she'd felt drawn to him, a bit of that bright-eyed girl returning, longing to be wanted madly. More fool her, she supposed.

The bell over the door rang loudly, jarring her into the present. She glanced at the clock, startled to see it was now afternoon.

"What have you done with it, you thieving little chit? Did you give it to him?"

Vexley's thunderous accusation broke the peace of the day and her muddled memories of the night before. *Damn. The forgery.*

Camilla twisted from her painting, stunned by the absolute fury on Vexley's face as he advanced, hands clenched at his sides.

Instinct made Camilla want to run far and fast, but some little innate voice warned her to stand her ground, that Vexley was mad enough to give chase and it would be far worse for her if he caught her then.

Camilla kept her voice calm and even. "I'm not sure what you mean, my lord. What have I done with what? And who have I given it to?"

"Do not play coy with me today! You know precisely what I'm inquiring about."

Vexley towered over her, a serpent ready to strike.

"Where is the forgery? I have spent the entire morning tearing my home apart and it is most certainly not there, so I'll ask you once again nicely before I stop being a gentleman, where is the damned thing, Camilla? Did you give it to Synton?"

She blinked up at him, hearing the words but having difficulty understanding.

If Vexley believed he was acting like a gentleman, then she might as well declare herself the Seelie Queen of Faerie.

"I haven't the slightest idea." Camilla's pulse roared in her ears as she focused on the most important thing he'd said. Surely she'd misheard him. "Have you lost it? Or moved it and forgot?"

"You think me a fool, Miss Antonius, but I assure you I am not. No, I did not lose it. It was right where I'd left it before dressing for dinner last night. And when I awoke, it was gone."

Camilla's mind spun. This was quite possibly the worst news. She'd been certain she'd have another chance to steal the painting back.

Vexley had to be wrong.

The alternative sent invisible spiders skittering across her skin. If someone else had the forgery now...

She straightened her spine, playing for time. "You had enough spirits to fell an elephant during dinner, Vexley. Are you certain you didn't move it and forget?"

"Don't." He leaned in, blue eyes wild. "You leave early. Not saying goodbye to anyone. And Synton also mysteriously vanishes. Then I awake to a missing painting. If you aren't in cahoots with him, then I wonder, what happened to Lady Katherine, too? What would her husband think of such unbecoming behavior, such scheming? Especially if it were to become the talk of the *ton*. Satire sheets simply love a scandal, Camilla."

"Lady Katherine knows nothing of the forgery, and you'd do well not to threaten her." Camilla held her ground, nose stubbornly a few inches from Vexley's own. "I went home at a respectable hour and that somehow makes me guilty? What of the dozen or so others who showed no such tact? You know as well as I do that Harrington or Walters would love to possess that piece for their private collections. They have no idea it's not the actual painting. Do you truly hold them in such high esteem as to think they wouldn't steal it, given the chance?"

"Were you not telling me this very week that you wanted our arrangement to end?" he pressed, spittle foaming in the corners of his mouth. "I may not be a detective inspector, Camilla, but that certainly sounds like motive. If you're working with Synton, there will be hell to pay."

His hand rose quickly to circle her throat. He rested it there lightly but with dark promise.

Trapped, Camilla went very still.

His gaze raked down the front of her bodice, pausing on the swell of her breasts in her morning gown. For one horrifying moment, she thought he'd rip open her dress.

"Deliver it back by week's end, or I will see you ruined."

The bell over the door tinkled pleasantly, alerting them that they were no longer alone.

Camilla's breath stayed lodged in her chest as precious seconds passed by and Vexley didn't unhand her. Instead, his pale eyes glittered with malice—he knew exactly what she feared, and he enjoyed it.

But finally, Vexley straightened, his expression changing from fury to lazy indifference before he finally stepped aside, pretending he'd been admiring the art behind her.

"Have that wrapped up and sent over to Gretna House, Miss Antonius. I rather like it after all." He fixed her with an even gaze. "The splashes of red remind me of blood. They're raw. Powerful. You know I've always found broken things darkly appealing."

His ability to don a new mask so swiftly was disturbing. Wondering how she'd never noticed it before made her unease grow.

"Of course, my lord." She accepted his ruse, even if her smile felt as strained as the tension still winding between them. She finally caught a glimpse of the door, where a satire-sheet columnist seemed far too intrigued by their interaction.

"May I assist you with something, sir?" she asked cheerily.

"Lord Vexley!" The columnist ignored Camilla, instead calling after Vexley, who'd swept through the gallery as if he'd suddenly remembered he had somewhere more important to be.

"A moment…is it true that Walters fought with a garden statue last night and lost?"

Vexley paused, debonair act reinstated. "Come now, Havisham. You don't believe I'll give up my friends' secrets that easily, do you?"

Vexley flashed his legendary grin, slowing his pace to saunter out the door, apparently without a care in the world. Camilla waited until he and Havisham had exited the gallery before dropping onto her stool, muscles trembling. She had no doubt that Vexley would make good on his threats if pushed. In fact, he'd seemed ready to kill her then. Her hands came up to her throat, the icy sensation of the lord's touch chilling her to the core. She'd known Vexley would be angry if she succeeded in stealing the forgery, but she'd never imagined him causing bodily harm.

He'd never been violent before. Nor had she heard any rumors of his being involved in fisticuffs. Vexley had convinced everyone he was simply a drunken, lovable rogue.

But what did she truly know of the lord?

No one respectable visited the dark market as often as he did. Silverthorne Lane was a place where magic slithered through the streets, drinking the life and emotion from visiting mortals. She'd seen it happen firsthand with her father, knew how dangerous a place it was. Once he'd started going there, life as they'd known it had ended.

Initially, as Pierre grew sicker, Camilla, too, had ventured there, damning all consequences. If that was where her father had fallen ill, she believed she'd find the cure there too. And she'd felt the power there, sensed the allure.

After her father had died, she'd gone only twice more.

The first time was when she'd met Wolf, the legendary hunter, tempted by the life beyond Waverly Green he might have offered her.

The second time, she'd gone to warn him away, to ensure that he kept their night of passion a secret. Camilla wanted to stay in Waverly Green, and no one could know she'd thrown her reputation away in a fit of desperation, needing to remember she was still alive, even in the darkness of her grief.

Wolf had left with a vow, but only after promising he'd return one day.

She still prayed that would never happen. Vexley and Synton were trouble enough.

Speaking of...she'd been a fool to think that just because Synton hadn't pressed her for more information last night, he'd leave it be. One thing she could agree with Vexley on was that somehow, some way, Synton had snuck back into Gretna House.

Camilla would be damned if she'd let one more man blackmail her.

If Vexley was actually going to ruin her, she would at least have the satisfaction of seeing that wretched painting destroyed by her own hand.

Furious, Camilla put a sign on the door informing patrons that the gallery was closed for the day, then went to hire a coach.

She had a sudden need to visit Hemlock Hall.

As she stepped out into the cobbled street, she sensed someone behind her. She spun around, noticing a man leaning against the building across the street. His features were hidden by a hat he'd tugged low over his brow, his size and form indistinguishable under a black cloak.

He had on leather gloves that gave her pause.

Camilla waited for him to push off the building and leave, but he didn't. He remained where he stood, silent, foreboding.

Vexley wouldn't have hired someone to watch her, would he?

The answer to that was a simple yes.

She swallowed and hurried to the end of the street, calling a coach. When she climbed in and glanced out the window, the man was gone.

THIRTEEN

Envy tilted back his head, considering the forgery he'd stolen earlier. The late-afternoon sunlight slanted through the window, gilding the dust motes he'd stirred with his pacing.

He'd been staring at the impressive painting for the better part of the day, pleased with himself for wrangling it out from under Vexley's nose while he snored.

The man was a total disgrace, sleeping on his stomach, his pimpled ass uncovered, passing gas as foul as his manners.

A savage part of Envy wanted to hang the forgery in his foyer, invite Vexley over for drinks, and piss a circle around Camilla's work, marking his territory until the game moved on.

Instead, Envy reined himself in, remembered that strategy was what won wars.

And certainly, a war was on. Last night his second attempt to secure Camilla's help had failed. He only had one more opportunity before he was disqualified. And while the rules surrounding any forfeit were still unclear, the realities facing his court were anything but.

Envy *needed* to win.

He'd been trying to keep a positive attitude, but things were bleak. He couldn't use his magic to influence Camilla—seduction didn't work.

Asking straight out had failed spectacularly.

"Fuck." Envy raked a hand through his hair, glancing up at the painting again.

Desperation made people messy, careless. Envy needed to focus. Stealing the forgery had given him a bargaining chip to use with Camilla. He'd seen how much she wanted it. So, when Camilla had tried to tear it from the wall, he'd used a tiny bit of magic to lock it in place. Collecting it himself was an insurance plan, a card hidden up his sleeve. Since it wasn't outright persuasion, it wasn't breaking any of Lennox's rules.

Now that he had secured the forgery, Envy considered what else he might focus on.

Preparations for the ball were well underway, as it was nearly upon them, only two nights away now.

The manor house was fully restored to its former glory and then some. The dark wood gleamed from its recent buffing, the new velvet draperies hung thick and lush. The artwork brought over from his real private collection was tastefully displayed across the estate, and he'd shown the staff how to prepare his preferred custom drink—the Dark and Sinful. It was a decadent concoction he'd created one evening of muddled blackberries, brown sugar simple syrup, bourbon, orange zest, and a splash of champagne.

They'd scoffed at the name, but none had protested after they'd sampled it.

Now he could turn his full attention toward attempt three. His spies hadn't unearthed anything of great importance on Camilla yet, only things he'd already known—although they had confirmed his suspicion about the secret tunnel her father had made. It was laid on top of a realm line, an invisible magical boundary that might open to other realms. Not many knew of them and even fewer used them. Particularly here in the human realm.

Envy hadn't sensed that the tunnel had been activated, so it wasn't presently in use. And he hadn't seen any runes or a portal key notch, although that didn't mean Pierre hadn't hidden one somewhere. And even if he had, Envy doubted he'd been able to unlock it.

Portal keys were only gifted by two species that Envy knew of: Fae, primarily the Unseelie royalty who ruled the dark court, or very powerful shape-shifters—like werewolves.

Instead of wasting the rest of the day with his growing frustration, perhaps Envy would pay the infamous dark market a visit. At least then he might learn more about what Vexley had been up to. He'd been so convinced that the man was another player, but after his baffling performance last night, Envy hoped this wasn't his competition. It'd be a letdown. But it would be helpful all the same to find out who else in Waverly Green might be privy to realm lines.

"So. This is where you've been hiding out."

Envy didn't turn around at the sound of his brother Lust's voice. "Let me guess. Pride's been gossiping like a courtier?"

"Probably. But I heard it from Gluttony, who mentioned hearing it from Greed."

His brothers were no better than the irksome columnists.

Gluttony at the very least ought to know better—he was currently involved in a war with his own reporter in the Seven Circles.

"With the curse broken," Envy drawled, "I would have thought you'd all have something better to do with your time. Though I can't really blame you—I am the most interesting of our brothers."

He called for Goodfellow and instructed him to put the painting carefully in his bedchamber. Envy had warded the room so no one could enter without his permission. It should be safe enough there.

"My visit to the Shifting Isles is hardly scintillating for you, though," he continued once Goodfellow had departed. Lust had made his way over to toy with the velvet drapes. "Surely you ought to be more intrigued by a certain death goddess than my…reprieve. Vengeance and lust do work so nicely together."

Lust chuckled, never one to fall prey to needling.

"From what I've heard, she's preoccupied with her puppies." Envy rolled his eyes at the cavalier mention of the werewolf pack. "Even if she weren't involved with that drama, I rather like my cock attached to my body at the end of the day. Plus, the little game you're currently involved in is much more interesting. Is it true an artist castrated you?"

Envy touched the jeweled dagger at his hip, contemplating returning to the Seven Circles solely to castrate Pride.

"Not that it's any of your concern, but rest assured, I am still the most well-endowed sibling."

"Debatable, but the masquerade you're hosting is enticing enough. My invitation seems to have gotten lost—an oversight I rectified for you by arriving early. I'm sure my influence will make it legendary."

Lust's voice held a note of teasing, always a sign of trouble. He'd finally moved away from the drapes and was considering the carvings of the mantel far too closely.

"Consider me your lustful goddemon, here to turn this into the most debauched event this realm has ever seen. Imagine all those stuffy, buttoned-up lords and ladies giving in to their pleasures..." Lust's tone turned wistful. "Your staff will be cleaning the tables and walls for weeks."

Camilla's face crossed Envy's mind, her eyes closed in rapture as someone dropped to their knees before her, tasting her sweet desire as she rode their face. For some reason, he pictured this occurring right on his dining room table.

"No." Envy finally turned, giving his brother a hard look. "Absolutely—"

"You!"

The door to Envy's studio crashed open, his second-in-command striding in after the little hell beast who'd charged in before him, silver eyes flashing.

"How dare you."

Alexei tossed his hands up. "I tried to stop her."

Envy flicked his attention over the artist, ignoring the giddy curiosity on Lust's face. Camilla's silver hair was arranged into an intricate knot held in place by a paintbrush, and her gown was a deep, sultry plum. If it weren't for the lightning in her eyes, threatening to strike him down where he stood, he'd have paid her a compliment. Camilla knew what colors to pair to elicit the most pleasing results, and her creativity extended well beyond paint on canvas.

"Try harder. Miss Antonius is all of five feet and a handful of inches," he finally said. "If you cannot handle her, Alexei, perhaps we ought to reconsider your position."

"You will do no such thing," Camilla said. "Aside from the promise of a vicious assault on his groin, I also threatened to bite him if he stood in my way."

Lust made a strangled sound.

"I see." Envy schooled his features into bland interest, giving away none of the amusement he felt at the thought of Camilla unknowingly sinking her teeth into a vampire.

He also could not recall a time when anyone had dared to give *him* a direct command.

Camilla stared up at him in challenge.

Lust let loose a low chuckle. "You must be the reason he's in such a foul mood."

"Pardon me, and you are?" Camilla asked, her tone still frosty as she looked Lust over, seeming less than impressed.

A considerable feat given that Envy's brother was the prince who ruled over pleasure, and his very presence usually incited skirt-lifting or trouser-dropping admiration within seconds.

Lust appeared wildly amused—and far too intrigued—by her lack of swooning. Envy felt the magic of his brother's sin slowly circle the artist, testing.

He gritted his teeth.

Lust bowed over her hand, letting a bit more of his sin out as his lips brushed across her gloved knuckles.

"His better-looking brother, naturally."

"Charmed." Camilla wrenched her hand away, then returned that impressive glare to Envy.

She hadn't been affected by Lust's power at all.

"I demand a private audience at once."

Lust flashed him a surprised look, clearly taken aback too by her complete disregard.

Envy raised a brow, then nodded to his brother and Alexei. "Very well."

Both men seemed cowed enough by Camilla's entrance to heed the request.

Once they'd closed the door, he leaned against the table where his drink sat untouched, puzzled by her ability to withstand a demon prince's influence.

"For someone who wishes to avoid ruination, demanding to be alone with me, unchaperoned, seems quite risky, especially after what I said last night. Unless of course you're here to fulfill that naughty fantasy."

He was curious to see whether she'd confront him about that.

She did not rise to the bait, instead pinning him in place with those moonlike eyes.

"Where is the forgery?"

"I assume you mean *The Seduction of Evelyn Gray*?"

"Do not play a game with me, my lord." Camilla advanced, only stopping when her skirts brushed against his knees. "Vexley visited me earlier."

Even though Vexley was nothing more than a pox on a pig's ass, irrational jealousy seared through him.

"I am disinterested in any lovers' quarrel you might be having."

"How unsurprising. It's safe to assume you're even less interested in the threats of bodily injury that were made with his hand around my throat, my lord. As you cannot be bothered with all that, just tell me where the forgery is so I can collect it and be on my way."

Envy stilled.

The heart he assumed to be shriveled and black pounded furiously as he looked Camilla over more carefully.

"He hurt you?"

One word, one look of confirmation, and Envy would have his demon blade in Vexley's gut within the hour.

Camilla drew herself up, glaring. "Not this time, but he has threatened far worse if the forgery is not returned immediately."

"That will not happen." His voice was laced with its own violence.

Camilla jerked back, her eyes rounding as she looked him over closely, seeming to understand that he meant it.

In fact, he found himself suddenly striding toward the door, plan whirling into place.

Perhaps once he was finished with the mortal, he'd gift him to Alexei for a meal.

If Vexley proved to be a player, it would be most beneficial indeed.

"You cannot murder him," Camilla said, sounding—of all things—partly aghast and mildly frustrated.

He didn't slow his pace. "I assure you, I can."

"Allow me to rephrase. You will not murder him."

Envy finally slowed and glanced over his shoulder, suspicion winding around him like a tangled vine. One look at her stony face and he knew: there was more to this twisted tale.

When it came to Camilla, he really shouldn't be surprised.

"Why?" he asked.

She swallowed hard, the column of her delicate throat moving slightly.

The very throat that Vexley's cursed hands had attempted to desecrate.

Rage surged again before he obliterated it. If Wrath could see him now, submitting to his sin on behalf of someone else... the smug bastard would never let him live it down.

"Why won't you allow me to kill him, Camilla?" Envy repeated.

He didn't think it had anything to do with morals. At least not fully. He waited, silent, watchful. Allowing her time to give him the truth.

"Because the forgery isn't the only thing he has of mine, my lord."

Several beats passed while Envy waited for her to elaborate.

Camilla's hands fisted at her sides, bunching in her plum skirts. Her anger and despair warred in the space between them.

"If he dies, so does my father."

PART II

A Deal with the Devil

FOURTEEN

"METAPHORICALLY SPEAKING, I mean," Camilla rushed to add, watching Lord Synton's face carefully, noting the exact moment he decided against hunting Vexley down. For a minute, he'd reminded her of an angel of vengeance: all lethal grace and divine punishment, charging in to completely obliterate a foe for their wrongdoing.

Looking at him now, at the cold calm and utter control he had over himself, Camilla had no doubt Synton would be capable of murdering Vexley and not sparing another thought once the dastardly deed was done. The fact that he *hadn't* done just that indicated that he'd weighed the advantages against the disadvantages and found Vexley to be safe from retribution.

For now.

She didn't think Synton would glory in the kill, but he certainly wouldn't mind being the one to dispatch Vexley.

Or, on second thought, as she saw his pupils constrict, perhaps he *would* thrill in the violence, welcome it with open arms. Which ought to make Camilla wary of him but somehow comforted her instead.

"How, exactly, does one metaphorically kill one's father?" he asked. "Should I believe one might have also metaphorically killed one's mother?"

Synton's tone was cordial enough, but there was a hardness in his eyes, a stiffness in his shoulders, and an undeniable feeling that the man standing before Camilla was nothing more than a feral animal trapped in the cage of expensive suits.

This man *liked* the darkness, welcomed it; the shadows were where he preferred to be.

Camilla imagined painting Synton that way—his beautiful face emerging from the shadows, the lushness of his lips set against the harsh lines of a harsher expression, wielding a blazing sword dripping with the blood of his enemies.

"Miss Antonius?"

Her name jolted her out of her vision. Camilla shook her head, clearing it. "I didn't mean it the way it sounded. And *of course* I didn't kill my mother. She left to travel the world. End of story."

"Enlighten me about your father, then." He bit out the words as if each syllable gravely offended him.

She took a deep breath. "Vexley is in possession of something that belonged to my father. Something I very much want back. If he's to be believed, it's secured outside Waverly Green, and only he knows its precise location. Should Vexley meet a foul end, I won't ever retrieve it. It's an object my father treasured, so losing it...it has a great emotional attachment for me, is all."

It wasn't the full truth. It had begun one wintry night. Camilla recalled Pierre grabbing a coat and rushing out the door, muttering about a story Camilla's mother had once told them, years before. This had been toward the end, when he was often caught up in his fantasies of the past, but this time had proved different. Pierre had gone missing for three days, coming home exhausted but proud, the owner of a magical key he'd claimed would change everything.

Camilla had gleaned that he'd bargained for that key on Silverthorne Lane. It was soon afterward that the secret entryways took over his world and the secret gatehouse studio was built.

He'd been a man obsessed, forgetting to eat, barely sleeping; it had been difficult to watch, to try desperately to pull him back to his life before Fleur had ruined it with her tales of shadow realms. But still, after he'd died, the key had felt important. Like it might reveal something Camilla had missed about his madness, if she herself found the right door.

Of course, now she knew she should have pawned it back at the dark market. Instead, she'd kept it secreted away, unwilling to part with it.

Sentimentality often grew fangs and bit a person in the rump.

If Camilla had sold it, Vexley never would have stolen it from her, and she'd not have one more chain wrapped around her now.

"Your father is really dead, then."

"Yes," she said quietly. "He really died a few years back."

There was a slight softening in Synton's features, like he understood what losing something irreplaceable meant. For a tense beat, Camilla thought he'd reach out, hold her hand, let her know she wasn't alone.

Then he slammed any empathy down, his expression going carefully blank as he stepped back, putting distance between them. He was wholly unreadable now.

Except for his clever eyes, which seemed to indicate that his mind was rapidly sorting through puzzle pieces and riddles, figuring out his next move and whether this information changed anything.

He slowly dragged his gaze over her, a new spark entering those shrewd eyes.

"I'm hosting a masquerade ball in two nights' time."

Camilla drew her brows together, not immediately understanding the giant shift in conversation. "My invitation arrived earlier."

He nodded, almost absently. "I will assist with locating the object that belonged to your father. I will also hold on to the forgery and keep Vexley on a tight leash, ensuring that he doesn't cause any problems for either of us. If you agree to paint the Hexed Throne, I'll return the forgery to you after it's complete."

He held up a hand, forestalling any argument.

"We both get something we want out of the bargain. Before you toss the offer aside, take time to really think it over, Miss Antonius. It's a fair deal."

It was a reasonable request, yet Camilla's pulse roared in her ears.

She *couldn't* paint that throne.

At least not without giving away one of her most closely guarded secrets.

But her choices were quickly dwindling.

"What is the true reason you want that painting?" she asked, knowing it was likely in vain. Yet if she considered giving him one of her secrets, he should return the favor.

"I told you. I collect intriguing art. Your talent is such that I'd like to own this piece."

Synton's expression abruptly shuttered, but she'd caught a glimpse of something desolate, something that seemed to span centuries, staring out from his emerald eyes. There had been no hint of humanity in that look, only coldness so impenetrable that she shuddered in its wake. She could easily imagine he'd lived lifetimes alone, tortured by something he'd never escaped.

"Very well," she said, inexplicably moved. "I'll give you an answer in two nights, at the ball."

FIFTEEN

Envy was surprised that Goodfellow had been correct about the Fae.

The dark market on Silverthorne Lane was cleverly named for the creatures that sold curious wares and made cruel bargains with mortals either foolish or arrogant enough to believe they could deceive those who'd practically invented deception.

Most humans believed the Fae were incapable of lying—it was a tale they'd spun themselves, as they often crafted folklore that suited them best.

Only one myth held truth—iron did lay them low.

If mortals were half as smart and superior as they'd like to believe they were, they'd fashion their homes and prisons out of it. Envy knew for a fact that every dungeon in his brothers' Houses of Sin was made of the material. Plenty of other lesser-known nasties roamed the realms, and iron did a pretty good job of holding them, too.

Shrewd vendors called out from the open-air stalls as he passed, trying to entice him to their tables.

"Memory stone?"

"Potion for never-ending lust?"

"Jacket to divert any foe and cheat death?"

Envy strolled along the cobbled street, glancing into each stall of questionable artifacts, hands tucked casually in his pockets. But inside, he was tense—sensing Fae magic pulsing all around, luring and tempting, like a song whose tune slowly sank into the listener's subconscious until they hummed it without thought. It was subtle, a charge in the atmosphere, a scent that hung thick in the air like a heady mixture of spice and storm clouds, unmistakable: the Wild Court's magic.

The Wild Court was the name given to the Unseelie kingdom, home to the dark Fae. As a species Fae were birthed into one of two courts. The Seelie—or the light court, who worshipped the sun and spring and summer—or the Unseelie court, the Fae who worshipped the moon and fall and winter.

Part of the island chain where both the Seven Circles and the Shifting Isles were located, Faerie loomed in the west, divided down the middle by an invisible boundary. The Seelie had settled in the east, where the sun shone the brightest, while the Unseelie had set up their court in the west, where the moon reigned supreme.

Of course, there were solitary Fae and exiled Fae as well, and each faced their own unique challenges. Being a member of a court was ingrained in their very beings, so parting from it willingly or unwillingly was difficult. Or so he'd been told.

Fae time moved differently even from other Underworld realms, too. A few days in the mortal realm could equal a few months in Faerie, though a few days in Faerie was only a week or two in the Seven Circles. Envy knew that personally, from a time he'd prefer not to think of. Yet, despite his ignoring the tricky Wild realms, over the years, rumors had reached the Seven Circles of discord in the Unseelie court.

It seemed that decades before, Prim Róis, the Unseelie Queen—legendary for her wicked games—had abdicated her throne for a time, delighting in the chaos her absence wreaked.

Mostly, she did it to needle the king. She was Discord, he was Chaos. Both as inconstant and changing as the moon they worshipped. Together they had ruled over the Unseelie, culling a court of nightmarish Fae for several millennia, twisted and gnarled and full of rot. The Unseelie kingdom itself had been broken into the jagged points of a star—with Prim

Róis and Lennox ruling at the top and their wicked heirs overseeing the remaining four courts. Envy knew firsthand that the Unseelie were similar to succubi, feeding on emotions, most associated with passion. He knew, too, that they enjoyed toying with humans.

So Envy and his brothers had kept a close eye on them, especially once the witches and vampires began circling Faerie like sharks, drawn to the scent of spilled blood. Malice Isle—home to the vampire court—was a mere stone's throw from the southeastern shore of the Seven Circles, granting them easy sailing to Faerie once they traveled west past the Shifting Isles.

Luckily, the Seelie at least had shown some sense, turning their attention to their own matters, unconcerned with their wicked brethren.

Envy drew himself from his dark thoughts, glancing around to be sure none of these strange, lone Fae might have deciphered where they'd gone.

Luckily, a stall on his left drew his attention. Paintbrushes made of gemstones glittered in the moonlight. One was carved from a single flawless emerald. Beautiful.

Envy plucked it up, feeling for any trace of magic or trickery, intrigued when all was as mundane as it appeared.

"Bag this up."

Copper eyes flashed. Sharp teeth gleamed.

"A fine choice, Your Highness."

His true title was nothing but a mere hiss on the wind, yet several pairs of ancient eyes turned to him. Before the Fae could spill any other secret, Envy's dagger was at the Unseelie's throat, the tip digging deep enough to draw its sparkling blood.

Envy's blade glowed, pleased with the offering.

"Tell you what. Give me information and I may be persuaded to keep your head attached to your body. Lie and I'll piss on your corpse's pyre tonight. Deal?"

A demon blade was indiscriminate as to who or what it killed. No immortal could withstand a strike. Except for his brothers.

The Fae seethed but inclined its head. Wise enough to ensure that it lived to see another wretched day.

"Have you, or has anyone you know, sold information to a man called Pierre Antonius? Give details."

"Yes. He wished to know of a way to travel realms."

"How long ago?"

"Two years."

"And?" Envy pressed. "What else?"

"We told him of realm lines."

Just as Envy had suspected.

"Did your king give him a key?"

"I no longer belong to any king or queen. What they do or do not give doesn't concern me."

An exiled Fae, then, more volatile than a solitary Fae. Exiled Fae were either furious at being without a court, or happy to be free. This one seemed to lean toward the former.

"Political bullshit aside, answer the question. Did he have a key?"

"Yes."

And Envy would wager that that was the object Camilla wanted to get back. The one she'd claimed held sentimental value. Given the secret tunnel and the passageways shown in Pierre's art, Envy understood why she'd want it back, even if she wasn't fully aware of what it did. That Vexley had it indicated he was more cunning than Envy would have believed. And almost certainly guaranteed he was a player.

"Why did he want to travel realms?"

"Same as all others. To live among his betters. To amuse us until we grow bored."

Which was an arrogant way of saying the Fae didn't know. Pierre could have been searching for a way into Faerie, or he could have been searching for shifters.

"Have you, or has anyone you know, bargained with a mortal named Vexley? If so, be specific as to what he wanted."

"Yes. He wanted information. About a key."

Envy's grip tightened on his dagger.

"The same key?"

"I would imagine so. Not many portal keys to be found these days."

It took every ounce of will he possessed not to go back on his word and stab the Fae.

"Did he secure information about this key?"

If so, then the odds of safely locating and retrieving the key were growing slimmer. Envy knew that if Vexley had had any inkling of what the key was worth, he'd have sold it to the highest bidder, easily lying about returning it to Camilla.

An argument broke out the moment before the Fae answered him, stealing Envy's attention long enough for the Unseelie to vanish beneath his grasp.

Cursing, he glared at the mortal fighting with the proprietor two stalls down, feeling a little less murderous when he saw who was making all the ruckus.

Lord Edwards. Katherine's husband.

Curious indeed.

Envy quickly considered all possibilities: Edwards could be another player. Or maybe he was one of the many who'd become addicted to Unseelie magic.

Envy could walk over, drag the man away from the fight, or he could watch from the shadows, see what other secrets there were to be gleaned.

Envy wasn't the helping sort.

He called upon his own magic, cloaking himself in shadow before drifting closer to the furious lord.

"I'll have you know that Peter did not take to the tonic as promised."

The Fae dealer gave the mortal a blank look.

"The rooster, for God's sake," Edwards said between clenched teeth. "You promised it would sire golden-egged riches. I demand my money back."

Envy briefly closed his eyes. Was Edwards really such a fool? Or was it possible he needed the rooster for his clue? Odd, but the game master did have a wicked sense of humor.

Though maybe Edwards was like any other mortal, wanting an easy way to secure more wealth.

Bored and disappointed, Envy continued down Silverthorne Lane, scanning the thinning crowd, trying to sort out the mystery of Camilla's father and his fascination with other realms. What had lured him—Faerie or shifters?

Or was Pierre's fascination simply that annoying human need for adventure?

Envy suddenly wanted to know more about Camilla's absent mother; she might very well hold the answers he needed. Camilla had been quick to end the discussion when he'd asked about her, and now he very much wanted to know why.

SIXTEEN

Camilla's maid cinched her stays tight enough to elicit a wince, then helped her into the most magnificent garment she'd ever seen, let alone owned before going to fetch her slippers.

After her father died, she'd used all her earnings from the gallery to keep the staff on. The gallery had come a long way already, earning a nice income for her, but she couldn't replace her entire wardrobe each season like she used to.

It was either pretty dresses and half the staff, or half the dresses and supporting those she'd known her whole life. The choice was easy.

The gown she wore now was beyond anything she'd dreamed of owning again. Indeed, it was a work of art—lavish, decadent, and undeniably stunning. Camilla felt like a princess in it, not just because the gown must have cost a small fortune, but because wearing it made her feel powerful. It had been a long while since she'd truly felt that.

She twisted one way, then the other in front of her full-length mirror, admiring the flow of the material.

The skirts were ethereal layers of fluffy white tulle, with silver sparkles scattered like glittering stars across the fabric. The bodice was made of diamonds encrusted with silver beads and downy white feathers. She looked like a moon goddess, ethereal, tempting, and completely out of any mortal's reach.

The gown had mysteriously shown up two hours before Synton's ball, along with a matching silver filigree mask. No note accompanied the package, but a beautiful new paintbrush was nestled on top of the dress.

Though calling it a paintbrush hardly did it justice—the handle was a solid piece of carved emerald, the exact shade of Synton's eyes, leaving no room for Camilla to mistake where the gifts had originated.

Surprisingly enough, though made from a gemstone, the brush wasn't heavy or hard to handle—it fit her palm perfectly, making her long for a few moments to sit at an easel.

Camilla often wondered if paint ran through her veins instead of blood. When she created, it was as if she made new realms, fantastical and beautiful and exactly where she wished she could escape to. With her art, somehow she was connected to the universe far beyond her small gallery. She could live a thousand and one lives, each more magical than the last.

Synton had chosen his temptation well.

The paintbrush was a cunning gift. It made Camilla seriously consider painting the Hexed Throne for him, consequences be damned.

She laid the paintbrush back on the crushed velvet, emotions churning. She needed to give him an answer about his proposed deal tonight.

She wished this decision didn't feel so much like a betrayal. She recalled the night before her father had died—he'd tried to draw her near, his arms shaking with the effort.

"Darkness... will... not... win."

"I don't understand," she'd said, tears stinging her eyes. Had he known? She remembered thinking, had he always known?

"You... are... good, sweet girl. Never... doubt."

It was the last thing he'd ever said to her. And Pierre had made clear throughout the years how he felt about hexed objects. How dangerous they were, to be avoided at all costs.

Mixed with Camilla's rare... talent... should she paint the Hexed Throne it might very well appear. Stories varied on what it did—from granting everlasting power and immortality to cursing all other rulers and even destroying immortals—but Camilla wasn't sure any variation would be good.

What did Synton want with the painting of the throne?

He'd claimed he wanted it only for his personal gallery, but Camilla didn't need his uncanny ability to detect a lie to know he wasn't being truthful.

Could she really risk giving someone like Synton access to an object with the power to do unspeakably dark things? Her father had taught her repeatedly that power corrupted even the purest soul. Synton didn't strike her as having a pure soul to begin with.

If Camilla painted the Hexed Throne, she would be responsible for whatever happened after. Maybe Synton wouldn't abuse it, but it could be stolen by someone worse.

A gentle knock brought her attention to the here and now.

"Come in."

Her maid dropped a polite curtsy then helped Camilla into her slippers. "The Lord and Lady Edwards have arrived."

Camilla glanced at her reflection one last time, then donned her mask.

One way or another, the woman who returned to this home would be changed. For better or worse.

The way her luck had been going didn't inspire confidence.

"Please, Father. Help." Camilla tried to summon a memory of her father, seeking his reassuring voice, but whatever being heard her plea in the Great Beyond laughed darkly, the chilling echo reverberating through her bones.

Camilla hurried from her bedchamber, hoping that haunting laugh wasn't a sign of worse things to come.

SEVENTEEN

Hemlock Hall was no House of Envy, but the prince of that circle was pleased enough with the restoration. And the turnout. Regardless of the ache growing in the pit of his stomach, or the way his attention kept turning to the clock. Much would be decided by the end of the night. He'd either be one step closer to victory, or he'd damn his people forever.

The fate of Envy's court depended on one stubborn mortal.

The irony was poetic, he supposed. Lennox had had decades to plan this game, and had probably chosen Camilla because of that very trait, knowing she'd not make it easy for any of them.

Still, Envy hadn't expected to come this close to losing so soon.

He focused on his breathing, on the role he needed to play of enigmatic lord. Inside, he churned like a violent sea. He wanted to pace the upper balcony, strum his fingers along the banister, release some of his pent-up energy.

Maybe he just needed to find a willing partner and fuck his way to serenity. Or better, restore some power by stoking someone's envy.

That shouldn't be too hard. He looked out at the first guests, arriving with great excitement at his glittering estate. He'd restored the circular drive, adding a fountain that boasted a statue of a winged beast, the water colored a sparkling pale green.

Every chamber, every inch of the grounds, had been designed to dazzle and to provoke his sin.

Nearly everyone in Waverly Green's mortal high society had accepted his invitation, well over a hundred nobles drawn to the manor house and its mysterious allure, if only to boast about it later. Envy had also made sure to withhold certain invitations. There was nothing to be envied about an event that everyone could attend.

He watched as a dozen or so couples swarmed into the ballroom, dressed in gowns and suits of the finest materials, their masks gleaming in the candlelight. Women circled the room, talking excitedly, while the men swiped drinks from passing trays.

Envy moved along the balcony overlooking the grand hall, listening in. Even wearing deep gold masks, he recognized the Lords Walters and Harrington from Vexley's party, and the man—Lord Garrey—who'd snuck off with Widow Janelle.

Lord Garrey was interesting. Apparently, he'd had a string of bad luck over the last few years, despite his family's impeccable standing. His youngest sister and then a woman he'd courted had gone missing, never to be seen again. Envy's spies had also uncovered his connection to Lord Edwards, a boyhood friend. Lord Garrey, too, had been seen frequenting Silverthorne Lane.

Knowing all this, Envy suspected that Lord Garrey was another player. Fae liked to take mortal women, lure them into Faerie. It would be something worth playing for—a chance to win one back.

Envy's hunch grew as the man excused himself to slowly wander around the edge of the ballroom, his attention sliding over each painting and sculpture. Envy had purposefully included art depicting Unseelie. He'd wanted to see who would notice. And like clockwork, that was where Lord Garrey paused now. The Wild Court.

Envy signaled to Alexei, who'd been waiting on the main floor, indicating that he should watch the mortal in question. His second nodded, then disappeared into the shadows.

Envy returned his attention to Walters and Harrington. Two buffoons, from what he'd observed, not likely players, unless Lennox was simply toying with Envy.

Whispers from that group of lords reached his ears, their voices tinged with jealousy. Apparently, Envy's invitations had done what he'd hoped they would. He'd stamped them with a two-headed wolf, the symbol of his House of Sin. And they had been printed on the finest card stock, the green so deep it was almost black, with silver ink that glimmered.

Gifts had also been sent, each tailored to the guests. Brandy, cigars, rare books—Envy's spies had been gathering careful intelligence for him. He'd made it nearly impossible for those invited to refuse. Harrington and Walters practically seethed from the audacity, the insult of the packaging being so wretchedly, wonderfully unique.

Camilla's gift, however, had been different. Envy had shopped for everything himself. And he'd given her far more than a simple party favor. Camilla might not be royalty, but he'd wanted to see her look like a princess tonight, unmatched in dignity, in grace. In part because her beauty called for it, and in part to show Vexley he'd never stood a chance.

Sparks of envy already flitted through the ballroom air, feeding his sin, and magnified by the seductive oils he'd placed throughout to stoke every human sense. Vanilla, ginger, jasmine, musk—each scent evoked a different feeling, promised a new delight.

Knowing he had to store up as much power as possible for the game, Envy had played into the darkness of sin through his chosen décor, too. Dark wooden tables and chairs, a black crystal chandelier. Sconces and candelabras made of iron, fitted with ebony beeswax tapers.

Below him, the ballroom floor gleamed like a meadow at night, the blackish-green marble buffed to clearly reflect the masked faces of the dancers gliding across it.

At his nod, his hired quartet began to play, and gowns in every hue unfurled like flower petals as they twirled across the large expanse of floor, each reflecting its own beautiful midnight blossom within the marble.

Envy's vision had come together exquisitely.

The mortals sensed the true grandeur, sipping their drinks, talking in little groups, growing bolder as the night grew later because of the masks they wore. Envy had guessed they'd allow themselves to indulge in sin a bit more if they had a sense of anonymity.

Although, thus far, the most scandalous thing he'd witnessed was men stealing more dances than society normally permitted.

He wondered what Camilla would be like, whether her mask would make her bold. Envy waited for a splash of silver to cut through the rainbow of colors swirling below, thinking of her desire in the tunnel several nights before. It had been so intense, so heady, it had nearly made Envy lose sight of his goal.

Envy pictured her silver hair, then thought about winding it slowly around his fist, angling her face up to his. Would she fight such a leash, or welcome it? In either case, he'd cover her mouth with his until she forgot her anger, forgot she'd ever wished to deny him what he wanted most. He could imagine her moans as he pushed his tongue into her mouth, possessing her as she'd wanted, up against that wall.

He'd been tempted by her then and was frustrated to realize he still was. Maybe Envy needed to get her into his bed, bargain aside, so she could remove herself from his head shortly after.

One night and then he'd finally be satisfied.

"Careful, brother."

Lust sidled up beside him, a tumbler of Dark and Sinful dangling from his fingertips.

"Some might confuse that expression for longing."

Envy remembered the role he needed to play. He was a Prince of Hell, debauched, insolent. Looking for the sort of fun to inspire his sin.

He wasn't a desperate male on the verge of losing everything.

"They would be correct," Envy said. "I long for the next clue."

Lust snorted.

"Stubborn prick."

"You sound like Pride now. Perhaps you ought to do as Sloth has suggested—branch out and be more creative."

"Since you are so unbothered, I'll happily bend Camilla over and shove my cock deep—"

Lust made a garbled sound.

Envy had exploded before he could think through his actions. Still, he squeezed his brother's throat tighter, his expression void of humor.

"Don't."

"Why? It's lust, not love. No need to act like our love-drunk big brother. Unless, of course, this game is different from the others." Lust's gaze sharpened; he'd been purposefully provoking Envy. "There isn't anything you'd like to confess, is there?"

A loud roaring sounded in Envy's head. Lust hid his cunning behind his jovial persona, but his instincts were nearly unmatched by any of their other brothers.

"Until she's mine," Envy said smoothly, "you know how I feel about sharing."

It was normally true. Everyone knew how territorial he could be.

"Good. For a moment it looked like you were thinking of tearing my throat out."

Lust flashed him a wolfish grin before his gaze darted behind Envy.

Envy dropped his hand and flexed it, poised to strike again.

His brother tossed an arm around his shoulders, turning him to face the dance floor.

"If you won't take the artist to bed, someone else will."

There she was—a shimmering blade cutting through the darkness. His princess of starlight, if only for one evening. The woman who held him and his court in her burning, deadly grasp.

"Gods fucking damn," Lust muttered beside him, whistling softly. "That woman."

Envy barely noticed Lady Katherine and Lord Edwards standing beside her, mere shadows in masks of blue and gray. Between them, Camilla held her head high, her otherworldly hair pulled back from her mask, curled and cascading down her bare shoulders.

His attention slid over her collarbones, admiring the dip in the gown that hinted at her curves but didn't reveal much. It was meant to tease, to

seduce, and Miss Camilla Antonius was enchanting the whole room. At Vexley's party she'd been shy, wanting to fade into the shadows, escape notice.

With her shining silver mask, she owned every ounce of attention that came her way now. She was a star, and she refused to dull her light for any mere mortal.

Which was fitting, since she wasn't meant for a mortal man tonight.

She was meant for Envy.

And after she agreed to paint the Hexed Throne, because he had to believe she would, he was going to enjoy every second of their time together. Worshipping her body until the sunlight streamed in through the windows and their night of passion ended.

Envy was ready to make his own grand entrance when he saw something that made his sin ignite.

Vexley had arrived as well and was already whisking Camilla onto the dance floor. His hand had settled far too low on her hip for Envy's liking.

Jealousy, ice-cold and ancient, frosted the railing where Envy stood.

Mortals peering over the next balcony shrieked as ice shot across their banister next.

Gods damn it. Envy used a tiny bit of magic to glamour the mortals' memories, making them forget the oddity they'd just experienced. Once they'd settled, he flashed his brother a warning look.

"Don't start."

Before Lust could needle him about his temper again, Envy was already descending the stairs.

Masked lords and ladies attempted to catch his attention, stepping into his path, clearing their throats. Envy carved through them like a dagger, aiming for the mortal who had a certain wish to die. Vexley's garish gold mask was about as subtle as his hands sliding lower on Miss Antonius's form. If they dipped any farther, Envy would chop them off.

Envy ignored gasps as he strode with purpose onto the dance floor. He didn't speak, didn't deign to ask to cut in. Vexley ought to thank his God that Envy didn't shove his blade through his heart right there. Or perhaps he'd stab the idiot's cock first, show him how it felt when someone took something that wasn't theirs.

Instead, Envy's arm slipped easily around Camilla, and he expertly drew her into a waltz without missing a beat. She stiffened for a moment, then relaxed, her gaze fixed to his mask. Vexley fumed, but the dance had soon left him far behind.

They circled other couples, but Envy paid them no mind. Camilla was a goddess to be worshipped, and tonight she was his.

He watched as she nibbled her lower lip, the action igniting an ember of heat low in his abdomen.

"Something you wish to say, Miss Antonius?" he asked, bringing his mouth to her ear.

He'd meant to tempt her, but that coiled warmth dropped lower, his body suddenly aware of each place they pressed together.

A shiver rolled down her spine—Envy knew, because he felt it beneath his light touch. Her skin pebbled from excitement. He drew her closer, not demanding or forceful, but steady. An edge shy of possessive.

Camilla didn't back away. Instead, she leaned in, as if matching his move. Daring him to up the ante. His hand gently stroked along her back, her sharp intake of breath hardly noticeable as they whirled.

"Camilla?" he prompted, his breath stirring the delicate silver curls near her neck.

"People will talk about what you just did, my lord."

Amusement laced his tone.

"And what would they say?" He guided her around again, moving faster, keeping pace with the music. "That I stole a dance? That I prevented a drunken ass from making a spectacle? Or that I could not care less what anyone thinks?"

She was quiet a moment.

"The paintbrush was lovely. But bribery is always tempting, isn't it?"

He smiled. "Consider it merely a simple gift."

"With all due respect, my lord, I'd wager nothing with you is simple."

His chuckle was deep and delighted. Miss Antonius was a formidable opponent. He might actually miss sparring with her when all this was through.

Envy maneuvered them to a shadowy section off to the side, affording them a moment of privacy.

"If I wished to coerce you, Miss Antonius, I can think of much more interesting ways to do so."

Camilla's gaze dropped to his mouth, lingering there a beat too long before she jerked it back up, quickly glancing away. A pretty blush stained her cheeks.

Interesting.

He considered tilting her chin up, tracing those full lips with his, kissing her right there. He wondered if she'd be scandalized by his behavior, or if the mask would make her daring.

A throat delicately cleared behind them, breaking the moment. Envy didn't immediately step away or drop his arms from Camilla. He shot an annoyed look over his shoulder.

"Yes?" he asked, tone clipped.

The brunette held up her dance card. "This dance belongs to me, my lord."

Envy blinked, realizing that the music had stopped, that a new song was beginning. He was about to dismiss the woman, who he suspected was Widow Janelle behind the white feathered mask, when Camilla stepped back, dipping her chin in a slight nod, then swiftly moved across the dance floor, heading straight for the refreshment table.

Envy stared after her a beat. He'd been so close to...what? Getting her to say yes, or gaining her trust? Maybe he simply wanted to kiss her in that moment, make Vexley and anyone else watching mad with envy.

The brunette shifted back into view, her gaze behind her feathered mask drinking him in.

"My lord?"

Envy pasted on a pleasant smile. Society games were already interfering, and he hadn't even had the pleasure of bedding a lover for his trouble.

He shot one last look in Camilla's direction, his sin igniting when he saw his pleasure-seeking brother sidle up to her, a fresh drink clutched in his hand.

Lust lifted his glass in Envy's direction, a smile curling his lips. Gods-damned prick.

Envy could imagine too clearly what Lust would say, how he'd probably attempt to use his sin on Camilla again. Jealousy seared through him as he gathered the masked woman up in his arms, purposefully dancing her closer to where Camilla stood.

He wanted to keep an eye on Lust to ensure that his brother didn't screw his best chance at saving his court. And perhaps he wanted to see how Camilla reacted to his dancing with another. He swore there had been something there, brief though it might have been.

And if Camilla had considered kissing him, perhaps she was also considering accepting his bargain.

Something like hope kindled in his chest. Tonight might prove to be worthwhile after all.

EIGHTEEN

"If you desire another dance with my brother, take it."

Camilla tore her attention from the man in the emerald mask waltzing across the dance floor and settled it on Synton's brother.

She hadn't noticed when they'd first met, but while he shared the same dark hair and bronze skin as Lord Synton, his eyes were a striking shade of charcoal that now nicely matched his mask.

He gave her a secretive smile that she couldn't help but return.

There was something infectious about him, something that made her want to enjoy his company.

The feeling was a bit unsettling, if Camilla was being honest.

"It's improper to dance more than twice with one man, Mr. Synton."

At that, he laughed, the sound filled with genuine delight.

"While I imagine my brother has laid claim to this already, please call me Syn. I think of myself as the premier prince of sin, no matter what my brothers may say."

Given the devious twinkle in his eye, she could imagine him in that role.

"Very well, Syn. How many brothers do you have?"

"There are seven of us, each more devilishly handsome than the last."

Seven Synton brothers, God save them all.

And not a one of them lacking in confidence, Camilla would wager.

He leaned in, dropping his voice to a conspiratorial whisper. "We're known as Princes of Sin. A title we take very seriously, I assure you."

Camilla snorted. She didn't doubt that at all. Though a slight trepidation crept along her spine. Seven Princes of Sin did exist, ruling over a realm called the Seven Circles, though some myths her mother had told her claimed there were once eight.

It couldn't be...

She studied the man next to her.

"I've heard the stories. Let's say you're really a Prince of Sin. What do you rule over?"

"If you haven't guessed already, I must not be a very good prince."

A frustrating nonanswer. Though Camilla was probably only hoping he and Synton were something other, something more legendary. She wanted an excuse for this irksome attraction. It was far easier to blame it on magic than accept the fact that she liked a scoundrel all on his own.

"Why aren't you out there dancing?" she asked. "Plenty of ladies keep stealing glances."

"I much prefer to stir up trouble from the sidelines."

He turned those unique eyes on the crowd, his smile growing more wicked.

"So much debauchery. It's good for the soul."

"Debauchery?"

Syn nodded to the dance floor. "Wickedness."

Camilla followed his gaze, then sucked in a breath.

Couples who'd been discreetly talking in the shadows of the room had drawn closer together, as if compelled to touch, moving their hands into daring positions on each other's bodies, their touches hungry and not at all restrained by prying eyes.

Camilla's attention darted around the room. Those on the dance floor didn't seem to notice the lapse in propriety. Most were laughing and swaying to the music of the string quartet. They'd all been sampling the drinks, their eyes glassy behind their masks, footsteps unsteady as they whirled.

But around the perimeter, far from the flickering candlelight, a few couples had begun to kiss. Throats, ungloved hands, lips, breasts...

"What on earth..." Camilla couldn't believe it. She blinked as if that would erase the scene unfolding in the darkest parts of the glorious chamber. Heat crept along her body, inching up her neck, down to her belly.

Beside her, she realized that one masked couple had begun to make love, right up against the wall, the woman's flushed skin emerging from under her dress as she wrapped a bare leg around her partner's back. Candles flickered wildly on either side of them until they went out one by one, keeping their secret.

Camilla's heart thundered in her chest. This couldn't be truly happening. And yet...

She looked at the silver trays that kept coming, the drinks flowing freely. Had something been added to them, something that lowered inhibitions?

"Well, there's a complication I didn't expect," Syn muttered. "Shall we take a turn about the garden, Miss Antonius?" He abruptly stepped in front of her, attempting to block her view.

But he was too late.

She ducked beneath his arm, watching in fascinated horror as the masked brunette rolled onto her toes and yanked Lord Ashford Synton's lapels toward her, leaning in for a kiss, right there in front of the entire ballroom. A few couples stopped dancing, lips parting in shock.

At least Camilla wasn't the only one who'd been rendered speechless.

And yet the cursed lord didn't immediately disentangle himself from the masked beauty.

Not that Camilla watched for very long—or even long enough to see their lips crash together. The moment leading up to the kiss was all she'd needed to feel ill. Without thinking, she spun on her heel, fleeing the ballroom before she could do something ridiculous.

"Camilla, don't!"

She ignored whoever called out for her, not wanting anyone to witness her jealousy, and pushed open the doors to the terrace, rushing down the stairs toward the hedge maze.

The damp cold of the autumn air stung her eyes and seeped in through the thin layers of her gown, chilling her to the core.

Camilla welcomed the feeling of ice—she wanted to feel nothing but numbness, to think of nothing but the cold.

Otherwise, she'd recall Synton and the way she'd wanted him to grab *her* earlier, press his mouth and body to hers until they couldn't figure out where either of them began or ended.

She wanted to drown in his kiss, submerge herself in untold passion.

Camilla was startled to admit it, even silently to herself.

When he'd danced with her, saving her from Vexley, she'd foolishly thought it meant something. Just like the gown he'd sent. And the paintbrush.

All it meant was that he wanted something *from* her; he didn't want her.

Camilla ran as fast as she could, rushing down one row of the hedge maze to the next, her slippers soaking in the dew of the freshly cut grass, icing her toes until each step felt like she was treading across tiny steel blades. The pain helped ease the ache in her chest.

She ran until the viselike grip of jealousy loosened, giving way to annoyance at herself.

Camilla should not suffer for a man who clearly didn't harbor any secret affection for her.

If Synton didn't wish to—

One moment the path ahead was clear, and the next she collided with the very man she'd been running from.

Lord Synton held her arms tightly, catching her before she stumbled and fell. Above her, his gaze was glittering and hard in the moonlight. He'd discarded his mask, and with it, any pretense of civility. Whatever looked out from his eyes did not seem human.

Camilla stood still, her pulse thrashing as his dark eyes dropped, taking special care to follow the line of her décolletage, then abruptly flicked back up to trace her jaw, her lips beneath her mask.

If she'd thought his expression was forbidding a moment ago, it was nothing compared to the brutally cold look he gave her now.

"Never show me your envy again, Miss Antonius. It won't end well."

"Do not threaten me."

Camilla shrugged out of his grasp, not bothering to deny her jealousy.

His lips curved into a wolfish grin. "It was a warning."

A strange, dark energy surrounded him out here, a mixture of shivering violence and burning lust, two opposing forces clashing together like a brewing storm.

Even with the charge sizzling in the air, she had the impression that he was holding himself back, aware of whatever power he wielded and the damage it could cause.

Her chin notched up.

"And if I don't heed it?" She met his eyes, unwilling to drop her gaze.

There was one strained beat of stillness, then all the control he'd been exuding snapped.

One moment she was standing there before him, the next she was up against the hedge, the evergreen branches poking into her with a delicious hint of pain.

Synton had pressed his entire length to her front, his hand tangled in her hair, his nose buried against her throat, breathing her in. His body was tense, coiled tight.

With a mere flick of his wrist, he had her mask off, sliding its silky ribbons down over her ears, across her cheek, before he tossed it into the dense shrubbery.

He tipped her face higher, seemingly to decide which he'd like to taste first, her lips or the flushed skin of her throat.

She was shocked to realize she wanted him to taste it all.

Synton angled his face closer, his lips tracing a line of fire along her jaw as he brought them slowly to hers, hovering for a moment in which she could taste the hint of bourbon and berries on his breath. Then, at last, his mouth brushed against hers. Tender at first, and then firmly, sending sparks of desire up her spine.

As he withdrew, his teeth tugged needily on her bottom lip.

"Some games should not be played unless you're certain you can win."

He ran a finger along the edge of her ear, gently settling her hair back into place. "Stoke my sin again and I will show you what it means to lose, Miss Antonius."

Without another word, he turned, leaving her alone. She could practically hear the thunder of her heart echoing off the hedge maze, followed a second later by the scorching flame of her annoyance. A dramatic mood shift. Once again.

"Damn insufferable ass."

She took a moment to collect herself, pulling free of the hedge, straightening her gown and fluffing her skirts. Her annoyance only grew as she plucked her mask from the nearby shrub. She picked a few stray leaves from it, the moonlight sparking off the mask to illuminate the abandoned maze each time she shifted it.

Camilla exhaled loudly, glancing back toward the large manor in the distance. She hadn't realized how far she'd run. Now the warm glow of the windows seemed like distant stars.

Perhaps she should go home. She was no longer in the mood to play Synton's games.

Holding her mask in one hand, she grabbed her heavy skirt in the other and trudged along silently, looking for the path out of the maze and to the front of the estate.

Surely Lord Edwards and Lady Katherine's driver would take her home. He could always come back for them.

A twig snapped behind her and she whirled around. A man stepped out from the next pathway, holding his hands up.

"I didn't mean to scare you, Miss Antonius."

Camilla strained to see him in the dark. "Lord Garrey?"

He stepped closer, hands still up as if to prove he meant no harm.

"You're a long way from the ballroom." He glanced around. "Shall I escort you back?"

Camilla's heart thrummed faster, her instincts warning her that something was off. Lord Garrey's gaze kept darting around, his head cocked to one side, as if listening.

His behavior wasn't what it ought to be, given the fact that he'd come upon her alone. He knew just as well as she did how this would look. He should have turned and left her immediately. Yet he lingered, his attention straying to her neck.

"You know we can't be seen alone. Please," she said, keeping her voice calm and steady, though inside she felt anything but, "leave before my reputation is ruined."

"I imagine that would be worth something to you."

She didn't like his tone.

"It's valuable to every woman in Waverly Green, my lord. I'm no different."

"But you are, aren't you?" he asked, taking a small step in her direction. "Different."

This conversation was heading down a road it shouldn't.

"If you're referring to running my father's gallery, then I suppose I am." She didn't bother pointing out that society was to blame for more high born women not running a business, that only her circumstances were different.

He nodded, almost absently, then sprang forward, like a fencer. Camilla was caught off guard by the sudden burst of violence.

Before she could fight back, Garrey had clamped a cloth over her face, preventing her from screaming for help. She clawed at him, nails raking down his skin so hard she drew blood.

"Hush," he said. "This will be over soon."

He yanked her around, slipping his hand beneath the chain of her necklace, but not jerking it. She whimpered as his grip on her tightened painfully.

"Give me the goddamn locket, Camilla."

She shook her head, tears welling in her eyes.

"Don't make me get rough."

He tugged at the locket but didn't use enough force to rip it off. Through the tangle of fear and rage she felt from the assault, this was odd enough to be noticeable. Why go through the trouble of attacking her only to falter now?

Instead, he shoved her down to the ground, pinning her beneath his body. He'd removed his hand from her mouth, but she went still when she saw the glint of metal. Garrey held a dagger to her heart, eyes dark.

"Give me the locket and this will be over." His voice was low. "I don't want to hurt you, but I will do what I must."

Seeing the blade pierce her beautiful dress, Camilla raged. She didn't want to hurt him either, but she, too, would do what she must.

"The locket isn't worth much money," she spat. "You won't pawn it for much."

"It's worth more to me than you can imagine." He motioned to it with the blade. "Give it to me with your own hand. Now."

"Why? If you want it, take it."

"Stop playing games, Camilla. Give it over. And be quick about it."

Camilla's mind spun. She could give him the locket. Make this encounter end. But it wasn't simply a necklace, and somehow, some way, Lord Garrey had figured that out.

A plan slowly formed.

"Let me up." She added a touch of submission to her expression, made her bottom lip quiver. "I'll have to stand to undo the clasp."

Lord Garrey looked her over, his expression pinched.

He didn't believe her, not fully, but she'd seen that wild desperation in his gaze. She knew, too, that he saw what everyone else in Waverly Green did—a young, aristocratic woman who'd been groomed to obey men.

While he might suspect a trap, he'd also been groomed to believe he could handle her.

He got to his feet slowly and offered his hand. His manners were obscene, considering what he'd just done. Camilla bit down on her retort. Instead, as she came to her feet, she wobbled, pretending her heel had broken in the scuffle.

"Oh!" she cried, falling forward, grabbing his arms to steady herself.

Generations of good breeding snapped in, just as she suspected they would. Lord Garrey dropped his dagger, catching her. And she used the movement to bring her knee up between his legs as hard as she could.

"Bitch!"

He doubled over and she attacked again, following him to the ground like a feral beast after a bone. Which, she thought wryly, she sort of was.

But as she drew back, she tripped over her damn gown.

He used the moment of distraction to counterattack.

He kicked her feet out from under her, knocking the breath from her lungs as she fell. Before she could regain her senses, he rolled on top of her, crushing her with his weight.

"Give me the fucking necklace or I swear I'll kill you."

His hands were around her throat, squeezing. Little black spots flickered at the edge of her vision, and she thought she tasted blood. Then she realized: she'd bitten her tongue in the fall. The metallic taste filled her mouth, made her gag.

She clawed at his hands again, now slippery with his blood.

"You bitch." He was in a rage now, his fingers tightening until she was certain he'd break her neck.

She felt around the ground desperately. Something had fallen, something she could... her fingertip stung as she found his fallen blade.

Blackness filled her vision. She had seconds left. Maybe less.

Her hand slipped over the hilt, the blood making it nearly impossible to clasp. She dragged her hand across the grass, succeeding in wiping some of it away.

"No one said you needed to be breathing," Lord Garrey said, his face a vicious mask of brutality. She had no idea what he meant. Who didn't say she needed to be breathing?

Maybe he thought she was too far gone to understand.

"Guess you'll give me the locket willingly when you're dead."

As the final air was forced from her lungs, Camilla grasped the dagger and brought it down, sinking it to the hilt into the side of his neck.

She twisted it, baring her teeth in a snarl, tears streaming down her face.

His grip loosened instantly, and his eyes froze open. Then, slowly, he toppled to the side. Camilla could barely see through the tears that were flowing faster now. She shoved and wriggled her way out from beneath him, trembling from the attack and what she'd just done.

She'd killed him.

She glanced at the dagger protruding from his neck, shivering at the sight. Lord Garrey wasn't exactly dead yet. He was twitching and choking on blood.

"No!" she cried, looking around frantically, then down at her blood-drenched silver-and-white dress. "No, no."

She grabbed her hair, pulling at the roots, trying to think. How had this happened?

Camilla dropped to her knees, reaching for the dagger, and was hauled back suddenly.

She fought and kicked and screamed.

"Shh. It's all right."

Synton's voice was an instant balm.

His arms were gentle but firm, his heart pounding so hard she felt it through her back, a rhythm hers instantly slowed to follow.

"I'm going to take care of this, all right?" He was far too calm for the scene he'd come upon, holding her head soothingly in place under his chin. "I want you to tell me exactly what happened. Then we're going to clean you up."

After a moment, she gave a half nod.

He slowly released her and walked in a small circle to face her.

His gaze darkened when it dropped to her neck. "He did that?"

She nodded, wincing from the pain she was beginning to feel.

Synton glanced over at Lord Garrey, his expression one of pure loathing. He looked like he wanted to take the dagger out and shove it through him a few more times.

He motioned to someone—Alexei, Camilla thought, still dazed—and before she knew it, Lord Garrey's twitching form was gone.

There was no sign of a skirmish.

No broken hedges or torn-up grass.

Maybe that wasn't true. How could it be true? Maybe it was all there, and she was incapable of seeing it any longer.

She shook violently, unable to reconcile the deadly turn the night had taken.

Synton pulled her to him again, hugging her against his chest.

"You're all right," he said softly, stroking her hair. "Close your eyes. Breathe."

Camilla did as he said, breath ragged as she tried to draw it in slowly.

His hands warmed as they gently passed over her neck, her arms, her gown. Like he was soothing away each injury.

There was nothing untoward about his actions. They offered only comfort and safety.

If Camilla hadn't been in shock, she might have wondered at the odd sensation flowing over her. Her skin stopped aching, her breathing evened out. The metallic taste in her mouth faded away. Gently, without attracting notice, she slid her hand up to her breastbone, feeling that the locket still rested there. Then she let herself go, leaning into Synton, who just held her in the circle of his arms, waiting for the storm to pass.

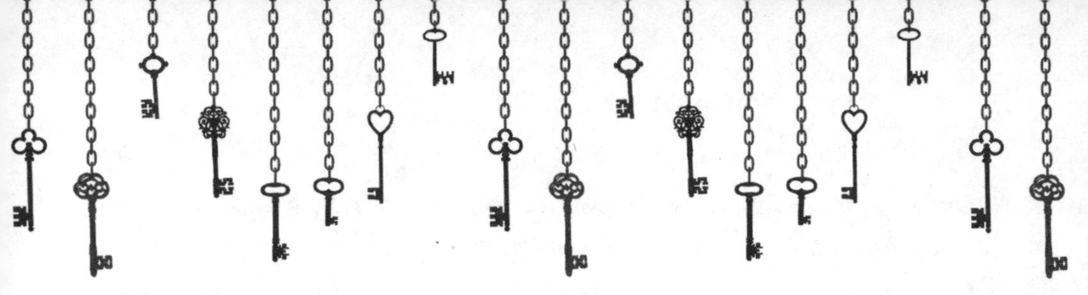

NINETEEN

Dear God, Synton. When Vexley suggested we all play hide-and-seek, he wasn't talking about your—"

"Don't finish that," Envy warned, ready to lay waste to the whole of Waverly Green.

Lord Harrington, Envy recalled. The dolt was making sure his voice carried across the hedge maze, drawing a second man, Walters, to bear witness. They were too drunk to notice how still he'd gone, or how dangerous that was.

If Envy hadn't been on the verge of whisking Camilla away, he would have heard the imbecile coming. Lord Garrey had proven himself to be a player, all right. And while Camilla had gotten to him first, Envy should have.

The bastard had nearly killed her on Envy's own property. Envy had made a horribly wrong call. He'd summoned Alexei to follow a second lord who'd been curious about the Unseelie art, thinking Garrey was still in the ballroom, dancing with Widow Janelle.

Garrey must have left shortly after Camilla did, following her into the maze.

Alexei would ensure that Lord Garrey succumbed to the wounds Camilla had inflicted. Envy's only regret was not being able to do the deed himself.

Camilla whimpered, hiding in his arms, and he jolted to their current dilemma. The lords moronic and idiotic were causing a scene.

"Are you giving it to that woman right there?" Harrington stepped closer and laughed. "Is that Miss Antonius? Vexley will have your balls."

With the power of his sin instantly rushing through him, and the heat of Camilla's body still lingering in his magic, it took enormous restraint not to murder the mortal right then. The last thing Envy needed was any other reason to attack him.

His restraint only grew more impressive as Walters swaggered over and called out too.

Camilla had already suffered enough. Envy was grateful he'd had the foresight to restore her gown along with her injuries with a bit of magic, and only felt marginally weakened from the use of it. No one would think anything violent had just occurred where they stood.

"Look what we have here!" Walters shouted. "Satire sheets will rejoice tonight!"

Camilla stiffened in his arms, finally breaking out of her shocked state.

Envy turned to further shield her from the loathsome lords and dropped his voice so only she could hear.

"Now would be a wonderful time to tell me if you accept the bargain or not."

Incredulity laced her voice.

"Why bother? It's too late—I'm ruined as we speak."

Like hell she was.

If Camilla was already ruined, then the forgery wouldn't matter, and Envy would no longer have a winning chip to cash in. He wouldn't go down so easily as Garrey tonight.

He felt the crowd slowly growing larger behind him, knew time was running out.

They were already falling down a cliff to ruination. The more witnesses, the harder it would be to dig themselves out of the mess.

He racked his mind for a new strategy, something he could offer Camilla that would save them both. A solution came to him. It was one he'd wanted to avoid at all costs, but he saw no other way out now.

And he paused for another reason too. Once he opened his mouth, this would count as his third attempt to secure Camilla's help. He had to hope this plan was the one to see him move forward.

"Camilla, look at me." He stooped a bit, to bring her level to his eyes. "I promised to protect you. Let's pretend we're betrothed until this scandal passes." She blinked. Did she understand? He tried again. "It's a good deal and you know it. You'll get what you desire and so will I."

She was quiet for a strained second that had his cold, black heart pumping fast.

Please, he silently urged, *don't damn my court*. Not now.

"You can't be serious," she finally whispered. "After what I just did..."

It wasn't a no.

Envy tugged his mask free, allowing her to see how serious he was. The stakes couldn't be higher for him. And now they couldn't be higher for her.

"I assure you I am. Deadly so. The choice is yours, Miss Antonius. Salvation or ruination. Quickly now. What will it be?"

TWENTY

TIME SEEMED TO stand still as Camilla considered Synton's offer.

It was the best option she had, she supposed, considering the circumstances. Although she couldn't understand why he'd want anything to do with her after . . . what she'd just done.

The violence, the blood, the pain. She exhaled, trying to push that attack from her mind.

Unlike Vexley, Synton wasn't blackmailing her or forcing her hand. He hadn't manufactured this discovery, had previously admitted to wanting to avoid playing any society games.

The fact that she'd just mortally stabbed someone on his estate, and he'd assisted in covering it up, was certainly something they'd need to discuss. But he'd protected her. Held her when she started to fall apart.

She glanced down at herself, wondering at her dress. The lack of bruising. If she went to the authorities, no one would believe she'd been brutalized. Had Synton used magic to heal her? It was possible if he'd visited the dark market like she'd told him to.

"Miss Antonius?" he prompted quietly. "Do you accept?"

If she was Synton's intended, Vexley wouldn't be able to try to coerce her into marriage himself. And if he tried to blackmail her again, she had a feeling Synton would be more than happy to dissuade him.

And if Synton succeeded in locating her father's key?

It was almost too good to hope for.

The lord's patient gaze was fixed on her face, his own expression impossible to read. But for one moment he'd given her a look filled with such hope, such silent urging, she'd known how desperate he was. She knew next to nothing about him, but her instincts said to trust him.

Camilla nodded.

"I accept."

In a flash he pulled a pear-shaped emerald-and-diamond ring from his pocket and placed it on her finger, its size wildly large on her tiny hand. The ring was beautiful, expensive.

Territorial.

No one would be able to miss the damn thing.

She pressed her lips together, wondering why he'd conveniently had this in his pocket. But her suspicions faded in the next second, as Synton twisted and punched Harrington in the mouth, the sound like a whip crack in the sudden quiet.

The lord cursed, stumbling back as blood poured down his chin.

Walters jumped back too and screeched before tearing off across the maze.

Camilla could only stare, unblinking, at the scene before her. Harrington wasn't a small man by any means, but Synton had dispatched him with only one punch. And it looked as if he'd restrained himself.

Exactly how strong *was* he?

"Are you bloody mad?" Harrington yelled. "You broke a tooth!"

Synton landed another solid blow to his opponent's middle and Harrington went down.

"Now you've got a matching rib. If you ever speak of my betrothed in such a manner again, I'll rip your tiny, limp cock off and shove it down your throat. Have I made myself clear?"

"What in God's name is going on here, gentlemen? Though I use the term *gentlemen* very loosely."

Lady Katherine rushed upon their little gathering. Tossing her gray mask aside, she looked between Synton and Harrington before scrutinizing Camilla.

A hundred questions were brewing behind her steady gaze, and Camilla knew she'd demand answers later, but for now Katherine seemed appeased and stared down at Harrington, shaking her head.

"How many scandals will you be involved in before you act as a man of your station ought to, Harrington?" Katherine asked. "Wasn't relieving yourself in front of the duchess lesson enough? You're not nearly charming or handsome enough to carry on like a buffoon."

Harrington wheezed as he glared at Synton. "I caught this rake with your friend. God only knows what he would have done if I hadn't come upon them and interceded."

"You interrupted my proposal, misread the situation, and proceeded to spread ugly rumors without giving either of us a chance to defend ourselves."

Synton wrapped an arm around Camilla's shoulders, drawing her near. She nestled closer without pause. His warmth enveloped her, reassured her.

"You insulted Miss Antonius and offended me. Count your blessings that I haven't challenged you to a duel."

"You're not engaged," Harrington scoffed. "You got caught with her tits nearly out and—"

Synton had him on the ground again.

By now half the masquerade had gathered in the hedge maze, watching Harrington get the life punched out of him.

Camilla ought to feel horrified or sickened, but the truth was she wished to land a punch of her own. That should have bothered her, given what she'd just done to Lord Garrey.

Synton's head whipped in her direction, his bright emerald gaze clashing against hers.

She could have sworn his lips twitched before his expression was once again hard.

"Would anyone else care to comment on my fiancée?" he asked, his tone deceptively calm.

No one, not even Lady Katherine, uttered a single word.

"Wonderful. If any of you consider changing your mind, I'd recall this scene before spreading rumors. Should any reach my ears, leaving Waverly Green as quickly as possible would only delay the inevitable."

He didn't say, "I'll hunt you down and tear you limb from limb," but the message was unmistakable.

"And now, my darling," he said, turning back to her, "shall we find something to toast?"

TWENTY-ONE

"REMIND ME ONCE again, Lord Synton. How did you say you two met? I can't seem to recall, with all the threats and punching and missing teeth," Lady Katherine asked as their carriage rolled down the cobbled street.

After Envy had sent everyone home, he'd agreed to ride with Camilla and her friends. It seemed like the sort of thing a lovestruck fiancé would do, but now he found himself trapped in a slew of questions. Lady Katherine ought to moonlight as a detective inspector.

"After I contacted Camilla regarding a commission, we began to exchange letters quite frequently," Envy lied smoothly.

"This was before you arrived in Waverly Green?" Lady Katherine didn't believe him.

"Yes. I asked Camilla to keep things quiet. I wanted to wait for the right time to announce my intentions. In fact, the ball tonight was supposed to act as the stage for my proposal, but then I realized I wanted to ask Camilla privately."

"That sounds plausible, darling." Edwards nodded brusquely from the other seat. "It was a rather extravagant party."

Lady Katherine kept her cool gaze locked on Envy.

"And when, exactly, did you give her a ring? Before you laid Harrington low?"

"Please, Kitty, leave it for now," Camilla said. "It's been a long evening and my fiancé is not the villain in this story. You saw the way Harrington acted. The man's a knob. Synton has been in contact with me for weeks and tonight I finally accepted his suit."

Envy looked his false fiancée over, impressed that's she'd given most of the truth without actually lying to her friend.

Lady Katherine seemed only partly mollified.

"I apologize for any uncivilized behavior," Envy said, trying to recall what might offend human sensibilities. "No ladies ought to bear witness to such violent acts, but Harrington never should have tried to ruin Camilla. He's fortunate a few missing teeth and a broken rib are his only worries."

At that, both women exchanged secretive looks before bursting into laughter.

Edwards rolled his eyes. "My lovely wife here was something of an underground pugilist before we married. They would hardly consider fighting a shock."

Humans never ceased to amaze.

Envy glanced from Edwards to Katherine to Camilla. Edwards was outwardly as stuffy as they came, yet he had a certain impish sparkle in his eye when speaking of his wife.

"Did you fight as well?" Envy asked, staring at his artist.

"Goodness, no." Katherine's eyes glittered with mirth as she cut in. "Camilla's always been more of a lover. She'd attend to illustrate the fights, though. Do you also box, Lord Synton?"

"Sometimes," Envy admitted, thinking of Wrath's legendary fighting pit. "My brother has his own private ring. Sometimes he invites our whole family to participate."

The carriage rolled to a stop and Envy peered into the night. A large, towering house took up nearly an entire block.

"Welcome to Birchwood." Edwards nodded to the estate. "Our city home."

"I thought we were escorting Camilla to her residence?" Envy said, trying to keep any frustration from his tone.

He'd planned on circling back after they'd dropped Camilla off. Now that she'd come to her senses, she needed to start painting at once. Time was quickly ticking away.

Lady Katherine cut an amused look in his direction. "And not celebrate your joyful news? Don't be silly. I cannot imagine sending you two off without toasting to your betrothal the way we ought to have done earlier. In fact"—she grabbed Camilla's hands—"I insist you both spend the night. We'll have a big celebratory breakfast in your honor too."

Camilla squeezed her friend's hands back and gave Envy a small, apologetic smile.

"That sounds lovely, Kitty, thank you. We'd be honored to have you host us for the night."

We would be no such thing. As if overhearing his internal thoughts, Camilla sent him a withering glare.

"As my lovely fiancée has stated, we'd be honored," Envy said tightly. "Thank you for your thoughtfulness."

At least they could retire to their bedchamber early and then work on the painting.

Envy was already hatching a plan to have Alexei bring the supplies they'd need when Katherine added, "Wonderful. We'll have separate rooms made up for you at once."

"Splendid," Envy said, grateful once again that he was now able to lie.

He'd simply sneak into Camilla's chamber later.

A feat that would be irksome but not impossible.

Or so he foolishly thought…

TWENTY-TWO

"What is that excessive ball of dander?"

Camilla glanced up from where she sat perched on her bed, following Synton's gaze to the mammoth long-haired gray-and-white cat that stood between her and her pretend betrothed. Bunny's initial purrs gave way to a grave look of disapproval.

Camilla's cat was a wonderful judge of character.

Or perhaps the cat simply did not approve of a late-night visit to Camilla's bedchamber.

Though Bunny probably sensed the inner war raging inside Camilla and was being overly fussy. Camilla was fairly certain Lord Garrey was dead. It was beyond difficult to grasp. She'd had no choice; he'd made it clear he was going to kill her. But still, she felt wrong for not regretting her actions.

Bunny nudged her hand, drawing her to the here and now.

"Lord Synton, please meet Bunny."

Synton closed the door behind him softly, his attention traveling from Camilla to Bunny, then back. She couldn't tell whether he was amused or concerned.

"Unless it's casting some powerful glamour, Bunny is a feline. You do realize that, correct?"

Camilla gave him a bemused look.

"With the spirit and claws of a great lioness, I assure you. Don't insult Bunny again, or you may live to regret it, my lord."

His lips twitched. "I'll take your warning under consideration."

"Very wise. My cat does not appreciate anyone who does not worship the ground she walks upon."

"Why is your cat at Lady Katherine's?"

"Whenever I spend the evening here, Kitty sends for Bunny straightaway. She adores riding in Lord Edwards's coach. They spoil her with her own silk pillow and bowl of warm cream."

"You spend the evening here often, then."

Camilla nodded. "We have dinner every week when Lord Edwards is out. I usually spend the night then."

His sardonic expression shifted to something more serious as he finally took Camilla in.

"Are you all right?"

She inhaled deeply, then slowly let it out. "Is he..."

"Responsible for his own sins?" he asked. "Then yes. Alexei got the full story from him."

He wasn't dead. At least not by her hand. The knowledge wasn't quite a relief, but a knot inside her chest loosened.

"I'm not going to ask why he wanted your locket," he murmured. "I suspect you wouldn't tell me the truth even if I did."

Camilla pressed her lips together.

"As long as you're all right," he said, looking her over again, "I'm going to bed. Sleep well. We'll start the painting first thing tomorrow."

He turned, hand on the knob. And her loneliness rose up in a rush.

"Wait."

He twisted to meet her gaze. Silent. Steady. When she didn't speak again, a wry smile tugged at his lips.

"Did you want something, Miss Antonius?"

She wanted him to hold her again, to make the coldness still clinging to her disappear.

His gaze darkened as if he'd read her thoughts, his attention slowly moving down.

She hadn't been expecting company, and a maid had already helped her into her nightgown and robe. Camilla had her own guest room at Birchwood, with items of hers stashed away for whenever she visited; Katherine wouldn't hear otherwise.

The robe was made of silk and the nightgown was soft knit lace, the material hugging the contours of her body with gentle grace. Given the nature of the material, much of her silhouette was easily visible. She loved to sleep in its soft luxury, never expecting anyone to actually see her in it.

Camilla was now exquisitely aware of just how little she had on.

Synton's attention was a hot caress as it slowly moved from her face and then downward. His perusal was thorough, sensual. He took his time, admiring every inch of her body before dragging his gaze back up again, just as slowly.

Camilla's mouth was suddenly as dry as the desert, her body growing warm and tight. Gone were any horrible memories of the hedge maze. The ghost of what had almost happened had been chased away.

"Was there something *you* needed, my lord?"

Camilla's voice drew Synton's focus back to her face but did nothing to douse the fire crackling between them.

Synton had the air of someone who indulged in his carnal urges often and was well versed in both giving and receiving pleasure. Camilla had never been one to fully submit to another in any capacity, but there was something tantalizing about the thought of being subjected to his every whim and demand.

Before she could stop herself from imagining his previous lovers, jealousy seared through her.

His expression shifted suddenly, the fire giving way to ice.

"Write up a list of everything you need from your home." His tone was clipped, impersonal. "Tomorrow you'll be moved into Hemlock Hall."

"What?" Camilla pulled her robe more tightly around herself, caught off guard.

"My staff will collect your things tonight."

Living under the same roof as this impossible man was most decidedly a terrible idea.

"I cannot live with you before we're married. People will talk."

"Not if you've been gifted your own private bridal wing by your protective fiancé. I want you with me from now on, lest anyone else try to harm you."

"Have I been?" she asked. "Gifted my own wing?"

His smile reemerged, turning positively feline. Bunny herself seemed to perk up from where she'd settled in a corner.

"Disappointed you won't be sharing my bed for our little ruse, pet?"

She was, rather.

Camilla also knew he was needling her with the endearment to distract her.

"You think very highly of yourself."

"I'm exceptionally talented at reading emotions. You desire me physically."

Cocksure. Arrogant. Damnably correct.

She lifted a shoulder as if it were common knowledge and she was unperturbed. "Well, you cannot keep your hungry gaze off me, either, my lord. Each time you look at me I think you're removing an item of clothing and trying to decide what to do next."

"Is that what you think, Miss Antonius? That I somehow lack know-how?"

Camilla sensed they were entering dangerous territory again.

She'd been fighting loneliness for the last two years. If she permitted herself this one indulgence, allowed him to make her forget her solitude... maybe the ache would disappear for another few years. They were already pretending to be betrothed.

Why not let that excuse set her free? She could give in to her desires for one night.

"I'm quite positive you're a proficient deviant when you wish to be."

Synton's sparkling gaze filled with challenge. His expression said Camilla was right.

"Tell me, Miss Antonius, are you ever a deviant?"

Camilla had been, that once. Had craved the touch of another ever since.

He mistook her silence. His tone softened to a purr. "Would you like to be?"

He waited, watching. Whatever he saw in her expression made him stalk closer. Like he'd understood she was silently daring him to act on his longings as well.

"Just for tonight," he said, gaze locked onto hers, setting new rules. Ones that intrigued Camilla, despite herself. "Our secret."

Camilla's breath caught. She hadn't expected him to agree.

"Take off your robe. Hand me the sash."

Camilla glanced around the bedchamber, thinking of her friend who was sleeping soundly two doors down.

"We shouldn't," she said, hand rising to rest on the sash, the cool silk a balm against the sudden warmth in the room.

God, did she want to let the soft material pool at her feet.

Synton uncannily read her thoughts again.

"Doing things one shouldn't is often so freeing."

He prowled a few steps closer, the charge between them growing more intense. Camilla felt like she was standing in the middle of a field, watching lightning strikes grow closer. She tugged to loosen her sash, just a bit.

"When was the last time you were a little wicked, Camilla?"

"What, exactly, are you proposing?" she asked.

"Only a kiss," he said, with a slight, teasing smile.

The way he said it, his voice a low growl of temptation... Camilla had never felt such heady anticipation. Her palms tingled, her breathing turned shallow. Her heart thundered in her chest. Excitement warred with desire, and admittedly, slight nervousness.

She wet her lips.

Synton stopped before her, gazing into her face. Noticing the gesture, his lips curled devilishly. "Hand me the sash, Camilla. Now."

She did. Sliding it from around her waist, she dropped the ribbon of silk into his open palm. As she shifted, her robe fell slightly apart, exposing her lace nightgown.

Synton admired her silhouette, then motioned for her to stand and turn around.

She did as he'd silently commanded, already hating the fact that her heart raced harder, thrilled for whatever he'd demand next.

Synton gently placed the sash around her head, covering her eyes, then pulled it taut and tied it. The long ribbon tickled her back, falling between her shoulder blades.

She was blindfolded.

With one hand on her shoulder, he slowly spun her to face him. She craved the reassurance of his emerald eyes but could only feel the soft wind of his breath against her mouth.

"How does that feel?" he asked.

All her senses had heightened—from somewhere deep in the house she heard the soft chiming of a clock. Closer still she heard the slight rasp of Synton's breath, the rustle of his own shirt before he slipped a hand beneath her robe. His touch glided effortlessly over her nightgown as he circled her waist and drew her nearer to him.

"Good."

His body was warmer than she'd imagined, his scent intoxicating this close by. She tilted her face up, lips parting in anticipation.

If he was only going to kiss her, she wished to enjoy every second of it.

"We can do much better than good, darling."

His mouth skimmed her neck, her collarbone, grazing lazily from one side to the other before drifting lower, past her locket to the lace above her breasts. She'd expected him to kiss his way upward again, finally pressing his mouth to hers.

But she soon realized that Synton was a man who enjoyed playing.

Camilla felt the air stir around her as he moved, closing his mouth over the peak of her breast, where it pressed against the soft fabric of her nightgown. The unexpected heat and wet of his mouth sent a shock of pleasure through her as his teeth grazed over her again.

A moan slipped past her lips as Synton's erotic kiss soaked through her nightgown, causing a different sort of wetness to form between her legs.

He held her steady, his big hands gripping her waist, nestled just above the curve of her bottom. His tongue began stroking softly, drawing as much pleasure from her body as he could.

He moved to her other breast, licking and sucking over the thin material until she could no longer think straight.

Too soon, she felt him straighten, her damp nightgown now clinging to her.

"My lord..."

He let out a low sound of amusement, and she could have sworn he whispered he was anything but before he walked her backward until her thighs brushed against the edge of the bed.

"Sit."

Camilla did, her body tingling and eager for his next kiss.

She couldn't see him, but she felt his gaze on her, searing and heavy like a physical caress. She knew with certainty that if she could see him, there wouldn't be anything cold or dark in his eyes now. He would be ravenous, filled with need. Just like her.

Perhaps that was why he wanted her eyes covered—so she wouldn't know the effect she had on him. She loved and loathed the blindfold—loved how it allowed her to anticipate his next move and loathed that she couldn't watch him perform it.

"Unless you'd like me to stop, I'm going to kiss you again, Camilla."

"Please," her voice was low and husky, "don't stop."

He firmly pressed her back until she lay across the bed. Strong hands closed around her ankles, tugging her closer to the edge of the mattress.

His touch sent shivers of pleasures through her.

Silence stretched, the air growing thick with tension.

Camilla wondered if he was staring down at her, and if he was, what his expression looked like now.

Another whisper of movement. Was he kneeling?

She jolted at the unexpected sensation of his mouth on her leg, her gasps turning sharp and uneven. He traced little lines of pleasure from her ankle to her calf, tasting his way upward.

Her breath caught when he paused behind her knee. His powerful hands settled on either thigh, palms flattened there for a moment, rubbing gently. Comforting. Seducing.

Camilla fidgeted, wanting to see him.

Then his hands were moving again, slowly pushing her thighs apart, exposing her aching flesh. She stilled. She'd forgotten that she'd taken her underwear off, wanting to sleep with nothing between her skin and soft lace.

He cursed, and she wasn't sure he'd meant to. The harsh word igniting her desire even more.

Then he waited, as if testing to see if she would balk. A woman of her station was taught to demur, to deny her passions. To feel shame when she shouldn't.

The blindfold made her bold.

She slowly widened her legs. Cool air kissed her most sensitive area, her heart pounding as she waited to see what he would do next.

He groaned, as if he could no longer hold himself back, the sound a tortured growl of pure need.

Then his mouth closed over her sex. The first swirl of his tongue was delicate, chaste almost. The second was criminal. His stroke more powerful, demanding. A lazy lick that turned decidedly wicked.

Camilla arched up from the bed, moaning as his tongue parted the folds of her, swirling and then stroking deeper.

"Fuck," he said, pausing for a moment to kiss the inside of her thigh. "You taste incredible."

His mouth was on her again, his teeth grazing the bundle of nerves.

A slight nip, a jerk of her body, then he lapped up her desire. It was pleasure with an edge of pain, and nothing had ever felt so good. Her body throbbed as he suckled her flesh, spreading her legs wider so he could feast like a king. He teased her by kissing along her inner thighs, grazing over her sex to the other leg, his breath hot against her arousal.

He certainly liked drawing out each move until she almost cursed.

He blew across her clit, then pressed another chaste kiss to it. Teasing. Maddening. Her flesh growing so slick and engorged it almost hurt.

"Please." She fisted the sheets, trying to remember why moaning was a bad idea.

"So proper and polite," he purred against her, his tongue touching her lightly.

She bucked as his mouth closed on her again, his tongue curling slightly inside her.

He did not seem to share her worry about noise. His groan was more animal than human when his tongue touched her again.

Then he kissed her again *there,* his tongue sliding over the most glorious place she'd ever felt, alternating between flicking and lathing. She arched up from the bed again, panting.

He kept up that wondrously sinful lathing, but her body needed more. She wanted him deeper. Inside her. Pounding in time to that growing, throbbing, aching sensation.

"Oh, my..."

He penetrated her with his tongue, driving deep inside her, and she swallowed a cry of pleasure. His tongue was glorious, thrusting, stroking. Heat bolted up her spine.

The Lord of Syn was making love to her with his wicked mouth. Camilla's legs opened wider, needing him to press closer, the fire lashing along her body as he owned her with his sinful kiss.

"Oh, my God."

Another growl.

"I assure you He has nothing to do with this."

Synton's hands hardened their hold on her hips, keeping her in place. As if she would move away now. She'd stay prone for all eternity as long as he kept doing that with his unholy, lovely mouth.

She still couldn't see him, but the image filled her mind—Synton kneeling between her legs, hands buried in her lacy nightgown, head bent to her as if he were an acolyte to her body.

Her hips bucked upward, needing more.

Synton tended to her with renewed vigor, his warm tongue gliding over and inside her with such perfection that Camilla didn't care if God or the devil himself was involved. This man could drag her down to hell and she'd gladly burn for eternity.

She wanted him to go deeper, to never stop.

He replaced his tongue with his fingers, sliding them across her folds.

It felt so good, Camilla had to bite down on her lip to keep from crying out. She thrashed as that delicious feeling continued to crest into a wave of pleasure, gripping the sheets so tightly she feared they'd shred.

Synton gently hoisted her legs over his shoulders, pinning her to the bed with one large hand as he feasted.

"Come for me, Camilla."

It was a command.

"Come all over my tongue. Now."

And she loved it.

Each glorious stroke had that bundle of nerves growing tighter, hotter, coiled and ready to send fire through her veins as her release found her.

Camilla rocked her hips forward, fingers threading into his hair, tugging his face closer, earning a growl of approval that vibrated so deeply, she went tumbling over the edge, her body taking flight as pleasure rippled through her in one hot wave after the last. She'd orgasmed before, but this was unlike anything else. This made her want to stay in this bedchamber forever.

He didn't let up, his fingers and tongue continuing to ride her through the sensation until another orgasm barreled through her. She cried out as the next orgasm sent her straight out of her body, floating somewhere far away.

Synton's ministrations slowed to languid strokes, not stopping until the final wave broke, leaving Camilla feeling boneless and spent. She collapsed back, breathing heavily.

"That..." Was a religious experience. If he was the Lord of Syn, she'd happily become the worst sinner there was.

He kissed her inner thigh one last time, then gently set her trembling legs down.

She felt the heat of him leave. His jacket rustled, the air stirred. Then all was quiet.

He couldn't have...

Camilla sat up, ripped off the blindfold, and blinked. The room was empty. She stared around her, emotions whirling from one extreme to the next.

There was no way he'd done *that* and then left. Without a word.

"Synton," she hissed, furious.

And unless she'd been in some suspended stupor from his talented mouth, he'd moved faster than anyone should be able to.

Still, he didn't return.

The immeasurable ass had in fact given her an orgasm to end all orgasms, then left.

She stared at the door, body still trembling from the aftershocks, wondering how Synton could go from such burning passion to cold indifference that swiftly.

If he was playing a game with her, he would regret it.

Camilla decided right then that instead of showing him how angry she was, she, too, could play. She'd adopt his mask of indifference. Let him be humbled too.

She tossed herself back onto the bed, staring at the ceiling, rethinking the whole encounter. It took far longer to get her annoyance under control than she cared to admit. But once she did, she puzzled his behavior out more clearly.

The blindfold.

The mention of only tonight.

The abrupt departure.

In some way, she was certain, he'd bared himself more than she had.

There was something he desperately didn't want her to see, which only made her more curious to unravel the mystery of his past. Forbidden things always intrigued her.

And Lord Synton, mercurial moods, gruffness and all, was *very* tempting indeed.

TWENTY-THREE

"The paint, canvas, and brushes are all here in the studio," Envy said by way of greeting, keeping his back purposefully to the artist he'd summoned at first light.

He'd left the Edwardses' early that morning, also sending a message of apology for missing the celebratory betrothal breakfast.

"I expect you'll work swiftly, Miss Antonius."

He turned then, surprised that Camilla did not betray any of her feelings upon entry. It wasn't like her to be so... quiet.

Envy had been certain she'd be furious that he'd left without so much as a goodbye. Or predictably lovestruck.

She was neither.

Her attention simply swept around the room, passing over him like he was one more canvas to catalogue. She gave no indication that Envy had been on his knees, nestled between her thighs, a few short hours before.

He bristled.

"Should you require anything else, Alexei will see to it."

"Thank you, Lord Synton," she said at last. "If you'll have him bring a cup of tea, that will be all."

Envy's brows hit his hairline. Did she take him for a servant now?

"What of scones and clotted cream? Shall he bring some of those as well?"

"Unnecessary, but thank you for being thoughtful."

Camilla ignored the obvious sarcasm in his tone, striding over to the wooden stool and easel, running a hand lovingly across the polished wooden grain before hoisting up her chosen canvas.

She'd dressed in a charcoal gown today, the color deep and rich in pigment. A line of pearls ran up the sleeves from her wrists to her forearms, and a second line traveled along the front of her bodice from neck to navel.

Envy wanted to pin her hands above her head and rip the pretty pearls off with his teeth.

"You may leave now," Camilla said over her shoulder, almost as an afterthought. As if she'd forgotten he was there. "I work better alone."

Envy stared after her.

Camilla did not drink at the party last night, so it wasn't as if she'd been in some drunken stupor. He was positive she remembered coming all over his tongue, sweet and warm like honey. Was she *choosing* to ignore that?

Certainly, last night had been shocking. But Camilla had survived the crisis of Lord Garrey and moved on. Had decided she wished to live, to celebrate life.

He'd found that highly attractive.

He hardened just recalling her soft moans, her rapture pure and free as she fully submitted to the pleasure he'd given her.

She'd bitten her lip to keep anyone from hearing, and thrashed across those sheets, tangling them up just as he'd wanted her legs to be tangled with his when he climbed on top of her.

When she'd started undulating her hips, directing him to the exact place she wanted him, it took everything in him not to sink his cock into her wet heat the way they'd both craved him to. Camilla was a surprisingly vivacious lover and he'd only had one small taste.

One being the operative term.

His rule of only bedding someone once typically included one night of lust.

Which usually included every possible position, every act of pleasure. Then it made sense that their time together was over forever.

There wasn't anything typical about how he'd gone about things with Camilla last night.

He'd left before he *couldn't* tear himself away.

The moment she came, he'd imagined pulling her on top of him, dragging her up and down along his hard length until they'd both been teased into a frenzy.

Envy wanted to make love to her properly.

If he was only going to have one night to experience Camilla, he wouldn't waste it. Plus, he'd promised not to ruin her, and had he given in last night, there was no way Lord and Lady Edwards would have missed the sound of Camilla's moans.

Propriety had fucked him again. He was a walking, frustrated ball of gods-damned virtue, even after tending to himself with thoughts of her taste making him so cursedly aroused, he'd come with a demonic roar. Several, increasingly frustrating times. Each time he came, he was less satisfied than before. He craved her and his hand did not compare.

And her indifference was driving him positively feral. If this were a game played between them, he'd have to admit she currently had the upper hand. All previous lovers had been near savage with jealousy after he'd graced their sheets, begging for more. And that was the way he preferred things.

"Was there anything else, my lord?"

Envy's attention snapped back to Camilla. She'd been watching him, and he'd been oblivious.

He was never oblivious.

That was antithesis to his very nature. Envy planned, he was meticulous, he missed no details. Everything was a puzzle for him to solve. If Camilla thought to best him in this game of seduction, she truly had no idea who she was playing against. If she wished to be indifferent, he would be doubly so. Use her move against her.

He gave her a cold look.

"Do not dismiss me in my own home, Miss Antonius. If it happens again, I'll be forced to remind you who serves whom."

Amusement ghosted across her features.

He had the distinct impression she knew exactly who'd served whom last night. Gods-damn it all. None of his shots were landing.

"I imagine that will be *very* hard for you, my lord."

Camilla's gaze slowly dropped to his trousers before she flicked it back up, mischief glittering in her silver eyes. His cock jerked in response, eager to draw her attention again.

"Since it appears that you'll have your hands full *thinking,* I really must get to work."

Saints curse him, Envy's arousal grew at her second blatant dismissal.

If this had been any other time, any other circumstance, he'd have taken Camilla right there on the paint, using her perfect little bottom and his handprints to capture each thrust of pleasure on the canvas.

Then he'd hang the damn thing in his foyer.

Let her dismiss him *then.*

Rock-hard and frustrated in more ways than one, Envy left Camilla to her painting.

Out in the corridor, his cursed brother leaned casually against the wall, carving thin strips off a pear and popping them into his mouth. For once, his expression was oddly contemplative.

"What?" Envy snarled.

"You're in trouble," Lust said, pointing out the obvious. "The lust coming off you would make *my* court blush. Ever think maybe Camilla was chosen to distract you?"

Envy had.

Which meant the game master had chosen her with care. And that enraged him.

Camilla deserved to be more than a pawn, designed to pierce him deeply.

"In a few hours, she won't be a problem anymore. I'll have both the Hexed Throne and the next clue."

And Miss Camilla Antonius would have a missing and presumed dead fiancé, one who'd left his entire mortal estate to his would-be wife.

It wasn't part of their original bargain, but once Envy got what he was after he did not plan on returning to Waverly Green, and it made sense to give Camilla an added boon. He'd surmised that her finances had taken a downturn after her father's death. Otherwise, he couldn't imagine why she'd resort to creating forgeries. It was the least he could do to repay her for helping his court.

He would also see to it that Vexley would never be an issue for her again. Nor would any other player. He had Alexei working with his spies now, tracking down anyone else who was mildly suspicious in Waverly Green.

He'd kill the whole realm before anyone else got to her.

Lust gave him a doubtful look.

"Bring her to House Lust first, when you visit. If she starts with House Wrath, she'll think we're a bunch of vengeful savages who don't know how to have any fun."

Envy rolled his eyes. From what his spies had revealed, Wrath and his wife were having lots of savage fun. All over their House. In fact, rumors were circulating that Wrath had barely seen his court since his queen's coronation. They'd been too busy playing with chains and knives, stoking each other's fury like deviants.

If they kept this up, there would be a hellish lot of nieces and nephews soon.

"Camilla will come to House Envy first," Envy said without thinking, immediately regretting it when Lust flashed a victorious grin his way. "Why are you still here?"

Lust lifted a shoulder and dropped it.

"Can't I just be concerned for my brother? I know something's wrong. We all do."

Envy's attention narrowed on his brother. It wasn't an outright lie, but he sensed Lust was fishing. And he was getting entirely too close to the truth.

"You and Gluttony have a wager going?"

"There is that aspect as well."

"Get out."

Envy turned and began walking toward the kitchens. Apparently, he had a cup of tea to request for Miss Antonius. Then he'd take another long, icy bath. Alone.

"She doesn't succumb to my influence, at least not strongly."

Lust's shift in topic drew him up short.

"Have you tried to use your power on her?" he continued.

"The rules of the game won't allow me to use magic," Envy finally admitted.

It was a weak excuse, one his brother didn't bother to call out.

"Wait until after she paints the throne." Lust was quiet for a moment. "Then try."

Lust didn't say it, but Envy knew what he was thinking: that Camilla might be very different from Envy's last mortal.

Lust, for all his incessant bed hopping, was a secret romantic.

But Envy had already decided how this story would end.

In his world the only happily-ever-after he sought was for his court.

TWENTY-FOUR

CAMILLA PULLED THE emerald brush from where she'd hidden it in her bodice, eager to use it for the first time, even if she wasn't as thrilled to begin work on the Hexed Throne.

Trepidation inched its way down her spine, making the fine hair along her arms stand on end.

She already sensed the wrongness of what she was about to do, felt the first gusts of dark magic blowing in around the edges of the room, like spilled ink bleeding its way across a fresh page. If her father's stories could be trusted, the Hexed Throne—from wherever it slumbered—was cracking an ancient eye.

Would it be curious or furious at being summoned?

Camilla would soon find out—after striking the devil's bargain with Synton, there was no getting out of this part now.

Perhaps she was giving her talent too much credit, perhaps it would only be a simple painting.

And Synton is only a simple art collector with no dubious aspirations whatsoever.

She all but rolled her eyes at herself. Denial never did anyone any favors. Damned or not, this was the fate she'd chosen for herself, and it was time to get to work.

A quiet tapping drew her attention to the window.

She walked over and peered out across the manicured grounds, not seeing anyone. Another chill of foreboding caressed her spine. It was probably just a wayward branch. But after her encounter with Lord Garrey in the hedge maze, she wasn't so sure.

Anyone could be out there.

She glanced up at the cloudless sky, the color an unblemished, crisp fall blue. There was no breeze today. No hint of any impending storm. She shook the odd sensation away and took quick stock of her supplies; oils, watercolors, pencils, charcoal, pastels...

Tap, tap, tap.

She jerked her attention back to the window. Had a shadow just passed? Chills raced over her. Surely it was just a bird flying too close.

Foolish. Her mind was playing tricks on her, that was all. After such a violent attack, that was not surprising.

Tap, tap, tap.

This time, the noise was louder, a definite knocking. When Camilla looked out the window now, her breath caught. Was that Lord Garrey?

Fear slammed into her. Not Lord Garrey.

A cloaked figure stood just on the other side of the glass, his face hidden from view in the garment's depths. A scream caught in Camilla's throat a half second before she recognized the figure as one that had lurked outside her gallery. He rapped gloved knuckles along the pane, jerking his head toward the latch.

"Synton?" she called out at last, backing away.

Somehow, the figure outside seemed amused. It made no movement to try to stop her, or to come in. Still, she retreated toward the door, keeping her attention on the man. He lifted a hand—probably to break the glass—and any calmness she'd been clutching at vanished.

"Synton!" she yelled. "Hurry!"

The figure tilted his head back, but all she could make out was one pale yellow wolflike eye that seemed to wink at her before he abruptly turned and darted away.

A beat later, Synton was there.

"What's wrong?"

Camilla stared at the window, recognition dawning, if not understanding. That eye...it couldn't be. She had to be mistaken. She dragged her attention to the lord, trying to find a reasonable excuse for her behavior. She couldn't very well tell him the truth, not now.

"Apologies, my lord. Do you have the tea?"

He gave her an astonished look.

Camilla cleared her throat awkwardly. "Once I begin painting, I'll need to be completely alone."

Synton frowned at her and then looked over the rest of the room, suspicion clear in his face. But there were some things she couldn't reveal, not after how hard she'd worked all these years, and the man at the window—however he'd gotten here—was one.

After a drawn-out moment, Synton finally left, still frowning, and came back a few minutes later with a tray. A silver tea service, some biscuits, and cubes of sugar.

"Will that be all, Miss Antonius?"

His tone was mocking, but she ignored it.

"For now. Thank you."

Once he left, Camilla fixed herself a cup of tea to settle her nerves. She didn't want to think about why the hunter had tracked her down, especially now, of all times. He might once have promised he'd be back, but no good could come from his visit right before she painted a hexed object. And how had he known she was at Synton's, anyway?

The more she'd tried to keep her world together after her father's death, the more threatened it had seemed to become. She'd made her choice, years ago. That should have been the end of it. But deep down she'd always worried that she'd only been granted a small reprieve from the inevitable. Her past was circling like a buzzard, waiting to dive down and drag her carcass off. The hunter was gone for now, she figured, and surely harmless. Until he tried to speak to her again, she might as well embark on the task at hand.

Camilla sipped her tea, a smooth Waverly Green blend, and looked around the space again, finally able to appreciate the details now that she was alone.

As if it were chiaroscuro made solid, the chamber was a study of bold, dramatic contrasts—on one side a wall of floor-to-ceiling windows let in bright sunlight, and on the other dark paneled walls cast nearly black shadows in the corners.

A long wooden table held stacks of sketchbooks, leather-bound and well-worn. Broken bits of charcoal, a few balled-up sheets of paper. And a crystal decanter half filled with deep amber liquid, with two matching crystal glasses.

A large limestone fireplace along the wall at the back of the studio held a gentle blaze that was giving off a warm, cozy glow. A leather settee and a handwoven rug were tucked in front, offering an artist a comfortable place to lie back and dream. Along the last wall, a few canvases were stretched and waiting on easels.

It was all perfect, exactly what she'd have chosen for herself. Synton was a man who missed nothing.

She'd need to be extra careful around him now. The faster she completed the painting, the faster she'd be free from their arrangement.

She pulled an apron from the nearest chair and tied it around her waist.

Camilla returned to her easel, situated before the wall of windows, and sat, her attention focused solely on her own work now.

With steady hands she undid her locket and tucked it into a pocket she'd had sewn into her dress.

She kept the ridiculously oversized emerald-and-diamond ring on; then she canted her head and closed her eyes, pulling up an image from her father's stories.

In all accounts, the Hexed Throne burned on one side only, completely unaffected on the other. Another stark contrast; another act of balance.

Camilla thought about her father's voice, telling her the Hexed Throne had been created by the First Witch, a supernatural being descended directly from the sun goddess, according to legend.

Her daughter had fallen in love with a demon prince—one of their mortal enemies—and the First Witch was so furious, she hexed several objects in hope of destroying the demons. The story claimed that the Hexed Throne was meant to entice the prince, then overtake him.

Camilla let her memory expand, releasing its boundaries, moving beyond its emotions, until her talent felt alive in her veins, rushing out to her fingers, into the brush, ready to leap beyond.

Deep in her mind's eye, the throne spoke to her, told her the colors it needed, the shape, the very manner in which it ought to be revealed.

Camilla waited until the whole image had presented itself before opening her eyes.

Now, when she looked at the canvas, she saw the entire composition as if it had already taken its rightful place. She understood that this wasn't how it worked for everyone, but somehow, this was how it had always worked for her.

She began. The background needed to be solid black to start—like the throne was emerging from deep within an abyss, a spark of life where nothing should survive.

And perhaps a bit of mockery for the Creator.

The throne held its own power now. Was its own god in its eyes. The witch who'd hexed it, given it power and life, was *nothing* compared to its glory now.

Oh, yes, the rumors of its being sentient were true. Except it wasn't mildly sentient, it was fully aware, had as many thoughts and emotions as any other being. The Hexed Throne knew what it was and liked playing games, considered itself quite the game master, in fact.

Camilla passed no judgment, felt no emotion other than determination to bring forth the piece the way it desired to be seen. She had become a vessel for it to inhabit as it saw fit.

When she used her talent, dove deep within that well of creative power, Camilla lost all sense of time. Seconds or months could pass, and she'd remain blissfully unaware, conscious only of her brush.

Her father used to say talent like hers was a long-ago gift, perhaps bestowed on her family by some powerful Fae, and that when Camilla delved into its power, she shifted into the time of Faerie or the shadow realms.

It was dangerous, Pierre would remind her, to meddle with unpredictable forces, to stand between realms.

The idea that she might not be able to control her gift annoyed Camilla, even coming from her father. The depths of her talent might be a gift, but she'd worked hard at her craft. To understand not just what called to her, but how to give it life, how to make it her own.

Something Pierre Antonius had once known too. Before he'd crumbled in the end.

Camilla set her brush down, rubbing at the knot that had formed in her chest.

Her heart ached when she thought of her father. Time was so precious, human or Fae. She'd give nearly anything to have one more moment with him.

The abandoned canvas sent out a subtle pulse of light, a shadow-like heartbeat.

The throne did not want Camilla's attention to stray. It was displeased.

It was the master of her universe now. And she would obey.

In an almost trancelike state, she picked up the brush, dipped it into the paint, and continued. From the darkness the throne had emerged, and now from the throne came the flames, burning bright, bold, insistent—

What felt like a moment later, she'd been roughly lifted off her feet. A hand firmly held her legs, and another pinned her backside while all the blood rushed painfully to her head.

Disoriented and half under the throne's spell, Camilla needed another long moment to realize she'd been unceremoniously tossed over a shoulder like a sack of potatoes.

Just as suddenly as she'd been picked up, she was dropped to her feet, the sound of a door slamming finally snapping her into the here and now at the same moment her back hit a wall. The impact wasn't strong enough to harm her, but it did jolt her into awareness.

Camilla blinked until her abductor's furious face came into view.

"What the bloody hell were you doing, Miss Antonius?"

Synton's normally cultured voice was nothing more than a snarl, his expression bordering on savage as his gaze raked over her.

Cold air kissed her flushed cheeks.

The temperature had suddenly dropped, as if each fireplace in the estate had gone out at once. If Synton hadn't been standing so close, she'd have rubbed her arms to escape the chill.

"Painting." She glared back at him. "Or have you somehow forgotten our bargain in the last hour, my lord?"

He gave her a strange look, eyes narrowing slightly.

He stared for an uncomfortably long beat, his expression remaining as ruthless and hard as ever as he slowly looked her over again.

After another intense sweep of his focus, his stance relaxed, and he stepped back.

Marginally.

A flicker of warmth returned to her skin.

"From now on, you'll only work on the Hexed Throne with me inside the studio too."

"Why?" she asked.

"Because I'm protecting my investment."

"That's not—"

"Negotiable," he interrupted, flashing a dark grin as her scowl deepened. "Willingly paint with me in the room, or I'll handcuff us together until it's complete, Miss Antonius. And I do mean the whole time it will take. The choice is up to you, pet."

TWENTY-FIVE

Envy knew Camilla would be furious if he called her pet, but that didn't stop him from doing it. Igniting strong emotions in her perversely amused him. He liked seeing her nostrils flare ever so slightly, liked seeing the uptick in her pulse and the narrowing of those moonlike eyes. He'd come to enjoy the second before she gave him a little bit of hell.

And right now, her clear-eyed aggravation was a relief. When he'd pounded on the door the first night and she hadn't answered, he'd gone to bed thinking nothing of it, knowing how easy it was to get lost to creativity.

On the second evening, after Alexei had spent the day outside the studio and reported that she hadn't emerged to eat or drink, Envy had grown suspicious.

Camilla hadn't lied when she'd told him she'd only been gone an hour—he would have sensed it if she had. To her it had only been that.

Meanwhile, just over two days had passed in Waverly Green.

Envy wasn't sure whether it was the game or the throne itself causing time to flicker, but whatever the cause, he would not be leaving Camilla alone again.

It didn't surprise him in the least that this clue was proving more difficult than the last. Lennox wouldn't give up his prize so easily this time.

Camilla tried to move out from beneath his arm and he blocked her passage, keeping her firmly against the wall.

"Now what?" she asked, fresh aggravation lacing her tone.

"It's getting late. You'll eat and drink something, then retire to bed.

We'll begin again after you've fully rested. You are of no use to me if you're ill or half dead."

Silence stretched between them.

Camilla's eyes sparked with anger.

"Nowhere in our bargain do I recall agreeing to specified bedtimes, Lord Synton. I work until I'm satisfied. You may either join me or see yourself to bed alone. Clearly your senses have been addled if you believe you have any right to order me around."

Envy looked her over, wondering what was so gods-damned appealing about this constant battle of wills. If this mix of intrigue and arousal was even close to how Lust constantly felt, it was a wonder he did anything aside from indulge his sin every moment of the day.

A muscle in Envy's jaw tightened. He wanted Camilla to continue painting for selfish reasons, and he was far from tired. If she wished to continue, then so be it.

He stepped back and swept an arm out. "After you, then, Miss Antonius."

Camilla brushed past him and walked into the studio, spine straight, as if entering a battle.

If a war ever did break out, he wouldn't be surprised if she eliminated her enemies, one by one. Her will was one of the strongest he'd ever encountered.

Camilla was all polite society darling until pushed; then a scrappy little warrior emerged, baring teeth.

Her savage side called to his.

She rolled her stiff shoulders only once and then sat, the emerald paintbrush he'd gifted her already in her hand and poised above the red paint. She'd kept his apron cinched at her waist.

Behind her, Envy poured himself a knuckle of brandy and leaned against the settee by the fire, his gaze snagging on the painting for the first time.

Camilla was much further along than he'd imagined.

Seeing the throne emerge from the canvas, he was reminded less of a chair and more of a blade, which made sense, considering the hexed object was precisely that: a weapon. Camilla had chosen a color somewhere between champagne and bronze, not quite warm in tone and not cool, either, but situated perfectly between the two.

Opposites melded together in perfect harmony.

Camilla had only just begun to add the flames on the left. She worked on them now, her brush dipping in and out of the blended paint on her palette.

As he stared at the image, the darkness around the throne slowly undulated, as if smoke were curling around the sides of the canvas. Curious.

If Camilla noticed the oddity, she didn't let on.

Envy sipped his drink, the burn satisfying as it traveled downward. Camilla was fascinating to watch, as present and free, a touch reckless, as she'd been while receiving pleasure. Her silver hair tumbled down her back, shimmering with her deft movements, and the emerald on her finger caught the firelight. In her hand, the paintbrush flickered with life, as if she were imbuing her very soul into the paint, breathing life into her art.

Envy's attention shifted once again to the painting. Now its background moved like the sea at night, as if a secret might be rising in the throne's wake. Somewhere in this image was the third clue.

Anticipation had Envy leaning forward, body tensed, ready to spring into action.

As if in response, Envy sensed another energy in the room, a sort of power, testing for any constraints, any magical boundaries set up to lock it in place.

His own magic snarled in response. Something otherworldly was definitely here.

Envy straightened.

This was *his* domain.

Camilla was completely unaware of the charge building in the room, of the shadows that began to slowly pour out from the canvas, leaching into the studio like a dark wave.

His heart thudded. She was close to finishing the piece.

And whatever had joined them knew it too.

The flames on the painting crackled like real fire. Across the studio, the flames in the fireplace flared in solidarity.

He'd never seen such a thing—Camilla was creating reality from fantasy with her brush.

For a moment, Envy forgot about the game, the prize, and what winning might mean for him and his court. Instead, he considered what it would mean to set his sights on the woman herself.

Could she truly create new realities?

Perhaps the painting wasn't the clue he'd been sent after; perhaps the artist was.

Envy considered the implications of that as the studio howled around them, the darkness now swirling angrily like a great gathering storm.

Any moment now, fantasy and reality would no longer be discernible; their world and whatever Camilla created would collide.

Envy tossed back the rest of his drink and set his tumbler on the table, hands flexing. His demon blade practically burned at his side, begging to be used on this intrusion.

"Miss Antonius."

Envy's voice cracked through the storm like a whip of lightning. She didn't seem to hear.

"Camilla."

She turned from her easel, silver eyes glowing like stars.

He'd swear that whatever looked out at him was not entirely human.

Did the throne overtake her?

His heart ticked faster.

Envy said her name again, his voice this time laced with the command of a demon prince, a magical demand that none could ignore, and she blinked, irises once again normal.

"Come," he said, his gaze fixed on the hulking form behind her. "Now."

Camilla glanced over her shoulder and then did as he'd bidden without argument, her paintbrush still clutched in her hand.

Once she was safely secured behind him, Envy smiled mockingly at the throne before them.

With a roar that would make the devil himself pause, all hell broke loose.

TWENTY-SIX

CAMILLA DARTED BEHIND Synton, praying they would be able to exit the room before the hexed painting did whatever it was about to do.

But it was too late.

Much too late.

An inhuman screech rent the air. Her body felt suddenly hollow, as if giving life to the hexed object had taken something from her in return.

Camilla grabbed Synton's arm at the exact moment he reached back for her, as they tried to take in whatever vileness she'd set loose.

From what she could tell, it was enormous, crouched or hunched before them, a dense shadowy form with glowing crimson-orange embers for eyes.

In all her years, in all her nightmares, Camilla had never seen the like.

Not in the stories her mother and father had told. Not even in the places her mind had roamed.

Whatever it was, she understood that it wasn't the throne itself; it had been the hexed thing living inside the throne, using its physical form.

Fire raged around them, growing stronger, wilder, like its shadow master.

Its hatred was palpable—its fury unmatched.

Camilla sensed it wanted to burn the entire estate, the whole city, until nothing but ash remained. Destruction. Cruelty. Chaos. Who knew how many years it had plotted revenge, locked within the confines of its prison? Maybe the old stories had it wrong, maybe the witch had hexed the throne to keep this creature far from the world. Maybe her hatred wasn't a threat so much as a protection.

Truth was often lost or rewritten over the centuries.

"What's happening?" Camilla shouted, her voice swept away by the next gust of sulfuric wind.

Synton squeezed her hand but didn't comment.

What was there to say?

The world was breaking and re-forming into a hellscape before their very eyes.

Camilla's mother had been less obsessed with the mythology of the other worlds than her father, but she had held fast to one rule: Pierre should never open his talent to a demon, and she'd raised Camilla that way too.

Camilla never would have painted the throne if she'd known what it truly was. And there was no way anything that malevolent was anything but demonic.

Winds howled in the most frightening manner, the air growing uncomfortably hot, smelling of death and ash.

Embers seared her skin, falling like some cursed snow from the devil's domain.

Terror seized her. This would not end well.

Camilla needed to get herself and Synton to safety. If she destroyed the painting...

She inched forward, determined to—

"Stop."

Synton barely raised his voice, but the creature heard him all the same. It stilled. And so did Camilla.

From deep within the bowels of the Underworld they now stood in came a sinister laugh.

It was layered, as if multiple voices in varying tones spoke at once.

"You dare to command me?" the hexed demon seethed.

Synton completely ignored the violence in the creature's tone. He took a step toward it as if it should fear *him*. "You have information for me."

Camilla wanted to throttle Synton. Did he not notice how much danger they were in?

Before she could pull him back, the demonic creature lurched forward, drawing in deep breaths like it was scenting them.

"So much power. So much... sin."

The shadowy form exhaled slowly, its eyes flaring a brighter red.

"Your Highnessssss."

Camilla went perfectly still.

Its head swiveled in her direction. In the next moment, it was *inside* her mind, speaking to her silently.

Talent is such a horrible thing to waste, it said. *Yours will be given back if you play the game until its end.*

What game? she thought back at it.

Did you believe he *wouldn't eventually force your hand?*

Inside her mind the Hexed Throne laughed wickedly. It had seen her realization.

Yesssss, it hissed, delighted, *you are now but another pawn to be moved around his board.*

It wasn't talking about Synton. The creature was speaking of someone much, much worse. And she felt it again, then: that strange hollowness from before, and she knew her talent was gone. Her heart pounded wildly. He'd stolen her talent, her very essence.

She didn't have long to dwell on that horrid revelation; she gasped as a crown shimmered to existence on top of Synton's head. Emerald-tipped, beautiful.

"Ahhh." The throne purred, speaking aloud again. "Prince of Envy. There you are. In hiding no more."

"What?" Confusion warred with Camilla's terror, winning for a moment.

Without glancing in her direction, Synton strode toward the throne, magic cracking around him—*from him*—with each mighty step.

If the throne was power, then, impossibly, the alleged prince was the source from which it sprang. She could feel the magic unspooling from him now.

Camilla's heart pounded a furious beat. What *was* Synton? Surely he couldn't be...

"Tell me what I want to know." Synton's tone was insolent, demanding. Royal. "Now."

The flames on the throne shot upward, a towering inferno of fury and chaos that the elemental creature danced before. The hexed object raged at the command, but just as Camilla was convinced it would strike out, it whispered, "Hush! Those goose, lose no text."

There was a beat of silence before the lord reacted.

"Send my regards to your king."

Synton's arm lashed out, and it shrieked, its many voices screaming in unison as a gleaming blade pierced through the shadow-like creature with ease.

Faster than it had begun, the fire, the embers, the wind, and the throne itself winked out of existence. In fact, the very painting she'd created had turned to a pile of ash. The only thing that remained was the emerald-tipped crown sitting atop Lord Synton's head.

The throne had called him the Prince of Envy.

A charge he hadn't denied.

Camilla watched as he finally shifted to meet her accusing stare, his expression cold, without an ounce of remorse. His gaze was fathomless, unflinching. Inhuman.

It all made sense, suddenly.

There was an ancient loneliness in his eyes because he was no mortal, brokenhearted man. Lord only knew how old he was. How many lives he'd lived, how many loves he'd lost.

If he was even capable of such an emotion. Maybe he'd simply shown her what she wanted to see, manipulated her to the full extent of his power.

Prince of Envy.

Now that the initial shock had passed, Camilla could think more clearly.

Most in Waverly Green believed the tales of the seven demon princes to be fiction, but she should have known better. She was well aware that it was unwise to write something off simply because you'd never seen it.

Many strange things were often found hiding in plain sight. The world was a vast, curious place filled with curious creatures. People rarely showed their true selves. But in all the stories she'd heard, demons couldn't lie.

She laughed then at the irony, the sound anything but amused.

"Lord Synton. Clever. You must have had a good laugh at all our expenses." Her tone hardened along with her expression. "You claimed you and Vexley were nothing alike, but here you are, nothing but a ruthless liar. And a miserable demon."

His hand fisted at his side, his gaze darkening.

A spark of temper ignited in his eyes now, burning away the iciness.

One thing had been true in his charade, at least—he did not appreciate being likened to Vexley.

"Not so miserable when I'm in your bed, Miss Antonius." His gaze mocked now. "You got a small taste of my powers."

Despite her anger, heat lanced through her. No wonder he'd pushed her so thoroughly out of her mind—he was a prince who literally ruled over sin. No human in this whole world could compete with his skill in debauchery; since the stories were apparently true, the princes had practically invented the term. He had owned her with his tongue, and like every other fool who ended up in his sheets, she'd willingly sold her soul for that taste.

He smiled then, a quick brutal flash of teeth.

"I sense your arousal, Miss Antonius. Even knowing what I am, even hating that I lied, you want me."

Attraction or not, it would be a cold day in hell before she invited him into her bedchamber now.

Another thought hit Camilla.

"Which brother did I meet?" she demanded.

At the ball, Syn had said there were seven brothers total. Truth as far as she knew. Probably the only bit of truth she'd been granted this whole time.

The Prince of Envy narrowed his eyes.

That look was definitely the sin he ruled over rearing its head. Good. Now she knew one of his weaknesses.

"Lust."

That certainly explained things.

"Which brother is Alexei?"

"He's my second-in-command." Envy's gaze glittered, dark and ominous. "Think twice before you threaten to bite him again, pet. Alexei is a vampire, and I promise he'll bite back much harder. Although his venom can give you untold pleasure. You'd come as you died and beg for more with your last breath."

Camilla knew he was trying to shock her, but most fiction spoke of vampires and their dangerous seduction, so the fact that Alexei's venom could create orgasms to die for was hardly the most inconceivable part of her evening.

Which was rather remarkable.

"Since our bargain is now complete, I highly doubt I'll encounter your pet vampire again, Your Highness." Camilla drew herself to her full height, wishing she weren't still wearing the damn painter's apron. But at least using his true title seemed to rankle the prince.

God save her. The Prince of Envy. A fairy-tale villain sprung to life, and he'd had her convinced she'd experienced heaven in his devilish arms the night before.

With nothing left to say to the lying scoundrel before her, Camilla headed toward the door, but paused with a sinking heart. She *couldn't* leave. To win her talent back, she needed to play the game. The throne was very clear on that. She wished she could claim she had no idea what the throne had meant, but she did. She subtly tried to summon her talent…to no avail.

Camilla took a deep breath. She knew very little of how the games worked, but she'd heard legends of their deadly stakes before, and of the sneaky game master himself. Losing her talent, her ability to paint, was the one thing he'd known she'd never endure, the one move he could make that guaranteed she'd play.

And if she was joining a current game, then odds were that was what Synton—Envy—damn it, whoever he was, had been up to all along. She felt her anger rising, but she reminded herself that if all this was true, then she needed Envy. At least until she figured out what she had to do next. Or she found another player to...

She closed her eyes. Of course. Lord Garrey. Recalling how Synton had helped him meet his end, she wasn't sure it would be a good idea to let the demon prince know he had a new competitor—her.

And it'd be an even worse idea to let him find out she'd kept her own secret all along too. For now, she'd not reveal anything about her stolen talent, either. He'd become suspicious.

What was one more secret, anyway?

When she opened her eyes again, Envy was standing directly before her, looking dangerous.

"Do you know what the throne said?"

"A bunch of gibberish." She tried to say it calmly, but her heart pounded so hard she worried he'd hear it.

"Hush! Those goose, lose no text."

"You are proving my point beautifully, Your Highness," she managed.

"It was a clue." Envy looked briefly offended. "An anagram. *Hush! Those goose, lose no text.* Deciphered it says, *House Sloth next. She goes too.*"

Camilla's mouth snapped shut.

The prince didn't miss a beat. His smile was victorious.

She kept her face blank. Her game and his were truly intertwined.

"So you see, my darling," he continued, "you have unwittingly become a part of the game I'm playing. A game I have spent many years waiting to win."

He had no idea how correct he was about that.

With his free hand, he made to reach for her, then dropped it before making contact, a serious look overtaking his face.

"I might have lied to you about my name and title, but you have to understand, I will use any means necessary to win." Then he gave her a wolfish smile. "And I love being a sinner too much to ever be a saint."

"No one would nominate you for sainthood."

"And be glad of that. Saints don't typically kill to protect their investments."

"Is that what you think I am? *Your* investment?"

"I think you're delaying the inevitable and wasting time."

"Perhaps I want you on your knees, apologizing before I decide what to do."

His expression turned dark with sinful promise.

"I've been on my knees for you. If you want me there again, just ask. But if you expect an *apology* while I'm down there, you'll be disappointed. At least in that regard."

She gave him a withering look but said nothing.

"Choose to accompany me, or don't, Miss Antonius. Either way, you're coming with me to House Sloth."

Heat coiled low in her belly. Most inconveniently. She *shouldn't* be aroused by the damned brute.

Camilla cursed that wretched little deviant inside her, the one who purred seductively at the villain for his unbridled vices and mocked the hero for his unshakable virtues.

Life would be so much simpler if she would fall for the male whose moral compass was as dependable as the North Star.

But helping Envy was the key to helping herself now. For better or worse, they were partners in this game, no matter that he didn't know that. At least not yet.

"Since you need me for whatever the next clue suggests," she said at last, "I want time to prepare, at least."

Her tone was firm, her stance clear. This would be a negotiation, or she'd find another way to play the game.

Envy looked her over. "An hour."

"Two."

He stared at her a long moment. His expression was carved from stone, but she swore she saw the faintest flicker of respect before he blinked it away.

"Two hours," he agreed, gritting his teeth. "Eat, bathe, dress warmly. We'll leave precisely at midnight."

She graced him with a single nod.

He held the studio door open for her. "Camilla?"

She paused on the threshold, glancing back.

"If you run, I will chase you."

She saw how serious he was. Envy would pursue his goal ruthlessly.

Part of her was intrigued by the intensity of wanting something so badly that no moral line would go uncrossed. A male that driven, that focused...fascinated her on the most basic level.

She spun around, heading for her chamber before he could see the tiny thrill she felt at that dangerous vow.

TWENTY-SEVEN

"Well?" Envy barked, staring out through the window at the dark hedge maze.

He'd been mulling over the chaos of the evening, as well as that strange moonlit glow in Camilla's eyes, trying to puzzle out what she could be, if she wasn't—as he was beginning to suspect—entirely human.

Envy had guessed she had secrets when she became the key, vital for him to receive the third clue. He hadn't expected the mystery of who she was to delve so deep.

He didn't need another complication right now. His mood was downright hostile as he sorted through theories—none of which satisfied.

Shape-shifters, Fae, even some peculiar combination of half-vampires could explain her talent. But he wouldn't know for certain until he learned all he could of her family.

He'd already sent his spies out with new instructions, to locate Camilla's mother and find out more, when he'd felt Alexei lingering in the corridor.

Whatever news he brought couldn't be good. "How bad is it?"

"I'd counsel seeing for yourself, Your Highness."

Envy glanced at the clock. He had more than an hour and a half before Camilla had agreed to depart, which would give him just enough time to travel to his court and return.

He turned to face his vampire second-in-command.

"How bad?" he repeated, enunciating each word.

"Two-thirds, Your Highness."

"Fuck."

Two-thirds of his court now lost to the fog. They'd be in serious peril if anyone else heard how vulnerable House Envy was right now.

Envy strode out the door, the vampire trailing along like a shadow behind him.

They traveled down several sets of stairs in silence, stopping once they reached the wine cellar. The limestone walls held a slight chill that had little to do with the lack of sunlight.

Envy had used magic he could ill afford to spare on crafting a portal here to enter his House of Sin.

"Watch Camilla," he said to Alexei. "Make sure she doesn't leave the grounds. I'll be back in an hour to escort her through the Sin Corridor."

Alexei inclined his head and disappeared back up the stairs.

Envy inhaled deeply, then held his palm to the wall. He whispered his spell, then walked straight forward, into the secret portal hidden in the stone. Immediately he was submerged in the dense energy connecting the realms, pushing through as if wading through water, but within seconds he'd broken free, striding forward on the other side.

He let out a breath, looking his private suite over. All was how he'd left it. His oversized four-poster bed was unrumpled, the nude portrait of himself still proudly displayed on the ceiling. Good.

The nightstands were polished, but not completely free of dust. A light layer coated the top of the wood, just enough for him to drag his finger across.

His notebooks were piled neatly, the letter that had begun the game tucked carefully between them.

No one had entered this chamber since he'd left.

He steeled himself for whatever would greet him outside this room.

Once in the hallway, the silence immediately struck him. There was no music, no movement. No shuffling of feet or hurried sounds of demons moving to and fro, bringing art, arranging it, admiring what he'd collected and curated throughout the centuries.

Envy's House had been crafted to give the feel of a museum. Each wing, each level featured a different medium. There was the Tapestry Room on the second floor, along with the Titans Room, and the Longest Night Gallery on the third, where one would also find the Gothic Stair, the Heritage Tower, and the sixth-floor corridor, which featured architectural fragments Envy had collected from across the realms, made of varying materials, his favorite being stone.

He had rooms dedicated to mortal art—Venetian, Renaissance, Baroque, Georgian, Ancient World, Old World. And even, though he'd bragged about it less lately, art from the Wild Court of the Unseelie.

Some wings were even designated by color, mixing and matching different periods. The blue corridor, red, pink, then the metallic wings featuring gold, silver, bronze, and copper. But the green art he'd collected, that was where the magic of his sin truly shone—he had gorgeous variations in shades not known to mortals, far beyond sage, hunter, emerald, deepest moss, or brightest grass.

Envy strode through the hallways, not seeing another soul. He paused to glance out the arched windows in the Mist Corridor, looking at the courtyard below.

Empty.

His courtyard was one of his favorite places. Usually it was alive with courtiers, some playing music and others setting up canvases along the gardens. He'd always delighted in their paintings and sketches of the water features, or the birds who nested in the magical winterbud trees he'd imported from the far north. He'd taken such pride in the unrivaled beauty of his home.

That was all before. Now only the statues and sculptures he passed watched his silent procession, their stone faces as lifeless as his court.

Alexei hadn't exaggerated. Things were much worse.

Envy's long stride ate up the expansive corridors, growing quicker the longer he went without seeing anyone. Near stairs leading to the upper level, where the nobility who preferred to remain at court stayed in luxurious suites, he paused.

There, in the distance, he heard it. Wailing.

Jaw locked, he aimed for the sound of grief, holding his worry and anger tightly in his fist, allowing no trepidation or dread to show on his face.

After an eternity he stopped before a chamber.

He raked a hand through his hair, despite his vow to look unaffected.

"Fuck."

This would not be good. For the first time in his immortal existence, the Prince of Envy considered running from his court.

Please, he silently begged any Underworld god who'd listen, *spare them.*

He hoped he wasn't too late.

The door he stood before belonged to Lord and Lady Casius, two of the higher-ranking nobles, the lady a member of his council, made up of demons he'd known for centuries. Who'd schemed with him, who'd searched for spells with him for decades now, hoping to delay the madness. Who'd found the one spell he could use to lie. Who'd believed Envy would see them all saved, in the end. They never blamed him for what he'd done, even though he deserved it.

If they succumbed...

There were few things in any of the realms that Envy could imagine being worse.

The Lord and Lady Casius had been blessed by the old gods, and before he'd departed for the game had brought three new demons into the world, even knowing the risks. The babes couldn't be older than six months, even with the time he'd been away.

Envy knocked gently, then pushed the door open, his nails digging into his palms as he entered the room.

It had been destroyed.

"Who are you?" Lady Casius screamed, her gown tattered and torn. "Who is that?"

"Shh," he soothed, "it's me, Piper. Prince Envy."

Tears streamed down her face, terror making her back away.

"I...I don't know you."

She wailed again, the sound echoing in the once finely appointed room. Glasses were broken, art ripped from the walls. As if a battle had been fought, blood was splattered across the wallpaper.

"I don't know him! WHO IS HE?"

Envy followed her pointing hand to the slumped form at her feet, blood pooling out from the lifeless body. She'd attempted to cover him with her bedding. Had torn the sheets from the mattress in a violent frenzy. A moment of clarity must have hit at some point.

He slowly approached, hands up, then knelt, already knowing what he'd find.

Dreading it.

He pulled the sheet back and quickly averted his gaze. Lord Casius had been gone for some time. Envy wasn't certain how he'd missed the scent of rot when he'd first opened the door. To kill a demon...it wasn't an easy feat. They were long-lived, perhaps not immortal like Envy and his brothers, but not casually lost, either.

Envy saw some defensive wounds on his friend's hands, knew if he'd still been in his right mind he wouldn't have struck his wife, even if she was repeatedly striking him.

Gods-damn. When Envy won the game and restored balance—because he refused to consider the alternative—Piper would never recover. Even if she got her memories back, she'd never forgive herself.

In so many ways, Envy was already too late.

He was struggling to figure out a way to remove his old friend when Piper's next words pinned him in place.

"Who are they?" she screamed, her tone shrill. "WHO ARE THEY? They kept staring and crying. WHO SENT THEM TO KILL ME?"

"Who are..." Envy had a sudden realization and couldn't bring himself to look.

But as the prince of this circle, it was his duty.

He would own this sin, allow it to scar his soul. These deaths, these murders...they belonged to him. If he'd never given the chalice to her...

He would solve the riddles, claim his prize, and make this right. No matter the cost to him. No matter who he had to deceive, kill, or toy with in the process.

Envy would win. Or his circle would be no more.

His eyes stung as he forced himself to scan the room.

There, in the corner, where the cribs had been...

Bile seared up his throat; he squeezed his eyes shut, closing off the unspeakable sight. It made no difference. The image was burned there, forever.

Envy allowed himself one moment of grief; then his resolve hardened along with his heart. He needed to set this right before he returned to Camilla. And he had little time left.

"I did it." Lady Casius fell to her knees, horrible clarity flashing in her eyes.

Envy knew it would soon pass like it always did; the memories would fog once again, and she'd be blissfully unaware of reality.

He needed to get Piper out of this chamber immediately, needed to see about—

A shriek filled the air.

Before he saw the blade, before he could cross the room, Lady Casius had thrust the dagger through her chest, her knees cracking against the marble floor a moment before her skull did.

Envy felt the blow as if in his own heart.

Cursing, he scrubbed his hands down his face, fighting down an unfamiliar panic, until his breathing was in control. Then he wrapped his heart in ice, the coldness erupting from him to coat the room in a layer of frost, and he set about collecting his fallen friends.

Once again, Envy had been too late to save them, and now he had five more deaths to add to his sins. Five more demons he'd sworn to protect.

He would not leave them here; he would take their bodies to where they had taken all the rest. At the very least, then, they would no longer be alone.

TWENTY-EIGHT

"WHAT MAKES YOU trust anything that hexed creature said?" Camilla asked.

Envy had been watching her closely. Too closely. She'd known from the moment she'd opened her chamber door that he was not in a pleasant mood. He'd scanned her, his gaze hard, his mouth a cruel slash as he took a step inside and all but bared his teeth.

"I told you to put on something warm. Get a cloak."

"Do not speak to me like that," she said firmly. "I'm not a child."

"Then don't act like one."

She narrowed her eyes. Something was certainly amiss.

Camilla wasn't sure what had shifted. If he'd had any warmth for her before, it was long gone. His coldness, the hard set of his mouth, the unforgiving glint in his gemlike eyes—here stood the villain of lore. The Prince of Hell wicked enough to inspire parents to tell their children terrifying cautionary tales.

She had no idea what could possibly have happened in two short hours to turn him into this harsh beast.

She scanned him slowly, looking for any clue. There was no blood, no wrinkle in his hunter-green suit, no crack in his icy façade or hair out of place. Yet she felt his dark energy roiling below the surface.

"What happened?" she asked quietly. "Did another player attack?"

"If we're sharing information now," he said, voice dangerously soft, "why don't you start by telling me about your parentage? Or perhaps about your charm?"

Everything inside her stilled.

"What?"

"Most mortals cannot conjure reality with a few strokes of their brush, Miss Antonius."

"Well, lucky for you, isn't it, that I could."

He took hold of her hand, whispered something in an ancient tongue, and in the very next breath Camilla suddenly stood on what felt like the edge of the universe.

The world of Hemlock Hall had vanished, replaced by something much darker, vaster, and colder.

Envy dropped her hand, stepped closer to her side, and murmured, "Welcome to the void outside the Seven Circles. This is the space that connects it to all other realms." He smiled grimly. "And before you are the infamous gates of the Underworld."

Camilla stared at the strange air around her, fear prickling her skin almost as much as the icy wind. Looking down, she was stunned to find herself clothed in a thick cloak, which had somehow magically appeared.

There was no sound at all, except for the prince's voice.

And the thrashing of her pulse. Anger made her spin to face him, eyes flashing.

"Are you completely mad?"

"Not yet."

Camilla had half a mind to leave him and strike out on her own. Except his clue had indicated that she needed to go to House Sloth too. Cursed game, and it'd only just begun. For her, at least.

"If you *ever* put your will above my own," she said, her voice lowered but laced with the promise of vengeance, "you will regret it, Envy."

"There are many things I regret, Miss Antonius, but taking you here isn't one of them."

He jerked his chin toward the gates.

"We have a long way to go before we settle for the night. I suggest moving."

Camilla tamped down her annoyance. She had to focus on the game, and she supposed the menacing gates were the only way to Sloth's court. Besides, she'd long had to tolerate brutish males. She could continue to do so, for now.

She turned to look at the strange cavelike chamber before her.

The gates Envy spoke of gleamed nightmarishly several paces in front of them, carved from bone and horn and fang. Creatures too wicked to live and too sinister to be forgotten, forever immortalized in a warning to all who passed through.

There was beauty in the Gothic feel of it, a dark beauty Camilla shouldn't wish to paint. And now that her talent had been stolen, she couldn't. Panic clawed at her as she tried to summon her talent, once again to no avail. Even with her magic bound, the shape of the arch called to her.

The shift from Waverly Green to this strange land was so abrupt, Camilla could scarcely wrap her mind around the truth of it even as the iciness seeped into her skin. The Prince of Envy had well and truly dragged her to the Underworld. No story ever could have prepared her for its majestic terror. Not even the darkest tales told by her father.

"We must pass through the Sin Corridor first," Envy said, breaking the spell. "It will test you to see which sin you have the biggest affinity for. You may experience some...odd...feelings as each magic attempts to seduce you. Don't worry, I'll be watching over you with the utmost interest."

"I'm sure you will," she said icily. Ignoring his attempt to distract her, she considered what that actually meant. She'd be tested for each of the deadly sins.

Lust. Greed. Envy. Pride. Wrath. Gluttony. Sloth.

Seven ways for this realm to do its worst.

Camilla determined right there that she wouldn't make it easy, on Envy or this forsaken place. Now that she was forewarned, she'd be waiting for the first indications of magic.

"Any questions, Miss Antonius?"

"What will happen in Waverly Green while we're gone? I have a business, a life. I cannot simply cease to exist while you play your game."

He arched a brow; she'd surprised him. Good.

"I'll have my people craft a plausible story for our absence. And I'll purchase some art in your gallery upon our return. Payment—"

"You will do no such thing. I do not need your charity."

"It's an exchange for the inconvenience, and time lost. You're a wise businesswoman, surely you see the value in that. Any other questions?"

She saw the value in that, all right. She would find the most expensive pieces in her collection and tally them up. This might even guarantee she could pay her staff for the next two years.

Mollified, she considered what else she needed to know.

"How long will each test last?"

"That depends entirely on you. This realm thrives on sin—the way oxygen and water are the fabric of life in the mortal realms, vice is part of this realm's being." He paused. "We need to travel on foot until the Corridor has completed its test. Other magic is forbidden until you've experienced each sin and have been aligned with a House, so even if I wanted to, I could not simply bring us to House Sloth."

"This realm needs to determine where I belong, even if I'm not staying? And you have no power over it?"

He assessed her before answering. "Vampires, Fae, shifters, and goddesses also dwell here, and while they do not normally choose to align with any demon House, the Sin Corridor will always be curious to see where you would do best. Think of it as a natural order, if you must. No matter how powerful a prince is, no matter that this is our domain, there are some laws of nature even we cannot break."

He guided her forward, their steps silent, lost to the surreal depths of the void.

Before them, the walls around the gates were cavelike—stone panels soaring higher than she could ever hope to see unless she sprouted wings, the color a strange bluish black.

Opaque, like thick slabs of ice.

Envy placed a hand on her back, urging her forward, and had them through the gruesome gates within seconds.

She wondered whether he was only anxious to be on his way, or didn't want her examining the gates too closely.

The moment they'd crossed the threshold, the gates closed behind them, trapping her in this strange new world of snow and ice.

Sounds returned, as ominous and wretched as she'd have imagined. Winds gusted, ice-coated branches clattered, and in the far distance she swore she heard snarls as of some great beasts.

It did not surprise her that humans had been told the Underworld was a land of fire when in fact the opposite was true. Places hidden from mortals were often disguised in an attempt to keep the humans from realizing where they were, should they ever stumble upon them.

She gazed around at distant mountains, the surrounding evergreen trees, and the steep corridor through them, yawning on and on in front of them, trying to orient herself.

Everything was buried under snow.

Even the sun—if it could be called that—was a dulled orb pinned to a twilight sky. Another storm was blowing in. The cold air smelled of nature's violence.

"You remain remarkably unaffected, Miss Antonius. Why is that?"

"I've been fed stories of different realms as part of my weekly sustenance for as long as I can remember. My father frequented the dark market from the time I could walk."

The prince waited for her to elaborate, his cool, aristocratic features as remote as this frozen land.

Of course the Seven Circles, the realm ruled quite literally by sin and debauchery, by seven dark and dangerous princes, were forbidding. Like the regal man next to her. Or rather, regal demon prince.

That would take some getting used to. Remembering he was no mortal man.

She tamped down the rush of excitement she felt, hating how the thought of his power affected her.

"That didn't answer my question." Envy was watching her curiously.

She lifted a shoulder but remained silent.

After lying to her and now this kidnapping, he would have to wait forever before she'd reveal any more secrets about herself.

Camilla drew in a deep breath, the cold air forcing her senses to heighten.

Envy hadn't lied, at least not about the Sin Corridor. She'd pretended to be unaffected, but she'd felt the magic of the world circling them like a pack of wolves sniffing out potential prey. She wondered which sin would strike first, test her mettle. She also wondered if the realm would be surprised at what it discovered.

"We'll travel as far as possible, but if the test hasn't finished, we'll need to shelter in the Corridor for the night," the prince said, breaking the silence.

Camilla flicked her attention to Envy, noticing the tension in his body, the strain.

He couldn't have seemed more on edge if he'd tried. From what she recalled of old stories, he did not need to remain with her.

He was choosing to do so. Probably to ensure that she didn't run. Or maybe it had to do with his sin. Envy wouldn't want her to stray too far from his side.

He looked her over clinically.

"Are you cold?"

She shook her head, then quickly gestured to the grand cloak. He was not the only one capable of withholding unnecessary details.

If he found that suspicious, he didn't comment on it.

Instead, he began their slow trek through the snow, remaining a few steps ahead to tamp down a path for her. It was practical, but also kind.

Camilla drank in each part of this realm as they walked, guzzling details and storing them away to paint when she returned home, theoretically with her talent again intact.

This was precisely the sort of scene that would make her name in Waverly Green. Her father had known that distinctiveness was the key; his whimsical fantasy pieces had been so unique compared to the religious or still life paintings so many others gravitated toward.

This would combine Camilla's love of landscape with the vibrancy of the fantastic. Something not quite as on the nose as Pierre's work, but so perfect for her, holding secret worlds that begged to be explored.

There was so much white, of course, but it was broken with deep, rich splashes of green from the trees, gray clouds in the sky, and a beautiful bluish tint where the ice was exceptionally thick. The colors were muted but rich, holding steady against the looming danger of the dramatic weather.

They traveled up steep hills and down sharp ravines. Sometimes the path was so narrow she had to turn to the side to pass, and other times it was wide enough to march an army through.

The farther they trudged, the more she understood that this realm was vast—much more so than she'd ever heard. It seemed to go on forever in every direction—the corridor only hinting at what majesty might lie beyond those high mountain peaks.

Camilla had never traveled far outside Waverly Green, except for her family's yearly outings to their country estate nearby. Still, her mother had loved to share stories of her previous travels across the mortal world, often painting a picture with her words as deftly as Pierre had with his watercolors. For many years, her mother and Pierre had seemed an exceptional match.

Yet her mother's restlessness had put an end to that.

After her father had died, Camilla had thought about following her mother's footsteps and leaving Waverly Green. Suddenly alone, she realized she could go anywhere, do anything. At home, it had seemed possible that the flood of loneliness and memories would drown her. But she'd made a choice, holding close her father's honor, choosing instead to run Wisteria Way.

Camilla had never really regretted her choice, but she'd still secretly dreamed of seeing the worlds from her father's stories one day. Although the reality that she was doing so now with the Prince of Envy at her side seemed more than she'd bargained for.

Every so often she felt the slight pressing of magic against her and mentally brushed it away. Wrath was only mild annoyance. Gluttony was a slight desire to keep feasting on the world. Envy was wishing she had a way to come here whenever she wanted to soak it all in and feeling jealous of those who could. Yet nothing overwhelmed her, nothing commanded her.

She was the master of her will. If only she could summon her talent as easily.

Envy kept his attention mostly fixed on the tree line, indicating that the snarls she'd heard earlier were in fact beasts. She'd heard legends of three-headed hounds and could picture those creatures making the eerie sounds they heard now.

Envy glanced at her a few times, his brow creased as if she were the one riddle he couldn't solve.

She waited, breath held, for him to question her, but he never did.

She studied him while his back was to her, openly admiring his powerful frame, the certainty of his confident, unhurried steps. Envy was at home in this harsh world, undisturbed. He was the greatest predator in this corridor and knew it.

And that knowledge made her annoyingly attuned to him.

Camilla watched the way even the snowflakes seemed to part for him, not daring to muss his hair or clothing, admirers merely sweeping to the side, bowing to their prince.

If she were to paint him now, here, she'd have the whole realm bending to his mighty will. Would show the earth folding in at his feet, kneeling too.

She snorted.

He'd love the idea of being worshipped by the very earth he stood upon.

He shot a look over his shoulder.

"Nothing," she said, answering the unspoken question in his eyes. "Just amusing myself."

"I can see that." His mouth curled up at the edges, the first flicker of playfulness she'd seen on his face since he'd brashly brought them here.

He turned and set an increasingly brutal pace.

On and on they walked.

Instead of Camilla's being fearful of the snarls and roars all around, a sense of adventure reemerged, her creativity spinning visions of what the creatures hidden in the forests might look like, how she might paint them when she won her talent back. Because she *would* win it back.

Would the creatures be great winged beasts, perhaps with the head of a lion and the body of a whale? Would their fangs be the size of her arms? Would they be covered in thick coats of fur, or in scales, or something wholly new?

The possibilities were endless.

Excitement rushed through her as the next roar sounded, vibrating through the ground. It sounded like it was directly over the nearest hill. Camilla thrilled at the pounding of her heart, the rush of her pulse.

Envy shook his head, his expression still mildly amused at her reaction, but remained silent.

Camilla realized that fear had shaken something awake inside her, made her want to shed her civility and become all animal too. Dangerous. Batting aside these pestering sins, it was the only thing that truly tempted her. Aside from the prince himself.

But he was dangerous for a far different reason. She sensed he could unleash in her all she'd kept locked away, hidden. And the idea of him unraveling her secrets was no longer as frightening as it should be.

Winds gusted with renewed vigor, the tops of the trees swaying, beckoning her to let go too.

The snow began falling more heavily, dotted with ice.

Envy stopped abruptly.

"We'll stay here for the night."

Camilla peered through the dense foliage.

Here was nothing but a battered cabin built from roughly hewn trees, barely large enough for her, let alone the two of them together. Not after this day of Envy tempting her so fiercely.

For the first time since she'd entered this realm, Camilla's heart raced for an entirely different reason. It seemed her true test of will was about to begin.

And this time, she had little hope of winning.

Brushing off magic was one thing, but ignoring her growing desire was something else entirely. And this sinful realm knew it.

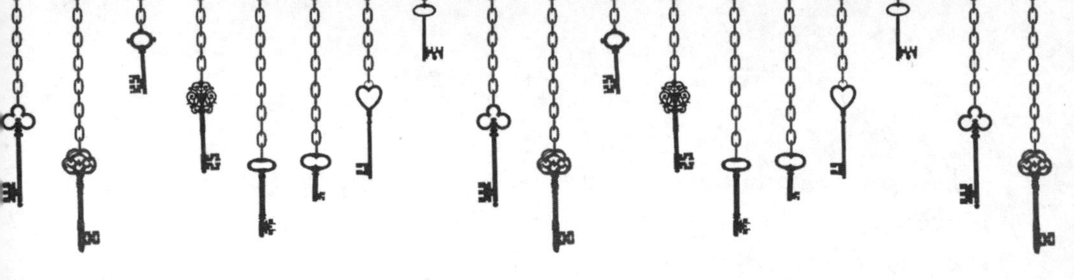

TWENTY-NINE

"After you, Miss Antonius."

Envy held the giant spruce branch back, fully revealing the tiny cottage he'd hidden beneath the giant evergreen the last time he'd brought a mortal woman into his realm.

He didn't like to think of that, of her, so he focused instead on his handiwork—though *cottage* was a generous term for the little cabin he'd made by hacking away at trees, fusing them together with bits of magic. Nothing too intense, nothing that would anger the Corridor. If he'd been able to conjure the building entirely, he would have done so. Alas, he'd rolled up his sleeves and had gotten to work.

Envy supposed he still felt some small sense of accomplishment.

Camilla seemed startled at first, but now looked the structure over with interest, just as she'd done with every inch of the Sin Corridor today. He hadn't known this blasted place to inspire such amazement or intrigue before; Camilla had surprised him with her enthusiasm for its arctic depths.

And even more surprising, thus far she'd seemed to avoid most influence, furthering his growing suspicion that she was keeping a secret. But Envy knew that when sleep eventually pulled her under, Camilla would succumb to the wicked realm. No being—not even the strongest vampires, shape-shifters, or Fae—could withstand the seductive pull of the Sin Corridor.

And that was without the physical attraction already sizzling between them.

He'd kept his connection to her senses open, ensuring that he'd know if she felt distressed or fearful at any point along their journey. If something attacked, he wanted to know immediately.

When they first arrived, she'd been burning with anger that he'd brought her without warning. What he'd neglected to admit was that he'd waited until he sensed her readiness, long before she'd formally given him an answer.

The true surprise came as she trudged through the storm behind him.

He'd felt a tingle of fear that had quickly turned to excitement. When her arousal slammed into him next, he'd nearly lost his footing. He'd glanced over his shoulder, and her gaze had raked over him from head to toe, carnal and untamed. He'd strained to feel any indication that she was being tested for lust, but he didn't think so. What she'd felt had been her own emotions. He wasn't sure she'd been aware of it. But he couldn't forget.

And now they were about to be trapped for hours, alone in the cabin with one large issue.

Envy reached past her and yanked the frozen knob until it twisted free, the small door popping open with a loud crack as its coat of ice shattered. The shards sparkled atop the snow like broken glass.

Camilla gave him a look, then stepped inside. Just past the doorway, she paused.

He knew why.

They were going to be *very* cozy tonight.

The tiny one-room cabin was dark and windowless, the square space taken up almost entirely by one large bed. And by *bed* Envy meant the thick layers of pine boughs he'd braided into a lush platform.

The "bed" was pressed against the far wall, leaving only a small path for him to open the door fully.

The air was stale but laced with the warmth of the pine. They'd be warm and safe from the elements. Hours had passed, and even if she wasn't tired yet, Camilla needed to sleep before the worst of the storm hit.

Envy gently nudged her forward.

She dug her heels in.

"There's barely enough room for the bed."

What she avoided mentioning was the fact that they'd practically have to lie curled around each other to fit upon it. A fact he'd been partly dreading, partly anticipating.

It was going to be his own sort of personal hell to have Camilla pressed against him while experiencing the sensation of sins.

"Apologies for the less-than-stellar accommodations, Your Highness," he mocked softly. "Next time we travel through the Corridor, I'll make sure to add another wing to the cabin."

She called him a gloriously filthy name under her breath but let him step past her, swirling his cloak from his shoulders and spreading it over the bed of boughs, like a sheet of sorts. He gestured that Camilla could lie down, which she did with a glare, crawling onto the mattress and testing its stability before moving to the far side. Envy closed the door behind him, making sure it caught firmly in its frame, and then climbed atop the mattress at her side.

Her warmth enveloped him almost instantly, her scent filling the space between them until all he could think of was how much he envied her perfume for touching her skin when he couldn't.

"Will we travel directly to House Sloth?" she asked. "Once we're… done here?"

"Yes," he said. "We'll travel a bit farther to please the Corridor, then I'll *transvenio* us to my brother's circle as soon as I can. We should arrive by midmorning."

"*Transvenio,*" she repeated quietly. "According to my father's stories, that's how demon princes travel between realms. Like shifting from one reality to the next. Which is how we arrived at the gates earlier. Correct?"

"Indeed."

"Won't we see your court first?"

He swallowed tightly. "There's no time for a visit."

He supposed he should send a missive to Sloth first before showing up unannounced, but to do so he'd need to stop at his House and await the royal admittance to the rival court, which meant Camilla would see the crumbling kingdom firsthand. Even if he brought her to his royal cottage on the outskirts of his grounds, too much could go wrong. Sloth would likely take his time responding, and that was the one thing Envy could not risk now: wasting any more time.

He allowed himself a brief fantasy of a different story unfolding. Of his House being robust, filled with life and art, and demons who collected all manner of objects and items to inspire his sin in their circle mates.

Envy wanted to see Camilla's gaze sweep over everything when it was as glimmering and wondrous as it used to be. He wanted to know if she'd like his House, his galleries, his curiosities. His bedchamber.

And that was dangerous.

He shouldn't want any of it.

She was quiet for a few moments.

"You said you're playing a game...that's what all of this is for. What's at stake?"

Everything, he thought. "An artifact I covet," he finally said. It was true enough.

"You're doing all this for an artifact?" she asked. "It must be very important."

He stared at the wooden ceiling, his jaw tight. They were getting too close to discussing his greatest mistake, especially here, where he'd once brought *her.*

Camilla rolled over to face him, but he didn't look back at her. He couldn't.

"Take off your cloak," he said instead. When he sensed her surprise, he finally looked over and gestured at their exposed bodies. "We'll use it as a blanket."

Camilla gave him a long, silent once-over, but she did as he asked, and he helped her to wrap the edges of the garment around them. As a final act of chivalry, he pulled off his waistcoat, bundling it up to form a pillow he placed under her head.

As she settled back, even more snugly situated against his side, Envy decided to count backward from one thousand, focusing on his end goal.

He hated Lennox and his royal Unseelie Fae. Hated them beyond anything he'd hated before. He would not only see his court restored but would see Lennox's Unseelie court obliterated in return. He'd toy with them all as Lennox had with him.

"Envy?" Camilla whispered, breaking his focus. He felt her stir under the cloak, and then a warmed finger emerged, which she reached over to run along his jaw.

He'd been gnashing his teeth.

He forced himself to relax.

"How many other players do you think there are? In this game?" she asked, removing her hand.

"Depends on how many others the game master has wronged. Could be five, or twenty. Or just down to two or three, by now."

"What happens to the players who don't solve their clues?"

"Their fate is decided by the game master. He can choose to let them leave peacefully, or he can kill them. Their lives are his from the moment they sign the blood oath."

Camilla's breath hitched. He finally dropped his attention to her. She was biting her lip, her expression pinched. He wanted to smooth the line between her brows but didn't. No good would come from such tenderness.

"What if they don't sign a blood oath? At the start?"

She looked worried, but he wasn't sure why.

"As far as I know, everyone who plays has signed the oath. It's what allows the game master to enforce the rules."

"What do you think we're looking for next?" she asked, rolling back over to look up at the ceiling now. "The riddle didn't give us a real clue."

He liked that she considered them a team.

Too much.

"My brother is quite the collector, and House Sloth is filled with books and artifacts. I imagine we'll find the next clue in one of his libraries. We'll just have to look for something that doesn't belong."

She rolled over to face him again, her expression wary.

"And this game master…I've heard the Fae play games. The Unseelie King in particular."

Clever woman.

He debated indulging her again but couldn't see the harm in admitting she was correct.

"They do. Lennox, the Unseelie King, is the game master."

Camilla grew silent. He wondered what stories she'd heard of the Unseelie King. Wondered if she knew just how dangerous he was when he wanted something.

Envy suddenly did not want her getting tangled up in all that. "Sleep. Tomorrow will be a long day."

Camilla had spun over to lie on her other side, and now she went still. He'd tried to respect her boundaries, ignoring his eagerness to spy on her feelings in this close space, but he couldn't help himself—he opened that channel between them again, and clearly detected her irritation.

"You must be surrounded by demons who kiss your royal ass often," she said suddenly, and he flinched. "Not everyone enjoys being ordered around."

Gods' bones. The woman drove him mad. Perhaps it was time to return the favor again, have a bit of fun before the search was back on.

"Normally, they're kissing my cock." Envy smiled as her jealousy swept through the cabin. "And they enjoy it very much when I order them around."

She kept her back to him, pretending he no longer existed.

Her jealousy gave him something to focus on, something to enjoy. He didn't like being back in this space, not after all that had happened. He couldn't help but taunt her a little, to remind himself how different this situation was.

"In fact, I give all sorts of orders," he said, shifting to stare at the ceiling, hands behind his head. "Some you might recall. Take off your clothes. Lie down. Spread your thighs." He paused, and then said slowly, "Come for me."

She swallowed audibly, her energy now tinged with arousal. Envy knew she was recalling that recent night in vivid detail.

"A good lover gives me orders too, pet. Would you like some examples?"

She cursed over her shoulder, telling him exactly where he could go. He rolled to the side again, facing her back, and dropped his voice into a seductive growl.

"Fuck me harder, deeper, faster. *There.* Don't stop." He was entirely too pleased by her sharp intake of breath. "I play along, Camilla, good and obedient for a time."

"I am completely uninterested in your conquests, Your Highness."

"Mm." He knew that was true without using his senses. But he also knew she perversely enjoyed thinking about him doing each of those things to her.

Realizing that he himself was more affected than he'd intended, he allowed silence to fall between them once more, trying to ignore the warm curve of her backside just inches away.

At first, he sensed her disappointment—she *liked* playing games, he realized—but then her exhaustion finally kicked in. He hoped she would sleep well now and put aside new worries about Lennox and his treacherous game. Sure enough, Camilla's breath finally turned slow and even. Sleep fell over her like a blanket of freshly fallen snow.

He waited until she'd been asleep for some time before stealing another glimpse. She lay curled on her side, the cloak tucked up firmly beneath her pointed chin.

Sleep didn't come for Envy; he doubted it would, and anyway, he'd prefer to stay alert. Few creatures in this forest would dare intrude upon him, but still, the game was afoot. He wasn't sure how much time had passed when she suddenly rolled back over, toward him, slowly clutching at the cloak, as if trying not to tumble into a dream.

Silver hair fanned around her in a halo, giving her the look of an angel.

Her lashes were long and dark, resting in little half-moons on her golden cheeks.

She looked peaceful, completely at ease. Like the male next to her was some kind of knight, and not a wicked prince.

Envy couldn't recall a time anyone had laid themselves so bare before him.

He slowly reached over, pushing a loose curl behind Camilla's delicate ear. Her lips parted, a contented sigh slipping through. She was deep within sleep now, fully relaxed. He thought to envy her such peace, but somehow, he couldn't.

He knew the Sin Corridor would show her no mercy now.

Envy rolled onto his back again, gaze fixed to the ceiling.

His whole body was tensed, waiting.

He tried to focus on what the next clue might be. Solving the riddles and winning the game should be the only worry in his head. And yet...the more he considered Lennox insisting that Camilla accompany him, the more he hated that she was here.

He should have left her in Waverly Green.

If he'd been a better male, he would have. Consequences be damned.

Camilla's breath shifted, broken by a slight catch.

He swallowed thickly.

And so the long night began.

Now her even breathing turned into little gasps of continual pleasure. His hands curled into fists as they merged into soft moans.

Envy tried to focus on the sleet outside, the howling winds knocking the door against its frame. Anything to avoid thinking of when he'd been between her legs, eliciting those same sounds. One taste of her had been dangerous—it hadn't remotely sated him.

As if in response, she thrashed against her cloak, rolling to face away from him, in the process exposing her neck. With a soft murmur, she seemed to draw closer to his warmth, her hips rolling until her plump little bottom found his side, where she rubbed against his hip, seeking friction.

She was undoubtedly being tested for lust.

Envy locked his attention on the damn ceiling, attempted to count the grains in the wood. Camilla was stirring again, her hands coursing up her body. Despite being buried below her cloak, he could feel their path as if it were his own. First they were sliding over her hips, pausing atop her quivering stomach, then up onto her breasts, where her fingers cupped her generous curves, no doubt finding pleasure in their tempting give as she squeezed.

Selfishly, he hoped she was seeing him in her sin-fueled dreams.

Recalling how it had felt as *he* made her come.

Despite his best efforts to be a gentleman, Envy's cock stiffened.

What he wouldn't give to push her thighs apart and sink into her, to slam their hips together until they shattered apart. He couldn't be tested by the Sin Corridor, but in that moment, he'd almost swear he was.

Envy brought a fist to his mouth and bit down hard, but the pain only focused his desire for pleasure.

Camilla was kicking off her cloak now and reaching down, drawing her skirts up, showing off supple skin contained only by silk stockings, made for worshipping.

He could no longer help himself. He watched, rapt, as she circled her hips, lifting them, lost in her phantom lover's caress. The soft exhale of her breath tangled with the rustling of her skirts, the scent of pine released from their bed with every movement. As if against his will, he felt his hand closing over his erection, stroking atop his trousers in a matching rhythm.

Camilla slowly opened her eyes and, to his surprise, stared straight at him. Seeing his own arousal, she pushed herself up to her knees, maneuvering gracefully as she straddled him, skirts billowing down as she braced her hands on his shoulders. Above her stockings her thighs were bare, and he could feel their smoothness where they tightened against his hips.

"Camilla," he warned, suddenly alert. "Wake up."

She smiled at him below her heavy eyelids, the most wonderfully devious, wicked curve he'd ever seen.

"Who says I'm asleep, Your Highness?"

THIRTY

Perhaps it *was* a bit wicked, but Camilla was having entirely too much fun torturing the prince lying stiffly beneath her.

He deserved to be toyed with after his lies and trickery. And especially after that stunt to make her jealous. It took her a few moments to realize what he'd been up to; she'd been thoroughly focused on trying and failing not to envy his previous lovers.

Once she pieced together his little game, she was irritated with herself for playing into it. He'd had entirely too much fun, stoking her envy, trying to whisper things to shock and tantalize, to build anticipation and need.

Camilla had been shocked, all right, shocked by how damp the area between her thighs had become at the mere thought of his rakish orders.

So when she had felt the testing tingle of lust, she'd decided to make the most of it. If Envy wanted a show, she'd give him one.

The sin's influence had long since receded, something she was surprised Envy hadn't even considered.

Although, feeling his full response to her, she'd almost forgotten this was supposed to be a cheeky repayment. His thick length was pressing against her, so hard and tempting it was difficult to remember where the boundaries of her playacting fell.

If there were any left at all.

She wondered how far they both might go, pretending neither was aware that the Sin Corridor wasn't responsible for their actions.

Another wicked game.

Her hands drifted back up along her sides, teasing the undersides of her breasts before circling the tight buds at their centers. Her bodice felt tight, constricting, and she could feel her flesh pushing against her neckline, threatening to spill over with her heaving breath.

She lifted herself up, then slowly moved down his body, getting lost in the sensation, the sheer power of him coiled tightly beneath her.

All that raw masculinity, all that animal grace, practically vibrating with barely leashed desire.

This might have started as a game, but she wasn't pretending to be aroused.

A strangled sound jerked her attention back to the prince, and she glanced down to see Envy's gaze locked on her, a tortured expression on his face.

He grasped her hips, strong fingers splayed around them, like he couldn't decide if he should help grind her against him or lift her off completely.

Camilla boldly looked him over, pleased he was still so... affected by her show.

"Camilla."

Her lips curved. His voice was low and slightly hoarse.

She imagined there weren't too many people who'd ever turned the Prince of Envy's own game against him.

"Would you like to know what I was just recalling, Your Highness?" she asked, circling her hips again, writhing up along that glorious length.

"No."

Liar, she thought.

"The night at Vexley's, when we fell off the mattress and landed, like this? For a moment, I had wondered what you'd do if I leaned down." She did so now, her lips hovering so close to his she felt his sharp intake of breath. "I wanted to see if you tasted as sinful as I hoped."

His throat bobbed and she lightly traced the outline of his mouth with her tongue. It was the shape of fantasies—full and seductive and made for kissing.

"Should I have? Tasted you that night," she whispered, bringing her mouth to his ear, noticing the trail of goose bumps rising along his flesh.

She didn't think he was breathing anymore. He looked pained.

Tension wound between them, so taut she wanted to pluck it like a string.

"I want you to answer two questions truthfully, Your Highness. Will you do that? For me?"

His gaze fixed to her face, scanned her eyes, then fell to her lips. His nod was a slight incline of his head, barely noticeable.

"Did you like the way I tasted?" she asked silkily.

He cursed, his grip on her hips tightening, his self-control slipping.

"Yes," he gritted out.

"Do you think about it?"

She sank into him, hitting a spot that made them both suck in their breath. Camilla realized she needed to be careful. Her body throbbed against his.

Envy hadn't answered her question. She leaned down, nipping at his lip.

"You promised to answer."

"Yes. I fucking think about it." He gave a tortured laugh. "Constantly."

"Thank you for your honesty." Abruptly, she pushed herself up, slinging her leg back over to settle peacefully on the bed next to him again. She gave him a victorious smile as she tidied her cloak around her, readying for sleep. "May your dreams be as wondrously sinful as your tongue, Your Highness."

Envy's teeth ground together, his jaw tight enough to cut stone.

Camilla thrilled, just a little, as she added, "And in the spirit of honesty, you should know, I might think about it too."

Morning arrived with another mighty storm.

As Camilla stretched and rose, she felt tired but ready to see what more this realm would bring her.

The prince didn't offer much in the way of conversation as he donned his cloak and broke through the fresh frost on the cabin's door. He seemed to be wound more tightly than usual. Whether it was because of their little temptation game the night before, or because his mind was on his true game, she couldn't tell.

They trudged through the endless snow, the landscape losing some of its appeal the colder and wetter and hungrier she got. After a few hours of endless walking, he finally paused.

"All right. We've gone far enough to satisfy the Corridor." He held out his hand. "Are you ready?"

She nodded, and without uttering another word, he magicked them away. Camilla felt the power of the air whooshing around them and opened her eyes to find an enormous stone castle ahead, nestled at the top of an impressively jagged mountain.

She spun in a circle, drinking in the castle, the mountains—bruised smudges of navy and white stretching far into the distance—and the mist that had descended like a funeral shroud.

Unless Envy had changed his mind about their plan, they were on the front lawn of House Sloth.

Envy strode up the wide stone stairs powdered with fresh snow, heading straight for the arched double doors at the top, tucked into an alcove flanked by two grand columns.

Camilla, too, trudged up until, unable to help herself, she stopped before the first column, admiring the intricate flora and fauna carved into what appeared to be limestone—or whatever the demon equivalent was. Whoever had done the work was exceptional: there was not a single chisel mark, no sign at all that the stone hadn't sprung forth already carved.

She peered closer. The scene depicted was whimsical yet dark: flowers shifting to become weapons and animals seemly engaged in battle.

Camilla understood. Nature was a violent mistress, her beauty a mask to hide her cruelty.

Camilla slowly circled the column, pausing on the most fascinating scene yet. A scorpion, vulture, and ibis, all dancing around a sphere. More animals and geometric shapes were spread throughout, but this grouping seemed different.

She laid her hand on the cold stone in reverence, wondering if magic had been involved in its creation.

Envy paused, glancing over his shoulder, his expression inscrutable.

"Stay there, Miss Antonius. No matter what."

The fine hair along her arms stood on end and she instantly became more alert.

He hadn't *asked* her to wait, there was steel in his command.

Now the carvings didn't seem so much enchanting as ominous.

"Is this not your brother's estate?"

Envy's hand flexed toward his right side, to the place where she knew he hid his dagger.

"In this realm it's considered an act of war if a prince shows up in another's circle uninvited."

"Yet you continue to waltz in, brother."

Before he could turn back around, the point of a blade erupted from Envy's chest.

It happened so fast Camilla's scream was ripped from her throat at the exact moment the blade was yanked back out of the prince.

Envy dropped to his knees, his expression one of cold fury as gold blood spurted from the wound, splattering brutally across the snowy steps.

"Touch her"—his voice was laced with malice, even as it faded to a mere whisper—"and I'll annihilate you all."

Even bleeding as horrendously as he was, Camilla felt the promise in his words.

Keeping one eye on his attacker, Camilla rushed to the fallen prince's side, but as she dropped before him, Envy vanished.

She frantically patted the ground where'd he'd been—had he been cloaked by some invisible force? But he was truly gone. Only a small pool of blood remained carved into the snow, its color a harsh reminder that he was Other.

She glanced up at Envy's killer, taking stock of what she might use to defend herself, quieting the voice that said she'd never stand a chance against him. She'd have to try.

His hair was a unique shade caught between silver and gold, his eyes the palest shade of blue she'd ever seen. They were like two diamonds gazing back at her, hard and cold. Utterly without emotion.

The demon was studying her closely too.

After an uncomfortably long stretch of silence, he slowly returned his dagger to its sheath. He'd said Envy was his brother, so…

"You must be the Prince of Sloth."

He gave an insolent half bow, then said smugly, "He had that coming for a good century."

"You murdered him." Camilla couldn't believe how cavalier the man was!

Amusement warmed those icy eyes a fraction.

"I assure you, he's only been sent back to his circle. He will probably return by nightfall, fully healed, but this time he'll have the decency to send a missive first. Come. Miss Antonius, was it?"

Camilla nodded, weighing whether she should believe him, but Sloth turned, giving her his back.

In his mind Camilla clearly posed no threat. She supposed she could use that to her advantage, if needed.

"Welcome to House Sloth."

THIRTY-ONE

House Sloth was unlike anything Camilla had ever experienced in even the most upper-crust homes of Waverly Green. She doubted even the king or queen of the realm could boast such wealth. She'd never seen their castle; they lived in Sundry, a city far north of Waverly Green that served as Ironwood Kingdom's capital.

And not simply wealth of objects, but of knowledge.

Inside, they entered a circular foyer.

Multiple corridors were accessible from the entryway, the rambling castle spanning beyond sight in all directions.

For all intents and purposes, it appeared to be an enormous library.

Every hallway she could see was lined with dark wooden shelves filled with leather-bound books. Brass sconces burned quietly along tasteful paneling, and plush handwoven rugs lined the hardwood floors.

"This is breathtaking." Camilla slowly spun to take it all in. "I've never seen anything quite like it."

Below their feet, a compass rose was inlaid in gold.

Sloth gave her a bashful look, so unlike his brother's arrogance. *And* unlike the dagger-wielding demon prince who'd just stabbed Envy through the chest.

"Come," he said, "I'll give you a tour while we wait for my brother to arrive. If you'd like," he added. "If you'd prefer to go straight to your guest chambers, that can be arranged."

Camilla smiled tentatively. She'd rather learn what she could, right now.

"If it's no trouble, I would love a tour."

Sloth inclined his head.

"I am curious, though," she said quickly, "about the column out front. The carvings were so beautiful. What do they mean?"

Sloth seemed pleased she'd noticed.

"It's our interpretation of the Twin Pillars, although unfortunately not an exact replica."

"I haven't heard of them," Camilla admitted.

"It was an ancient site dedicated to the stars and night sky, though some argue it signified the Seelie and Unseelie courts. The pillars attract lightning, and when it strikes them, they glow, and the constellations carved onto them are meant to project into the amphitheater where they sit. One pillar is said to be good, and to reflect harmony and prosperity, gifts from the old gods. The other is rumored to be evil, and to depict cataclysmic destruction, offering a warning in a sense. Or so some of the more plausible theories go. No one is really sure, of course. What we do know is that they offered the Fae a direct pathway to the mortal lands."

"I would love to see the real ones someday, then." Camilla could only imagine what a sight that would be. How magical it must feel to see the heavens greet the Underworld, a union that shouldn't exist.

"Unfortunately, they're now hidden below my brother's circle, bound there by magic."

"Why?" Camilla's heart sank at the thought of the ancient site being defaced.

"The Unseelie King's obsession with mortals grew in such a way that it endangered them and the boundaries of our world. Lennox was warned to stop his antics, but he didn't take kindly to being commanded by a demon, no matter that my brother rules over all Underworld realms. Lennox felt that as the Unseelie King of his own island to the west, he, and his court, should not be held to the same rules. So we had to limit his access, for the good of all."

"One person ruined it for everyone."

"Not a person," Sloth said gently. "It's imperative to remember that no beings you meet in the Underworld or any of the shadow realms are human. No matter how human they appear."

"Right, of course."

He gave her a tight smile, then motioned ahead.

"Inside, House Sloth comprises two hundred and thirty thousand feet of shelving."

Camilla was still considering the Pillars, but Sloth drew her attention back to him.

"Last count there were one hundred and eighty-seven thousand books, sixty-four thousand specimens, twenty thousand pieces of art, including sculptures, and nineteen hundred weapons. Each artifact is housed within the reading chamber most suited to its subject."

Camilla couldn't wrap her mind around those figures, but she saw he wasn't embellishing the number. The ceilings in every direction soared at least thirty feet, and shelves with ladders utilized the entire space.

House Sloth was utterly magnificent but somehow still retained a sense of warmth and invitation, despite its size and grandeur. Perhaps it was the overstuffed chairs arranged in alcoves throughout, or the large oak beams, weathered from age, decorating the vaulted ceilings. In any case, a part of her wished to immediately curl up with a book and lose all track of time.

There wasn't a hint of pride or ego in Sloth's tone as he tallied his collection, she noted; he spoke as if only doling out facts.

"I cannot begin to imagine how many years it's taken to curate such an extensive collection," she said at last.

"Too many, I'm sure, but such is the burden of my sin."

He nodded toward the wing in front of them. Above it a carved plaque read SCIENTIA.

"Each wing of the estate is broken down into sections like this one. Every book in this wing relates to science; different rooms within that wing are dedicated to different subsects. Flora, fauna, anatomy, astronomy, archaeology, and so forth. Then there are history, geography, art—and within that wing it's broken into illustrations, oils, time periods, and artists, or even, for fun, 'the art of seduction' or 'flirtation' or 'culinary arts'—and then there are the poems, plays, fiction, and of course tomes sorted by species. Fae, vampire, werewolf, demon, witch, goddess, mortals, halflings, changelings, shape-shifters, and so on. There are also birth records for the supernatural royalty throughout the ages, and sections dedicated to the occult. Spells, curses, hexes, enchantments, alchemy, riddles, puzzles and games."

Camilla's heart felt as if it were about to sprout wings and take flight.

"How on earth are you able to obtain so many birth records?" She shook her head, the answer swiftly coming to her on its own. "Spies."

"Umbra demons—the most unique of the lesser demons—are mercurial creatures at best, but being incorporeal lends them a certain finesse. You simply need to ensure that you're paying them the highest amount. They are loyal only to themselves. And my brother Pride, mostly."

"Your collection is all quite impressive, Prince Sloth."

He pursed his lips, and Camilla wondered what she'd said that had displeased him.

"Pardon me, Your Highness. If I've overstepped—"

"You haven't, Miss Antonius." He gave her a warm smile. "I go by Lo. Please do away with any formalities. Only my brothers call me Sloth, and it's typically to get a rise out of me."

Lo guided her down a long, winding corridor that was easily twice the size of her town house. He paused before the next hallway, glancing up at the plaque.

HABENTIS MALEFICIA.

Witchcraft.

"Some wings are more . . . sentient. They often rearrange themselves—nothing too disconcerting. Windows and doors switch places, furniture changes. One hour you might find a settee, the next a barstool. Sometimes spells we investigate go awry. Witchcraft doesn't come easily to demons."

"Do you do much investigating?" Camilla asked.

Lo lifted a shoulder, shrugging noncommittally.

"My court dabbles in a little of this and a little of that. We enjoy being well-rounded."

Which was demon evasion for yes, she thought wryly. Maybe he hadn't written her off as a threat quite yet.

"Would you be able to find something out of its place?" she asked, thinking of the game.

"Of course; we keep strict records of each and every chamber."

Records were wonderful, but they'd still need to search through each room. And that could take a lifetime, she was realizing.

They continued into the next corridor, each one more impressive than the last.

Instead of hardwood, this floor was made of what appeared to be black marble with deep crimson specks.

Lo caught her curious stare.

"Heliotrope. More commonly known as bloodstone. It's mined from just outside Malice Isle. The seat of the royal vampire court."

He didn't elaborate and Camilla didn't press. She'd heard whispers in the dark market of the vampire prince—it was said he always heard his true name when it was spoken aloud, no matter where or when—and she did not wish to draw his attention if those rumors were true.

"Most ladders are enchanted," Lo said. "Simply call for one and direct it where you'd like to go." At her surprised look, he added, "We are quite capable of physically moving ladders, of course, but why not enchant if one can? We may prefer mind over brawn, but don't forget, we are demons. House Sloth will battle just as ruthlessly as any other House of Sin."

He'd said it so casually one could almost miss the underlying threat.

"Duly noted, Lo. I have always believed that the mind is more fearsome than the sharpest blade. It alone can devise many ways to cut an enemy down."

Camilla had not fallen into the trap of believing he was simply a harmless book aficionado, but she could understand how others would. Easily.

She wondered if that made him even more dangerous.

How many others had foolishly underestimated the Prince of Sloth? Had mistaken his penchant for reading all day for laziness instead of what it truly was—honing the best weapon in his arsenal: his mind.

If knowledge was power in this circle, then the prince standing before her, hands tucked carefully into his pockets, dripped with it.

He gazed back at her with the precision of a scientist, and Camilla knew there was no detail he missed, no subtlety or nuance overlooked or cast aside.

Lo was not a lazy, slothful male by any means.

He was infinitely patient. Calculating. Wickedly intelligent. Lo took his time, studying until he was satisfied with all potential outcomes.

If he was currently without a partner and sought one out, God help the person he fell for. Camilla knew he'd leave no stone unturned as he investigated them to the fullest degree, plotting and planning his seduction so well they wouldn't stand a chance.

Not that anyone would want to. Underneath that unassuming appearance lurked a warrior just as deadly and ferocious as his brothers.

"Your guest suite is just down the next corridor." His expression had returned to indifference as he continued at a leisurely pace. "Please make yourself at home. My brother will likely turn up within the next hour or two."

Camilla bit her lip, stalling.

"Might I be permitted to look around more?"

Lo drew up short, eyeing her closely. "What subject are you interested in?"

She wondered if he knew about the game, how much she should reveal.

"Honestly, I'm looking for a clue. It's for—"

"Envy's newest game, of course." Lo sighed. "I'm not sure how you've gotten involved with it, but you seem like a good person. Don't let Envy's obsession with winning just to boast about it destroy you. These games are seldom worth the price."

That didn't feel true, from what Camilla had seen. Envy was driven, focused, yes—but his intensity didn't seem like something frivolous. He hadn't told her otherwise, but she'd begun to suspect the game meant more than Envy was letting on. To anyone.

Instead of drawing suspicion to that, she asked the question that had become the most nagging and persistent. Which she immediately wished she could take back.

"Is your brother...attached?"

"Aside from what he calls his curiosities, my brother doesn't form attachments."

"Ever?"

Lo cocked his head to one side, considering.

"Envy hasn't told you of his rule."

It wasn't a question, so Camilla didn't answer.

Sympathy entered Lo's expression.

"Envy spends only one night with a lover. No matter what you feel, or what you think he might feel, that will not change, Miss Antonius. My brother is incapable of change."

Envy hadn't told her that part outright, but thinking back on that night in Kitty's house...he'd told her it was only that evening. *Their secret.* The fact that they hadn't slept together meant their one night technically wasn't over. Which made her mind spin with possibilities.

"Because his heart was broken before?"

"Because his sin will not allow him to be satisfied with what he has," Lo said gently. "Envy will always desire something new. Until he gets it. Then he is envious of the next item he covets, the next person claimed by someone else. He'll pursue you, become wildly territorial until he successfully captures you, then toss you aside. He isn't cruel. He's simply ruled by his sin like we all are."

Camilla wanted to cast the warning aside but thought of Vexley. Of how quickly Envy had despised him. She'd thought it was about defending her. But if Lo was to be believed...

"You're saying there was never any heartbreak?"

"I never said that." Lo's smile was a slow twist of his lips. "If you want my advice, guard your heart and forget my brother. He is content with his games and riddles and plots."

It was a warning meant to dissuade her, but it had the opposite effect. Camilla liked those things too. Each day, lately, she liked them more and more.

A servant made his way toward them, a bookish demon wearing spectacles. His pace was unhurried.

He handed a note to the prince, then bowed.

Lo read it over, then tucked the paper into his waistcoat.

"Bathe. Eat. Rest. My brother is already requesting reentry." Lo smiled again, although this smile didn't quite reach his eyes. "I'll make him wait a bit more just to remind him who rules House Sloth."

THIRTY-TWO

"Gods-damned prick."

Envy crumpled the missive in his fist, seconds away from declaring war on his bastard of a brother Sloth. Said war was only narrowly avoided by the surprise visitation request from his *other* prick of a brother, the gold-eyed demon staring at him now.

Envy glared at Wrath, who was dressed impeccably from head to toe in his signature black.

Gold rings gleamed on his fingers. Only a fool would think they were a simple fashion ornamentation. Envy knew firsthand how they could sharpen a blow.

His brother had come prepared for a fight, and Envy was feeling vexed enough to oblige. Decades ago, Wrath had refused to get involved the first time the game master screwed Envy. A fact he'd never fully forgiven his brother for. If anyone had stood a chance at swaying Lennox back then, it had been Wrath. But he'd chosen diplomacy instead. It set into motion their underlying friction and Envy's least favorite role he played: the conniving, heartless villain.

Animosity aside, Envy had recently pretended he wanted to steal something his brother coveted. What no one knew was that Envy had his spies secretly feed Prince Greed the location of the two missing goddesses. It was *that* precious information that set into motion the eventual destruction of a curse. Envy had done his best to push and prod everyone into action, using any foul means necessary, always thinking of his court and their fate.

No one suspected Envy's true motivation, they all only saw the game player. Which suited him fine.

The demon of war gave him a mocking grin.

"I missed you, too." Wrath tossed a bag his way, the scent of sugar and cream immediately filling the air. "Not as much as my wife, though."

Envy glanced inside the bag, a strange feeling thawing his irritation slightly.

Emilia had made cannoli for him. He stared at the bag a long moment, no discernible ulterior motive surfacing, nothing aside from...friendship. Emilia loved cooking, loved nourishing those she cared deeply for. Envy was admittedly a little touched that that now extended to him.

He fought the urge to try one when he realized how closely Wrath was inspecting him.

Envy folded the bag up again, tossed it carelessly onto his desk.

"Gratitude." Wrath's tone was amused. "That's the foreign emotion you're experiencing. I'll pass along your thanks. For some reason, Emilia thinks you're friends now."

That pleasant feeling in his chest expanded painfully.

Envy squashed it at once.

"Shouldn't you be home tending to your deviant wife? I've heard all about the manacles."

"She's visiting her sister." Wrath's golden gaze pinned him, all humor draining away. "And if your spies watch my wife again, I'll come for you."

Envy sighed.

"Contrary to popular belief, no one cares about your sex life. Don't bend your wife over every hard surface you encounter outside the castle if you seek privacy like a mortal."

"Your spies shouldn't be in my circle, those wards—"

"Why are you here?" Envy interrupted; best not to travel that path.

Wrath stared at him, hard, proving he knew exactly what Envy was up to.

"Where is your court? The corridors were quiet."

Envy's stomach tightened. Wrath had been escorted by Alexei, taken directly from the front door to Envy's study. It had been risky to allow Wrath access, but dismissing the request would also have raised his brother's suspicions.

He'd warded the corridor to divert any confused members of his court, keeping them far from the demon of war's watchful gaze.

"A new Iron Age exhibition was recently installed on the upper terrace."

It wasn't a lie. Unlike a human, any demon prince would detect deception. Envy had worded it carefully to keep Wrath from sensing any untruth.

Wrath scanned him, gaze sharp. He was clever enough to know something was off, but there was no direct lie to call out. Thankfully, House Wrath recently visited House Envy, and even if his brother was suspicious, Envy's court had appeared mostly intact then. Wrath would never imagine how far they'd all fallen and how fast.

Envy adopted that bored look his brothers associated him with.

"If you're looking to make Emilia jealous, I'm sure you'll find someone to your liking here. Feed my sin while you're at it."

Wrath leveled him with a look that indicated Envy was pushing him too far.

"You need to work off some anger. I sensed it from my House."

Envy *was* wound tightly. But he didn't need assistance. He needed to be searching House Sloth for the next clue, and he'd grown tired of his meddling brothers. Eventually, one of them would figure out why he was so tense. He needed to get rid of Wrath before he became an issue.

While Envy had waited for his wound to heal, he'd ventured down into the kitchens. Smoke had drifted up, snaking through the corridors and stairwells. A demon was facedown in the fires, the cause of their death not immediately obvious.

Envy had found Franklin, his butler, wandering in circles before he'd snapped himself together and bowed. He'd briefly forgotten who Envy was.

A sign his memories were growing foggier by the day. Soon he wouldn't remember who he was, what vital role he played at the House. Envy had sent him to his chambers with instructions to rest, then took care of the kitchens himself.

He'd just scrubbed the scent of burnt flesh from his body when Wrath's request arrived.

"Well?" Wrath pressed. "Do you feel like fighting, brother? Or do you think you're going to attempt to take my throne?"

"Trust me, I'm in no danger of vying for your sin. Unlike you, I don't need to fight in order to get myself under control. *Non ducor, duco.* I am not led, I lead."

Wrath didn't move to strike, but Envy felt the charge build in the air all the same.

"House Vengeance is stirring up enough discord as it reestablishes itself. Your game had better not incite a war within our ranks."

Envy didn't let his intrigue about House Vengeance show. Aside from the slight gossip Lust had shared, whispers hadn't reached his ears yet about Death's mysterious domain. In fact, Vittoria had been surprisingly quiet since she'd taken her shifters and returned to her House.

"I mean it." Wrath's menace shook the floor. "We've got enough to worry about with the witches, we don't need problems with the Fae because you can't handle your shit. When will you stop playing games?"

Envy's own annoyance grew. Wrath had no idea how fucked they'd all be if Envy lost this game. It wasn't his fault the rest of the realm had gone mad. That was not his mistake, and he refused to shoulder any more blame.

"The witches were nearly annihilated in that last skirmish. You know as well as I do that it will take them decades to pose any true threat again. And when do we ever have peace? Sursea, the so-called First Witch, is immortal. We could wipe the realms of all witches, but she'd just spawn more. Peace is a concept that is unattainable, and you well know it."

Wrath's hands curled into fists, but Envy pressed on.

"Pride might hate Sursea, but he'd never allow any true harm to come to the mother of his wife. Your quest for peace would incite the very war you claim to want to avoid. Pride would strike your circle without second thought; his entire focus is on finding Lucia. You, out of everyone, ought to know what that feels like. So, demon of war, should I truly believe *you* suddenly wish for harmony? When wrath fuels you?"

Envy's smile was all teeth.

He wasn't done stoking his brother's sin. Not by a long shot.

"If one foe falls, another will rise in their place. Such is the way of the Underworld. And you *like* it that way. The monotony of peace was exactly why we all fell to begin with, if you'll recall. You schemed your way to that throne like the rest of us. No one remains defeated or down forever. No one remains at the top for eternity, either."

The floor in Envy's private study rumbled with Wrath's legendary anger. "Is that a threat?"

Envy gave him the indolent look he knew infuriated his brother.

Perhaps he *was* looking to fight.

"Have you only come here to annoy me with bullshit talks of peace, or is there an actual reason for this visit?"

Wrath looked like he was silently weighing the benefits against the disadvantages of striking Envy, but he eventually leashed himself. Ever the diplomat.

"Lust said the woman you've taken an interest in doesn't succumb to his influence."

Lust was going to find himself with a dagger to the balls.

"That sounds like Lust's problem. I haven't taken an interest in anyone."

Wrath's attention sharpened. Envy silently cursed himself. He'd lied. Demons were proficient with omissions and word play, but *never* outright lying.

Envy would never reveal the lengths he'd gone to to overcome that curse. The pain. The cost. He hadn't been certain lying would be necessary for the game, but he had planned and searched until he'd found one ancient legend that could make it come true.

He'd die a True Death before he revealed that secret to anyone.

"Lie." Wrath prowled closer, his sin igniting once more. "How?"

"You don't honestly expect me to share my secrets. Why bother asking?"

"Do you care for the woman?"

"I am intrigued with her talent," Envy said truthfully. "You know I covet unique things."

"Allow me to rephrase, do you care if harm comes to the woman?"

Envy's pulse raced. Wrath would hear it, ever attuned to the hunt. The area between his shoulder blades burned with the sudden need to release his wings. Wings that he couldn't summon. Wings he'd lost with the fall of his court.

"You bore me with your drivel. But yes. I would care if harm came to her. The game wants her in play. Therefore, she holds value for me."

Wrath narrowed his eyes, silent as he assessed Envy.

"Choosing not to answer the question directly is as good as answering it, Aethan." His brother was exceptionally cunning when he wished to be. "Perhaps it's time to stop playing, then. She could get hurt."

Envy couldn't have stopped the game even if he'd wished to. And Wrath standing there, acting superior, as if Envy had no clue how much danger Camilla was in, made him want to lash out.

"Do not use my true name in that perverse shorthand again. And do not come to my circle and lecture me. My patience only stretches so far."

Wrath's expression didn't shift. He still wore the cold, mocking smile Envy wished to punch off his face, his gold eyes glittering.

"Spoken like a demon in love."

He turned then, his muscular frame taking up the entire doorway.

"Pride wagered invitations will be sent out by year's end," Wrath said. "After today, I'm calling three months."

Envy knew he was being goaded.

"Invitations for what?"

"Your wedding."

Something ancient and restless reared itself inside his chest. Envy would sooner drink from the Fatal Chalice before he married anyone, even Camilla. True, he might enjoy her company, might desire her physically, but it would never go beyond that.

He wouldn't allow it.

"I look forward to collecting my fortune, then."

Wrath chuckled darkly, broad shoulders shaking.

"Don't bet against yourself. Or Greed's coffers will finally be larger than yours."

Before Envy's sin could snap out, someone knocked on the door.

Fear had his breath lodged in his throat before Alexei stepped in.

Envy's attention shot to his second's hand, to the note he'd been waiting for from House Sloth.

He tore the wax seal open and read. Fucking finally. He'd been granted permission to enter Sloth's domain.

He glanced up, annoyed that Wrath was still standing there. "Don't you have a wife to tie up? Why are you still here?"

Envy sensed it a moment before it happened.

Wrath's dagger flashed, striking into an invisible foe. An Umbra demon formed, slumped and dying at the demon of war's feet.

"Keep your spies away from Emilia."

He crouched to wipe his blade on the dead spy's tunic, then stepped over its body. Before Wrath could leave on his own and stumble across anything he shouldn't, Alexei escorted him back to the front doors.

Envy folded his arms across his chest. "Report."

The second Umbra demon materialized, partially.

"The human—Vexley—disappeared shortly after you left that realm. No one has been able to scent a trail."

Envy gritted his teeth. "And? What about the artist's mother?"

"No family in Waverly Green. No blood or hair in the house."

Which meant there was no way to know if she was a shifter.

He supposed he could cut a lock of Camilla's hair, have it tested by spell. Find out one way or another what she was, if anything. But if that jeopardized the game, counted as interference…

Envy sighed.

"Keep searching."

THIRTY-THREE

Apparently hours after he'd arrived at House Sloth, Camilla finally received word that Envy was on the premises. She felt immediately annoyed that he hadn't bothered to check on her. After bathing quickly, she'd wandered around for the entire day, doing her best to hunt down their next clue. Alone.

Not to mention that the last time she'd seen him, he'd had a dagger sticking out of his chest. Instead of letting her know he was indeed all right, he'd gone straight to a chamber on Fae history.

If Camilla harbored any misconceptions about where his priorities lay, they were dashed now. Clearly his one and only focus was on the mysterious game.

"Despite our introduction, Lo seems very personable. And he is rather handsome," Camilla said by way of greeting, curious to press Envy's sin to see how much of a rise she could get.

Envy snorted but didn't lift his head from the book he was flipping through. His sin had not been invoked. Maybe he didn't feel for her. The thought rankled.

"You clearly disagree. Why?"

Envy flicked his emerald gaze to her.

"After stabbing me, did my lovely brother happen to explain why he goes by that name?"

She slowly shook her head and his devious grin emerged, alluring dimples and all.

"Because he delights in laying his enemies low. Sloth is as wicked as they come. I'd advise never falling for his *personable* veneer."

"Although one ought to be thankful I at least make an effort, right, brother?"

Lo leaned casually against the doorframe, a pair of spectacles hanging from a chain around his neck. He'd discarded his tailcoat and rolled his shirtsleeves up, exposing toned arms and what appeared to be a tattoo of some phrase peeking out.

"My court is searching through every chamber as we speak. If there's anything out of place, they'll find it."

He glanced between them, his expression difficult to read.

"It's getting late, so I've instructed my cook to send food up to your suites. Since we'll be working around the clock to locate the clue, we don't have time for a formal dinner. I hope that will suffice, Miss Antonius."

Envy clapped once.

"Well done. You skirted the truth beautifully."

At Camilla's inquisitive look, he added, "Sloth prefers to snack in his chambers while reading. Whenever he can avoid a large dinner gathering, he will. His House motto is *Libri Ante Vir.* Books before man. He probably has it permanently inked on his ass."

Lo didn't deny the charge.

"Should you need anything, Miss Antonius, please don't hesitate to ask. My cook is more than happy to make whatever you'd like."

"Have some of my preferred cocktails sent up. And some demonberry wine for Miss Antonius to try."

Envy leaned back in his chair, kicking his feet up onto the table, the picture of arrogance. He'd just ordered another prince around, in a circle that did not belong to him. Even Camilla understood that that was deeply insulting.

Lo pressed his lips into a line. He was probably debating whether to strike Envy again. This time Camilla imagined he'd stab deeper.

"Don't forget the muddled blackberries and brown sugar," Envy added. "It's going to be a long night."

Camilla smiled as Lo rolled his eyes and exited the chamber. Envy would be lucky if she didn't stab him next.

"What, exactly, are you hoping to find in this section?"

Envy cut a look her way, then held up the book he'd been immersed in. It was a history of the Unseelie King.

"Lennox thinks himself a god, but he must have a weakness. Once I find it, I'll exploit it."

Spoken like a true villain.

But that was just another mask, she guessed. She considered her response carefully, knowing that how she proceeded here would either set the stage for him to share what drove him and open up, or it would make him close his heart off entirely.

She'd start slowly.

"You've met the king?"

The air chilled several degrees. "Next time we're in the same room, one of us won't freely walk away."

Hatred, ancient and colder than ice, laced his words. It was a dangerous vow.

Camilla shuddered. The Unseelie King must have well and truly done something terrible.

"I imagine the Unseelie are no worse than any other creature in this realm," she hedged. "Why do you hate him in particular?"

A servant quietly entered the chamber, depositing a silver tray laden with bourbon, syrup, orange zest, and blackberries, and an interesting bottle of wine. It was dark and sparkled like stars.

"Wine or bourbon?" the prince asked, changing course.

"Wine, please."

Envy got up immediately and fixed them both a drink, handing her a glass of demonberry wine before downing his first cocktail in one go. He made another and sipped it.

He looked her over with slitted eyes. "Were you all right here, alone?"

His question surprised her.

His tone was quiet, casual, but she sensed something dangerous writhing below the surface of his placid expression. It could indicate that what Lo said was true—that Envy would be territorial until their time together ended. Or it could be something else he'd already learned.

He was extremely difficult to read when he wished to be.

"Yes. Your brother gave me a tour." She paused, observing the way his hand tightened on his glass. "It was all very impressive. I must have asked about everything, but he answered all my questions with a smile."

"How very generous of him."

"I asked about you," she said.

Envy's brows rose fractionally. "And? What secrets did my dear brother reveal?"

"You have a very interesting rule."

He looked like a panther that had just scented prey. He sat forward, his half-empty glass dangling from his fingertips, gaze locked onto hers intently.

"Did he fill your head with fairy tales, Miss Antonius? That I am somehow wounded and in need of the right salve?" His smile was all teeth. "I like who I am. I like the challenge of the one-night rule. The way it drives lovers wild. Their jealousy sustains me. Gives me power. And there is nothing I enjoy more than gaining power. You'd do well to keep that in mind, over a fantasy."

"Maybe it's your power I'm after, my lord."

She said it to provoke, but the words didn't ring untrue.

He smiled at her then, showing off his dimples for the second time that night.

"Remember this conversation *after* you visit my bed."

There was that damnably cocksure prince again. At least he was amused.

She wanted to steer him back to their original topic. "You were talking about the Unseelie King, about why you hate him."

"I'd much rather we discuss our night of passion. How do you feel about wings?"

Wings would be very interesting indeed. Her expression gave away nothing.

She knew he was trying to distract her. But Camilla didn't take the bait this time. She sat silently, waiting for him to either open himself up to her, or close the door firmly instead.

He topped his drink off, then exhaled, the sound half contented, half resigned.

"Lennox took something from me. Not once but twice."

Envy sipped his bourbon, his gaze fixed on some faraway point.

"I made the mistake of becoming intrigued with a mortal once before."

Camilla held her breath, heart pounding at the idea that it was happening a second time. She knew that whatever he said next would be terrible, knew that whatever had transpired had deeply wounded the prince.

"Before Lennox decided to play the first game with me, I used to receive invitations to visit the Wild Court on occasion. Their art is unlike any other, and a party in Faerie...they are legendary for good reasons. Chaos, debauchery. It fuels those who are beings crafted of sin. And the dark Fae are far wickeder than my brothers."

Envy finished his drink, his attention sliding back to the bottle before he decided to continue.

"That night...something unsettled me about the invitation. It was not just for me, but for...her. However"—he lifted a shoulder and dropped it—"I wasn't sure if my envy was clouding my judgment. Perhaps I didn't want her to go because I didn't want her to be fascinated by anyone else. Perhaps I didn't want someone to see what I had and manipulate her. Or perhaps I was a selfish, controlling demon, as she'd accused me of being."

"She went to the Wild Court on her own," Camilla ventured, her stomach twisting into knots. It was no place for mortals.

"Fae are seductive by nature, especially to humans. You know well—humans grow up on stories, most of which don't relay the full truth of the Folk. So she went to Faerie, tempted by adventure, tempted by a fairy tale that no one had bothered to reveal is actually a nightmare.

She drank their wine, ate their food, and danced with their king. I arrived late, tried to save her. Then I was banished."

It felt like a bird's wings were beating inside Camilla's chest.

"I asked my brother Wrath to intervene, to help me break the ward, but he declined. Wanting to avoid a war with the Unseelie."

Rumors and legend claimed that the Unseelie King could create wards so intricate not even the strongest being could break them. She knew how powerful Envy was, knew he would have tried repeatedly to slip beyond those impenetrable threads. That his brother had refused must have hurt tremendously, but Camilla wasn't sure even Wrath would have succeeded.

"From what I know, Lennox didn't tire of her for a long time. When he finally did, instead of keeping her there where she could live forever, he dumped her back in the mortal world, at the queen's behest."

Envy's gaze when it met hers was void of all emotion.

"Do you know what happens to humans who remain in Faerie too long, Miss Antonius?"

A tear slipped down her cheek. Envy watched it fall.

Time moved much differently in the Fae realm. If the king had kept her there for a long time by his standards, that meant hundreds of years had likely passed in the human world. When the king sent her back, she would have aged instantly and died.

There would have been nothing Envy could do to save her.

"I'm sorry, Your Highness. Truly." Camilla was surprised by how fully she meant it, considering how deeply this mortal woman had clearly affected the dark prince before her.

"Don't be. It accomplishes nothing."

Envy grabbed the bottle of bourbon and stood, heading for the door.

He paused before facing Camilla again.

"Promise me something?" he asked.

Camilla nodded but didn't speak, unwilling to make a vow without hearing the terms.

"Don't ever trust an Unseelie royal, Miss Antonius."

He was gone before she could respond.

With his confession still weighing down her heart, Camilla was slow to realize he'd only given her part of his story.

When he first began his heartbreaking tale, Envy had said the Unseelie King had taken from him twice. If the mortal was the first thing, then what else had the king stolen?

If she solved that mystery, Camilla suspected she would finally have the answer to what Envy was after, and why winning the game was worth any cost.

THIRTY-FOUR

ENVY STARED AT the bottom of another empty glass, wondering what had possessed him to share that story with Camilla.

No one knew the whole truth.

Not even Alexei. And one of the main reasons Envy had taken the vampire on as his second-in-command was to rally certain members of the vampire court to his cause, should a battle between House Envy and the Unseelie King ever happen.

It had been nearly two hundred years since Alexei had come to House Envy, and he'd been present for a handful of previous games throughout that time. All had been frivolous back then. But Lennox had also been less sadistic, more interested in Fae trickery than true torment.

Envy had slowly seen the change in Lennox, sensed trouble simmering in the Wild Court. If he were to actually win this game, he wanted to prepare for any outcome.

He'd been less cunning back then. He would not make the same mistakes now.

Envy had spent the years since then becoming someone new, someone who could not be defeated. Now every move he made had a purpose, a strategy.

He planned for all possible outcomes, slowly moving pieces into place, waiting for the chance to make his ultimate move.

Envy fixed himself another Dark and Sinful and sat on the overstuffed sofa of his sitting room, where Lo's staff had laid a crackling fire.

He'd lied once again; he knew exactly why he'd told Camilla about the Unseelie King. He needed to ensure that the artist would not be tempted by Lennox. Envy had little doubt that their paths would inevitably cross as the game drew closer to an end.

If Camilla knew how dangerous the Fae were, she stood half a chance of surviving an encounter with them.

The knock was quiet but drew his thoughts into the present.

"Enter."

Sloth shut the door behind him, his gaze slowly sweeping the room.

The scheming bastard had placed Envy and Camilla in a shared suite connected by a bathing chamber and this sitting room. He'd claimed it was to keep them close together for their comfort.

Envy had taken one look at the rumpled bed she must have napped in earlier and headed straight into the communal room, needing distance from her scent and his swirling thoughts about those sheets.

"Miss Antonius isn't here," he said, jerking his chin toward her room.

Sloth nodded as if he didn't already know that.

"Good. I wanted to discuss something with you privately."

Envy motioned for him to get on with it.

"I used my sin on her."

"And she resisted it."

"It happened with you as well," Sloth surmised.

"No, Lust attempted to seduce her in Waverly Green. At first, I assumed it was because that realm dampened his power somehow. I believe she succumbed in the Sin Corridor, but barely."

Sloth nodded again, taking it all in.

Envy knew he was sorting and compiling facts, taking his time.

Finally, Sloth spoke. "An amulet warding against dark magic is the simplest explanation. Or perhaps she has an enchantment inked onto her person?"

He looked Envy over clinically.

"Have you noticed any tattoos hidden on her yet? Maybe a symbol or initial?"

"You know my rule."

"And I suppose she's still here, so perhaps you don't know."

"I thought you'd interrogated Camilla?"

Envy suddenly wished to know what else his brother had talked with her about. Camilla had mentioned a tour but had changed topics quickly. Now he wanted to know why. What had his damned brother tried?

"Easy, your sin is infringing on my circle."

Though his words were light, Sloth's tone held a warning.

He was especially testy, making Envy wonder what *he* was preoccupied with. Hopefully some secret lover was driving him as mad. Sloth didn't feed his passions often or as widely as the rest of them, but he'd had a few serious relationships over the centuries. First Liam, then Ivy.

No tragedy or heartbreak was involved—the relationships simply ran their course, ending amicably each time. Sloth avoided drama. The bore.

"I'm simply suggesting you get on with it and pay attention to any marks on her body," he said, as if exhausted by Envy's antics.

"I'm not going to bed her for information."

Sloth grinned at him, slowly, immensely amused.

"What?" Envy snarled.

"Morals look interesting on you, brother. Did you ever stop to wonder if she might be your next clue? She'd make for an interesting riddle, and you know how cunning Lennox is."

Envy was silent. Of course he had. The moment he'd deciphered the last clue, he'd considered that Camilla was a larger part of the puzzle, but he'd since dismissed it.

Mostly because he didn't *want* her to be part of the game. That Sloth had also landed on the possibility indicated that it was something he needed to explore.

Envy had said time and again that the game was all that mattered.

It was time to prove that. He didn't think she was a player, but something was driving her, something more than simple curiosity. He'd almost sensed it before he took her to the void between realms, then she'd walled that emotion off.

Maybe he was wrong. Maybe she was a player, and he was just a pawn on *her* board.

"If you don't want to seduce her for information," Sloth continued, "simply pay attention when you make love to her. Knowing you, you'll make your one chance quite . . . thorough."

"I will not take her to some borrowed, subpar bed here."

Mischief glittered in Sloth's eyes.

"This wing is warded for privacy. No one will hear her, if that's your concern. I know modesty is a consideration for most of her species."

"Humans."

"Mm. I assume you haven't felt any power in her either."

"No." Envy debated the merits of keeping the next bit of information to himself. "She does possess a rare talent with art, but other than that, I haven't sensed anything."

"Care to elaborate?"

"It doesn't concern you."

"Interesting."

Envy truly despised it when he said that.

Sloth studied him very carefully again, like Envy was nothing more than an insect for him to pin down and dissect.

"Did you see the latest gossip?" Sloth asked at last, far too casually. Envy stared until his brother elaborated. "Gluttony's reporter printed this just today."

He pulled a newspaper from his pocket and slapped it against Envy's chest.

Envy glanced at the headline, then scanned the article.

RUMORS ABOUND!

A mysterious game seems to be afoot, drawing players to the Seven Circles from across the realms. Some insiders claim the Unseelie King is up to his wicked ways, pulling the strings of our very own Prince Envy.

The prize is rumored to be something worth killing for, tailored to each player and tempting enough for them to sell their souls. Though it's unclear if murder is or is not permitted this time around. We'll hope to find out.

A few more farfetched theories speculate as to whether this game is a darker, more nefarious plot by the Unseelie King to take advantage of how distracted the demon courts have been of late by the Goddesses Fury and Death of House Vengeance.

With the Seven Circles in peril, might Lennox slip his leash and sneak into the mortal land again?

The Unseelie King's obsession with mortals is well known, giving credence to this theory. What we know is that two strangers were spotted here in the past week. Both players?

Before this article was submitted to print, the ever-lacking Prince Gluttony was questioned about a guest he'd hosted the previous night, but he refused to comment or confirm any part in the game. This same guest was seen heading toward Bloodwood Forest in the predawn hours.

He hasn't been seen since.

Some have posited that the unidentified male was heading there to find the Crone who's believed to frequent the magical forest. When asked directly, Gluttony remained mum, hinting only that it was likely a lover sneaking out after overindulging in sin.

That the prince would attempt to play coy and fail spectacularly is unsurprising. Gluttony is the least clever of his brothers.

Multiple witnesses have spoken in anonymity about a certain white-haired solitary Fæ who's been seen lingering near the woods in different circles. Should this prove to be true, it begs the question why. Is Lennox spying on his players or is there another mystery in need of solving? Or perhaps this Fæ is hunting his true love.

If you have any information, do contact us at once.

Lastly, it has been noted that the usually boastful House Envy has gone silent. It leads one to believe the stakes might be higher than the prince may admit. Why else would Envy lock his circle down at the same time as the game's rumored start? Others are wondering why he hasn't been seen taking flight in the wake of the curse's end. Where are his wings? And could the two be related?

Envy crumpled the paper in his fist. "Tell me you're not believing gossips now."

"Is it true?" Sloth asked, watching as Envy tossed the paper into the fireplace. "Did you lock your circle down?"

"Would it matter if I did?"

Sloth was silent for a long moment. They stood, watching the flames devour the page, each lost in their own thoughts.

"Summon your wings," Sloth said, finally, lifting his icy gaze to Envy's face.

"Shall I roll over or fetch next?"

"Levi—"

"Where are your wings, brother?" Envy shot back. "I don't recall seeing them recently. Should I write in to the paper? Give them something else to speculate over?"

Envy needed this line of questioning to cease at once.

Who gave the reporter her cursed information? One fact Envy had gleaned was that there were at least two players who had also made it to this realm. Gods damn it all.

Hopefully they were the only other players left.

"She could be Fae," Sloth said casually, changing the subject so abruptly Envy almost missed who he meant. "Seelie Court, perhaps. Maybe even half Fae."

"Camilla isn't Fae." Envy gave him a hard look. "Shifters also resist most influence and have talents. And they appear human for the most part. She sometimes..."

"She sometimes," Sloth prompted, goading.

"She sometimes has their temperament," Envy said.

Sloth didn't press the issue. It was as plausible as his guess. If anything, Camilla's being a shifter made the most sense.

Envy just wasn't sure. He didn't get wolf, but there were other rare shifters that weren't pack creatures.

It would explain why her mother had left, at least. That innate need to roam, to keep moving. Most shifters who weren't pack creatures found living in one place extremely difficult. It also lined up with *when* her mother left. Camilla had just come into adulthood, no longer requiring her mother's guidance. If only the gods-damned woman could be found.

"Of course, if you simply do not wish to sleep with her, there are other ways of obtaining that information," Sloth said. "I have taken the liberty to set something up, in the event you weren't amenable. Technically, one only needs to see her nude form to look for any suspicious marks."

"What have—"

"Oh!" Camilla burst into the room, then stopped short, her smile faltering as she took in the princes. "I didn't expect you to be here. Is this...should I come back?"

Envy had taken his dagger out before he realized it. Clearly, his need to protect was heightened.

Envy stepped away from Sloth but didn't put his weapon away.

"Is everything all right, Miss Antonius?"

Camilla bit her lower lip, the move signaling her hesitation. A flash of when she'd done that same thing in bed crossed his mind.

"I was hoping to find Lo here, actually."

Sloth shot Envy a smug look over Camilla's head.

"Why, exactly, were you hoping to find him in your bedchamber?" Envy asked, sharply.

Camilla's expression darkened.

"Do *not* take that tone with me." She glared at him for another moment, driving home the point that she was not his to be ordered around, then looked at Sloth. "Perhaps we should postpone my visit to the steam room. I find the idea of relaxing impossible now."

"I'm sure my brother doesn't truly mind. Do you?" Sloth asked, the picture of gods-damned innocence.

Envy was too riled up to respond right away.

This was what his cursed brother had meant about setting something up. Bringing her to his steam room? Envy had to mentally restrain himself from throttling his brother.

Sloth crossed his arms over his chest, his obnoxious smile growing as Envy's sin chilled the room. The conniving sadist. His brother had played a dirty game, but Envy needed to leash his sin, lest he be thrown out of this circle. Again.

"Shall we?" Sloth asked, offering Camilla his arm, ever the perfect gentleman. "Unless you'd prefer some time alone with Miss Antonius, brother? Remind me...was there something important you wanted to ask her? Maybe you should escort her to the steam room in my place. You are looking like you could do with a bit of the treatment."

Envy was sure he did look that way, thanks to his vicious brother.

Camilla did not make this easy on him. She raised a brow, waiting to see what his next move would be.

Envy positively *loathed* their teaming up.

"Get the fuck out, Sloth."

His brother flashed him another victorious look before slowly swiveling to Camilla. "Alas, my brother is feeling testy. I'll send some refreshments up. You'll need them."

"Thank you." Camilla smiled warmly. "That will be lovely. Another time?"

A beat after Sloth left, an enthusiastic knock sounded at the door. Envy attempted to pull himself together, adopt his mask of indolence.

He drew in a deep breath and opened the door. Sloth had indeed played filthy yet again. The demon standing with a tray of refreshments was classically handsome and far too intrigued with Camilla as he craned his neck into the room, smiling brilliantly at her.

He gave her an appreciative look as he held up a robe.

His arousal hit Envy like a hammer.

"Hello, miss, I brought this for you and some—"

Envy hauled off and hit him, his fist landing squarely in the demon's mouth, his jaw cracking like thunder as it dislocated.

The demon clutched his face and darted back into the corridor, his covered tray and plush robe clattering to the floor.

It was probably the fastest anyone from House Sloth had ever moved.

Without turning, Envy said, "You and I need to discuss some things, Miss Antonius."

Like what secrets she was keeping and why.

Envy finally pivoted to face her, his expression void of warmth. He would no longer play the game of flirtation with her.

None of this was about passion or seduction.

This was about winning.

This was about his court.

And Camilla needed to understand that whatever had passed between them would remain in the past. His brothers were getting the wrong idea about their arrangement.

Others would likely follow suit. Namely, the Unseelie King.

Camilla's expression was impossible to read. Perhaps she'd just remembered what he truly was. Or maybe she was unwilling to part with her secrets. She might even already sense what he was about to try to uncover.

"Sit." Envy closed the door to their shared suite and jerked his chin toward the sofa. "Better yet, take off your clothes and put on the robe. We're going to test a theory."

THIRTY-FIVE

Camilla swallowed hard; her focus fixed to the demon prince, who was gazing back without an ounce of emotion on his face.

She hadn't realized how often Envy had started looking at her with fire until it was replaced by ice. Perhaps she'd underestimated the control he had over his sin.

She certainly hadn't expected *this* reaction from a simple trip to the steam room.

Envy had to be well aware that there was nothing romantic involved with a trip to the spa, a place of relaxation Lo had told her was one of the jewels of his kingdom. Disrobing didn't automatically equal sex. Being aroused and acting on it were two very different things.

After the story he'd shared, did he truly expect her to run off with his brother?

She and Envy might not have any sort of relationship, but she wouldn't be heartless.

Even if she *had* just overheard the last part of his conversation with Lo.

"Unless steam rooms are entirely different in this realm, copulation was not an option, you do realize that, correct?" she asked. "Out of respect for you, I would not have come back to this room to find Lo if it had been."

His expression turned thunderous.

"How very thoughtful indeed, knowing that you would have gone *elsewhere* to find my brother, Miss Antonius."

"You know full well that's not what I meant. Why are you behaving like this?"

"I'm the one who's behaving oddly?" he asked. "You seem quite at home here. In the Seven Circles, the Sin Corridor. My brother's House. Why are you so at ease around demons? Do you not find *that* strange? I certainly do. What are you hiding, Camilla?"

"You cannot honestly be annoyed that *I* might have a secret. You. The Prince of Secrets. Why not tell me about the prize you're after? If you'd like to have an open and honest conversation, we'll start there."

She folded her arms across her chest, waiting. If he gave her one secret, she'd return the favor. But he would never get something without sharing in equal measure. If she caved now, it would set up a disastrous dynamic where he expected her to give while he withheld.

Sure enough, the demon remained stubbornly silent.

"I didn't think so." She was frustrated beyond measure now. "Since this conversation is traveling down an avenue I'm sure you'll regret, I am removing myself from it."

Camilla headed for her suite, and Envy had the audacity to follow her into her private bedchamber.

She whirled on him, truly annoyed. "What are you doing?"

"You wish to relax. I can assist."

"How are you proposing to do that?"

"Take off your clothes, put on the robe. I'll rub your back down with oils."

"And you are *so* altruistic that you're offering to do it for me without ulterior motives?" She laughed humorlessly. "Tell me, what exactly were you and Lo discussing before I entered the room?"

Envy scrutinized her.

"Eavesdropping is unbecoming."

"So is scheming." She smiled sweetly. "If you have a question, asking is usually the easiest route. Don't you tire of all the plotting?"

He looked at her as if she were an alien species.

"You hate the Fae so much, yet you play just as many games, Your Highness."

"Mostly just the royal Unseelie's," he interjected, a poor attempt to break the tension.

That admission didn't help at all.

"What is the second thing Lennox took from you? Is that what makes this game worth winning at any cost?"

"It doesn't matter."

Camilla shook her head.

"You are so tangled in Fae and the game that you cannot see straight anymore. Of course that matters. You withhold information, tell me half-truths and partial stories, yet demand I lay myself bare at your feet whenever you wish me to. And you give nothing in return."

She waited for him to say something, to share one small piece of himself. Instead, she saw his expression shutter, saw the mask slip back into place.

For once, she stuck with brutal honesty. "It's clear you've been hurt. That you're angry. I suspect it all stems from whatever else Lennox took from you. But you'll have to forgive those who've hurt you and forgive yourself above all. Or else you'll keep carving yourself open, bleeding yourself dry. And I can't imagine that's pleasant for an immortal."

"They don't deserve forgiveness."

"It's not for *them*." She threw her hands up in exasperation. "They will never care. They probably don't even remember. It's for you. It's for your brothers, your court. And it's for me."

She brushed past him and closed the door to her room.

Camilla would find a way for them both to win the game, and then she'd go back to her quiet little life in Waverly Green, no matter how difficult that might prove to be now.

THIRTY-SIX

A RUSTLE OF FABRIC from the other side of Camilla's door stopped Envy from chasing her.

Wonderful. Just what he needed to complete his night. She was disrobing and now his mind was envisioning the slow, seductive removal of each garment instead of focusing on methodically uncovering her secret layer by layer.

Even through a thick wooden door she knew the best moves to use on him, knew how to get his mind focused on her, teasing and distracting.

The same way you tease and distract her.

Camilla had not only figured out his game, she was playing it better than he was.

He strode into the sitting room between their two suites and made himself a Dark and Sinful. Double. Minimal ice. Fuck the berries.

He drank it down, barely tasting the liquor he usually savored.

He poured another glass, then went to his private bedroom and dropped onto an overstuffed leather chair. Each sofa, settee, chair, and chaise in House Sloth was made to entice one to lounge, to curl up and lose oneself.

Envy was losing himself, all right, to annoyance, irritation, and a glorious woman with more secrets and puzzles than he had. Two more drinks in, part of him could admit he liked her refusal to show her hand. Camilla made him work hard for each kernel of information, giving him just enough to crave more without ever fully satisfying his curiosity.

She remained a riddle. A vexing, beautiful riddle begging to be solved. He just didn't have as much time as he'd like to puzzle out the mystery of her.

Envy kicked his feet up onto the arm of the chair, attention straying to the clock on the mantel. Midnight. And restless.

He was frustrated. With the gossip spreading through the Seven Circles, with the twisted game, with each second that passed and his court grew more weakened.

He wanted to unfold his wings and catapult into the sky, leaving this hell behind. And that needled him too. The fact that he *couldn't.* That he'd need to win to do so ever again.

Envy had to reserve as much power as he could. One thing the columnist had gotten correct: part of his circle was warded against anyone coming or going without his permission. And it took most of his magic to maintain that lock, leaving him weaker than he'd like to be.

He closed his eyes, leaning his head against the back of the chair, emptying his mind.

Then he thought of Sloth's attempt to stoke his sin and bolted out of his chair, pacing the bedchamber like a caged wolf.

The reporter had said two players were in the Seven Circles.

One heading toward Bloodwood Forest. Perhaps he would get lucky and find a player; then he'd have one less worry to taunt him. Sleep wasn't going to be happening, so he headed for his door, set on hunting down his competition.

He wrenched his bedroom door open, then halted.

There, sprawled on her stomach across the chaise in their common room, half dressed in shadows, wearing nothing but her soft-looking short stays and reading a book, was Camilla.

Check fucking mate.

Camilla had upended his game board with this move. He had to grudgingly admire it.

She'd lit and arranged several candles to strategically cast shadows along her body, composing the artistic scene with impressive precision, positioning herself in a way that gave her the appearance of being fully dressed, allowing a glimmer of the truth to flicker into focus whenever she moved.

Which she did now, legs bent above her and crossed at the ankles, slowly swinging back and forth like she hadn't a care in the universe. She flipped the page of the book propped in front of her, completely undisturbed by Envy's presence.

Corked bottles of oil sat on a tray on the low table next to her, the robe Sloth had sent for her folded neatly on the carpet near her feet.

Their conversation and his taunting words from earlier drifted back to him.

Take off your clothes, put on the robe. I'll rub your back down with oils.

A smile ghosted across his lips. Clever, clever woman. Camilla was tempting Envy to massage her. She knew he wanted to see her bare flesh, to see whether any mark or spell or enchantment had been inked onto her skin.

And likely, she was thinking of his rule—by his own decree, they'd only ever have one night to make love.

And she lay there, almost entirely undressed, daring him to make his move.

Envy didn't bother to stop his attention from following the artful lines of her body—from her shapely thighs and calves to the generous curve of her bottom—as she turned another page. Upon closer inspection, he saw that she'd removed her underwear but kept her thigh-high, lace-edged stockings on.

He admired the sight of her like he'd do with any great work of art. Camilla was the painting, the sculpture, the most exquisite thing he'd ever seen. Silver hair, golden skin, all draped in a tantalizingly dark mystery.

From where he stood in his doorway, he didn't notice any immediate signs of ink. Though he wondered why she'd kept her stays and stockings on, whether it was a ploy to get him to undress her the rest of the way, torture him, or a means to hide the information he was seeking.

The ivory stays hit just above her ribs and dipped low enough to show the tops of her breasts. From the little he could see, they laced up the front, not pulled tight enough to restrict, but allowing her golden flesh to spill out the top.

Two tempting bows tied each strap, making for ease of removal.

She wanted to play. And he was always game.

Envy leaned against the doorframe, folding his arms across his chest. "I didn't know you enjoyed reading."

"I suppose it's one more secret I'm keeping, Your Highness."

Camilla didn't bother to glance up, his second clue that she was toying with him.

Even knowing that he was playing into her scheme, Envy couldn't stop himself from striding over. He knelt down, gently pressing the book back to read the cover.

"Of course." He scoffed. "You're looking for a Prince Charming."

"Just because I occasionally enjoy romance novels doesn't mean I'm looking for a prince. I find most royals to be tiresome, arrogant bores who don't know the first thing about being charming."

She gave him a pointed look, then tugged her book back and continued reading.

Arrogant, most certainly guilty as charged. But tiresome or boring...

Envy plucked up the bottle of oil, uncorked the stopper, and inhaled. Vanilla and bourbon. Sweet and sinful, just like their little game.

He contemplated his next move. Going to Bloodwood Forest wasn't the most practical use of his time. The likelihood of finding another player wasn't high, especially since they'd been seen heading there last night. If they had entered the forest, they'd be long gone by now.

He could waste time and energy he didn't have running down that old lead. Or he could play this little game with Camilla, hopefully solving the riddle of her, and maybe even stoking her jealousy before the night was over—thus refueling his power.

If she had a magical tattoo inked onto her skin, he'd know she was Fae.

If she didn't, his theory of her being some kind of shape-shifter would be proven likely.

He stood and drizzled the oil over her back without warning, enjoying her slight hiss as the cool liquid dribbled across her skin.

Envy didn't stop at her back. She was offering him an unobstructed view of her body, and he was going to tend to *every* inch of her, searching for answers to the questions he had.

Hopefully he'd succeed in solving one mystery tonight.

He poured a light line of massage oil over the round curve of her bottom, then set the oil aside. He slowly rolled down one stocking at a time, pulling them off to expose her bare flesh. He wound the stockings around his fist, considering tying her to the chaise with them, but tossed them aside. He wanted Camilla freely squirming tonight.

Envy grabbed the oil again and continued drizzling it down the backs of her thighs and all the way to the soles of her feet.

"What are you doing?" she asked, breathless.

Camilla was excited by the unexpected path he'd laid out.

"Showing you why Prince Charming isn't what you truly desire."

Envy gently gathered her loose hair, then swept it aside, giving himself access to her neck and shoulders. He rubbed the backs of his knuckles against the line of her stays, slipping a finger under the strap, tugging it gently.

"Is there a reason you left this on, Miss Antonius?"

She shot him a look over her shoulder, part irritation, part anticipation.

"If you wish to see me fully nude, Your Highness, I'm afraid you'll need to dirty your hands."

He smiled faintly at that.

"You ought to know one thing about me, Camilla darling."

He reached around, gently pulling one side of the bow on her shoulder straps. He moved to the other side, unwrapping the next ribbon. Then he loosened the ties along the front, freeing her breasts as he removed the garment and tossed it aside.

"I *like* being filthy."

Her breathing sped up, her arousal hitting him hard.

"I'd wager the mere thought of how dirty I can be arouses you."

He took the book and set it aside, then guided her back down, pressing her firmly onto the chaise so he could stroke her shoulders, kneading each muscle until she slowly relaxed.

Envy rubbed the backs of her arms, followed each down to her wrists and hands, tending to every area with care. His attention was sharp on her, cataloguing any freckle, any hint of magic at play. By the time he'd worked his way down to her lower back and run a hand over her tight little bottom, he hadn't found a single indication that she was glamoured.

He wasn't sure whether he was relieved or even more skeptical.

Envy rubbed the oil into her legs, ending the massage with her feet, releasing any ache she might have felt from their long trek through the Sin Corridor.

She hadn't complained once of the miles they'd traveled on foot.

He listened as she sighed contentedly, her body languid from his ministrations. Her desire, though—that had continued to build with each stroke.

It was time for him to up the stakes.

His hands lightly trailed along the backs of her calves before he flattened them against her thighs, rubbing larger circles across her uninked skin. He fought the urge to lean over, bite the plump flesh of her bottom before soothing away the sting with a kiss.

Still, the air around them felt thick, tense. Her breathing had all but stopped as she waited to see what he'd do, where he'd touch next.

Envy took his time, plotting, dreaming of all the divinely sinful ways he'd make her call out his name. Slowly, he drizzled oil into the palm of his hand, allowing it to warm slightly before sliding it down to his fingers.

He began rubbing it over her bottom, again and again, on each circle his hand dipping deeper between her legs, beginning to stroke that lovely place he wanted to bury himself inside.

"Well," he purred softly as her hips lifted to meet his touch. "Looks like I was correct. You want it dirty too."

She was drenched, her arousal almost as slick as the oil on his hand. He lazily traced the seam of her body, dipping the tip of his middle finger inside her. A harsh curse escaped her pretty lips, her face half hidden under her ethereal hair.

"You crave a demon, do you? One who fucks like a sinner because he is one."

He withdrew his finger before she could push herself onto it, sliding it back across her body, spreading her wetness.

"I promise, sweet Camilla, you won't be shouting for God when I'm buried inside you. I'll be ruthless when I grace your sheets."

His finger circled her clit, and he bit back his own groan. It was so swollen with desire she must ache. At the touch her hips bucked against his palm.

Envy finally slid one finger inside, giving her what she wanted. Camilla arched up and back, seeking more. His filthy little deviant wanted him to fill her. He plunged a second finger in, her soft moan making his cock rock-hard. She was so wet, so hungry for more.

Camilla propped herself on her forearms, her book long forgotten as she glanced back at him, watching as he continued to pleasure her.

"You'll be shouting my name, Camilla. I will be your God, your Creator, your Destroyer, and every depraved dark thing in between. And I promise you'll find religion on my cock. You'll get on your knees for it, pray for it, worship it with every fiber of your being."

He withdrew his fingers, then gave her clit a tiny little pinch, adding a twinge of pain to enhance her pleasure. Camilla moaned, the sound pure bliss. He thrust his fingers back inside her, pumping them, his own breath ragged as she quietly demanded he keep doing *that* to her.

"You won't think of Prince Charming again. I promise you that."

Envy lightly slapped her slick flesh, her body jerking toward him.

Camilla cursed softly, arousal glistening down her leg.

Envy played gently with her clit, one flick, another, before plunging his fingers deep inside her again. She began grinding against his hand.

The way her body responded to him was fucking glorious. He could watch her seek pleasure from him all night.

She clenched around him, slowly riding his fingers.

His free hand drifted down to his erection, stroking it gently over his trousers as he watched her. It would be easy to give in and give them both what they craved. He could pull her hips up until she was on all fours, bend her over the arm of the chaise, spread her wide, and end their mutual torment. But the lure of this particular game was even more potent than any fleeting physical satisfaction.

Camilla's breath caught as she rolled her hips, seeking friction. He stroked himself harder, his balls tightening as his own pleasure increased. He imagined how good it would feel to slide his throbbing cock across her slickness.

But tonight wasn't that night. Tonight was about her alone. He stopped touching himself and focused on her again. She was getting close.

He pumped a few more times, drawing out the sensation, listening as her breath turned ragged, then withdrew his fingers.

Camilla must have sensed the shift; she glanced back at him, back still arched, searching.

"You stopped."

She didn't ask why. But her frustration was written plainly across her face, as was her lust. Instantly, Camilla knew...He'd won this round.

Envy flashed her a grin, then bent forward and nipped playfully at her fleshy bottom, his tongue soothing over the mark, indulging his earlier fantasy.

He stood, straightened, and handed her the bottle of massage oil.

"Use this when you touch yourself later. It'll be almost as good as when I make you come again."

"What?" she asked, her tone incredulous. "You can't be serious."

He gave her a slow, wicked smile. "Sweet dreams, my filthy little darling."

Envy returned to his bedroom and shut the door, chuckling softly as she called him every cursed name in the book.

THIRTY-SEVEN

"That is absolutely not a clue," Lo said for the fourth time. "Put it down."

Camilla closed her eyes, praying for some sort of divine interference. After she'd slept for only a few short hours, more frustrated than ever after Envy's win last night, they'd all had breakfast, then immediately began their day of hunting.

By now, they'd been searching for the next clue for ages and the demon princes were driving her well past the point of madness. She was feeling downright murderous.

Perhaps that had something to do with the fact that she'd done exactly as the antithesis of Prince Charming had suggested, unable to sleep without finding release after he'd driven her wild once again. That he'd somehow outmaneuvered her at her own game ought to be criminal. Next time, she'd have to plot her victory better. Clearly, he'd been repaying her for the Sin Corridor.

Game on, demon.

This morning they'd all been methodically searching through one chamber after the next, deciding that the three of them, plus two research assistants, would complete a more thorough search if they worked together, room by room, shelf by shelf, using Lo's meticulous records to compare what was in the room with anything that might have been added.

Which sounded fine in theory until one factored in the princes' inability to work with each other without fighting. Every. Cursed. Minute.

Camilla scanned the room, her attention pausing on an artifact that looked like a dark moon. Glass, smoky and opaque. A few shelves over, an enormous nautilus shell was displayed, measuring at least two feet in length, larger than any she knew of in the mortal world.

"Give it to me now," Lo said to Envy.

Using gloves, Lo gingerly plucked the illustrated manuscript out of Envy's hands, setting it back under a glass encasement.

"You're certain it's not a clue?" Envy asked. "I don't see it listed."

"This book has been part of this collection for three hundred years. In a House with this many artifacts and tomes, it's unfortunate that one was missed in the ledger, but not unheard of. Put it back down."

"If you're sure Lennox didn't plant this clue back then," Envy said, "show me the proof."

"Tell me why you need to win so badly, and I'll consider sharing my court secrets," Lo lobbed back. "This game just began in the last month or so, correct?"

"Lennox has been known to plant clues whenever the opportunity arises."

"You're not answering my question," Lo said.

Best of luck with that futile inquiry, Camilla thought crossly.

"Maybe the gossip column was correct. Maybe you're playing for much more this time."

Camilla's brows rose. "Gossip column? What did it say?"

Envy shot his brother a contemptuous look. "It didn't say anything."

"How very odd," Camilla said, "that a paper should print nothing at all. Yet here we all are, discussing something."

"Bloody hell, do you ever cease with your games?" Lo said. "The paper is public knowledge." He shook his head and looked at Camilla. "Rumors suggest Envy's circle has been magically warded. No one has been able to go in or out. It started just when the game did."

"I don't see how it matters whether it is true," Envy said.

Camilla watched him closely. His demeanor had shifted slightly—it was nothing very noticeable, but he'd tensed for the briefest moment before adopting that frustratingly blasé attitude. As if he couldn't be bothered about the rumors.

Which was categorically false, as he'd just tried to keep that rumor from her.

She couldn't sort out why he'd attempt to downplay its significance unless he was hiding a much darker truth.

"Exactly," Lo said, interrupting her thoughts. "You refuse to tell me any of your court secrets, so I have no desire to share mine."

As the princes continued to bicker, Camilla wished to throttle them both. They'd now been at this particular disagreement for an hour. She half wished they'd pull their cocks out to compare sizes and get on with it.

Envy's attention snapped to her.

"Mine's much larger, Miss Antonius."

She rolled her eyes. Leave it to Envy to pick up on that.

Lo glanced between the two of them, brows knitted at their silent conversation.

"Nothing." Camilla waved her hand, irked. "Please, continue this scintillating argument. I'm sure we have several more hours we can dedicate to it as well."

The two males picked up where they'd left off, completely missing her sarcasm.

At the rate they were going, they'd never make it out of House Sloth.

Perhaps this was evidence of the prince's sin at work. They were moving at a snail's pace, and Camilla had never realized before how inactivity drove her mad. At home she was always in motion: drawing or painting or curating the gallery or visiting Kitty. Tending to Bunny and waltzing her around the town house, kissing her fuzzy little peanut head.

Now Camilla was... losing her mind.

She missed her big gray-and-white cat.

She wanted to find the next clue as much as Envy did, but she, at least, refused to be waylaid by petty feuds and court politics.

Thinking of clues, Camilla briefly wondered if she should be searching for something else for her first riddle, but no note had magically appeared with any game rules for her, and no blood oath had been signed. So was she not quite a player? She supposed she was a pawn.

A fact she hated.

Just as the game master had known she would. He'd made his move expertly. This had been the highest form of blackmail, proving there really was no honor among thieves.

If she'd never agreed to Envy's bargain, she would never have painted a hexed object. And she'd not be in this predicament now. It had all been plotted brilliantly.

Camilla needed to get her talent back.

But it wasn't Envy's fault. One way or another, her path would always have ended on this road. She'd known that the hunter's return was an inevitability, as was the lure of the Fae. The clouds of her past had been looming above for some time, gathering into this perfect storm.

She closed the book she'd long since stopped scanning and glanced around the chamber again. They were in a room dedicated to emotions, and the only thing she felt at present was irritation. Everything looked to be in place. No book stood out to her, no object, except...

Her attention returned to the giant nautilus, then drifted over to that smoky glass ball.

It wasn't unusual to find an object or artifact tucked into the shelves here, but something about this object kept drawing Camilla's eye. Perhaps it was simply shiny and pretty and like a magpie she had a fondness for sparkly items.

"Hand it over," Envy said, continuing the argument with his brother.

"As outrageous as it is to consider, your game isn't responsible for everything in this bloody realm," Lo shot back, equally annoyed. "If you can't tell me why this is so important to win, don't expect me to put my court in peril."

Camilla crossed the chamber to get a better look at the gleaming nautilus shell.

Her fingers glided over the smooth surface, marveling at the burnt-umber stripes running along its curved outer edge.

She turned it over carefully, admiring the mother-of-pearl interior and the clever spiral pattern the mollusk was known for. Nature was the greatest artist.

She replaced the shell and picked up the glittering ball, holding it up to the light.

Her mood shifted from annoyance to wonder. The ball was even more magical up close. What she'd initially believed was opaque glass was actually thousands of little ebony grains that moved like sand within an hourglass each time she turned it.

The object was lovely.

Something about it made her want to smash it to pieces.

She'd raised her hand, intent on doing just that, when one word broke her trance.

"Stop." Magic laced Envy's voice, the power winding around her until she couldn't have ignored him if she'd tried.

The prince was slowly approaching, hands up, like she was a wild animal ready to attack.

"What?" she asked.

"Put the Orb of Golath down. Slowly."

Envy kept his gaze on her, steady, calming. Yet his demeanor only succeeded in making her more nervous. Her attention shot around the room. Lo, the two male research assistants who'd been quietly thumbing through each shelf, *everyone* had stilled, watching.

She looked down at the object she held, noticing the strange pulse for the first time. It beat like a phantom heart, like a distant drum. Somehow she felt like all the fears in the universe had been collected and were pounding at the thin glass to be freed.

"Oh, it's doing... something."

Envy moved slowly but steadily, his voice low and commanding. "Look at me. It will not harm you so long as it remains intact."

Of course, that statement made her want to toss the damn thing far away.

"It's pulsing." Camilla suddenly feared she'd hold it too tightly and shatter the glass by accident. Then she worried she'd not hold it tightly enough and it'd drop.

It undulated in her palms, the feeling twisting her insides into knots.

"Whatever it tries to do to get you to drop it, you must ignore it," Envy said. "The orb wants you to break it."

"The orb of what?"

"Gods' bones," Envy muttered. "Did you even see the cursed thing sitting there, Sloth?"

"Must have been glamoured from us." Lo sounded shaken.

"Why?" Camilla asked, trying to ignore the slick, cool feeling of the glass. It shifted again, now reminding her of a leech as it suctioned to her skin. "Why wasn't it glamoured from me?"

"That is the question, isn't it?" Envy asked, his tone curious. He shifted to his brother. "It wasn't part of your collection, correct?"

Lo shook his head. "No. I don't have an orb on the premises."

"Then this is definitely our next clue." Envy faced her again, face grim. "Try to set it down now, Camilla."

"I...I don't think I can."

"You can and you will." Envy seemed coiled to strike out at the orb. "Once it's been touched, only the person who picked it up can set it back down. I can't take it from you."

With fear surging through her veins, Camilla gently set the orb back on the shelf, mindful to step away as slowly as she could in case it decided to take a tumble on its own. She exhaled only after it was several feet away from her.

Envy drew her behind him.

"Where should we destroy it?" Envy asked.

Camilla stared daggers at his back. "Breaking it seemed like a very unwise idea a moment ago."

He glanced over his shoulder, his expression inscrutable. "You're more...breakable."

"Give me a second," Lo said. "I'll draw a containment ring. It should be safe there."

One of the assistants brought the Prince of Sloth a piece of chalk, and while he drew a perfect circle and added runes she assumed were for protection, Camilla racked her brain for what it was. She couldn't recall any stories.

"What is the Orb of Golath?" she asked again.

"Golath is known as the Fear Collector, an ancient being often thought to have possessed the first spark of evil," Envy said, still standing guard over the ball. "No one knows how many orbs are in existence, but they open doors even we demon princes fear to pass through. That one is here indicates we need to seek Golath next. He gifts them when he has a message. Or when he has a fear to collect."

The Fear Collector.

Of course, the next clue had to be some ancient evil. Why not the Wish Granter? The Dream Weaver?

And she'd been the one marked to find this clue.

Envy's attention remained locked on the orb, his expression set in hard lines as he concentrated. He'd dispatched the Hexed Throne with barely any effort, so to see him taking such care was anything but comforting.

"Are you ready to break it?" Lo asked, looking up from the containment circle.

The Prince of Envy took a step toward the orb, then glanced over at Camilla.

"Stand as far from the circle as you can, Miss Antonius."

She moved to the far corner of the room where the two assistant demons were crouched, books clutched to their chests. They'd likely been intrigued by the hunt for information, the excitement of finding a clue. Judging from the way they trembled, they hadn't expected things to get so dangerous. An oversized desk sat between them and the circle, which didn't seem like much protection at all.

Lo and Envy exchanged long looks, their conversation silent before Lo inclined his head, agreeing to whatever his brother had asked.

Without looking at Camilla again, Envy finally grabbed the orb.

He walked straight into the chalk circle, gave his brother one last hard look, then shattered it at his feet.

Camilla inhaled sharply.

A mammoth, nearly incorporeal creature reared up. It had the head of a goat and the body of a muscular man. Its horizontal irises landed on Camilla, taking her in.

It remained silent, cocking its head, its gaze never straying from where she stood.

"Golath." Envy's voice carved through the tension building in the room. "Where are you?"

"What are you, when are you, these are more interesting queries."

The creature didn't remove its dark gaze from Camilla. A forked tongue shot out between its overlarge teeth.

She remained very still, willing it to look elsewhere.

"Golath," Envy warned.

"You know where I am, Prince Envy. Below. Far below. Beneath the place where the tombs burn and the ground withers. Come find me if you dare. Bring the silver-haired one. I do so enjoy gifts."

The Fear Collector spun its nearly incorporeal body like a cyclone and disappeared into the circle, vanishing the shattered orb with it.

A heavy silence fell. Envy remained where he was, attention fixed to the floor, as if waiting for the creature to spring back and attack. But once it became clear it wasn't returning, he stared directly at Camilla.

His expression was carefully blank. Lo didn't look at her at all. Nor did the other two demons.

Unease clawed at her. She did not want to be that creature's gift.

"Grab your cloak," Envy said to her softly. "We're traveling below the flaming tombs. The fire that burns there produces ice, not heat. Making survival... unpleasant."

"No."

The only one who didn't seem surprised by her refusal was Envy.

He expelled a frustrated sigh.

"Unfortunately, this isn't a negotiation, Miss Antonius. If the decision were up to me, you'd remain here. Better yet, I'd deposit you back in Waverly Green. Since we are both without choice in the matter, grab your cloak."

Camilla's attention slid to the others in the room. She did not want to debate in front of them.

"Sloth, a moment of privacy, please?" Envy said, surprising her.

Once the other demons had left, Envy pulled her against his chest.

"Let's play a little game of truth, Miss Antonius."

She nestled against him, nodding.

"I won't permit anything to hurt you. True?"

"Yes. But—"

"There is no but, pet. Nothing will harm you." He smoothed a hand down her spine. "Do you trust me?"

She laughed, pushing back from his embrace. "Not at all."

He gave her a wolfish grin. Then seriousness entered his features. He pulled a small dagger from inside his suit. It was silver like her eyes, its sheath carved beautifully.

She hesitated for only a second before taking it. It wasn't made of iron, but it wasn't any metal she was familiar with either.

Envy tucked her hair behind her ears, then stepped back.

"You can trust me with your life, Camilla. That is something precious. Something I'd never play with. No matter what game is happening. Truth?"

Camilla held his gaze for a long moment, then went to fetch her cloak.

The tunnel below House Sloth was exactly what one should expect from an underground labyrinth deep within the bowels of the Underworld, home to creatures so terrible they do not seek the light.

Walls of frost-coated stone had been carved out to form the tunnel, the passage narrow enough that Camilla's shoulder brushed against the prince's as they walked silently.

Envy had had Sloth enchant her cloak so it regulated the temperature, ensuring that she wouldn't freeze to death, but the air was still brutal on her face. He carried a flameless torch, which didn't burn but provided enough light for them to see.

In many places the stone walls were gouged by claws, splattered with what had probably once been blood. There weren't any bones or skeletons—Camilla got the impression that whatever dwelled this far into the realm didn't leave such delicacies behind.

Occasionally they heard screams in the distance.

Once, when a yowl so terrible it made her shiver rent the air, Envy held a finger to his lips and grabbed her hand, pulling her down another winding passage, not slowing his grueling pace until the infernal wailing was a distant nightmare ringing in her ears.

He hadn't let go of her after that.

The closer they got to the land below what Envy had called the flaming tombs, the colder it got, like the world itself was warning travelers away.

Camilla had thought it couldn't get any worse, and it proved her wrong. If it hadn't been for the magic cloak, she would have frozen.

Her eyes stung, tears freezing on her cheeks. Panic made her want to cry harder.

Will my eyes freeze shut?

Envy abruptly pulled her in front of him, wiping her tears away with his thumbs. Her skin heated immediately, warming from his magicked touch.

"Breathe, Miss Antonius. The tunnel is meant to induce fear. Golath feeds on it."

Another less-than-comforting thought.

He waited until she found her calm center; a feat that was more difficult than she'd have imagined.

She nodded after another moment and they continued on, Camilla feeling marginally better.

Finally, after another long descent into an abyss, Envy stopped. He kept his hand wrapped around hers, his grip unyielding.

"Golath." Envy's voice had been low, but it rumbled along the darkness.

Her heartbeat quickened again as the creature appeared from the shadows, peering at them curiously.

Camilla simultaneously couldn't take her attention from it and never wanted to look upon it again. Here, where it chose to live, it was no longer nearly incorporeal. It was fully flesh and bone, its goatlike eyes glowing a sickly yellow in the dark.

Camilla couldn't make out much more than its horns, and that was only because of the light given off by its eyes. She couldn't see its mouth but sensed its smile.

"Interesting companions make for interesting stories. Come closer, curious mistress."

Its voice was deep, elemental. Different from that of the Hexed Throne, but somehow similar.

Camilla held her ground—she was not prey, no matter how much this tunnel wanted her to believe that—and the creature moved closer.

"Ah. What a tale there is to tell." Its yellow eyes flicked to Envy. "Master of secrets, prince of the dark, how peculiar to find yourself trapped in it. Moons are such chaotic things. Inconstant, flickering. As is new blood."

Envy tensed.

"What information do you have about the game?"

"What are games but opportunities to either boast of victory or taste defeat? Have you not already won?" The Fear Collector's gaze flared. "Proceed with caution, for there's much to lose."

Envy's grip on her tightened, but she sensed it had more to do with frustration than anything else.

"Speak plainly. Or is this a riddle I need to solve?"

The Fear Collector watched Camilla with slitted eyes.

"There are many riddles, many games, many players. If an ice prince falls, will a crimson one rise? I suppose that depends on who does the slaying. Blood must spill."

It slunk back into the shadows.

Envy swore. "We're not done."

"Curious are those who hide in plain sight. Beware, young prince. There are many slithering, venomous snakes in this sultry garden. Deception is the most wicked game of all."

Suddenly a name popped into Camilla's head—Prometheus—as if the Fear Collector had placed it there for her, bright and bursting on her tongue like a ripened strawberry.

She wanted to spit the name out, shout it into the void, but clamped her teeth together.

If the Fear Collector wanted her to do something in its presence, she would hold off for as long as possible.

She wondered if he'd done the same to the prince but refused to ask until they were above ground again.

"Is that it?" Envy asked.

"Memories, like hearts, can be stolen. My whispers echo through shadows, across realms, across times and dimensions, following and finding those who need to hear them. You never heed the warning, young prince. Will you now?"

With a troubled look, Envy ushered them back down the tunnel, away from the Fear Collector, and didn't once turn back.

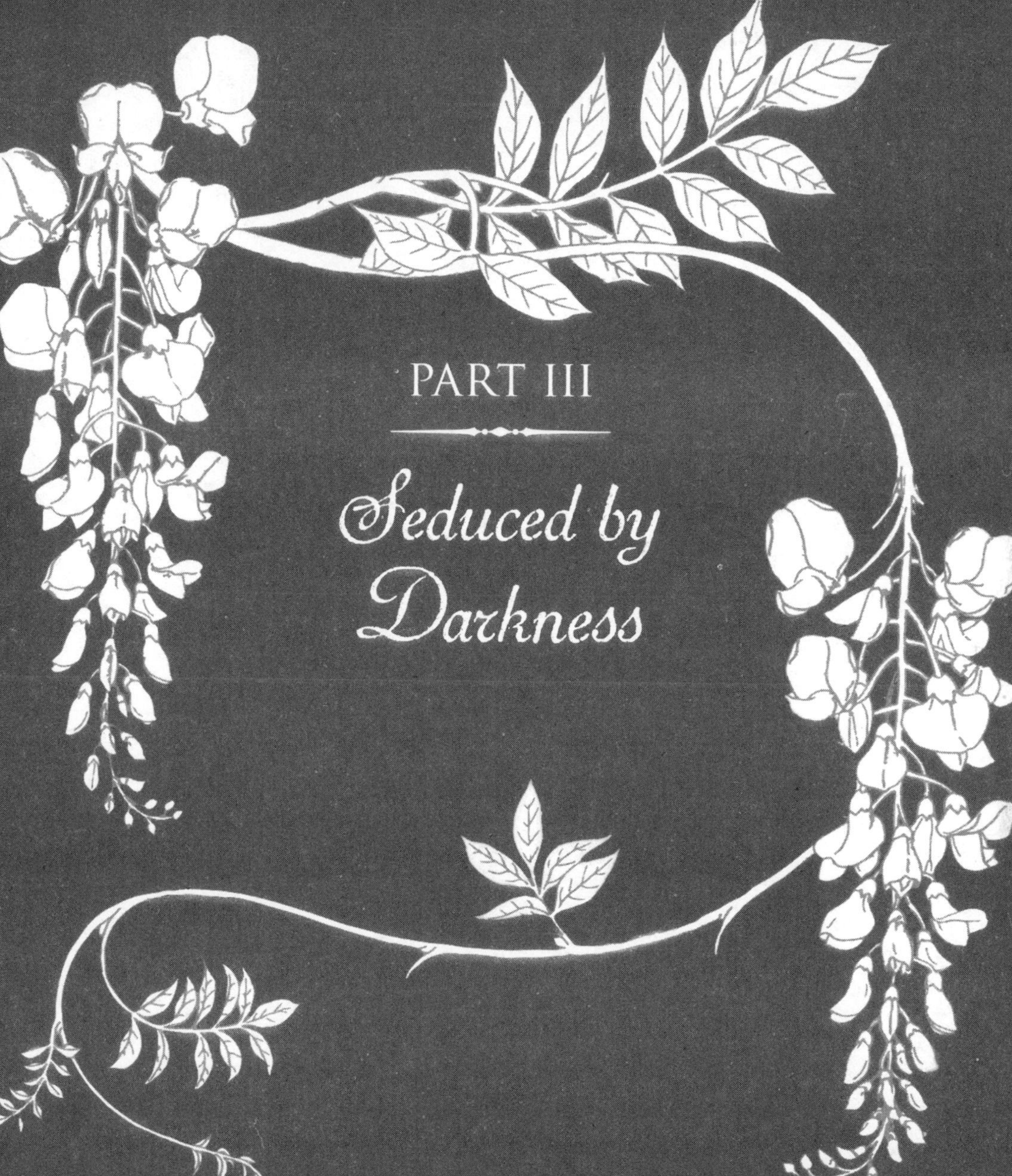

PART III

Seduced by Darkness

THIRTY-EIGHT

THE UNDERGROUND SPIT them out near the edge of Bloodwood Forest, an area not far from the border of Envy's circle where using magic was forbidden.

He cursed the Fear Collector for the parting gift. Envy had planned on retracing their steps, but the ancient being clearly sought amusement and had deposited them where Envy couldn't easily return to his court. It wasn't lost on him that another player was rumored to have visited this forest two nights before. Maybe he'd find some trace of them.

Once they safely reached his domain, he'd magic them to a private cottage near his House, where he could think without interruption.

Envy strode ahead of Camilla, wondering once again what secrets the artist was harboring and how they might possibly fit into his game. He wasn't one who usually found himself in the dark. And he didn't care for this growing mystery.

It was one thing for Sloth to be suspicious—he was wary of everyone he met until he'd fully investigated them from conception to birth to present day—but for the Fear Collector to sense something...his warning had been clear. Camilla was hiding something.

Variables and unknowns were a sure way to lose. And losing wasn't an option.

No matter how passionate Camilla had been delivering her little speech about leaving the past behind, some scars shaped the future. Envy had made a mistake. A mistake he couldn't forgive himself for. His entire court was suffering the consequences, and he needed to make it right.

He held his loathing for the Unseelie royalty tightly in his grasp, never forgetting the role they'd played. It was a concept she wouldn't understand; her life was a mere flicker in time.

Until she'd lost and let others down and felt the weight of responsibility press onto her shoulders, she couldn't lecture him on only seeking sunshine and completely forgetting that the world also needed rain to thrive.

Darkness was never as appealing as the light to most, but that didn't mean it was any less integral to life. Too much sunshine withered the soul.

Balance was the key.

"Who is Prometheus? Is it the actual Titan of myth?"

Her question drew him up short.

Had she understood what the Fear Collector had rambled on about in that circuitous way of his?

Envy held a finger to his mouth and glanced around the empty path, listening carefully. The woods were quiet, save for the gusting winds, whining and howling through the bare branches like scared mutts.

They were almost to his domain, where he could use his magic without issue.

"Do not say his true name aloud again." Envy's hand was on his dagger, his attention sweeping the woods again. "The vampire prince and his spies are always listening."

Camilla's face paled.

"I thought his name was Zarus."

Envy's eyes narrowed.

"For a mortal who's never been to the Underworld, you know a lot of interesting information."

"I think the Fear Collector planted the name in my head," she said defensively. He didn't have time to wonder about that oddity before she added tartly, "And the second was because my father had a lot of tales to share."

Envy's grip on his patience snapped. "Ah, yes. The man who was so obsessed with realm lines that he built a secret tunnel on top of one. Tell me, Camilla, why was your father desperately trying to find a way into Faerie? Or was he looking for certain shifter realms?"

Camilla's mouth pressed into a straight line, her gaze darting away.

She remained silent.

"The woman in that painting didn't happen to be the queen, did she?" he asked. "And I do not mean the mortal monarch. I know for a fact that Prim Róis likens herself to Eve. Strange that the painting was named for Evelyn. Perhaps your father had an affair with the Unseelie queen?"

If her mother *had* been a shifter, she would have despised the affair even more. Shifters and Fae mixed as well as oil and water.

Camilla's steely gaze clashed with his; he'd struck a nerve.

His smile was as sharp as his words had been, but he needed to push her until that hard wall she'd erected broke. It was high time he knew what he was dealing with.

Lennox wanted her to accompany him to the Underworld.

The Fear Collector had given her the next clue.

He wanted to know why. Why her. With her rare talent. With her expansive knowledge of his realm. With her ability to withstand most demonic influence.

Who *was* Miss Camilla Antonius?

He was damn well going to find out.

No more waiting, no more games. If he had to be ruthless, so be it.

Envy took a step toward her, impressed she didn't retreat. Males twice her size would cower before a Prince of Hell.

"My spies have unearthed lots of curious information on your father."

Camilla froze.

"You spied on us?"

She'd spit the question out like it tasted foul.

He inclined his head. Envy didn't like sparking emotions tied to his brother's sin, but the angrier Camilla got, the less likely she was to hold on to all her secrets.

"What are you, Camilla? Immortal? Halfling? Or just a deviously talented human liar?"

Fury laced her tone.

"What other absurd theories would you like to add, Your Highness? A lioness? An eagle? I know," she mocked, "maybe I'm a dire wolf."

"Why do you intrigue so many dark beings, Camilla, if that's even your true name? What do they sense that my brothers and I cannot? Why are you a necessary piece to the game? Lennox chose you. Why?"

Her expression shuttered completely.

And something inside him went feral.

He stalked closer, needing to know what she was hiding, needing to know *her.*

This little game had reached an end.

His sin lashed out. There was a wall between him and her will and he barreled into it, driving his power at it over and over, envisioning it like a wall of ice.

Nearly impenetrable until he made a tiny crack.

A tiny fissure was all he needed for his sin to finally burst through.

Camilla responded to envy, he'd seen it before. Envy projected images into her mind, both to fuel his power while he drained himself and to entice her true emotions to surface.

He pictured the Goddess of Death, when she'd fucked his second in front of him. Her ancient lavender eyes had locked on Envy, attempting in vain to stoke his sin.

At once, both he and Camilla were in that memory together, reliving his thoughts beat by beat as Camilla watched, confused, through his mind.

His focus traveled over her gown, obviously chosen with this tableau in mind. Vittoria always was the theatrical twin; it was a wonder she and Emilia had ever convinced his brothers—and the whole realm—that they were one entity all those years ago.

Vittoria's dress was nothing more than two swaths of lavender material that covered her breasts, then gathered at the middle before pooling to the floor. Long sections of bronze skin flashed with each of her movements.

Envy kept his emotions from that night away from Camilla, only showing her the goddess as Vittoria watched him, her desire for him bleeding through his memories, funneling straight into Camilla.

He neglected to reveal that he *hadn't* been aroused and never would be by Vittoria.

He recalled more of that encounter, how his second's hands had roamed the goddess's body, how her low moans had started; he stoked Camilla's jealousy until he was nearly drunk on it. He could sense her pushing back at his mental grip, shoving and trying to force her way out, but it was working. Camilla was wild with envy.

"You're playing with fire," he said to Vittoria in the memory. "Quite literally."

"And I do so love the burn." Vittoria spun in Alexei's arms, pressing her backside against his groin, and slowly gyrated. From this new position, she could watch Envy while she worked the vampire into a lust-fueled frenzy. A task she'd already completed if Alexei's curses and moans were any indication.

"If you're trying to stoke my sin," Envy drawled, "you'll have to do better than that."

"Oh, Envy. If I wished to stroke *your sin, I would." Vittoria's hand slipped inside the vampire's trousers, her fist pumping in a steady rhythm as he groaned. "You're welcome to watch. Or join..."*

Camilla was nearly feral in his mind, clawing the memory to shreds.

Her jealousy was unlike anything he'd ever felt before, it was a deep chasm inside her, seemingly endless. She'd been keeping her emotions locked away inside.

And he'd only just begun to discover how deep that well went.

One moment he had her in his mind; then suddenly, without any warning, Camilla pushed a memory into *him*. She'd chosen her return fire well.

Envy watched as Camilla braced her hands on the male's thighs—the material of his trousers pulled taut against the breadth of them—then leaned forward, tongue darting out to wet her full lips.

With nimble fingers, Camilla unlaced his trousers, slowly pulling his erection out. Envy strained to see the male's face, wanting to mark it for future notice, but could only see what Camilla permitted from this memory.

And Camilla's focus was entirely on the rock-hard cock twitching in her face.

Envy strained to release himself from this scene, but Camilla latched on, fed him more.

In the memory, she repositioned herself, then tentatively closed her mouth around the head, her cheeks hollowing out as the man instructed her to suck.

Envy wanted to put his fist through a wall.

The other male's long fingers plunged into Camilla's silver hair, threading it until he guided her into the motion he preferred. In the memory, Camilla nearly choked as the male pumped into her mouth. His grip in her hair tightened, his thrusts hitting the wall of her throat. Memory Camilla felt like she was choking—it thrilled and scared her. Tears streamed down her cheeks, as the bastard fucked her mouth so hard and fast she couldn't breathe.

Envy shouted in the memory, needing to be out. He didn't care that she'd been with someone else, but seeing it…It drove him mad. And the bastard—whoever he was—hadn't been gentle. He'd unleashed himself, uncaring of the woman's comfort.

He didn't realize she'd stopped provoking him—had somehow managed to tear them both free of the memory and backed him against a tree—until she pulled the dagger Envy had given her from her bodice and held it to his throat, her silver eyes flashing just as menacingly in the night.

They were both breathing hard, their eyes twin flames of envy.

Envy thought she would slit his throat right then and there. And he'd deserve it. Maybe he wanted her to—after that memory, he needed to be put out of his misery. The image of her on her knees, pleasuring someone else, was too much.

"Go on, pet. Hurt me." His chest heaved with his heavy breath.

Instead, she tossed the blade to the ground and dragged his face to hers, their mouths crashing together.

Hunger overtook them. Or madness.

He knew it wasn't madness but pure, unadulterated jealousy.

She didn't ask about Vittoria, and he didn't ask about the male in her memory.

They both needed to forget that other lovers had come into their lives, needed to imprint each other in their newest memories. Their game had taken a turn.

Camilla's tongue was suddenly in his mouth and his fist was in her hair and the kiss was unlike any other he'd ever had. She drew back, raking her gaze over him, possessive and filled with raw need, then ripped his shirt open, kissing up the stubbled column of his neck.

She stopped again when she reached his jaw, long enough to run her hands along the front of his body, tracing his tattoos, the ridge of each muscle along his abdomen. The dark hunter-green ink placed just below his belt line was a Latin phrase he admired. But it was only one of his tattoos. *Non ducor, duco.* I am not led, I lead.

"Beautiful." Her painter's hands followed the lines as they dipped lower. "Powerful."

The groan that escaped him was all demon.

"Camilla."

He pulled her against him, roughly caressing her breasts as she nipped at his throat.

"Kiss me," she whispered against his mouth, "like I'm the only thing you think about."

She already fucking was.

Envy flipped her around, pressing her up against the same tree, yanking down her bodice to finally liberate those glorious breasts. They tumbled free, beautiful and golden in the shadows of the trees.

He deepened their kiss until she moaned, arching against him.

He was going to devour her right on the cursed path, make her forget that anyone else existed on this realm.

And Camilla was all too willing for him to do just that.

Envy fitted himself between her thighs and began a slow, rhythmic grinding of his body against hers, a promise of what was soon to come.

Camilla pressed back, giving as good as she was getting.

He cupped her breast as she bit his lip, rolling her nipple between his fingers until the nub hardened; then his fingers dipped lower, curling around the hem of her dress before he fisted the material, tempted to rip it to shreds.

Camilla made an impatient sound in the back of her throat as he slowly exposed her stockinged thighs, and then the bare flesh above them, where she hadn't donned anything at all.

His knuckles skimmed the area he wished to be buried in, already damp with her arousal.

Envy wanted to take his time, to fulfill each of her fantasies and make her come until she couldn't take another ounce of pleasure, but his cock ached.

He could no longer wait. It was sooner than he'd planned, but what they'd just done...they'd gone too far. Now he had to claim her.

Envy didn't care what her secrets were, who he was or what his goal was, he wanted to shed civility and fuck like animals.

In one preternaturally fast motion, he had Camilla on the ground beneath him, her legs curling around his body, pulling him closer, locking him against her.

As if he'd leave now.

Envy didn't think about the game or what she'd set into motion, his thoughts were only of her. Their mouths and tongues and teeth clashed, their hands gripping and tugging as if they were battling to be inside each other's souls.

He began that slow, driving motion again, this time with his trousers against her bare flesh. One little piece of cloth separated him from being fully seated inside her.

"Tell me to stop, Camilla."

If she didn't, he would claim her. Right now. Ruin her for all other lovers.

Maybe she'd do the same to him.

His hips ground against her, harder, faster, finding a spot that made her claw him closer, her nails carving half-moon crescents into his skin, marking him, too.

Camilla's eyes fluttered shut. He pressed that spot again, loving the way she gasped. Her fingers dug into his shoulders, holding him tightly to her.

"Don't you dare."

Camilla was unlacing his trousers when he heard it.

A beat later he was on his feet, dagger in hand, scanning the woods.

He'd moved so swiftly Camilla didn't even call out.

Nothing was there, but he sensed another presence. They'd been reckless.

He'd been reckless. Envy never should have let passion and jealousy cloud his judgment. He knew how dangerous Bloodwood Forest could be. He knew what the Fear Collector had done, and still he'd let desire take over his reason.

Envy held out a hand, keeping his attention locked on the woods, waiting.

"Come along, love. We'll finish this at House Envy."

Camilla didn't reach for him. Didn't utter a word.

He glanced down.

She was gone.

"Fuck."

The game had already made its next move.

Where she'd been sprawled and eager a moment before lay only a card, the Immortal Heart facing upward. It was the symbol of the vampire court.

Zarus had been listening and wanted Envy to know.

Well, he certainly knew.

Envy stared at the infamous symbol—an anatomical heart, struck through the center with a skull-headed dagger that dripped blood—his breathing turning slow and even as a killing calm overtook him.

The vampire prince might be *un*dead, but there were still ways to change that.

THIRTY-NINE

EVERYTHING HAPPENED SO swiftly, Camilla didn't sense she was in danger until it was too late.

One moment she'd been on the brink of being swept up in a sea of erotic, unending lust, begging silently to forever be linked to her dark prince.

The next she was tumbling through realms. Her body felt like it was being torn apart, needles pricking and biting like teeth along every inch of her flesh. Her abductor remained a mere shadow until the portal—or whatever magic transported them—violently spit them out.

A large, cold hand shoved her to her knees.

She spun around, furious.

Whatever grit she'd clutched onto died.

Every instinct in her screamed that she should run. It wasn't the man's appearance as much as it was whatever she sensed comprised the fibers of him.

Tension thickened the air as they considered each other.

Outwardly, he looked like any other member of court. His clothing was simple but fine. A shirt any lord would wear tucked beneath a dark swallowtail coat. Tawny breeches fit snugly on long, toned legs. Supple leather riding boots rose to his calves.

He was powerfully built, a male made to fight.

His short chestnut hair was tousled like he either couldn't be bothered to tame it or preferred to look wild and inspire wicked thoughts. His penetrating eyes were framed with a fringe of thick, dark lashes.

It was those arresting eyes—crimson bordering on black—that gave away *what* he was.

Vampire.

She swallowed thickly.

"It would be unwise to give me trouble." His voice was gravelly, rough.

A trickle of fear paralyzed Camilla.

He crouched, leveling her with a hard look that promised violence if she didn't play nicely. Even from this new position, nearly kneeling before her, he exuded power.

"Understand?"

Camilla nodded, her mouth suddenly as dry as the beach they'd landed on.

He looked her over once more, then stood.

"Get up, little lamb. Fix your gown."

Camilla clutched her bodice and adjusted herself; she'd forgotten that the Prince of Envy had wrested it down in a fit of passion. It felt like hours had passed since she had been in his arms, not minutes. If she could run far enough away...

She glanced around at their surroundings, stomach sinking as her worst fears came to life.

There wasn't anywhere *to* run.

Not that she would outrun a vampire. They were no longer in the woods or even close to the frozen tundra that signified the demon prince's domain. They were on a seemingly deserted beach with black glittering sand and matching water, tendrils of fog drifting along the shore.

A pair of crimson moons hung in the sky, two watchful eyes from hell.

The air was warm, uncomfortably so.

A fact that wasn't surprising, as vampires didn't produce body heat.

Lord save her, Camilla was *in* the vampire realm and the Prince of Envy was nowhere to be seen.

As if reading her mind, the vampire said, "Your lover won't be joining us. His kind is currently unwelcome on Malice Isle."

Malice Isle. The island nation home to vampires was aptly named.

The very atmosphere felt threatening, foreboding, like it wanted to sink its teeth into travelers and taste their deepest fears.

To their left a tropical forest—or what had once been a tropical forest but was now thick with rot and death—stretched as far as she could see.

In the distance beyond that a Gothic tower rose high into the clouds, like a demon rising up from the Underworld, surveying its fiery domain.

A bruising shade on the horizon indicated that sunrise was not far off; if she could make it for another few moments, she stood half a chance.

"Move, little lamb."

"Where?" Camilla asked, stalling.

She didn't comment on the name he'd given her. The warning was clear: In his mind Camilla was on her way to slaughter. He saw no need to name his meal.

He jerked his chin to the left.

A cave mouth yawned wide, a bastion of safety for the twilight creature and certain death for Camilla. If the vampire trapped her inside, she would stand little chance of escape.

"I don't care for the dark," Camilla said. "Mr...."

"Blade." He smiled, fangs gleaming. "Now move before I *make* you."

Blade didn't give her a chance to act on her own, he hauled her to her feet and roughly pushed her toward the cave. He didn't hide his supernatural strength, didn't pull back like Envy must have been doing each time he touched her.

Blade dragged her across the sand, the grains seeping into her slippers, chafing her skin as she kicked her feet, scrambling for purchase. They were just outside the cave and no amount of struggling would break the vampire's iron grip.

Blade brought his mouth to her neck, and she stilled. "Don't forget to bow."

He shoved her across the cave opening.

Instead of finding herself inside the cave as she'd expected, she staggered into a beautifully appointed chamber. She blinked at the gleaming black floors, her reflection wide-eyed and wild where it stared back at her.

The cave was a portal to the castle.

Camilla immediately schooled her features.

Looking like prey in a place where she *was* prey wouldn't serve her.

Her attention drifted along the polished floor to the walls, black brocade shot through with crimson threads.

Her heart pounded. Her attention slid farther, to the center of the room.

A dais, a throne, and...there sat the vampire prince himself, hair pale wheat, eyes ice blue, an inhuman expression on his ageless face. He was taking her in, his gaze traveling from the top of her head, pausing on her neck, then continuing down to her feet until he dragged it back up and fastened it to her face.

He did not seem impressed. It was either very fortunate or extremely unfortunate.

Recalling what Blade had said, Camilla went to her knees, dipping her chin to her chest. Far better to play the game and live than choose defiance and end up dead.

Or worse.

She kept her attention fixed on the floor in front of her, even as a pair of buffed boots silently stepped into her line of sight, the toes gleaming silver.

He moved like a shadow.

Two icy fingers lifted her chin, forcing her to gaze back. Into the eyes of a monster.

A beautiful monster.

Camilla's mouth went dry, her command over her body drifting away. She'd heard rumors that royal vampires were the most lethal, the most powerful, especially when they touched you. Those stories were horribly true.

The prince hadn't even spoken yet, hadn't done more than gently press two finger pads to her skin, and Camilla's body was ready to give him anything he desired.

An overwhelming need to please him, to arch her neck or offer her wrist, allowing him the honor of penetrating her skin with his fangs, overtook her.

What made it more terrifying was that she remained *aware* of the danger, the terror of what he was doing, but she was powerless to resist. Her body *wanted* his venom.

His gaze turned molten as it traveled along her skin.

A few moments earlier, even more flesh had been exposed from when she and Envy had been mad with desire. Camilla silently thanked Blade for telling her to cover up; that tiny mercy was a lifeline.

The prince held up her arm, his thumb stroking the pulse point at her wrist.

Terror gripped her mind, but her body buzzed. She *wanted* to cry, but only managed a small whimper that sounded suspiciously close to need.

"Your Highness."

The cool voice cut through the heat.

"This is the one who said your name. I found her with Envy."

The prince dropped her arm, his nostrils flaring, scenting her.

She stumbled back, no longer caring if she offended him. Camilla wanted to be as far away from his deadly touch as possible, though her body still angled toward him, yearning. His hold over her hadn't dissipated fully yet.

He looked her over with new interest.

"Envy's paramour."

The vampire prince's voice was silky, designed to seduce. She wondered how many mortals had lost their lives to that sinful sound.

"Or a diversion, Zarus."

"One way to find out."

"I would strongly counsel sending her back," Blade said. "Wrath is primed to attack. We don't need to lose a potential ally in Envy, too."

The prince's smile was razor-sharp.

"Bathe her. I want the demon stench removed before dinner."

Camilla didn't return to her full senses until Blade dragged her out of the throne room and slammed the door shut.

He whirled on her.

"Do you wish to start a war, little lamb?"

"It doesn't seem to matter what I want," she said, rubbing her arms.

"Allow me to impart some advice." Blade advanced on her, rage burning in his crimson gaze. "Do not offer yourself up to the prince. Pitting two courts against each other won't end well for anyone."

"As if I had any choice. You do realize his touch removes all bodily control?"

His gaze darkened with suspicion.

"Not possible. That only happens when he gifts a mortal with his tongue. Terror should be clawing at your heart. Not desire."

Blade's attention swept the corridor, and she could see he was thinking quickly. He yanked her forward again, his voice low.

"Does Envy know what you are?"

No, but he's been trying hard to figure it out, she thought.

"I'm an artist."

Blade slammed her up against the wall.

"No amount of magic hides the truth in blood."

Blade looked like he was considering biting her. She held his stare, silently daring him to.

She swore he'd regret it.

"Act afraid next time you're near Zarus, or he will become curious. I saw your reaction. Be thankful he wasn't paying attention. I promise intrigue is the last emotion you'd like to invoke in him. Do you wish to leave here?"

Camilla nodded.

"Then fight your true nature. Or find yourself his new princess." He finally loosened his hold, and she peeled herself away from the wall.

"Why are you helping me?"

"I am helping my court. We are standing on a knife's edge at present, thanks to a foolish play our prince recently made, and I will protect these vampires at all costs. If that means feeding you to the wolves, I won't hesitate to do that instead."

He leaned past her and opened a door she hadn't realized they'd been pressed up next to.

"Lock the door. Do not open it for anyone until I come for you again."

He didn't say the precaution was to keep the prince away, but Camilla knew that was what he'd meant. The warning was there, flashing in his eyes. The only reason she hadn't already been bitten was because Blade had intervened. Twice.

Camilla didn't want to owe him any more favors. She sensed they didn't come for free.

She ducked under his arm and did as he'd suggested, wondering, as the bolt slid home, how she'd control her senses the next time Zarus touched her. It seemed there were indeed some truths she couldn't run from, no matter how hard she tried.

Blood will out, as they say.

A castle filled with vampires was perhaps the most dangerous place for someone with secrets like hers.

Blade returned directly after her bath, looking freshly bathed as well.

Camilla couldn't help but feel disappointment when she heard his voice on the other side of the door. She'd never been the type to turn to religion, but she'd prayed Envy would be standing there, looking suspiciously close to an angel. Something she knew he'd hate.

While she'd been alone, she'd had time to go over the events leading up to her kidnapping.

The Fear Collector had given her that name, Prometheus. It was the vampire prince's true name apparently, which made sense. Otherwise Zarus would be inundated by too many creatures speaking his name on a daily basis. The Fear Collector had either known—or bet—Camilla would say it out loud.

She was certain of it. Which meant this *had* to be part of the game. All she had to do was survive until Envy puzzled out the clue, if he hadn't already done so.

Unless this was part of the game *she* needed to solve...her mind raced with new possibilities. If she'd been tricked into coming to the vampire court, the game master had a reason for it. There had to be something here he wanted her to find. But what?

Blade gave her an icy once-over when she kept the door half closed.

Instead of ushering her into the corridor, he pushed his way into her chamber.

"Give me your wrist."

She clutched it to her chest. The gowns she'd found waiting for her after the bath left much of her skin bare. The sleeveless dark plum one she wore now was the most decent, and its neckline plunged to her navel. The right side of the skirt had a slit to her thigh, and the silk clung to her every curve, as if she'd dipped herself in paint.

Two little straps held the top in place, but barely. One quick move in any direction and she'd be on full display. She shuddered to imagine being so bare in front of the vampire prince.

"No."

"Do you prefer to offer me your throat?"

His mouth curved into a taunting imitation of a smile as his gaze dropped to the dress's slit. There wasn't anything heated or sensual in his look, only mockery. Blade enjoyed reminding her that she was only a warm meal.

"There is always your femoral artery if you're feeling a bit more daring."

She leveled him with a hard look.

"Have you been drinking?"

"An idea came to me."

He casually dropped onto a high-backed chair, his gaze running over her again, this time contemplatively.

"Vampires are highly territorial by nature. Even the prince wouldn't touch what belonged to another, at least not without making a grand show of fighting for the prize. Should you be bitten by someone else, he'd have to submit an official challenge."

"Let me guess," she deadpanned, "*you* wish to own me."

"No, darling, I wish to get rid of you. As easily as possible."

He leaned forward, his hands clasped loosely in front of him. If it hadn't been for the hunger taking over his expression, he would have looked deceptively relaxed.

"One bite. One mark. Zarus won't move on you again."

In life things were rarely as simple as Blade was making this out to be.

In fact, whenever someone promised an easy solution to a difficult problem, it was wise to run as far and fast in the opposite direction as possible.

Camilla knew one thing with certainty: if Blade wanted her blood, that was precisely what she wouldn't trade. He clearly had his suspicions, and she would not confirm them.

At least not willingly.

Some secrets were worth holding on to for as long as possible, no matter the cost.

"There must be another solution," she said.

"Your demon prince won't come, lamb. It's you and me or you and Zarus. Unlike the prince, I won't turn you. And I won't try to fuck you."

"You could simply help me escape."

Blade's chuckle was deep and dark.

"Where would the fun be in that?"

Camilla didn't comment. She hadn't expected him to help her, so his rejection was unsurprising.

He rose from the chair, a dark omen in the flesh, and motioned for her to follow.

"It seems you've made your choice, then. Move. We're going to be late for dinner."

Camilla glanced down at her silken gown again, at all the tempting skin it left on display. Blade had made it clear he didn't view her as anything other than food, but other vampires wouldn't feel the same.

"I sincerely hope I'm not the entrée this evening."

She wasn't trying to be funny, but Blade's fathomless gaze suddenly twinkled with amusement.

"That all depends. Try to keep your wits about you and you'll probably be fine."

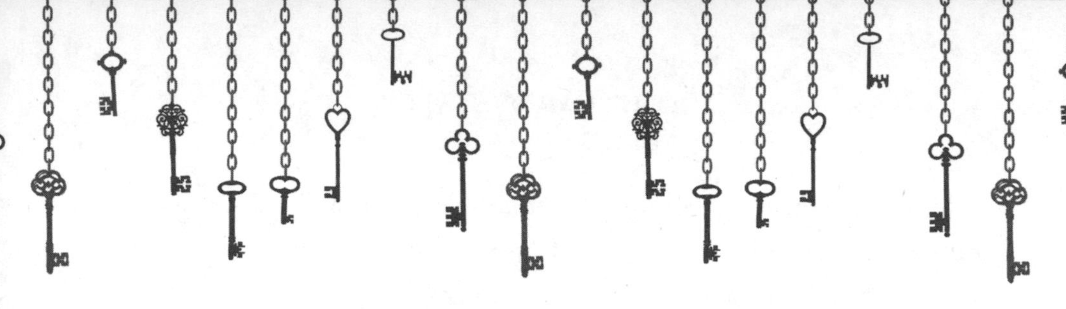

FORTY

ENVY STRODE THROUGH Bloodwood Forest toward his House of Sin, the Immortal Heart burning a hole in his pocket. Zarus had taken what was Envy's. Right out from under him.

Literally.

He carved his way through the dense wood and underbrush, the unnatural bark gleaming like bloody fingers in the moonlight. Fog wound its way around the base of the crimson trees, dense enough to obscure the ground and any nasty trap that might be set.

Envy didn't slow his stride. He barely glanced at his surroundings at all.

Between the escalating tension of the memory game he and Camilla had played and the abduction, he'd turned into a primal, territorial creature driven by instincts to take back and protect what was his. There'd been no cunning prince. Only snarling demon.

Envy supposed it was a result of feeling too much of his sin after so carefully doling it out over the last few years. He'd been distracted. He'd almost forgotten who he was, what was at stake, and nearly raced off to the vampire court without a plan.

But exploding into the vampire court would have been a terrible move.

His envy eventually cooled to that dangerous place he sought deep inside, clearing his mind until each piece of the last few hours had come together at last.

There are many riddles, many games, many players. If an ice prince falls, will a crimson one rise? I suppose that depends on who does the slaying. Blood must spill.

The Fear Collector's message was meant to be misleading, but Envy understood which part had been the real riddle when Camilla said that foul name.

It had clicked into place at once: The vampire prince must die. And a crimson-eyed heir must take his place.

"Gods' bones." Would this game never end? Lennox clearly had a deeper goal than even Envy had imagined, using his players to move much larger pieces around the Underworld on his behalf.

Unless having the vampire prince die was only about causing chaos—Lennox thrived on chaos, created it as often as he could. The Fae and their eons of life found it broke up the monotony of immortality.

Envy already knew that Wrath and his brothers would not be pleased with what he'd have to do next. It would be too risky, cause too much upheaval. But Envy had no choice.

Camilla was gone and Lennox would have his chaos one way or another. Envy's court's falling would also cause upheaval in their realm. And he vowed to protect his demons at any cost.

He'd made no such vow to the vampire court. So he'd orchestrate a regicide. Even if it furthered the Unseelie King's plot.

Pulling it off wouldn't be easy. Envy would need to somehow convince the only red-eyed royal he knew of to murder his crown prince in cold blood.

It would unveil Blade's secret. One he'd kept hidden from the rest of his court for two centuries. Until he'd been sired, there had never been another crimson-eyed royal.

At least not to Envy's knowledge.

Envy would need Alexei to deliver the message. It would be the only way to ensure that Blade took the request seriously and didn't tell Envy to go fuck himself.

He'd send Alexei immediately, then he'd—

A giant silver tree with gnarled wood and ebony leaves with silver veins drew him up short. The Curse Tree.

Envy's mind spun to a painting he had in his collection—and the silver plaque he'd had made to explain the fable surrounding this magical tree. He'd read it so many times over the years, he'd memorized the damn thing.

CURSE TREE FABLE

Deep in the heart of Bloodwood Forest lies a tree planted by the Crone herself. It is said, among other favors, the tree will consider hexing a sworn enemy if the desire to curse them is true.

To request the Crone's Curse: Carve their true name in the tree, write your wish on a leaf plucked from its branches, then offer the tree a drop of blood. Take the leaf home and place it beneath your pillow. If it is gone when you arise, the Crone accepted your offer and has granted your wish. She is the mother of the Underworld—beware of her blessing.

Envy's skin prickled. He drifted closer to the tree, picking his way over the rotted roots littering the ground, making forward movement trickier. The roots looked like broken bones jutting up from the earth in a failed attempt to free themselves from this cursed forest.

Mist slithered around his boots, wrapped around his legs. Whether drawing him closer to the tree or trying to push him away, it didn't matter. He could have sworn he'd seen something carved into it that made his pulse quicken.

He crunched over brittle leaves that had fallen, pausing at the wide trunk, then swore.

LEVIAETHAN

Not many guessed the correct spelling of Envy's true name; it was one of the most highly guarded secrets a demon prince could keep. The princes were always known by the sin they ruled over, keeping their true name from anyone who'd attempt to bind them.

That his name was carved into the Curse Tree was highly troubling.

He scanned the area, noticing fresh sawdust blanketing the frost-kissed leaves near the carving. Whoever had carved his true name had done so recently. Probably within minutes.

He thought of the gossip column, of the rumored player who was seen heading to this very forest. There were no coincidences while the game was underway.

He pulled his House dagger from its sheath, canting his head to listen. Bugs chirped and buzzed, the sound drowning out any footsteps.

But the player was close. Envy sensed it now. Swore he felt the air holding its breath along with whoever dared to curse him. As if he weren't already cursed enough.

He circled the wide tree trunk, listening. Watching.

The fog and mist played with his senses, like smoke and mirrors, causing shadows to flicker around his peripheral vision. The player was using it to their advantage.

Or so they foolishly thought.

Envy was the predator in these woods. And he enjoyed a good hunt every now and then.

He moved like a shadow, senses reaching out.

There.

Crouched behind an evergreen bush.

The coward ducked his head to his knees, keeping his face turned away.

Envy raised his blade, his intent clear.

A twig snapped behind him.

Envy stiffened.

"Don't touch him."

The voice was familiar, and unwelcome.

The Goddess of Death had arrived.

"He's mine."

Vittoria appeared as if from nowhere and drifted over to the player, running her hands through his hair. Assured he was still living, she then tugged him to his feet.

He did as she commanded.

Envy recoiled. The player was Fae. Not human. His elongated ears were pierced several times, the little suns signaling the Seelie Court. Vittoria leaned in and kissed him, completely unfazed by the demon blade Envy still held.

Envy gritted his teeth. "He's part of the game. He belongs to Lennox."

Vittoria ignored him, stepping back.

"I know. But he came to me." She gave the Fae an appreciative look. "He was *very* persuasive with asking for my help in his little game."

Envy drew in a deep breath. It didn't take his annoyance away.

"You gave him my true name."

She finally glanced over her shoulder, lavender gaze raking over Envy. "Not outright. He had to work hard for it. I gave him a nearly impossible task. He won."

Envy sensed she wanted him to ask about the bargain she'd struck but refused to do so. It didn't matter. The end result was all he cared about.

Predictably, Vittoria's frustration grew. She turned on her Fae. "Show him."

The male had the good sense to look scared.

The Goddess of Death was not known to be merciful. When she wanted something, she got it. If someone refused, she made them regret it. She was one of the few beings in the Underworld who could kill an immortal with True Death. Not that Envy wanted to think about that.

"Now," she said, eyes glowing as her power churned.

The Fae spared one last look at Envy, then... his glamour fell over him.

Envy stared at a mirror image of himself.

"Your obsession with me is getting sad," he drawled. "Fucking someone wearing my face still isn't the same thing, darling."

Vittoria's demonic hand darkened at the fingertips, death charring her own skin. Soon, Envy knew, her fingers would lengthen and end in talons. The better to pluck out hearts with.

"It has nothing to do with you," she said, voice pitched low. "Only what bedding you can do for my purposes."

"You know just what to say to make a male feel wanted."

"Would you rather I stroke your ego?" she asked, her voice a purr. "Tell you no male will ever please me like you? I think you hear that enough."

"Only when warranted."

"Maybe I wanted to let the fantasy of it ride me again and again in my dreams."

"It wasn't the fantasy or dreams, darling, but the Fae riding you."

She gave him a withering look.

"Our joining is inevitable. You cannot deny me for eternity."

He knew exactly why she wanted him. Only to see whether his brother Pride would become jealous. Her games were never-ending but held no appeal for Envy, unlike Camilla.

She motioned to the Fae wearing Envy's skin. "Go on. Pull his cock out and see how it compares to yours." Her smile grew wicked. "And then I want you to worship it."

The Fae dropped to his knees, hand already on Envy's trousers.

Envy halted the Fae's movements.

"While I appreciate the artful way of telling me to go fuck myself," he said, "I'm bored. I have a game to win. Aside from riding me, I'm sure we can find something else you want."

Vittoria's attention roved over him again, he could practically see her scheme. She'd known all along it would come to this. She whispered a spell that put the Fae in a trance.

"Your heart for his death. Before you open that troublesome mouth of yours, know it's my only counteroffer. Accept and he dies, or decline, and I escort him safely from these woods." She motioned toward the silver tree behind them. "Less you forget, he already carved your name. If he lives, you yourself will be cursed."

Lennox must have spies in the Seven Circles, ones who were well aware of his last run-in with the Goddess of Death. It was one more twist of the knife, quite literally.

Vittoria had removed Envy's heart recently, and it had significantly weakened him while it slowly grew back. His power was already slipping, thanks to the ward he had to keep up around his House of Sin. He didn't have the energy needed to regenerate a heart in the middle of the game.

But if the player left these woods now, placed that leaf under his pillow before he slept tonight, Envy would have another set of unknown troubles to watch out for.

It was a gamble he couldn't risk. The Fae had to die.

He kept his emotions locked away, mind reaching for any other solution. He didn't want to be the cause of another death, but his court was at stake and he'd do anything to save them.

Vittoria's gaze shimmered with dark victory. She knew he'd take the deal.

Hearts were one of her favorite sources of power.

Seeing no alternative, Envy gave a slight jerk of his chin.

"What was that?" Vittoria asked sweetly. As if she didn't damn well know. "You accept?"

He allowed every last drop of hatred he felt for her to shine through in his expression.

"Yes. I accept."

Her smile was as nefarious as they come. With lightning quick reflexes, she punched a hole through the Fae's chest and tore out his heart.

The Fae dropped into an unmoving heap, trance broken, he reverted to his true form, his eyes wide with shock. He was dead before he'd hit the ground.

Vittoria's demonic hand dripped with sparkling blood as she pivoted to Envy, clutching the throbbing heart close. She looked at it with approval only once before magicking it off to her secret chamber, where she kept them in jars.

Gods only fucking knew what she did with that morbid collection.

"Will he rise again?" Envy asked, toeing the body.

Vittoria gave him a bemused look. "He was given True Death."

He shot her a sharp look, not liking her tone.

"True Death is not what you're giving me," he said. "Remember that."

"Don't worry, little prince. I'm not finished playing with you yet. A deal is a deal."

She moved to stand before him, her talon carving his shirt open as she slowly dragged it downward, cutting some of his flesh as she exposed his chest.

She licked her lips, then flicked her gaze to his.

"This will hurt."

He'd no sooner braced himself for the pain than her talons ripped into his chest.

She clutched his heart in her demonic hand, feeling it beat a few brutal times, before wrenching it out.

Her delighted, cruel laughter was the last thing he heard.

Darkness descended and Envy collapsed.

FORTY-ONE

CAMILLA REALLY OUGHT to stop searching every shadow in the vampire castle for Envy.

Blade was correct about one thing: the demon prince *wasn't* coming to save her.

Maybe she'd gotten it wrong, and the Fear Collector hadn't somehow implanted the name in her mind. Or maybe the next clue had brought the demon elsewhere.

Envy had his game, and Camilla had hers now. She vowed to pour her energy into plotting her own escape and would not think of the prince again.

They had no true future. Engaging in a dark flirtation was not the same as falling in love.

Camilla wouldn't confuse any game with reality.

With each step she took deeper into the vampire court, she released herself from thoughts of Envy, or anyone else, for that matter. Camilla was her own hero and would plot her way out of this.

She and Blade strolled along a darkened corridor, the floors the same gleaming black as the throne room, the walls papered in a deep burgundy brocade.

Tapestries hung every few feet, giving the corridor a bit of texture and color. Even being in the heart of enemy territory, she couldn't help but admire the art they passed, until she saw the scenes that had been captured.

Bloodbaths, literally. Every which way a vampire might dine on a human, shape-shifter, or Fae was immortalized in the morbid art.

Camilla's heart pounded a wild beat.

Blade slowly glanced in her direction, his attention fixed on the pulse point in her neck.

Another couple emerged from the opposite end of the corridor, making her heart race faster.

Blade had her up against the wall, his body blocking the other vampire's, his eyes burning crimson. He brought his lethal mouth to her ear.

She snapped, bucking against him.

He clamped down on her, using his weight to pin her.

"Calm the fuck down *now*."

Tension coiled inside her, ready to lash out.

Blade shook her until her teeth rattled.

"I'm trying." She focused on her breathing. In, then out.

"Try harder." He gripped her waist painfully. "Your pulse is like a beacon. You'll attract every forsaken vampire on this isle if you don't relax."

Steps approached them, louder, closer, driving Camilla's heart rate up.

Blade cursed, his hand shooting down her leg to the exposed skin. His icy fingers shocked her into stillness.

"Pretend, lamb. Pretend you're enthralled. Or this will turn ugly."

Camilla froze, her body tense, as the sound of the other couple drew nearer.

Blade's cold fingers traveled higher, then pinched her, drawing her attention to his cruel face. Anger replaced her fear. Which, from his slight look of relief, was exactly what the vampire had been trying to do.

"Prick," she murmured, earning a wider grin.

His icy fingers only roamed higher, drawing her ire.

There was no passion in his crimson gaze, only a warning.

His hand traveled up until he grabbed her bottom, the move meant to indicate possession.

"She smells *divine.*" The female's voice was throaty, sensual. "Share her or take her to a private chamber, Blade."

Camilla dared a glance over Blade's shoulder, and any residual fear melted away at once. She wasn't looking at the female, she was staring at the male beside her.

The human.

"Lord Vexley?"

He gave her a haughty look.

"Miss Antonius."

He acted as if they were at another boring party in Waverly Green, not thrust deep into the bowels of the vampire court.

"What are *you* doing here?"

"Don't be so surprised by my otherworldly connections, darling," he sneered. "Did you think I only held power in Waverly Green?"

Camilla didn't think he held much power there, either, except, of course, through blackmailing *her.*

The female vampire stroked his chest, purring as he puffed it up more. The fool was going to entice her to bite him right then and there.

Vexley looked Camilla over disdainfully, his cool blue gaze raking over every inch of skin he could see past Blade. His attention fell to the slit of her gown, narrowing on where Blade's hand moved beneath the silk.

Camilla gritted her teeth, hoping she hid her snarl. The damned vampire was stroking her bottom, his smirk daring her to ruin their show.

"When you tire of the vampire," Vexley said at last, "come find me. There's a chance I may forgive your transgressions. Especially now that you're so... uninhibited."

Camilla was going to murder him. She tried to shove her way around Blade, but he was as immovable as a mountain range.

Blade jerked his head in a quick approximation of a *no.*

Camilla glared at him, wondering when they'd formed this uneasy alliance.

"Let's join them for dinner, my love." The female vampire's hands were now caressing Vexley in places Camilla never wished to witness. "It promises to be fun."

Vexley grabbed a fistful of her silky black hair, guiding her to her knees.

"Convince me, lover."

Blade shoved off the wall and escorted Camilla quickly toward the dining chamber, leaving Vexley and his vampire to their games.

Once they rounded the corner, Camilla paused.

"Is she going to kill him?"

Blade shook his head.

"He's been granted asylum."

"Why?"

"When the Unseelie King submits a request, it's wise to accept it. Even Zarus recognizes that."

Camilla's blood chilled.

"Vexley is playing the game."

"Appears so."

"Do you know what's at stake?"

Blade slanted a look her way.

"Don't know, don't care to know. It's nothing good if the Unseelie are involved."

Blade stopped outside a wide set of double doors, carved with more scenes of death. They were an off-white like bones bleached in the sun. Camilla realized with a start that they *were* bones bleached by the sun. Human bones. Hundreds of them.

Looking at them closely, she saw places where they'd been gnawed, the teeth marks unmistakably created by fangs.

She stepped back, a surge of fear urging her to run the other way.

"*Don't* run."

Blade's tone implied he'd chase her and that would be ill-advised. He was a predator first, the need to hunt in his blood.

His large hand gripped her arm, a cold manacle tethering her to his side.

"Try not to speak to Zarus or draw his attention. We'll sit as far away as is acceptable. At the first opportunity, we'll leave." He looked her over, his expression harsh. "If you cannot control yourself, I *will* bite you. Understand?"

Camilla inhaled deeply, then nodded. If she lost control around the vampire prince again, she *wanted* Blade to bite her. Hopefully it would bring her body back under her control.

With his free hand, Blade pushed the doors open, revealing a dining room that was more bordello than banquet hall.

Sultry immediately sprang to mind. The chamber was a study of deep, rich colors, the favored ones being deep purple and black. Dark, decadent, and tempting; the sort of room that invited you to come in, lie back, and indulge each of your senses.

Floor-to-ceiling windows opened onto a wide terrace overlooking the sea, the warm, salty breeze snaking lazily through the chamber.

A long dining table was divided by a deep plum runner straight down its center.

Glasses filled with various dark purple and red liquids—wine and blood and God only knew what else—were placed at each setting, while trays of purple fruit sat untouched in the center. Plums and grapes and figs and fruits she had no names for glistened in the soft candlelight.

Several alcoves were fitted with sheer panels that fluttered with each sea breeze, showing off private areas stacked with pillows where vampires lounged.

Some talked, some made love, others sipped from chalices filled with what could only be blood. The moment Camilla's gaze landed on the prince a wave of panic rolled through her; thankfully he was otherwise preoccupied and hadn't noticed her.

Blade tugged her toward the end of the table and slammed a glass down in front of her.

"Drink." Blade blocked her view of the prince. "Now."

"Wine is the last thing I need," she whispered. "Are you mad?"

"If your bodily senses are dulled slightly, you might not succumb to royal appeal so easily if he touches you."

That logic made little sense. When the doors opened behind them, bringing two more blue-eyed royals into the chamber, along with a new wave of fear that rivaled the one caused by the prince, Camilla downed her glass. Blade had been correct; it somehow eased the power of their magic.

He poured another.

"Sip this only when necessary."

Camilla settled into her seat more comfortably, then slowly took in the room.

Murmured voices carried toward them, low and soothing. If it hadn't been for the occasional biting, it would have seemed like a quiet, intimate affair among close friends.

Perhaps a little *too* intimate. Skin slapping against damp skin, softened by dewy perspiration, added a sensual applause much too close by. Camilla certainly was *not* in Waverly Green anymore. She didn't look even when the heavy breathing turned to soft moans of rapture.

Blade slung an arm around her chair, his head canted toward her. To anyone observing them, he would seem interested. Possessive. Like she belonged to *him*.

He twirled a strand of her hair around his finger, almost absently, but she knew Blade didn't do anything without reason.

Camilla hid her cringe when a group of humans was brought in, dressed even more scantily than she was. They paired off with vampires immediately, and Camilla could sense the new couples drawing the approval of the room.

As the first bites took place, Camilla watched the bliss unfold. The human woman nearest to her was already climbing onto the table and lying back, her legs spreading wide in invitation. Two female vampires moved to stand near her feet, each caressing a different leg, drawing her skirts high, then leaning in to suckle the artery in each of her upper thighs. After they'd sipped her blood, they began licking at the woman's sex.

The mortal arched up from the table, her fingers trailing down her breasts, dislodging the flimsy fabric of her dress. Her hands traveled down, across her stomach, then slipped into her own folds while the vampires began lathing her breasts.

A male vampire strolled over to join their little group, standing across the table by the mortal's head. When she noticed him, she cried out, begging for him to let her taste him. The vampires around the table called out in approval. One of the vampires replaced the human's fingers, pumping her own in and out as the woman moaned.

The vampire at last released his cock, then granted the woman's wish, pulling her toward him until her head hung off the table, allowing her to take him fully down her throat. The two other vampires continued pleasuring her—one stroking her sex, the other tending to her breasts while the male thrust into her mouth.

It couldn't be comfortable, Camilla thought, having the blood rush to her head, allowing the male to guide himself even deeper.

Still, he took the human's wrist, fangs at last penetrating her flesh, and groaned with pleasure as he drank.

Camilla couldn't look away.

The passion, the desire, it flowed as freely as the blood they sipped, and no one batted an eye. The vampires sitting nearest them turned back to their conversations.

It was as if an orgy weren't happening while they mingled with old friends.

Camilla couldn't imagine Waverly Green's nobility witnessing such an act and remaining as cool and calm, they'd all been scandalized by the kissing at Envy's masquerade ball. She laughed softly at the absurdity of her thoughts. Camilla had been just as shocked that night.

"Dinner and a show," Blade said, startling her. He, at least, understood this wasn't par for the course. At least not in Camilla's world.

Soon the whole quartet was moaning, pleasure rippling through them as the first waves of their orgasms hit.

Envy's taunt came back to her. *You'd come as you died and beg for more with your last breath.*

"My brethren have unique tastes." Blade leaned in, his voice dark with amusement. "But I've never understood the appeal of playing with one's food."

A shock of blond hair skirting the perimeter caught her attention.

Vexley and a new vampire had arrived. This female wore something much bolder than the last—leather that hugged her curves, showing off flawless skin and a pair of batlike wings Camilla hadn't noticed on anyone else. She had a whiplike tail she was using to swat at Vexley, which he didn't appear to mind in the slightest.

They went straight to one of the private alcoves, her long wavy hair flowing behind her.

"Do you have wings?" she asked Blade.

He leaned in, breath cool enough to make her shiver as it whispered across the shell of her ear.

"Nyghtshade is a succubus."

Camilla's attention shifted back to Vexley. Of course he'd get tangled up with a demon who lived for pleasure almost as much as he did.

Perhaps they'd have long-tailed demon children and live happily ever after in hell.

One could only hope.

"Zarus won't allow anyone to harm him until the game ends. But he'd better be gone before then. Asylum only lasts so long. Like I said, *I* don't play with my food, but others obviously enjoy it."

Camilla was relieved that Vex the Hex wouldn't become someone's dinner this evening. If he was stupid enough to outstay his welcome and bed every vampire and demon that caught his attention, then he deserved whatever fate he was dealt.

"I need to speak with him again."

Blade pressed his lips together, his attention sliding toward the end of the table where the prince now stood, his face buried in the neck of a handsome human. The mortal dropped his trousers and stroked himself as the prince fed, a beatific expression on his face.

If Camilla wasn't careful, that could be her.

"Make it quick."

Blade pulled her chair out, escorting her around the far edge of the chamber, keeping as much distance between her and the royals as possible.

He flicked the sheer curtains back, then followed her inside. Two large velvet pillows were unoccupied, so Camilla sat on one and Blade took the other, his knee brushing against hers.

The slit on her gown parted, baring her almost entirely. There were no undergarments in her suite, not even daring lingerie. Years of human modesty kicked in and she gripped the two sides of her skirt, attempting to cover herself, to no avail.

Blade dropped his tailcoat in her lap, his look cautioning her not to comment.

Vexley lay back, one arm bent under his head, the other fondling the succubus kissing her way up his neck. He watched Camilla get situated, eyes slitted as he slipped a hand down the front of his lover's pants.

"Crawling back so soon, darling?"

"I know you're playing Lennox's game."

Camilla had been wondering what Vexley's clues might have been and had a sinking suspicion she knew exactly what he'd needed to find.

"What was your first clue?"

Still fully clothed, the succubus climbed on top of him, grinding against his arousal to reclaim his attention. Wonderful. They were going to fornicate right there.

"Vexley," Camilla hissed.

He paid her no mind. The succubus pulled his erection out, her gaze hungry.

Vexley grabbed Nyghtshade's bottom, squeezing and kneading, his focus entirely diverted. He slapped her leather-clad rump with a flat palm, lips quirked on one side.

"Take these off, love. Then hop up and ride me backward."

"Vexley," Camilla said more loudly. "Stop."

Nyghtshade's clothing vanished from one blink to the next, her tail whipping back and forth like a cobra being charmed from its basket. She flipped around, then sank onto Vexley's less-than-impressive erection, giving him an unobstructed view of her bottom and that tail as she began bouncing up and down along his length.

Camilla was completely taken off guard at the sight, but Vexley wasn't at all concerned. As if it were commonplace to take someone with a forked tail to bed. In front of an audience.

He grabbed the tail, winding it around his fist like rope. Or a length of hair. Then thrust up, fucking the succubus with vigor.

May the gods be merciful and burn the image from my mind, Camilla silently begged.

Unsurprisingly, no divine interference arrived, wiping that hellish scene from her memory. Camilla wished to be anywhere but sitting there. And Blade looked like he felt the same. His lip curled back as he shook his head.

"Vexley," Camilla gritted out. "What was the first clue you needed to solve?"

He rolled his eyes.

"I had to get the key."

Time seemed to freeze. And if it hadn't been for that horrid wet noise and Vexley's grunts, Camilla would have thought time *had* frozen.

"My key?" she asked, her voice rising.

Vexley gave her an annoyed look.

"Honestly, Camilla. Let it go. It's just a key."

My father's portal key.

Just as she'd suspected. She moved without thought, knocking the succubus off the lord, her hands fitted around his throat.

"How could you! *We* had a deal."

Camilla wasn't that strong, but she was furious and had taken the lord by surprise.

Vexley thrashed, bucking wildly, but she held on, intent on murdering the idiot. If he'd given the key to a Fae, there was little hope of her ever retrieving it.

"Where is it?" she demanded, hands digging into his flesh. "Do you still have it?"

"No," he spit out. "I gave it to a contact in the dark market for my next clue."

Vexley went to hit her, but Blade's hand clamped around his fist.

"Do *not* put your hands on her, mortal."

Vexley glowered but dropped his hands. "Get her the bloody hell off me, then."

Blade hauled Camilla to her feet.

But Camilla knew exactly where the key would have ended up. In the game master's wretched claws. She went to dive for Vexley again.

"Stop," Blade growled low in her ear. "You're drawing—"

"Tsk, tsk. You know the rules, Blade. Dinner is a time for fucking, not fighting."

The voice was temptation, desire, seduction, and death knitted together.

And it was entirely too close.

Lips brushed against Camilla's neck, a cool balm against the warm room. Her body wanted to lean into it, while her mind screamed to run.

"It's under control, Your Highness. The female was jealous. An emotion to be expected considering who she was with earlier."

Blade's tone was almost as hard as the grip he had on her arm. He was subtly trying to pull her farther away from the prince.

"We were just leaving."

"Actually," the seductive voice murmured, "there is a matter you need to see to. Now."

Blade's grip tightened, the pain a lifeline Camilla clung to.

"I'll see her to her—"

"She stays."

Zarus's command brooked no argument.

And suddenly Blade was leaving her here, with him. Death.

Camilla watched as Blade inclined his head, then left without a backward glance. He'd warned her he'd toss her to the wolves if it meant saving himself.

Her throat tightened as she glanced around, searching for a glass of wine to help dull the vampire prince's appeal.

Cool fingers wrapped around her wrist, drawing her nearer. Her body instantly forgot why it wanted to dull his appeal, why it would ever wish not to fully experience *this* feeling.

Beyond passion, beyond lust, there was no name to give the sensations his touch alone provoked. If he should kiss or bite her... Camilla felt boneless as she sank against a hard chest. Cold and smooth like marble. And just as still. No heartbeat thudded. Nothing but venom flowed through his veins.

A chair appeared, or perhaps it was a throne.

One moment Camilla was on her feet, the next she was perched on the vampire prince's knee. A mere brush of his fingertips had rendered her body under his full control.

In the distance the slow pounding of a drum began, the tempo akin to his missing heartbeat. She looked blankly out at the chamber, her senses addled the longer she remained in the vampire's arms. Whatever had seduced her clearly impacted everyone else, too.

Everywhere she turned, couples gave in to their desires. Males pleasured males, females pleasured each other, and mixed groups kissed and bit and sucked whoever caught their fancy.

Humans slashed their own flesh, allowing multiple vampires to lick and caress them.

Never killing, only tasting, pleasuring.

Blood lust took on a whole new meaning in the vampire court.

Camilla didn't realize that the prince's lips hovered along her throat until he pulled her closer, his hands skimming her shoulders, brushing her hair aside.

She struggled to remember why she needed to be alert. A game, a clue...

Camilla vaguely remembered what Blade had said about not appearing seduced by the prince's touch alone. She tried to remain alert, to tense.

To behave as if she were fearful and not yearning.

His breath was on her neck, his tongue so close to her skin. Envy had said a mere lick could cause her to come. She fought as hard as she could with her mind, trying to twitch even one finger, blink one eye. Anything to prove she was stronger than this.

Zarus's fingers angled her chin, tilting until her neck begged to be suckled.

A shiver finally shot down her spine. In pleasure, not fear. But she hoped the vampire prince couldn't tell the difference.

She mentally cried out for a miracle, for anything.

His mouth came down on her, fangs scraping along her skin, sending cold fire as he punctured—

But then he was gone, crashing backward against his throne.

Camilla went toppling from his lap, their connection and his control vanishing. Her screams finally broke free from her throat.

And she fell directly into the Prince of Envy's waiting arms.

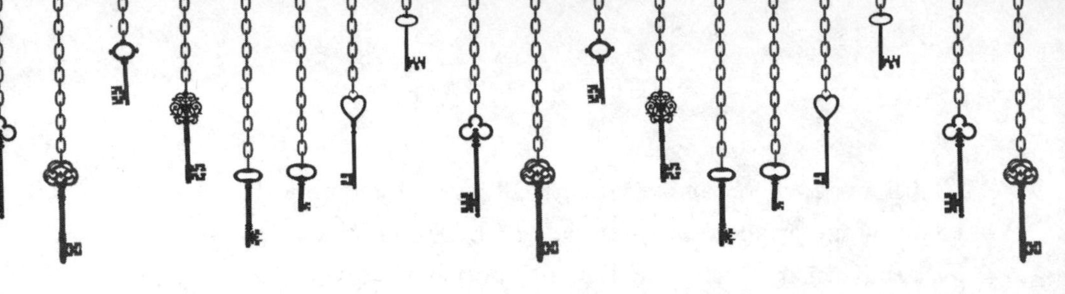

FORTY-TWO

ENVY HELD CAMILLA tightly to his chest, hoping she was too distracted to notice his lack of a pounding heart. He didn't want his confrontation with the Goddess of Death known.

Zarus would use the information to his benefit.

Yet, even in his weakened state, Envy's sin chilled the whole cursed dining room. Frost coated the chamber in thin sheets, the vampires hissing like the reptiles they secretly were as the temperature plummeted. His arms shook with the exertion of using his power, but he kept on.

He'd almost been too late. If the vampire had turned Camilla...

Zarus recovered almost instantly, flashing his fangs as he brushed imaginary lint from his suit. He plucked up the dagger Envy had thrown, sneering at it.

"You always know how to make an entrance." His gaze was hard. "Though I'm a bit insulted you used this blade instead of your House dagger."

That blade was mortal steel washed in holy water. It didn't kill a vampire, but it stung like hell. Next time he'd coat his blade with rosary peas, which would do a lot more than sting.

Though, if all went as planned, there wouldn't *be* a next time.

"Apologies, Zarus. I hate to stab and dash off, but you rudely interrupted us earlier. I'd like to get her back to *my* bed."

Zarus arched a brow. Arrogant twat.

"The woman said my name, which makes her *mine*."

The room chilled further. Envy had little power to spare but didn't bother trying to hide his darkening mood. Camilla was *his*.

Zarus grinned. "Unless of course you'd like to offer up a challenge."

Envy kept the smile from his lips. That was precisely what he'd come to do.

Camilla stared up at him as if she'd seen a ghost, her gold skin pale.

She hadn't thought he would come for her.

It was a wise deduction. One that should please him. He'd told her the game was his only focus. She wasn't entirely wrong. He was here because of it.

A twinge of *something* twisted deep inside him, though. Something not at all pleasant.

He *would* have come for her sooner if he hadn't run into trouble. But to admit that...

He flicked his attention around the room. Envy would prefer to have Camilla tucked safely into the guest cottage on his estate while he tended to this situation on his own.

There were at least twenty vampires, three of which were royal.

Zarus warded the castle using blood magic, so Envy couldn't just magic Camilla away to his House of Sin. Even not fully recovered, Envy could almost take down the vampires on his own, but Camilla complicated matters. He couldn't guard her *and* fight them all, at least not without posing a great risk to her. If he'd been uninjured, it would still have been too risky.

"Then I offer a challenge." Envy's voice was laced with boredom. "Your life for hers."

They were sent back to what must have been Camilla's chambers while preparations for the challenge were made. The entire journey down the hall, she'd clutched onto Envy's hand so hard his bones ground together. If he'd been mortal, it would have bruised him or dislocated something.

Once in the room, she whirled.

"You cannot fight him," she said.

Not *Hello, wonderful to see you, thank you for stabbing my enemy.*

"If he kills you..."

"Your confidence in my abilities is overwhelming, pet. Zarus may be strong, but he's not more powerful than me."

Camilla scrutinized him.

"Is that hubris speaking or truth?"

"Did anyone harm you?"

She pursed her lips at his blatant change of subject and refusal to answer her question. Aggravation was good. It meant she was scared but otherwise all right.

"No. Blade guarded me. For a while."

Envy cocked his head, listening.

"Speaking of the crimson-eyed bastard."

The vampire slipped into the room, eyeing Envy as he crossed his arms over his chest and leaned against a far wall. Blade was wise to keep space between them.

With the image of Camilla sitting on Zarus's lap, his tongue on her skin, fangs just shy of penetrating her, Envy wasn't feeling very charitable.

His sin was still raging, searching for an outlet.

Blade knew that.

"You owe me," the vampire said, voice low.

Blade kept his attention fixed to Envy.

"Not if you get everything you want out of the deal," Envy said. "You spoke with Alexei about the details, I assume."

"Yes. I don't like it."

"You don't have to. You've seen what he's been like. What he did with Wrath. He tried to steal Wrath's wife Emilia. A move that no sane creature would make. Is he still really fit to lead your court?"

Camilla glanced between them, a slow realization dawning.

"You're one of his spies?"

"Associate, darling," Envy said. "No one likes the term *spy*."

"Mutual associate," Blade added.

They were reluctant allies when circumstances forced them to be. Other than that, neither he nor the vampire had much use for the other.

If it hadn't been for Alexei, Blade wouldn't have dealt with Envy at all. The vampires were brothers in a sense, each turned by the same sire. For some reason Blade's eyes were crimson instead of blue, but he was still royal. Not many knew of the connection between Envy's court and Blade.

And Envy kept it that way.

Camilla stalked over and slapped Envy's face. She knew it wouldn't harm him, so it was more a show of temper than anything else.

He raised his brows.

"To what do I owe that honor?"

"You work together?" she asked.

"Occasionally. I fail to see the issue."

"Did you have me kidnapped?"

His eyes narrowed.

"When, exactly, would I have had time to arrange a kidnapping? Before you shoved that memory into my mind, or while we were rolling around like fiends in the dirt? Surely I would have chosen a much more convenient time to have you abducted."

"You deserved the slap. If only for that memory you shoved into my mind first."

She turned those flashing silver eyes on Blade. He didn't hide his grin. The scourge of Malice Isle was amused. Blade *liked* her.

"You could have mentioned this association instead of saying he wasn't coming," Camilla said. "Or were you hoping to bite me?"

Blade's smile turned as sharp as the weapon he was named for.

"I'd even bite *him,* foul-tasting demon blood and all, if it suited my interests, lamb."

"If we're through with the pet names," Envy drawled, growing more annoyed as his sin ignited, "what information do you have?"

Blade's attention zeroed in on him, a knowing look flaring in his eyes as he glanced between Camilla and Envy. The vampire would be wise to keep his observations to himself.

"The challenge will begin an hour or so before sunrise in the arena. Gladiator-style in front of the entire court. Zarus wants to stir as much drama as possible. With a ticking clock, the tension thickens. He plans to use poison."

As if that would kill Envy. Though weakened as he was, it wouldn't be pleasant.

He kept his face a mask of nonchalance. No one could guess there was a chance he'd lose. He couldn't even think it himself.

"And?"

"The poison will act only to slow you, dull your senses and power. Much like his venom does. Once it takes effect, he'll remove your head and limbs and burn the pieces on a pyre."

Envy rolled his eyes.

"Pyres are so dull. Leave it to your prince to be so uninspired. Though I suppose he is still stuck in the Middle Ages."

Camilla looked stricken.

"Can't we escape through that cave?"

"We could." Envy reached over, tucking a silver lock behind her ear. "But that doesn't solve the problem. Zarus would just send someone else to collect you. And next time he'd strengthen his borders. Best to end this now."

Blade pushed himself off the wall and headed for the door.

"I'll return if there's any news."

Envy nodded, turning his attention back to Camilla. He waited until the vampire could no longer be heard in the corridor before speaking.

"Should anything go awry, Alexei will take you to House Wrath. Don't fight him. My brother will see to your safety, and his presence will make Zarus think twice before attacking."

"You just said you are more powerful."

He hesitated for a beat.

"Winning is not always about power. It's about who wants it more.

Zarus will not fight fairly or lay down his sword easily. He will make me earn that victory."

"It would be easier if you just left me here."

"You know I'd never do that."

Envy's hand curled around her chin, his touch gentle as he tipped her face up. She'd romanticized him again. Giving him a golden halo while ignoring the fact that his had broken long ago.

Because *he'd* shattered it.

"But you haven't asked the all-important question, my darling Camilla."

She scanned his face, knowing he was leading her into a trap, unable to see where it lay.

"Why?"

"You are much more than you seem, aren't you, Miss Antonius? Not human. But what? I have a feeling that if I knew that, I'd know why you're part of the game. Care to enlighten me?"

She held his gaze, offering a slight negation as her answer.

Whether she was admitting to not being human, or answering his question about enlightening him, it didn't matter.

"Why wouldn't I ever leave you here?" he asked again, bringing his mouth close to hers.

She'd wanted to taste the seam of his lips, and he wished to taste her lies. He brushed his lips against hers, the kiss barely anything at all.

Camilla's breath hitched.

He drew back.

"It appears you've forgotten the game, Miss Antonius. You are a requirement for me to win. Were you listening to the Fear Collector? I am exactly where I need to be."

Camilla winced, tried to jerk away, but he held on, forcing her gaze to remain locked on his, even as it turned hateful. He thought of the book she'd been reading at Sloth's. Knew there was more to the choice in her fairy-tale romance than she'd let on.

Better for her to despise him now.

Envy wasn't incapable of change. He simply didn't *wish* to change.

"I will never be your Prince Charming, Camilla. For now, you hold immense value to me. When your value runs out..."

He stroked her jaw, watching her eyes turn hard as steel.

She wanted to hurt him. It was written all over her pretty face.

"Best hope that doesn't happen until the game ends, pet. Or else you might see how wicked I truly am."

FORTY-THREE

A FEW TENSE hours later, Camilla sat beside Blade in the royal box overlooking the arena, her knuckles bone-white from gripping her fists tightly in her lap.

Far below them a circular patch of white sand stretched wide, surrounded by matching high, smooth walls designed to keep fighters on the ground.

Unlike the black-sand beach they'd arrived on, the snow-colored grains and stone were clearly chosen to show off spilled blood, something that could prove dangerous in an arena filled with vampires.

Camilla didn't want to think about what might happen if blood lust took over. Given how high up she was, there would be no way out but down through the thick of it.

Dawn was still a ways off, the strange double moons of Malice Isle casting an eerie red haze along the sand. Torches burned—the acrid scent of smoke rising on the thick, humid air.

Camilla's gown clung to her like a second skin from the oppressive heat, adding to her discomfort. *That* was the reason she couldn't sit still or take more than a few shallow breaths at a time. It was a necessary lie she kept silently repeating to herself.

Vampires poured into the tower from several entrances, filling the seats beyond capacity, their cheers creating a terrible cacophony as they pounded their fists and stomped their feet, waiting for the battle of princes to begin.

She glanced around, looking for Vexley, but he was either seated in the raging throng below or had decided to spend his time with his mistresses from hell.

Soon the metallic scent of blood mixed with the smoke. Tray after tray of blood cocktails was served and the crowd, already dangerous, was now drunk and raging.

"One thing is certain," Blade said, gaze locked on the pit below. "It will be interesting."

She was grateful he hadn't lied and said it would be all right.

Even with Envy's confidence, there was no telling how the fight would end. Immeasurable ass that he was, Camilla didn't want any harm to come to the demon prince.

Alexei entered the royal box, nodding to Blade as they silently exchanged places.

Camilla slanted a look in his direction. He was already watching her.

"His Highness said to wear these."

He held up two beautiful cuffs: wide silver bands fitted with what looked to be a hundred ruby shards.

"He said, and I quote, put them on and pretend he's cuffed you to his bed."

She rolled her eyes. Even now the demon was trying to distract her. He could say whatever he liked about only keeping her safe for the game. His actions said otherwise.

Alexei handed her one cuff at a time.

She noticed he only touched the silver.

"Aversion to rubies?"

"Not quite." A smile ghosted across his face. "Rosary peas mixed with rubies. Highly lethal to vampires."

"He expects I'll need them?"

"A precaution, Miss Antonius."

She gingerly took the cuffs and put them on. They fit as if they'd been forged for her.

"They were," Alexei said.

"Why is it that everyone in this realm can read my mind?"

"Your expression tells your thoughts. It's minute," he added, "nothing a mortal would notice. But you're no longer surrounded by mortals. Creatures here pay attention to everything; no detail is too small. You need to constantly wear a mask."

"I suppose being surrounded by other predators keeps one sharp."

He inclined his head in agreement but didn't comment further.

Instead, he handed her a matching necklace he pulled from a satchel she hadn't noticed, his cool fingers accidentally brushing hers before he quickly drew back.

She searched his blue eyes for answers. She hadn't felt any loss of her senses, and his eyes identified him as royal.

"Your touch doesn't impair me the way Zarus's does. Why is that?"

His attention sharpened.

Bollocks, she cursed silently. She remembered too late that she was supposed to be human. Alexei looked at her for a long minute, then finally answered.

"Zarus is a blight." Alexei's icy gaze hardened. "He needs adoration almost more than he needs blood. In his mind he is a god, and he wants to be worshipped as such, even if he manufactures it through abuse of power. He rarely listens to advisors, and his hubris damages his court. He recently provoked Prince Wrath, which resulted in..." He shook his head. "Zarus's reign ended when he made that move. It's only been a matter of *when* he is deposed."

Camilla was surprised any predator felt a moral obligation to use their magic only when necessary.

"If Prince Envy defeats him, will you take the throne?"

"*When* His Highness defeats him," Alexei corrected, "I will return to House Envy."

"Is that what you want?"

"Yes."

Alexei glanced at the billowing white sheer drapes separating the royal box from the chaos beyond, the chalices of alcohol-spiked blood, the mortals being seduced and bitten.

If he longed to indulge like his brethren, he didn't let it show.

"I *choose* to be His Highness's second-in-command. There is much to learn from the way he runs his court. One day I might decide to return here, but for now our arrangement is mutually beneficial."

"Does Envy know you're studying his court?"

Alexei's smile broadened. "Of course. It was his idea."

Trumpets blared near the fighting pit, three short blasts that made the hair along the back of Camilla's neck rise.

Alexei shifted his attention to Blade, a silent conversation seeming to take place between them before the latter inclined his head and stepped into the shadows.

"Relax," Alexei murmured, "Envy will not lose."

Relaxing in a tower full of blood-drunk vampires while one of the only allies she had in this realm battled to the death wasn't possible. If Envy didn't make it...

Camilla wasn't sure there was much hope that she'd find her way back to Waverly Green. Alexei might try to bring her to House Wrath, but what chance did he stand of getting them to safety if the demon prince fell?

She perched on the edge of her seat, staring down.

Camilla fixated on the white sand below, on the two gated caverns on opposite sides from which she imagined each prince would emerge.

A giant humanoid creature wearing a crudely made wolf head helmet that completely hid its face strode out, muscled chest bare, tattooed arms and thighs the size of an elephant. It had to be at least twelve feet tall and was built like a mountain.

Camilla couldn't imagine anyone fighting it and walking away with their life.

Alexei scoffed.

"Canidae. Unoriginal as far as taunts go. But that's Zarus."

"How is it a taunt?"

It certainly didn't seem like a taunt to her. It seemed like Death walking.

"Envy's House symbol is a double-headed wolf. A green-eyed monster. Canidae, known as the Wolf of the Western Isles, was chosen to mock the prince."

In one meaty hand it swung a flail that had two spiked balls attached via chain. It was positively medieval—a weapon made popular in ancient blood sports, of which she'd seen many gruesome paintings throughout the years.

Camilla supposed that was exactly what this was: blood sport.

The giant creature swung its weapon at the crowd, the cheers growing impossibly louder as it swaggered around the arena.

It thrust its unoccupied hand at the stands, taunting, daring someone to come and fight.

To her horror, she realized it wasn't wearing a helmet—the creature had a wolf's head with a man's body; it was barking and growling as the crowd tossed someone over the wall, directly at the monster.

Without seeing its eyes, she couldn't tell whether the victim was a human or a vampire, but she saw how terrified he was; a steady trickle of urine glistened down his leg, earning more jeers from the raging crowd.

Everything happened quickly after that.

In a blur of metal flashing and flesh shredding, the creature had beaten the male until he was an unidentifiable mass of raw meat, his dying screams bloodcurdling as they echoed up the tower.

Blood coated the male from head to toe; part of his arm hung off, severed at the wrist, dangling by a stubborn tendon. His left eye had been bashed out, oozing something foul-looking.

Camilla squeezed her eyes shut, fighting the overwhelming urge to vomit.

The creature had been aiming for the male's skull, and she did not need to witness what happened when that killing blow connected with its target.

Silence fell, metal cracked bone, then the crowd went wild.

Vibrations from the seats below rattled *her* bones.

"It's over," Alexei said, leaning close. "The body is gone."

Camilla's stomach twisted violently as she stared down at the pool of blood that had just contained someone's life. It was beyond horrifying.

Beyond a nightmare.

And it was only just beginning.

With blood still dripping down the smooth stone walls, Envy strode into the arena looking like an indolent royal out for a stroll among his adoring court, completely unconcerned with the giant storming toward him, flail swinging, gore from its last victim splattering the mixed crowd of vampires and their human pets in the nearest stand, its muzzle nearly black with entrails.

Camilla realized with sudden horror that the body of its last victim was gone because Canidae had *eaten* it. No bone, no flesh remained.

Still, Envy walked out, his body language bordering on bored.

The demon prince wore a crisp suit, a stylish waistcoat, and a pair of freshly pressed trousers tailored to him exceptionally well. Not ideal fighting clothing.

Camilla wasn't sure whether he was brilliant or mad. Perhaps a little of both.

"What's happening?" she asked, searching for the vampire prince. "Why is he fighting that creature?"

"Zarus will strike as soon as Envy is focused on Canidae."

"Isn't that against the rules?"

Alexei flashed her a grim look.

"There are no rules."

The wolf-headed creature, Canidae, descended like a storm. The way it had been fighting earlier... it had been only halfheartedly.

Canidae focused on Envy with singular brutality.

Its footsteps shook the arena, its war cry the most terrifying thing Camilla had ever heard. It sounded like all hope had been lost, like blood and death had been its only friends for millennia. And Envy threatened to take them away.

The demon prince didn't move, didn't tense as Canidae thundered closer, its snarls making her recoil almost a hundred feet above it.

Camilla's heart nearly broke out of her chest, it was pounding so furiously. She stared, her attention fixed on the prince as if it had been magically stuck to the scene.

"Run," she urged quietly, "please. *Run.*"

Impossibly, as if he'd heard her whisper from the pit far below, Envy raised his gaze, finding her in the crowd instantly.

He stared into her eyes, mouth curved, as his hair ruffled in the breeze of the flail sailing near his head. He'd stepped out of its path only at the last second, sending Canidae into a seething rage as it barreled past him, whirling and wild-eyed.

Its size worked against it. The creature wasn't agile; any sudden movement from its opponent worked against it.

Camilla's knees knocked together, her hands bouncing from where they rested on her lap. She wanted to run and scream and wake up from this horrible nightmare.

Then she realized what Alexei had said. There were no rules.

Envy could use magic.

But why doesn't he?

Canidae had charged again, mere feet from Envy, when the prince suddenly unleashed himself. Whatever animal, whatever that uncivilized creature was that she'd sensed lived beneath his skin, it was no longer caged by propriety.

Envy was no longer a prince. He was every inch the demon.

And he was magnificent.

From one breath to the next he'd ripped his jacket and waistcoat off. The sound of his fist connecting with Canidae was audible all the way up to where she sat. The crowd, the jeers, the pounding fists and stomping feet, nothing drowned out the sound of that punch.

The creature flew backward, crashing into the wall, a crack shooting halfway up the tower from the impact. The demon had tossed the giant as if it had been nothing at all.

Camilla recalled when he'd hit Harrington—Envy must have been holding back. A lot.

Envy whirled, his House dagger drawn, as the vampire prince leapt from behind, fangs bared.

Zarus had taken the coward's move, trying to attack from behind.

Envy was faster, more powerful, more ruthless.

The demon thrilled at violence.

Camilla watched, rapt, as he fought with the sort of brutal grace that was hauntingly beautiful despite how horrible it was.

If she could paint him now, she'd focus on the harsh lines of his face cast by shadows, the glittering promise of death in his eyes, and the violent slash of his mouth as it twisted into a vow of pain and torment.

Suddenly, it all took a terrible turn.

Canidae removed a barbed whip from its belt, cracking it more loudly than thunder.

Another great beast, this one with the head of a lion, charged into the arena while the vampire prince stalked closer, still aiming for Envy's back.

Camilla was out of her seat, leaning over the edge, shouting for Envy to look.

Alexei grabbed her, hauling her back. She nearly turned and punched him.

"Do something! He cannot fight against three."

Alexei's gaze sparkled. "Zarus is attempting to make it a fair fight."

"How is three on one…" Camilla's voice trailed off as the answer came to her. "Envy is that much more powerful."

"Not quite."

Alexei nodded to the arena, where another two giant creatures emerged. One had a bull's head with the body of a man, and the other had the head of a bird of prey. Five. It took one vampire prince and four giant beasts to even the fighting field.

"Exactly how strong *is* Envy?"

"The Kiadara each possess the strength of two hundred men. They are rumored to be the by-blows of the old gods. Because of their taste for blood, they've aligned themselves with the vampires."

Camilla's mouth went dry.

Envy was fighting the equivalent of eight hundred mortal men and a vampire with immortal strength of his own.

The demon prince turned, saw the raging beasts descending, lifted his dagger, and smiled.

FORTY-FOUR

Envy hadn't had a decent fight in a good long while.

He was glad now that he hadn't taken Wrath up on his recent offer. He channeled his less dominant sins into weapons to be used on his enemies, stoking his wrath and gluttony and lust for killing.

He saved the best for last.

Envy summoned an image in his mind, one that made *his* sin snarl. For once he let his envy out of its cage, let it consume every thought, save one. Zarus had touched Camilla, knowing it was only a matter of time before Envy arrived on his doorstep.

With the memory of the vampire's hands on her body, his teeth scraping across her neck as he used his powers on her, Envy spun, sinking his dagger into a leg.

The vampire's growl was animal, the splurt of blood satisfying.

He'd aim for Zarus's unbeating heart next.

Ice shot around the arena, a result of Envy's power. He needed to pace himself, rein his magic and emotions in, or he'd burn out too fast. Already he felt breathless, the strain of moving his body more difficult without his gods-forsaken heart.

Sadistic Death goddesses.

The Kiadara used claw and fang and might, falling on him like starved animals in a frenzy. Daggers made of his ice stabbed the creatures.

Envy landed punches that sent them flying back, took some hits, and quickly realized they'd come prepared to win using any means necessary.

The Kiadara coated their claws and blades in toxins, slowing his already sluggish healing abilities.

If he had to guess, based on the searing pain shooting down his back, they'd made hellebane. If he'd placed a bet at House Greed, he'd have wagered Zarus had done the same.

Blade had said Zarus planned to poison Envy, but hellebane was different. The plant was only found in the most remote regions of the Seven Circles, and wasn't toxic unless burned to a powder.

A barbed whip slashed between his shoulders, right where his wings were still tucked away. Hellebane seeped into his flesh, scalding. The pain honed his fury.

Envy spun, punching through Canidae's chest to rip out its still-beating heart. He tossed it to its brethren, who grew ravenous as they fought over it. The Kiadara's hunger knew no bounds—they'd eat their own severed limbs if blood lust had taken them.

He raised his blade to the vampire, his teeth bared. This needed to end.

Quickly. But he'd still make a good show of it.

"Come play."

"I'm going to make that little bitch come before I suck her dry," Zarus sneered.

It was the wrong thing to say.

Regardless of how drained he was, Envy moved with as much of his immortal strength as he could muster, dragging his blade across the vampire's neck.

The wound was superficial, a warning that Envy was still playing.

He spun and struck again, this time sinking his blade into flesh until he nicked bone.

Zarus howled.

Envy barely noticed the hellebane-coated blades as they tore at his flesh.

His gaze was fixed, hungry, on one target.

He brought his dagger down on the vampire's right knee, bone shattering from the impact. Zarus, for the first time, lost his sneer. He hobbled back, wincing.

Envy stopped playing. Only one of them was walking out of this arena and it sure as fuck was going to be Envy. Fear entered Zarus's eyes.

Vampires healed fast, but bones took time to mend.

Envy struck again, breaking his other kneecap. It shattered to dust.

Zarus wouldn't be standing again.

The Kiadara circled them both, spittle flying, landing in acidic hisses on the sand. Envy was momentarily distracted, and one of Bovinae's bull horns pierced his shoulder, going clean through.

The wound didn't begin to heal.

Envy gritted his teeth, swinging his blade up and through the Kiadara's rib cage, despite the ripping pain in his own chest.

His earlier wound had split open, but at least the Kiadara had crumbled into a heap, twitching.

Zarus had summoned the other two Kiadara to his side, forming a meager line of protection. His knees likely wouldn't heal until he feasted on blood and had a day's rest.

Zarus would not see sunrise.

The remaining Kiadara growled and screeched.

Envy's grip on his dagger tightened.

Lion or Falcon. Panthera or Falconidae.

In the end it didn't matter where he started. Envy felt no satisfaction in destroying these creatures, descended from gods. It was a waste.

And one more reason he would kill this vampire who took life without care.

Not kill, he reminded himself. That final blow belonged to another. Envy might be a soulless demon, but Zarus was a rotten bastard. His court deserved better.

Panthera roared, the sound vibrating the ground with its force.

Until this point, Envy hadn't paid attention to the crowd; he'd tuned them out, focusing instead on the sounds of his blade, meeting and tearing and shredding flesh. Now he heard their jeers, their cries for blood. They didn't care whose it was.

He wanted to look for Camilla again in the stands, to know she was still secure, but didn't. Alexei had his instructions. He'd die by Envy's hand if he didn't follow them.

Panthera prowled in a circle around Envy, closing in slowly.

Falconidae let loose a shrill call meant to distract. They would come at Envy as a team.

The wounds in his back bled freely, the drops turning to gold as they hit the ground. The creatures scented it, their gazes turning fully black. Envy was damned, but his blood was still divine; one taste was worth dying for. Or so he'd been told.

"I know I'm pretty. But are you going to stand there mentally undressing me all night?"

They leapt in tandem, each striking out at him. Envy narrowly missed Panthera's teeth but wasn't as fortunate with Falconidae's sword. It carved into his side, hitting a rib.

Hellebane made the wound twice as painful, his breath turning sharp with each damned inhalation. His gold blood mixed with the red and black of his opponents and their previous victim, spilling faster than it had ever done before.

Fucking hell. He was getting... dizzy.

Panthera used the distraction to knock Envy to the ground.

Sand ground into the wounds on his back as Panthera's teeth gnashed at his throat. Where its saliva hit his skin, it sizzled like water hitting hot rocks.

Envy bucked, sending the lion flying across the pit, its body hitting the stone wall with such power that it fell, limbs and head crooked, dead.

Envy did not pity the final creature. Falconidae.

He charged the raptor-headed monster, dagger puncturing one eye, then the next, before he tore the creature's head off and tossed it aside, panting. The hellebane continued to burn beneath his skin. He needed to clean his wounds soon. And the fight needed to end.

Envy was weakened, more so than he'd ever admit.

Zarus, however, was trying to drag himself away, trailing his useless legs.

Envy walked over and drove his blade through Zarus's hand, pinning him, then crouched in front of the wounded vampire, arms propped casually on his knees. The position hurt like nothing he'd ever experienced. But his expression didn't let any pain show.

It would be so easy to rip Zarus's head off and feed it to the flames right now. But the game hung in the balance, so he waited, wounds searing. The Fear Collector had given an unmistakable command.

He wondered, briefly, if the vampire had known all along what was at stake today.

If he'd agreed anyway. The Unseelie were excellent at stoking egos, making a win seem inevitable instead of improbable.

"Hubris, the great destroyer of man and beast alike." Envy tsked. "Whatever the Unseelie King offered, you should have refused. You had a good life. Blood. Lovers. A whole court to serve and please you. Yet you dared to stand against a Prince of Hell."

Zarus coughed up black blood, but his expression remained a vicious mask of defiance.

"She'll...never...be...yours."

Something twisted in Envy's chest, as painful as the hellebane.

"Did Lennox tell you this would happen?" he asked. "That you would fight for more than your crown?"

Rage flared in Zarus's ice-blue eyes.

"...promised...his...daughter."

"I certainly hope he specified which one. He has more animal-like half-breeds roaming around than any of the mortal gods. He might have promised a sacred cow to you."

Zarus's lacerated tongue darted out, as if savoring this final blow.

"...one...four."

Envy's brows knitted.

There were four blood heirs in the Wild Court, two Unseelie princes and two Unseelie princesses. Each was rumored to possess magic with untold capabilities.

It would indeed be enough of an incentive for Zarus to risk it all.

Not only would his court be aligned with all Unseelie Fae, but his princess would be fearsome, powerful enough to keep enemies from his shores.

Any Unseelie princess would be as wicked as her parents, though, eventually ending her vampire prince for sport. Or, more likely, to claim more territory for the dark Fae.

Lennox never offered something of value unless he believed his investment would triple. The vampire either didn't know or didn't care about that. He probably thought he'd trap the princess with his venom.

Zarus gurgled on his own blood, trying to say more.

Envy supposed it was poetic justice in a sense.

He yanked his gaze away, finding Blade in the cavern just outside the pit. Thanks fucking be. The hellebane was so painful now, he was nearly brought to his knees. He needed to siphon some envy soon, replenish his depleted power.

Teeth gritted, Envy hauled Zarus's limp form up.

Blade's crimson eyes glowed with violence as he stepped forward. It was time to crown a new prince.

Zarus finally caught up with the truth of the situation, his fingers clawing at Envy's arms.

"Mercy. I forfeit!"

"You never should have attacked my brother, or abused your own people," Envy said quietly. "Taking Camilla was your worst move yet. Never touch what's *mine*."

Blade's attention remained locked on the prince, his fangs gleaming as the sun slowly began to rise. In a move that was at once graceful and brutal, he tore out Zarus's throat, then held the severed head high. Envy felt the crowd's shock trickling down.

Blade didn't play with his targets; he'd always been one to strike hard and fast, dispatching with precision.

Envy sent a bit of magic to the bodies piled on the sand, creating a pyre.

Blade brought the prince's head to the flames, holding it there as the fire burned it to ash. Zarus had been so ancient, his papery skin caught like kindling.

The crowd's hysteria hung like a dark mist.

"Silence." Blade's voice cut off the cries of terror that had erupted.

"By blood." He indicated the charred head of his predecessor. "By blade." He dragged his weapon over his heart. "By might. I've taken the Immortal Throne."

Envy watched the crowd; they didn't seem convinced.

Blade would need to get them to his side before the shock wore off and another heir stepped up.

Blade knew this.

He pulled out two curved daggers, holding them as he spun slowly, staring into the stands.

"Bow before your new prince. Or die by my blade."

Tension hung as thick as the smoke in the air, and the sun continued to slowly ascend. Soon the vampires would need to retreat. But Blade had guards at the exits.

He would see them burn if they did not bow.

Next to Camilla, Alexei beat his fist to his chest, then took a knee. His proud voice carried down over the stands.

"Rightful ruler of the Immortal Hearts. I honor thee. Prince Blade."

A tense pause stretched out. Finally, several other vampires followed suit, offering the vow and kneeling.

Soon the whole arena knelt, their whispers filling the air.

Blade had taken the Immortal Throne.

A crimson-eyed prince now ruled. The first as far as Envy knew.

Envy glanced at Blade, hoping he hadn't made a mistake by putting a stronger vampire on the throne. Zarus was cruel, conniving, brutal to his own people, but Envy knew how he ruled.

Blade was an unknown, but hopefully he would be the prince his people needed.

Time would certainly tell one way or another.

Hopefully over the next several months, Blade would be too busy establishing his court and his rule, his attention set on finding a consort to join political forces and smooth things over with vampire nobility, to want to start any trouble with demons.

If not...

Wrath would undoubtedly hold Envy responsible for allowing a greater threat to emerge.

They would have to cross that bridge when they came to it.

For now, Envy needed to tend to his wounds before anyone discovered his growing weakness, collect his next clue, take Camilla away from here, then win this gods-damned game.

FORTY-FIVE

Camilla paced inside the chamber, feeling caged.

The battle had ended more than an hour before, and Envy hadn't returned to the room yet.

Alexei had deposited her, locked the door from the outside, then left.

She'd rattled the handle, then tried to pick the lock, to no avail. The vampire said it was a safety precaution, but it felt like *she* was the prisoner.

She rummaged through the room, finding a little satchel filled with medicinal jars and a slim dagger and sheath she could hide on her person. The dagger Envy had given her was lost to Bloodwood Forest, so this would do nicely for now. A hastily scribbled note read: *For the prince's wounds, reapply as needed. Never forget: Strike hard, little lamb. Blade.*

Camilla smiled. Despite how they'd met, she wished Blade well too.

Footsteps rushed past her room, again. A thousand people must have hurried past since she'd been locked in.

Bits and pieces of conversation reached her, confirming that the court was in total chaos.

Apparently only royal vampire heirs had ever deposed a prince before, and Blade's crimson eyes were making this unusual.

No one knew what to do about Blade's new position or claim.

Some were saying he *was* a royal despite his eye color, and then fights broke out over that.

The vampire court during such an internal upheaval was the last place she wished to be.

Camilla thought of her gallery, of her friends and her life back in Waverly Green. She thought of Bunny and wished more than anything else that her sweet furry friend were with her now. She tried to summon the feeling she thought should be gripping her tightly. To no avail.

Aside from her cat and her friends, Camilla didn't miss much else.

She sat on the edge of her bed, removing the rosary pea cuffs and necklace. A noise outside her chamber drew her attention and she sprinted to the door, banging.

"Hello?" she called.

"There you are." Vexley's drawl sounded from the other side. "Camilla, darling. Open the door."

She thought about banging her head against the wall.

"It's locked. From *your* side."

"Oh."

Click.

The door swung open, revealing both Vexley and his new girlfriend. The succubus waved her pointed tail, then shoved Vexley against the wall, running her tongue over him with a wink before striding off.

Camilla was too grateful for her assistance with breaking the lock to be disgusted by how aroused Vexley now was. She kept her eyes on his face.

"Are you going back to Waverly Green?" she asked, peering down the corridor.

No Alexei. No Envy. No guards rushing to lock her away.

"I am. Although if you're asking for a way back, it will cost you more than another forgery, my love." Vexley smiled and stepped closer. "This time I want you to accept my marriage suit."

Camilla wasn't surprised he'd use this situation to his advantage, but she *was* surprised to realize she hadn't been asking for a way back to Waverly Green.

If ever there were a time to escape, to run headlong back to her normal life, this was it. No more games, no more Underworld, no more vampire battles or Houses of Sin. But as much as she wanted her cat, she did not want to return home just yet. She still needed to win back her talent.

She retreated from Vexley, slowly shaking her head.

"You misunderstand. I don't wish to leave."

His hand clamped down on her wrist, grinding her bones together.

"*You* misunderstand. It's not a choice. Zarus's death has prevented me from obtaining my next clue."

"I don't see how that has anything to do with me."

"I've lost the game, Camilla. It's over for me. But you're here for a reason too—you'll ease my pain, won't you?"

"Let go."

His grip had tightened, but his expression remained perfectly calm. It frightened her more than his outward fury ever had. His tone was pleasant, cajoling. Like she simply needed him to bring her to heel, to make her see reason.

"This is the way, Camilla. You will return as my wife. We'll sell more forgeries. Make so much coin, we'll buy our way into immortality."

"That's why you played? To become immortal?"

Vexley's placid expression faltered. "I have my reasons, darling. Now come along."

"I said, *let go*."

The mask of calmness shattered, revealing the truth of the man she'd seen once before.

"I'm not leaving without a prize, Camilla. Even if that's you." Vexley's gaze had turned cold, his mouth twisting into a cruel sneer.

He shoved her back into her chamber, quickly pinning her against the wall.

"First, we'll put an heir in your belly."

His free hand slipped between them, tenderly caressing her stomach as if he weren't speaking of forcing himself upon her. As if there were anything gentle or sweet about his proposal.

"Vexley," she said again, trying to remain calm. "You don't want to do this. Let me go."

She glanced around wildly; the damn dagger Blade had given her was still in its sheath, too far out of reach.

Vexley leaned in, eyes menacing.

How this man had ever fooled society into believing he was carefree was a mystery. Camilla now saw that his lopsided grin also indicated how off-kilter the scales of right and wrong inside him were.

She channeled her fear, her rage, feeling it collect beneath her skin. She would give him one more chance to unhand her.

"Let go of me, Vexley. Now."

Her voice was calm, steady. It was a deception. One Vexley fell for.

He leaned into her harder, as if he could force their souls to twine right there. *He* wished for marriage. Till death do them part. She would grant him at least part of that wish.

He ought to have been paying attention to the silver in her eyes, gleaming like assassin's blades, not the swath of skin between her breasts.

But Vexley wasn't wise or observant. His selfish behavior would be his undoing.

His grip on her didn't loosen. But she no longer cared.

Using that connection, every single place he touched her, she let that strange feeling under her skin loose. Perhaps she was mad. But she'd had enough.

Years of torment, of fear, of folding into herself instead of pushing back, exploded in a torrent of suppressed emotion. Like a dam breaking, everything she'd held back flooded her.

"What the—"

Camilla's force surged through them both. Vexley's eyes rolled, showing the whites.

His hands, now fused to her, couldn't have unclasped her if he'd tried.

She watched distantly as he shook, his body violently convulsing, spittle forming at his mouth—like foam collecting on a churning sea.

She smelled the piss, the excrement, just before the pig collapsed onto his filth, his body twitching one last time.

Camilla stepped back, gaze fixed to the unmoving form, feeling void of emotion. In the distance, perhaps only in her mind, familiar female laughter snaked down her spine. She thought, for one dark second, that her mother would be proud.

She couldn't say what made her look up; perhaps she knew he'd been there, watching from the shadows. Perhaps she'd simply wished him there and he'd come, summoned by the depravity of what she'd done, or the way she felt not an ounce of remorse.

Envy moved into the light, his attention locked on hers. He said nothing of the man lying dead at her feet. No judgment crossed his features, no fear or revulsion.

Camilla said nothing of the wounds leaking ichor from *his* body.

Or the brutal way he'd killed in that arena, the pleasure he'd seemed to take in death.

Maybe they were both damned, wicked things, broken in all the right places so they lined up, jagged edge to smooth.

He extended his hand, waiting.

Before she went to him, she grabbed the satchel Blade had gifted her. She didn't spare another glance at Vexley as she stepped over him. Right now, Camilla wasn't capable of regret, or worry. Not even shock.

Whatever feelings she'd stored up had emptied, as if she'd used them all.

Clasping Envy's blood-speckled hand in hers, Camilla gave him one nod and braced for his magic as he whisked them away from the carnage of the vampire court.

FORTY-SIX

ENVY PULLED CAMILLA behind him, his battle senses on high alert, the pain inflicted by the hellebane still searing through him, honing his senses to a sharp blade.

They stood outside the private cottage on the outskirts of his grounds. He wanted a chance to speak with Camilla, to process all he'd just witnessed, and to clean himself up before deciding whether he should risk taking her into his castle. He'd need to walk his House first to ensure that the worst of his court's failing would be hidden.

Now that would have to wait.

A shadow moved along the forest's edge, bringing with it that sense of darkness that indicated one thing. Fae.

"Step into the clearing, slowly," Envy commanded.

The Unseelie did.

The male had a shock of white hair, pale yellow eyes, and lashes blacker than ink. His brown boots were scuffed but well made, his shirtsleeves rolled to show off dark bronze forearms, toned and lethal. The shirt was wrinkled, but even in the dark Envy saw the fine weave of the linen. The Fae wore a hat tugged low, hiding his elegant pointed ears.

He looked like a mortal hunter who'd dashed out from the woods, weapon missing, but most didn't realize *he* was the weapon.

Envy recognized him by reputation instantly.

"You're a long way away from hunting maidens in the woods, Wolf."

"Rumors abound." The Fae smiled, revealing more of his face and discarding his human disguise. "They say you crowned a new vampire."

Wolf's voice was melodic, mesmerizing, and had been used to seduce more than a few mortals over the years. His voice was a sign he'd once held rank in his court, though he was a long way from home now.

Envy didn't miss the fact that he'd referenced the gossip column. Wolf had likely come to see if the rumors about House Envy were true, testing the ward's boundaries. They were true, of course, but the ward Envy had placed was smaller than most would guess, surrounding only his House.

"You have a message from Lennox?" Envy asked.

The Fae drew closer, suddenly curious about Camilla. Too curious.

Envy's dagger was in hand, the blade still faintly glowing from its recent offerings.

The Unseelie noticed it and stepped back, smiling as if amused.

"Rumors, as I said." Wolf's grin spread. "Lovely little *shocking* rumors."

He was still looking at Camilla, fixated in a way that wouldn't end well.

Envy stepped forward, dripping menace.

"My patience wanes."

"I have no message from the king," Wolf said. "I was simply curious whether the rumors were true. I see that they are. Delightfully so."

"If you were curious about the new vampire prince, why come here?"

"Those two are unrelated." The Fae flashed another smile, this one as wolfish as his name. "I'll be seeing you, fair winter lady. Shifting seasons are always so beautiful."

Before Envy could run him through with his blade, the Unseelie was gone, shifting from one reality to another.

Envy glanced back at Camilla, his sin threatening to emerge. For a moment, she looked as if she'd seen a ghost.

"Have you met him before?" Envy asked, suspicious.

Her gaze darted to where the Fae had disappeared.

"Everyone's heard of his legends."

"Try not to appear so enthralled." Envy's mood soured further, noting she hadn't answered his question. "He hunts women."

"Those stories aren't exactly true." Camilla bit her lower lip after the admission.

"Oh? Do enlighten me, Miss Antonius."

"Wolf prefers women, but he doesn't hunt them to eat. Well"—she cleared her throat—"at least not in the way the stories tell it. Wolf's appetite is...most in Waverly Green believe he tricks maidens into letting him inside their homes. That's the cautionary tale told by men, at least, but from what I've heard, maidens are only too pleased to see Wolf. A night with him is...enough of a threat for men to weave such tall tales."

He'd battled a vampire and legendary monsters, and Camilla's face had flushed only when recalling lurid stories of the cursed Unseelie Fae and his bedroom skills. Envy stalked up the stairs to his cottage, wounds stinging.

As if Envy himself hadn't given her an orgasm with *his* legendary tongue.

Jealousy, cold and unrelenting, lashed through him.

"Come," he said, his tone frosty and *perhaps* a little petty. "Unless you'd like to wait for Wolf to return and see to that."

After Envy had shown Camilla to her private room and attached bathing chamber, he retired to his own bedroom suite. The cottage was large and well-appointed, fit for a prince who wished for others to envy him. It also happened to be the perfect place to entertain Camilla while he privately checked his court. After tending to his wounds.

He hissed as he slowly peeled off his shirt. His cuts had only partially healed, causing his skin to freshly rip again when he removed his clothing.

Another thing was stinging Envy too. Directly after the battle, he'd waited for the next clue to be delivered. But no message had come.

And as for Camilla…he'd suspected she had secrets, but she'd seemed momentarily stunned by the magic that crackled over her skin like little webs of lightning.

Whether she knew she possessed the skill or it had been a shock remained to be seen. Creatures in nature held such power—electric eels, for one. Leading him to think she might be a shape-shifter.

If she wasn't fully shifter, she could have some unique parentage; shifter blood from a distant relative would show in such ways.

Fae also possessed skills like hers—magic, and talents. But he hadn't gotten any indication she had Seelie blood. Her ears were those of a mortal. Until tonight, he hadn't seen any hint of magic. After he'd massaged her, there had been no sign of an enchantment inked onto her skin. And a glamour could often still be detected, even slightly.

If not Fae or shifter, then what else could she be?

Envy's hands were on his trouser strings when he heard her sharp inhalation behind him.

He hadn't looked in the mirror; he'd already known the wounds on his back weren't pretty. They were deep, down to the bone in some places, and the hellebane ate away at his flesh.

They might even scar, for once.

The tattoo that symbolized his House, starting just above his elbow on his right bicep before winding across his shoulder and onto his chest, might even need touching up.

"They didn't hold back," she said softly.

Her touch was featherlight and far too tempting.

He knew what those painter's hands were capable of.

"Miss Antonius." Envy meant for his tone to come out harsh, but it was too low, too inviting even to his own ears. "You should go back to your suite."

"I have a salve."

Her fingers traced his shoulder muscles, bunched and tense, until they slowly relaxed from her ministrations.

"And some herbs for your bath. They were gifted from Blade."

Envy smiled at that, appreciating a smart move when he saw one.

The new crown prince was already strengthening their alliance, making amends for the previous ruler. Envy doubted the Unseelie King would be pleased that this particular game had landed so smoothly. Lennox no doubt had wanted to create chaos and discord, to shake up the courts.

Not to mention, now that Envy knew Lennox had promised Zarus he'd unite their courts through marriage, Lennox would be spitting mad when he found out Blade intended to take a vampire bride. He'd already announced that he'd choose from one of the noble families in Malice Isle, further securing his claim to the throne.

It was another wise move. Now all the nobles who might have plotted to take Blade's crown would plot to have their heirs ruling beside him. The new vampire prince wouldn't risk marrying a Fae and causing any more strife.

Besides, Blade refused to fall for anyone who could be food. He'd made that abundantly clear. And that was partly why Envy had known Camilla would be safe near him. He'd only ever heard of the vampire deviating from his rule once—when he'd gotten tangled up with a werewolf.

Enemies made interesting bedmates.

Lennox must not have known, or thought Blade could be swayed to his side.

"Your arm and chest... twin wolves?" she asked.

He swallowed thickly. Thankful the ink was still intact.

"A double-headed wolf. My House symbol."

Envy imagined Camilla taking in the piece, how it covered his entire upper arm, then the right side of his chest. The lower portion of the wolf's body began right above his elbow; it stood on its hind legs, body reaching up to his shoulder. Its first head angled toward his chest, curving across his shoulder, its muzzle closed and somehow peaceful, contemplative.

The second head was set lower, taking up his pectorals, and was vicious. Its jaws hung open, teeth snapping at an unseen enemy.

With the exception of their vivid green eyes, Envy had chosen the tattoo without color, wanting the contrast cast by the shadows to give it stark beauty. Chiaroscuro always fascinated him, the study of light versus dark.

His wolves were forever chasing after something just out of reach.

Never content. Monsters, green-eyed and vicious. Like him.

Without any warning, Camilla slathered Envy's first cut with the salve. It burned like hell. Envy gritted his teeth as those lovely little hands continued to slowly torture him with the herbs. Admittedly, the first wound already felt better.

In no time she'd tended to each claw mark and laceration.

The hole where the bull's horn had pierced him was worse, but soon that, too, slowly began to stitch itself together, the skin itching and stinging like fire ants had nested there.

Camilla pressed a hand to his good shoulder, turning him until he glanced down at her.

She winced as if feeling his pain firsthand, though most was only a dull ache now.

His chest held only one wound, but it was by far the worst of them. Panthera had gotten one good hit in, its claw nearly gutting him.

Her gaze followed the jagged line from his chest to his navel.

Some emotion flickered there.

She touched his chest softly, her brow knitting. "Your heart..."

If it could have pounded, it would have been doing so now.

Envy gently withdrew her hands. "Will grow back soon enough."

Horror washed over her features. "What? How?"

"Let's just say I would have followed you to the vampire court sooner if I hadn't run into a slight...issue."

Camilla stared at him, seeming unsure of what to say.

"I'm sorry," she said, quietly, softly.

It made something primitive inside him sit up, snarl.

"I don't recall you wielding a blade, pet. Do not apologize for someone else."

"Let me rephrase." Silver eyes glimmered with annoyance. "I'm sorry, but this will hurt terribly."

Camilla smeared the salve down his front, her touch no longer gentle as she coated the wound, leaving no minute section untended.

He swore and jerked back, but the little hell beast moved with him, finishing the job with brutal efficiency.

"There." Her tone was clipped as she twisted the cap back on the salve. "That should be sufficient. Blade's note said to reapply if necessary."

She slapped a bag of herbs to his still-healing chest.

"Add two generous pinches of this mixture to your bath and soak for twenty minutes. It won't improve your attitude, but your wounds should heal nicely."

Cursed saints above, he was hard as granite. Again.

She turned to leave, and he snatched her hand, drawing her close against him.

Her desire hit him harder than any blow he'd taken in the arena. It was the first powerful emotion he'd felt from her since they'd come to his circle.

"Allow me to properly thank you, Miss Antonius."

Before she could offer him another smart comment, his mouth came down on hers.

FORTY-SEVEN

CAMILLA HAD JUST killed a man for less. But Envy's brazen kiss... brought her back to life.

If she'd been trapped in a cocoon of ice, frozen from the horror of what she'd done, she'd broken free now. His fire ravished all the dark, cold places in her soul, warming her, making her feel *everything*. Protected. Safe. Alive. Passionate.

Strong hands touched everywhere: her hair, her throat, cupping her breasts, running over her hips and thighs, stroking each area like her body was his favorite canvas.

Her gasps were his paint, her lips his greatest inspiration.

He tasted and teased, nipped and owned. Never relinquishing her mouth for long, his tongue tangling with hers in a dance she never wanted to end.

The kiss was a battle, a plea, a path to salvation or their greatest destruction.

Their game had become intimate, each move he made provoking one of her own. When she teased him, he returned the favor until they were clawing at each other's clothes, shedding them as quickly as they'd shed any notion of restraint.

Camilla didn't care what it was. Masterpiece, chaos, it made no difference. It was pleasure: intoxicating and pure, and she drank it down, sip after decadent sip.

His callused skin was rough against her softness, the friction a wonderful, unexpected delight for the senses. Camilla had hated this scrap of a gown in the vampire court; now she relished how much skin it exposed, the access it granted him to stroke and caress.

She touched him back as freely, flattening her palms on his bare chest, marveling at how soft his skin was there despite the hard muscle underneath, despite how torn it had been only moments before.

The intricately crafted tattoos marking his arm and chest were just as beautiful as the hunter-green ink at his belt line; she traced them all, listening to the rasp of his breath as she moved lower, along the line of his trousers, slung so low on his hips it ought to be criminal.

Despite his injuries, he was already aroused, the thick length of him straining against his pants.

Camilla wanted to pull him free, offer him the same release he'd offered her.

She went to undo his trousers.

His arms, capable of slaying giants, were gentle when they came around her, drawing her closer, staying her movements.

What had started as hungry, greedy kisses slowed into something more tender, gentle but never shy. Their lips began to savor, to move as if—for once—they had all the time in the world to learn all about each other, explore.

It was languorous, drowsy. The sort of kiss that made knees weak and heartbeats strong. It took her a moment to appreciate the shift, enjoy the sweetness of it.

His tongue touched hers, heat pooling low in her belly from the lazy stroke, invoking memories of when he'd made that same movement between her thighs, kissing the apex of her body until her back had arched off the bed and heat bolted up her spine.

When his hands moved over her now, it was less about possession, less about feral need; it was a question that made her breath catch, an answer that threatened to undo her.

All the teasing, the private games, the allure of knowing they only had one night, and she'd wanted to make it last, draw it out for as long as possible. It had just been a fun game. A way to forget her loneliness for a while, a lighthearted way to pass the time.

What Envy was doing now, this move…it threatened her carefully constructed walls.

Camilla had thought she knew the rules of this private game, but now he was kissing her like she meant something. Like this wasn't just about winning one night.

Like he might be playing to win something more.

And that awful realization, that he might in fact still be playing at all, made her face a truth she wasn't ready for.

Camilla felt as if she were falling, plummeting from the heavens to the earth, and he was the star she clung to, their desire lighting the whole damn sky.

Or maybe they were a comet, destined to crash.

Camilla drew away, touching her swollen lips; they tingled, seeking the press of his.

Envy brushed her hair back, cupping her face between his hands as if she were precious, the most intriguing piece of art he'd ever laid eyes on.

Those hands still had blood on them. But his violence didn't frighten her.

She watched as his palm slid to her chest, feeling the beat of her heart instead of tracing her peaked breast, still aching with want.

The way Envy looked at her now was dangerous. So, brutally dangerous.

More than the dagger he'd wielded with ease, or the cold, efficient way he'd dispatched creatures twice his size. The sharp edge of his lust had been honed to a finer point by something…else, something that could strike with more precision, travel deeper until it pierced a vital part inside her. Whatever game this was…it could slip between her ribs faster than he would slip out from beneath her sheets after their one night together ended.

His gaze never wavered from hers, so she saw the moment when he realized what she had seen, before banishing it from his face. A flicker in a storm, there one moment and blown away the next. But Camilla had seen it for what it was, knew it would never last.

This would always be a game to him. And the tender move, the sweet kiss...this play knocked her wildly off-balance. Only to worry she was tumbling all by herself.

"I should go," she said tightly, suddenly needing space.

Seeming to understand, he clasped her wrist in his hand, drawing her palm to his lips.

He pressed a kiss to her skin, then stepped away.

"Bathe. Rest," he said, backing into his bedchamber, giving her leave to exit.

A chasm opened between them, stretching wide, where moments ago there had only been closeness. A desire to breach all that separated them. At least on her end.

The tenderness was gone, replaced once again by his cool indifference.

Envy was content with their game as it was. And she'd broken the unspoken rule. She'd fallen for the illusion.

"I'll see you in a little while for dinner."

Camilla opened her mouth, to call him back, to explain why she suddenly needed to protect her heart, that this private game had somehow started to mean something it shouldn't. She wanted to cry out that *she* wasn't who he thought she was, but the only words that came out were a softly spoken lie.

"A bath sounds good."

Camilla's head rested against the lip of the tub, her silvery hair pinned high to avoid getting wet, the water's warmth finally soothing her. She was trying to forget Vexley's attack and subsequent death. The way he'd looked so broken and fragile as she'd stepped over him.

Then there was Wolf. He'd wanted to speak with her, for a while now. Had played a dangerous game, trespassing on the prince's land.

With the real game underway, Camilla knew she couldn't ignore Wolf forever.

Then there was Envy…

Excitement was something she'd craved while living her quiet little mortal life in Waverly Green. And so she'd been a willing player in their flirtation. Had enjoyed it thoroughly. There'd been a dark sense of pleasure in constantly upping the ante with him. She *liked* that he didn't hold back, that he made his move boldly and ruthlessly, that he'd pursue her, then pull back, waiting to see what she'd do, delighting when she bested him. He'd treated her like an equal. His constant playing exciting her on multiple levels, not purely physical.

Their dynamic had been working wonderfully until that kiss tonight.

She knew what she needed to do next: end their game. And not by giving in to the heat that burned between them like flying near the fiery sun.

Camilla needed to put distance between them, set new boundaries. She'd focus on the game master, on helping Envy win, since that seemed to somehow be tied to her role; then she'd win back her talent and return to Waverly Green.

It was a good enough plan, even if she didn't feel thrilled by it. It was the safe choice, the one that guaranteed she'd remain free of more heartbreak. She'd already experienced enough of that to last a lifetime. And Envy…even if she wished to share her secret with him, she couldn't bring herself to. It was best to end their game now and walk away unscathed.

Her eyes drifted shut, the promise of sleep tugging her conscience under. Much too soon a quiet knock broke the serenity.

"Come in."

There was no logical reason for Camilla's skin to suddenly pebble as if a cold wind had snaked through the warm bathing chamber, yet goose bumps rose along her flesh, her body aware of what her mind had yet to notice.

Her eyes cracked opened. As if her thoughts had conjured him, Prince Envy stood there, looking as sinful as Lucifer the moment he'd accepted his wickedness and fallen from grace.

She should demand he leave. She'd already concluded that this flirtation needed to end.

Camilla did not speak at all.

She wanted to know why he'd come. Maybe he knew that kiss had been too much. Had come too close to meaning something they both knew it didn't.

She raised a brow, waiting.

He could explain himself; then she'd send him away.

Envy's attention slowly meandered along the lines of her neck as if cataloguing the shape to later have painted. It was something he'd done before, like that unassuming swath of skin fascinated him, called to his need to have someone capture it on canvas.

"Two things drove me here, Miss Antonius," he began. "First, I considered apologizing for my behavior."

Her heart pounded faster. She'd been correct. The kiss was just another move.

A moment passed, followed by another.

She wondered if he hadn't quite worked out his apology and why simply saying "I apologize for being a tremendous ass and ruining our game" seemed to be such a monumentally difficult task.

When he didn't attempt to speak again, Camilla's patience dwindled.

"What's preventing you from accomplishing just that, Your Highness?"

His mouth curved, and Camilla knew at once he'd laid a trap. He'd been waiting for her to take the bait.

"I realized I would be lying. I'm not remotely sorry."

"For which part?"

Curse her. That was *not* the question she'd intended to ask.

"You know which part."

"That's not the way this is supposed to work."

"Do you want me to suddenly play by the rules?"

He knew she didn't, the damn beast. His smile was victorious. He hadn't come here to apologize at all; Envy had come here to restart their flirtation, to up the stakes once again.

"Were you to say the words, I'd have you out of that tub and on the bed this instant." His voice was sin incarnate.

He continued, more slowly now, taking another step into the room.

"As an artist, I'm sure you can envision my tongue on the canvas of your bare body. I imagine we could make quite the masterpiece together. *If* you don't forfeit now."

Camilla's breath hitched, but she forced herself to stay calm. "You have no morals."

"True. But yours are as gray in tone as mine, my dear."

"That's hardly true."

"What a cunning little liar you are."

She was indeed.

"What is the second thing that brought you here?" she asked. She couldn't let herself get caught up in this again, no matter how aroused she was feeling in the bath.

Heat kissed her cheeks that had nothing to do with the warm water.

He smiled, noticing her pinkened skin. "Thinking about my tongue, Miss Antonius?"

Camilla's thighs squeezed together.

"No. I'm thinking of dinner."

His attention moved to the bathwater, rippling from the subtle movement.

Hunger flashed in his eyes.

"Lie to me all you like, Camilla. But this isn't over yet, and you know it. When you're in bed tonight, fingers trailing over your deliciously swollen clit, you'll be dreaming of my hand doling out your pleasure."

Before she could argue, the damned demon gave her a mocking bow, then left.

Frustrated and highly aroused, Camilla slipped her hand beneath the water, doing exactly what the prince had said.

As she came, she made sure her moans were loud enough for the demon to hear across the cottage, hoping to drive him as wild as he'd driven her.

FORTY-EIGHT

"WHAT HAPPENED IN the vampire court once I left?" Envy had his back to Alexei as he asked, attention fixed on the cocktail he swirled in one hand.

It was well past the hour he *should* have retrieved Camilla for their dinner, far past when he should have checked on his court, too.

He'd made no move to leave the cottage.

He'd felt victorious after leaving Camilla aroused in the tub until he heard her orgasm through the walls. She'd knocked him clear off his high horse with that move. He'd grabbed some oil, fisted his aching cock, and stroked himself to orgasm while envisioning her.

"How many tried to take Blade's throne?"

"Two heirs, Your Highness." Alexei sounded amused. "Their heads are on spikes. One outside the throne room, the other outside Blade's bedchamber. With a warning that he's always watching."

"Brazen, bold. A bit dramatic." Envy snorted. "Glad to see Blade is taking to the role as expected." He turned. Alexei cocked his head. "No clues, then?"

His second shook his head and didn't elaborate. With a tight nod, Envy dismissed him.

He went back to considering his drink, playing over the encounter with Wolf.

Envy did not believe in coincidences.

The world was far too vast, the realms too plentiful, for anything to be random. Especially while a game was in play. Somewhere, buried in the seemingly random interaction, had to be the next clue.

There was no other good reason for Wolf to risk entering demon grounds uninvited. And the fact that he'd once been Unseelie nobility added to the possibility that Lennox had used him to deliver the next riddle. Of course, Envy couldn't stop his mind from spinning with far-fetched theories about how Camilla had responded when she'd seen the Fae, too. Envy had scrutinized Wolf, wondering if he'd been the male Camilla had shown him in that memory.

He gritted his teeth. He shouldn't be thinking about that cursed memory still, but his sin needed an outlet, and feeling envy brought his senses into sharp focus.

Envy tried to use that now. He focused on the very first words the Unseelie had spoken, arranging and rearranging them a hundred ways.

Rumors abound.

It was a throwaway answer, given casually. The fact that it had been the gossip-column headline made it almost innocent, something easily overlooked. So of course, he was suspicious.

If it was an anagram, there were several possibilities.

O, absurd on rum.
Sob around rum.
Armor bound us.
A mob surround.

He was getting nowhere.

Absurd on rum could be Gluttony, he supposed. He'd probably sob after imbibing too much liquor too, especially if the reporter bested him again in a battle of wits. *Armor bound us,* perhaps Wrath, the war-seeking deviant. *A mob surround* might speak of Pride.

Previous clues had left Envy feeling certain of what he was after. None of these clicked into place as soundly, felt as right.

Envy swirled his liquor again, the darkness spinning wildly around a giant cube of ice. The rattle soothed him. As did the liquor itself. He was stalling.

The truth was, he didn't want to see his court. The last time had been horrific. Children...they were the line that should never be crossed. And it was all *his* fault.

What he'd find now, after more of his court succumbed...

His next clue had to be from that conversation. He had to move forward.

Envy shifted to when the Fae had been speaking to Camilla. In the moment, he'd allowed his sin to take over, cloud his judgment. Imagine all the ways the male would—or had—pleasured Camilla.

It was a mistake.

Envy was starting to wonder whether Lennox wanted Camilla with him for the final part of the game to distract him. If it had been the Fae's plan, it was working. Even being aware of that fact, Envy couldn't stop himself from succumbing to it. She interested him on too many levels.

Her parentage, her talent for painting reality, her clever mind, and that magical little lightning show. She was a puzzle he'd not yet been able to solve. And he wasn't the only one intrigued by her. Wolf made it seem like there was another secret he either knew or suspected.

I'll be seeing you, fair winter lady.

Envy set his drink aside and used a tiny bit of magic to summon his journal. Moments later he was scribbling down as many clues as he could form.

Fair winter lady.
Fear it inwardly.
Fire at inwardly.
Finality redraw.
Radiant wiry elf.

Envy cursed. The clue *had* to be there. The more he grasped at it, the more it seemed to slip through his fingers.

I friendly at war.
Fairway tendril.

He focused solely on *winter lady.*

Envy was suddenly aware of Camilla's scent. She'd entered the room on silent feet, and her presence now burned like a candle behind him. Or a strike of lightning, he thought wryly.

He straightened, glancing over his shoulder. She wore a hunter-green velvet gown—*his* signature color—that made the silver of her hair and eyes glimmer like the moon. She looked ethereal, otherworldly.

Entirely forbidden.

He followed her silhouette with his gaze, struck silent by how regal she appeared, how elegant. How different from the tousled woman he'd pictured moaning in the bath, the one who'd had him cursing as he found his own release.

"You look..." *like a personal disaster.* His face tightened. "I suppose that will do."

Her eyes narrowed, but she didn't call him on the lie. She nodded at the several sheets of paper he'd torn out, crumpled all over the floor.

"Cause for concern?"

"Deciphering riddles." He motioned to the ground. "Poorly."

She strode over, careful not to touch him as she leaned in, tracing the letters he'd scribbled in his journal.

He'd sensed her shift in emotions earlier, how she'd wished for something he refused to give. Camilla wanted a fairy tale. And he'd been serious when he'd said he'd never be the hero.

Envy did not believe in happily-ever-afters, only stretches of time that could be more enjoyable than others. He liked Camilla's company, thrilled at their push-and-pull flirtation, but he didn't want friendship. And she needed to get back to her world, her gallery, her life.

"Dearly twin?" she tried.

His blood iced. As did the chamber.

Camilla instantly shivered beside him, drawing back to rub her arms.

He knew of twins. And he despised one of them. The one who'd just removed his blackened heart once again.

Gods-damned Lennox.

"It was only a guess...," Camilla said quietly.

He yanked his anger under control, offering her a quick smile.

It did little to comfort her.

"An excellent guess. I believe you solved it, Miss Antonius. I just don't like what comes next."

He strode past her to the door, pausing to look back.

"I won't be able to be at dinner. But please feel free to dine without me." He snapped his fingers and a servant appeared. "The cottage also has a studio stocked with paints and canvases. And a library. You are welcome to explore and use whatever you'd like."

"Where are you going?"

"House Envy."

"Am I not coming with you?"

Envy hadn't imagined the subtle edge to her question, the hint of disbelief. They'd never played the game apart like this. At least not intentionally.

"No. You'll remain here."

He made a show of straightening his suit, pulling at his cuffs, as if he wished to look his best. He allowed innuendo to drip from his tone.

"I have a private matter to tend to. I'll be gone for hours, so don't wait up, Miss Antonius."

He'd told her once before that if he took a lover to his bed, he'd need hours.

She hadn't forgotten.

Camilla flinched.

Envy had never felt more like a villain.

But he left her standing there alone, looking like he'd broken her heart, then cut her with its sharp pieces.

To save his court and also keep Camilla safe, especially if Vittoria was still involved, he'd do much worse.

FORTY-NINE

CAMILLA STARED AT the door long after the prince had left.

He'd lied to her. Pretended he was seeking a lover when his expression looked as pained as hers. Had the idiot even realized he'd glanced away, his throat tight at that most crucial moment?

"What an ass."

He was an even bigger ass if he believed she'd simply stay put. As far as Camilla knew, she was a guest in his circle and as such she could travel wherever she pleased.

Before deciding where she'd like to visit first, she plucked up a few discarded pages, scanning more of the clues he'd tossed away. Interesting. He believed Wolf was the messenger.

Camilla had a slightly different suspicion.

She called for a cloak and thick wool gloves, which took far longer than she'd expected. The maid who'd arrived was flushed, her eyes bright, almost feverish.

"Apologies for the delay, miss. Staff is short..." She trailed off, glancing back down the corridor. "Were you needing anything else?"

Camilla followed her gaze. No one emerged from what she presumed were the kitchens below. Typically, a cottage of this size was considered a country estate. Envy should have a full staff—butler, footmen, maids, and cook.

"Are you alone?" she asked the young demon.

The maid nibbled on her lower lip. "Just me and one footman left."

Camilla's brows knitted. Something in the way the demon had said they were the only ones left caused unease. Before Camilla could ask her to expound, the maid dropped a polite curtsy, then darted back down the hall.

Camilla stared after her for a few more moments, but Envy's choice to keep the cottage barely staffed wasn't really a great mystery. Maybe he didn't use it often. Maybe the others were preparing for Camilla's arrival at his House. Or the supposed guest he was expecting tonight.

Either way, she had bigger things to focus on.

Camilla donned her cloak, pulled on her gloves, then stole into the snow-covered night. Excitement thrummed through her as she inhaled the cold, spruce-scented air. The Seven Circles were under a constant cover of snow and ice, the realm a winter wonderland.

Her breath puffed in front of her as she darted along the tree line, her steps crunching on the frost-coated ground, sinking into the soft coldness below.

She glanced behind at the cottage, the windows glowing with warm gold light. She'd half expected Alexei to emerge, but wherever Envy had gone, his second seemed to have followed. Envy probably expected her to stay inside the cottage.

A renewed sense of annoyance had her pressing on, searching for the far western edge of Envy's circle. Soon enough, the howl rent the air due north of where she'd paused. The sound raised an army of goose bumps along her arms.

Camilla tossed a quick glance around once last time, to be certain she wasn't being followed, then plunged into the woods. The animals grew silent, watchful.

A predator lurked nearby.

Several minutes later, she found him sitting on a mound, a brook fighting against the elements nearby, the trickle nearly frozen but refusing to submit to winter's might.

"Wolf."

"What a delight." His teeth gleamed in the moonlight. "Our paths cross again."

He'd discarded his hat, allowing the full majesty of his Fae glory to shine.

He knew what he was doing. And Camilla allowed herself to admire him for a beat.

His white hair was tousled from the gusts of arctic wind, his ears on full display. His star-kissed appearance like the night in all its glittering charm.

He was still beautiful, still as ageless as the last time she'd seen him up close, two years before. His Otherness reminding her of how quickly he'd enchanted her, how fast she'd wanted him in her bed. But he was a reminder of her past. Of a choice she'd been given years too late.

"You had a message," Camilla said. "Give it now."

Wolf tsked.

"Is that any way to speak to an old friend?"

He unfolded himself from the rock and was suddenly before her, her hands clasped in his as he swung her around. He danced them across the snow, humming a tune that would enchant any mortal who heard it.

"My sweet little lover," he crooned against her ear. "Come to court. Imagine the fun we could have. Twisted in sheets, twisted in our dark souls. Don't you wonder what it could be?"

She did. And that was the problem. She shouldn't want to go to the dark court at all.

Camilla allowed him his moment, then halted, feet stubbornly fixed to the ground.

"You brought me out here in the dead of night, I came. Give me the message. I'm sure you have many mortals to charm."

"Some immortals, too." His chuckle was filled with sensual promise. "Why deny what you are? You hide under that façade, dimming your light. Year after year."

He trailed a nimble finger along her ear, his expression sad.

"Do you even remember what you are? Or has playing pretend for the humans made you think you are one?"

She batted his hand from her ear, then strode away, furious. "I am not here to debate my choices."

Or lack thereof.

"Then tell me what you are. Prove you still know."

Camilla's throat tightened, her hands curling into fists. She had not admitted the truth out loud since the first day they arrived in Waverly Green and her mother had forbidden it.

Wolf's animal-like eyes glowed dangerously.

"Shall I remind you what it was like, to finally be with an equal?" he said quietly. "Not to have to hold back?"

She was breathing entirely too fast, her nails carving crescent moons into her palms.

"You wanted me, Camilla, because we are the same. When you came to me in the dark market, you knew I could give you what no mortal man could."

"Yet you take mortal women to your bed. Do they not give you what you desire?"

"You know as well as I do, I cannot truly fuck a mortal without glamour. It will never be the same as it was between you and me. Flirt with your demon now, but when the time comes, you'll mate with a Fae. There is a place for you in the Wild Court."

This was not at all the way she'd wanted this conversation to go.

"Is that why you were outside my gallery and Hemlock Hall? You're trying to stake your claim."

"Partly. But I was also sent to watch the game players. You were a pleasant surprise." He sighed and stepped back, looking her over. "It would be a poor move on my part if I didn't make my intentions known now. I'm here to offer a way back. If you agree, I want you to do so as my mate. It doesn't have to be about love. An alliance is far more valuable."

"Would you bring me back to Waverly Green?"

"Wherever you wish to go." His yellow eyes drank her in. "Mortal realms. Fae courts. My bedchamber. The offer has a time limit, I'm sure you understand."

Camilla knew what he wasn't saying. If she chose to return to Waverly Green, she wouldn't be able to leave again. Such was the subtext of Fae bargains. This offer hadn't originated with Wolf, it was from the game master himself.

She chose her next words with care.

"If you're serious about forming an alliance, answer a question for me."

He smiled, intrigued. "One question, one kiss."

"No kiss, one question, no assault on your favorite head."

His booming laughter filled the night. "Very well, let's play by your rules tonight."

"Where is the dearly twin?"

"Old name. Older than me."

"Ancient, then. My question remains."

"Old ones call them the dearly twin..." His focus briefly turned inward. "The Twin Pillars of Faerie. It's an ancient Fae site, now abandoned. *That* is where you wish to go?"

No. That was where she wished to go *without* him. And it was also not at all what she'd expected. Thankfully he didn't seem to realize he'd given her much more than she'd hoped.

"You didn't answer my question."

"There is a portal not far from here. One of the demon prince's guards watches it." He flung his hand out, motioning in the general direction.

"Which prince?"

"If you want me to take you there, that detail doesn't matter. Come."

Stubborn male.

"Good night, Wolf."

She started walking back in the path she'd made, unsurprised to hear the Fae curse and come after her.

"You need to give me an answer, Millie."

She spun, eyes flashing.

"Do *not* call me by a nickname. We fornicated. A lifetime ago. That is the beginning and ending of any affection we shared. And yes, I could give in to all my passions in your bed. I could ride you for as long as I liked, as hard as I liked, and know you'd be just as wild and hungry. That's ancient history now."

"Doesn't seem so long ago. And you didn't mind that nickname when I was pushing inside you."

Wolf's attention dropped to where her locket lay nestled against her chest, barely visible under her cloak. His expression imitated mortal sadness perfectly. He'd been practicing.

"What a curious little trinket...did your—"

He reached over, gently brushing the gift from her mother, then drew his fingers back with a hiss. He glared at her. As if she should have warned him that the charm repelled Unseelie males.

"If you leave, the offer is revoked."

"Of course it is."

Camilla's laugh was cold, void of humor.

They expected her to make a life-altering decision in only a few moments. A future wasn't something to throw away on a whim, to be forced into by fear.

When Camilla chose her fate, she wanted to do so for herself, because she'd had time to think about what *she* wanted out of life. She'd never gotten to decide that before.

"Good night, Wolf. Travel well."

"Wait."

His voice had lost its teasing edge.

She turned back, waiting.

Wolf surprised her by yanking her close, attempting a hug that ended up being a stiff pat to the back. Foolish Fae. She melted against him for a moment before disentangling from his embrace, then stepped back.

"I appreciate your hunting me down," she said. Thanking a Fae wasn't wise. Acknowledging an action was the best course to take, one that wouldn't leave you indebted.

"Don't go yet. Camilla, I need to hear you say it. I need to know you remember."

She knew what he meant, even if she wasn't sure why he was so desperate for her to say it out loud. It was a plea, not a threat or a demand. A choice. She thought about her mother, about how she'd commanded Camilla never to speak her truth aloud again.

"I may be Fae," she whispered softly, "but that doesn't make me part of your court."

"Doesn't it, though?" His smile was reminiscent of his name. "Be safe, fair winter lady. Remember, I am not your enemy."

Oh, but he is exactly that, isn't he? At least for now.

This time, when she plunged back down the path she'd made, the other Fae didn't follow.

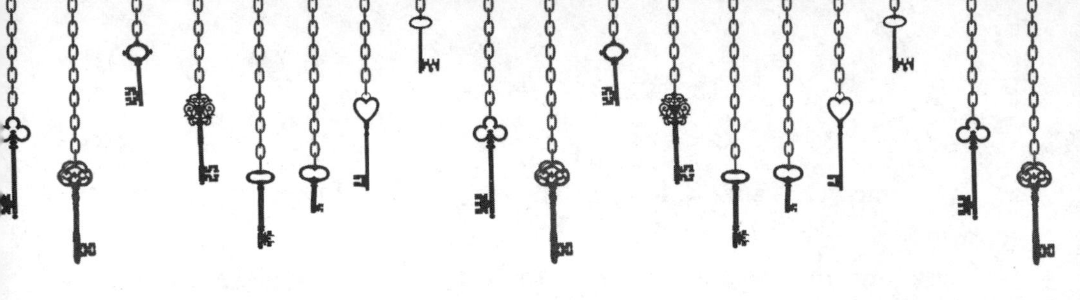

FIFTY

"Alexei." Envy's voice carried a magical summoning, alerting his second no matter where he was on the grounds that Envy needed him.

A moment later, the air stirred behind him.

"Your Highness?"

"Vittoria is on her way; I need this"—he motioned to the bodies of his fallen court members slumped throughout the corridor leading to his throne room—"taken care of before she arrives. No one can know the extent of our... problem."

Envy finally turned, looking his second in the face. The vampire's gaze was hard. Alexei had known the court was falling to the memory madness, had scented the blood behind closed doors well before the violence reached the corridors.

Lennox had many enemies; Envy only wished one would have taken him off the playing board centuries back. His second looked like he was considering doing just that.

Alexei could have returned to Malice Isle decades before. Envy knew he'd never admit it, but the vampire felt at home in these corridors. Had taken to the demon realm more than he'd ever taken to the politics of the vampire court. He wanted to see this game over too.

Wanted to rip the throats of their enemies out, bathing in their blood, making them pay for the suffering of the demons here.

"Of course," Alexei finally said, twisting to the nearest body. His mouth had a grim set as he hauled the first body up.

Envy lifted another, his anger and hopelessness growing. These members of his court looked like they'd turned on each other. When you couldn't remember anything, everyone wore an enemy's face.

Together he and Alexei worked quickly, bringing the bodies to a chamber where they could be properly tended to later. Demons didn't have religious practices like mortals, but there were sacred funeral rites observed by each House in the Seven Circles. Ways of honoring the fallen.

Once the corridor was cleared, Envy went to his bedchamber and changed into a fresh suit. Vittoria would scent death better than anyone else, given her true role as the goddess who ruled over it. He used more of his magic to cloak the scent. It was draining too much power, but he had no other choice.

Initially he'd only used his power to keep a select group of his guards and staff as clearheaded as possible, hoping they'd be able to take care of the rest of the court. Then Envy had had to ward his House. When he'd arrived tonight and seen the state of his court, he'd decided that no matter how much of a drain it caused, he needed to use his magic to stave off any more madness in his circle, as long as he could.

Now he was fueling too many demons with his personal store of power and barely keeping the memory fog at bay. He wasn't siphoning enough magic back to replenish what he was using. And it was taking its toll.

Being weakened going into what he assumed was the final leg of the game was not ideal. He had to hope other players were just as ragged.

Alexei stood in the doorway, arms folded across his chest. "I don't like this."

"Lennox doesn't design the game based on what we like."

"We don't even know if Vittoria has the next riddle or clue."

Envy blew out a breath. He knew that, but he couldn't risk not seeing if she did. "Do you have any better ideas?"

Alexei's mouth pressed into a firm line.

Vittoria might not be the key to the next clue, but they were almost out of time.

"If you're going to go through with it, then we'll make it count. You need to siphon more of your sin tonight," Alexei said, echoing his own worries. "You'll never last to face off with Lennox if it comes down to it."

They both knew it would. Lennox enjoyed lording over the winner, mostly to boast about his cleverness as game master.

"You won't like it," his second continued, "but Miss Antonius—"

"No."

"I don't mean stoking *your* jealousy." Alexei smiled. "If Miss Antonius sees you with someone else, I'm sure she'll provide a great deal of envy for you to siphon."

Envy couldn't argue. It was the best way for him to regain some of his power to continue funneling to his court. And yet...

"It's our best hope," Alexei said, more softly. "If Vittoria doesn't have a clue, you'll still have gained something from this meeting."

Envy glanced toward the window. Somewhere on his grounds, Camilla was in his cottage. Part of him wanted to go back there, forget his reality for a few more delicious moments.

"Vittoria will be here any second. I can set up an opportunity for Camilla to happen upon you." Alexei gave him a hard look. "Do what needs to be done."

"You know Vittoria only wants to make my brother envious."

"And?" Alexei challenged. "Are you suddenly taking the moral high ground? Now?"

Envy flicked imaginary lint off his lapel. Alexei was correct. He didn't have to like it, but he needed to do whatever it took to keep his court standing. Camilla's envy would give him enough power to fuel them all. He already knew from that taste in the woods.

They descended the stairs in silence, winding their way toward the throne room. Two guards stood on either side of the door.

"Once I call for the doors to close, no one is to enter," Envy said, infusing a bit of magic into his command, ensuring that they remembered their orders. "Are we clear?"

"Yes, Your Highness."

Envy strode toward the dais; the damage from the fire had long since been cleared away, his throne untouched by the magical flames that had taken the life of one of his council members. Rhanes had been a wise voice for many years, had the respect of almost everyone. His loss was a great hit to the court. As were the lives of the other council members who'd fallen during that first clue.

Envy settled onto the plush cushion of his throne, the hunter-green velvet soft and decadent. It was strange, glancing around the empty chamber, once home to so many lords and ladies, all vying to be the envy of their peers. They'd wear their finest jewels and silks, draping themselves in a sea of riches, all artfully displayed because of their prince's love of art.

Now there were only himself and Alexei in the great, cavernous chamber. The silence was oppressive. It felt as if the eyes of all his slain court were watching, wondering how far their prince would go to right this wrong.

Alexei climbed the dais as well and clapped Envy's shoulder before he took up his place of honor as right hand to the prince, standing just behind and to the right of the throne.

They'd only just settled into their roles when Vittoria strolled in, eyes glowing, brunette hair flowing.

Envy motioned to the guards and they closed the doors, sealing Envy, Alexei, and Vittoria in. Alone, for now.

He swallowed the revulsion down, adopting that indolent mask.

"Vittoria."

"Envy."

"I didn't expect you so soon."

She gave him a long once-over. "I'll always come for you."

Alexei mumbled a low warning. Envy had apparently made some sound of disgust.

Vittoria's gaze traveled over his second. "Alexei," she said. "Always a pleasure."

Innuendo dripped from her tone. The last time she'd seen the vampire, she'd been riding his cock in the corridor outside Envy's bedchamber.

Her blush gown had clearly been chosen to provoke—split up both sides, it fluttered open as she walked to the throne. Two tiny scraps of silk looped from her waist over each shoulder, covering her breasts only in part. She looked like temptation and sin. Her two favorite things aside from death.

"As wonderful as it is to see you again so soon," she said, pausing on the first step, "what do you want? I have werewolves to wrangle and a House to reestablish."

To see your head on a pike outside my House, Envy thought.

He felt Alexei's gaze boring into the back of his head, reminding him to set his personal feelings aside.

Camilla's silver gaze flashed into his mind. He shut it down.

"Perhaps I simply was bored, dearly twin."

Vittoria's expression didn't shift at the odd phrase. Maybe she wasn't part of his game. Or maybe she would make it difficult for him.

"And?" She climbed up another step. Only two steps separated him from the Goddess of Death. "Are you finally ready to play?"

His gaze sharpened on her. It was impossible to tell whether she was hinting at the game or was simply baiting him.

"Is that your price?" he asked, steeling himself.

"If we're negotiating, I want a sample first." Victory flared in her eyes. "See what it's worth to me."

She ascended another step, then the final one.

"Any objections, Your Highness?"

Vittoria leaned over, slowly pushing his legs apart and settling herself between them.

Her palms flattened on his thighs, slowly stroking upward, her thumbs following the inner seam of his trousers, stopping just shy of his cock.

It didn't so much as twitch.

Vittoria arched a brow. "Well, now. This is rather surprising."

She raked her nails over the tops of his thighs next, attempting to spark some sensation. His cock had no intention of playing along with his scheme.

Envy wasn't sure whether he felt like laughing or cursing.

Vittoria grew annoyed.

"Do we need to bring someone else in for our fun?" she demanded, attention flicking to Alexei. "Perhaps your second should join us."

Alexei came around to the front of the throne, his expression cold. "Should I get the woman now?"

Vittoria's head cocked to one side; then a wretched smile curved her lips. "No. Our little prince here is going to close his eyes. Think of this woman."

Envy gritted his teeth but attempted to summon an image of Camilla, no matter how wrong it felt. He closed his eyes, closed out the throne room, recalled Camilla soaking in her bath earlier. How the water had caressed her curves, the steam mixing with her floral scent, her gaze sharp as he teased her.

He'd wanted to shuck off his clothes and step into the tub with her, drawing her onto his lap as he dampened a cloth and dragged it over every inch of her glorious skin, her nipples pebbling from the sensation, making his mouth water from the sight.

He jolted from his memory.

"There it is."

Vittoria was licking her lips and rubbing his erection. She'd only gotten the first lace of his trousers undone when he softened. She glared at him.

"What seems to be the issue?"

He scrubbed a hand over his face.

"I don't know," he lied.

"Are you in love?" Vittoria asked, her tone dripping with accusation.

"Of course not."

She pushed to her feet, her cheeks flushed with annoyance. "Your bedroom skills are legendary. Am I to believe the rumors are all false?"

"I'm tired. I have a lot on my mind," he said. "And you know I don't particularly like you."

"And you've *particularly* liked everyone you've fucked before?"

He hadn't, further complicating matters. He tossed his hands up, frustrated. "I'll try again."

Vittoria folded her arms across her chest, clearly annoyed. "What does this mystery woman look like? Glamour works wonders."

Everything inside him seized at the thought. He did not want to fuck someone wearing Camilla's face. When he took her to his bed, it would be *her.*

His mouth pressed into a firm line.

Alexei shook his head at his refusal to play along, answering for him.

"She has silver hair and eyes. Stands a little over five feet three inches tall. Gold skin. Full mouth, slightly upturned eyes."

Vittoria flashed another crooked grin. She moved around to the back of his throne, leaning across his shoulder.

"Close your eyes, Prince Envy."

Her hand shifted, slowly undoing the top button of his shirt. He hid his flinch. The last time she'd been near his chest, her taloned hand had punched through it.

She slowly licked down along the column of his throat.

He fought the urge to leap up and put distance between them.

"Let's pretend your silver-haired beauty is here." Vittoria's skin brushed against his. "In your deepest, most secret fantasies, does she close those full lips around your thick length while you sit back on your throne?"

Her fingers trailed lower.

"Or does she bend over this armrest here"—she traced the spot where his hand curled over his throne, his grip tightening—"and let you take her from behind?"

Envy thought about what Alexei had suggested earlier. He didn't need to actually have Vittoria in his bed to incite jealousy. He only needed to give the appearance that he was aroused by the Goddess of Death.

Vittoria continued whispering sinful tableaus in his ear, tempting him with thoughts of Camilla. He closed his eyes, imagining everything Vittoria said.

Slowly trailing his fingers up the back of Camilla's legs, the slight swishing of silk as her skirts lifted off her body. Her bare skin, soft and welcoming. He'd draw her gown farther up, baring her as he slowly pushed her up against his throne.

He'd go to his knees, kissing his way up, his hands drifting over the curve of her bottom, then sliding around to hold her hips, and dip within, ensuring that she was wet and ready.

Vittoria had painted a vivid picture, her hands roaming down his chest. But Envy had stopped listening to her, thinking only of the woman in his fantasy, glancing back at him over her shoulder as he finally dragged his cock against her entrance.

Soft, throaty laughter sounded from behind him.

Envy had gotten so hard from the erotic image, from the look of impatience on Camilla's face, as she pushed herself onto him.

He was so lost to the fantasy that he almost missed the commotion outside his throne room.

FIFTY-ONE

"I NEED TO speak with the prince."

The gray-haired butler's expression was one of deep contemplation as he barred Camilla from entering House Envy. How odd.

"The prince..." He trailed off.

"Envy," she said, watching for any flicker of recognition.

If the prince hadn't brought them here, hadn't told her they were in his circle, Camilla would have thought they were somewhere else entirely.

"Is the prince here?"

Clarity flashed.

"His Highness. Prince Envy. Yes. Yes, of course."

The demon nodded several times, almost absently. Then turned on his heel and began striding in the opposite direction, not looking to see whether she followed.

She waited on the palace's front step, debating whether she should return to the cottage.

Cursing, Camilla closed the door and hurried after the demon, wondering at the strangeness.

They traveled down a long corridor, silent save their footsteps. No demons or courtiers lingered, no staff. All was eerily quiet and still.

"Where is everyone?" she asked.

The butler didn't turn, didn't acknowledge her at all.

Camilla drank in every detail of the hallway, fingers trailing over the statues lining the wide passage, appreciating the way the art had been set up. If she hadn't been in such a hurry, she'd have wanted to spend days admiring each piece. From the brief glimpse into the prince's House, it was like a museum or art gallery.

It was the home of her dreams.

The floor tile was oversized black-and-white marble laid in a checkered pattern, broken only by a long hunter-green runner. Frames were gilded, sculptures were marble. The ceiling was painted with a wonderfully detailed fresco.

Camilla wanted to lie on the floor, staring up at it.

She glanced back at the floor, squinting at what first appeared to be droplets of paint. Little splatters of dark reddish brown marred the otherwise shining surface of the checkered tile. She kept the butler in her sight but drifted to a closed door. Dried blood smeared along the handle, pooling under the threshold.

She jumped back, heart hammering.

"What on earth?"

Now that she was looking more critically, other cracks in the beauty emerged—the thin layers of dust, the shattered marble and defaced art up ahead.

Camilla grew more concerned the deeper they traveled into House Envy.

She stepped over what appeared to be a smear of blood, strikingly similar to how it would look if a body had been dragged down the corridor.

Bits of broken glass crunched under her boots, the artful sconces smashed and hanging from the wall. If the blood hadn't been dry, and if the dust hadn't settled over the mess, Camilla would have thought Envy had encountered something horrible here earlier.

Is this why the game is so important? She imagined so. If his court was failing, she understood exactly why he was so driven to win.

The butler kept glancing over his shoulder, seeming to grow more concerned by her pursuit, as if he couldn't remember speaking with her. And worried she was stalking him.

This was why Envy had kept her in the cottage. And it was why he'd kept his indifferent act up so insistently. Envy had been playing another role. Wearing the mask of someone who needed to hide his desperation, who needed to plot and scheme and save his people at any cost.

She rushed around the corner of the next hallway after the butler, who'd finally paused by a set of arched double doors. Two guards stood to either side, ignoring the demon as he spun to face her, brows tugged close.

"May I help you, miss?" he asked.

Camilla was unsure how to reply.

"The prince," she said delicately. "You were taking me to His Highness."

"I was?"

The butler screwed his eyes shut, then blinked them open. Without uttering another word, he darted down the corridor, disappearing.

Playing her own game of pretend, she smiled warmly at the guards.

"Hello, I'm—"

"No one is permitted inside."

"Is the prince here?"

"No one is permitted inside," the guard repeated, his tone unchanging.

Camilla glared at the barrel-chested demon barring her from the throne room.

"This is a matter of urgency."

"No one is permitted inside." The guard flicked his attention over her, a tiny furrow appearing in his brow before smoothing away as quickly. "Order stands. For everyone."

"He *is* inside, though, correct?"

"No one is—"

"—permitted inside," she finished. "I heard you the first three times, sir. *Please.* I need to know if the prince is here; I assure you he will want to know what I've come to say."

The guard pressed his lips together. This was ridiculous. Envy wanted to win the game and Camilla had the location of the next clue. What on earth could he be...

Soft, feminine laughter spilled out from the other side of the door.

Camilla shot an accusing look at the guard.

"I thought *no one* was permitted inside."

The demon averted his gaze, square jaw set. He would no longer answer any questions. Not that he'd answered any before. He seemed only capable of repeating that one phrase. As if it was the only thing he'd been trained to say and he refused to deviate from his orders.

Why would Envy keep me locked out…

A sick feeling burned inside her.

Envy hadn't lied. He hadn't changed tactics. He *was* entertaining someone else.

Someone who had a sensual laugh. Who probably wouldn't balk at spending only one night with him, who didn't selfishly desire more than he wished to give.

It could have been her. It *should* be her.

Envy had wanted Camilla earlier and would have given her a night of pleasure she'd never have forgotten. But it hadn't been enough. For that one confusing moment earlier, she'd wanted more than just his body.

And he'd made it clear his heart was strictly off-limits.

It hadn't taken him very long to find another willing bedmate. Camilla almost doubled over.

There it was again, that uncomfortable dark feeling she refused to acknowledge, bubbling below the surface, a scalding geyser preparing to erupt.

Pretty, husky laughter sounded again, farther away this time, still as sultry as a summer evening. Inviting and warm, like sweat-dampened sheets and whispers spoken against pillows.

The prince was being charming, funny. How wonderful.

Camilla hadn't yet seen the throne room, but she imagined they were slowly making their way to the dais, dropping pieces of clothing faster than their inhibitions as they disrobed each other, hands frantic, searching, kisses searing, messy. Tongues and teeth clashing, fighting for dominance.

Or would Envy kiss the woman like he'd kissed Camilla earlier? Sweet enough to make her dizzy, slow enough to make her believe it could last forever.

More likely he'd have her skirts bunched in one fist, hair wrapped tightly around the other, bending her over the throne.

Jealousy, pure and unending, barreled through Camilla.

She blamed being in this circle, this court, blamed the whole damn demon realm for its proclivity to induce sin. But mostly, she blamed the prince for daring to take another lover while she was sequestered.

Did he think he'd come back, sated, and Camilla would be waiting?

She would not be so easily dismissed.

Camilla turned away, noting the moment the guard relaxed his stance, then spun back and darted past him, shoving the double doors hard with both hands. Luck was with her; they were unlocked. They crashed against the wall, two cracks of thunder, warning of her impending storm.

She rushed in and ran hard, halting at the base of the dais, staring up at the prince.

Envy was indeed on his throne, his expression pure, glorious indolence as he casually lounged back, eyes closed. One leg was kicked over an arm of the chair, the other was planted firmly on the floor. His trousers were tented in the front, his arousal straining against the material. His hair was mussed, as if someone had run their fingers through it.

That *someone* being a stunning brunette standing behind him, playing with the unbuttoned collar of his shirt, whispering something in his ear.

Her gown was blush, ethereal, and practically nonexistent. Her eyes, a light purple hue, glowed softly as they flicked up to drink Camilla in. She looked like she ate lovers alive and picked her teeth with their bones.

Recognition slammed into Camilla. It was the female from Envy's memory.

Whoever the female was, she wasn't human. Power churned in the space around her, not visible, but Camilla sensed it there. Her mouth twisted into a delighted smirk, her hand disappearing under Envy's shirt, exposing a triangle of the prince's smooth, bronze skin, which she leaned over to slowly lick.

Perhaps she thought Camilla was here to join them.

Camilla cleared her throat.

Envy's eyes opened, his attention sharpening when it landed on her, his nostrils flaring ever so slightly. Maybe he was furious about the interruption. Or maybe he'd scented her envy. Too late she recalled what he'd said about showing that sin to him again.

The guard had her in hand at once. "Apologies, Your Highness. I—"

"Leave her." Envy motioned to the guard. "Get out."

Camilla didn't turn to watch but heard the hasty retreat.

"Miss Antonius. We seem to have a problem."

No warmth was present in Envy's voice or his expression.

No hint of the male who'd held Camilla a few hours before, kissing her like he was damned and willing to fall further for another taste.

"I can see you're terribly busy," Camilla said, not hiding the bite in her tone as her attention dropped to his arousal. "What with all the clue-finding you're doing."

"Allow me to introduce Vittoria, the Goddess of Death," he said. "She is the *dear twin* of my sister-in-law."

Camilla drew in a deep breath. He *was* trying to solve the riddle. By seducing the twin. But she knew deep in her bones that she was correct. And this goddess damn well knew it too.

"Ah. The silver-haired beauty." Vittoria looked Camilla over with appreciation. "No wonder he's distracted."

The goddess toyed with a lock of Envy's hair, then raked her nails down his chest, dropping dangerously low.

Camilla's jealousy reared its head, a territorial snarl close to ripping from her chest.

Vittoria watched her with slitted eyes, her hands now drifting to Envy's belt.

"Should we take turns, now that he's... up for the challenge?" she asked.

Camilla's jealousy was spinning wildly out of control.

Vittoria kept her attention on Camilla as she dragged her tongue along the prince's neck, then slowly drew back, lips quirked. She knew what she was doing, was getting a perverse pleasure from it. Envy hadn't moved, hadn't stopped her. But his gaze was flaring with some emotion...something that burned ice-cold, not hot.

Seeming to tire of her toy, the goddess descended the stairs of the dais, walking a slow circle around Camilla.

"Perhaps we should pleasure each other." She gave Camilla a secretive smile. "See if we can tempt him to join. Or maybe we'll decide against it. Play with his sin a little." She looked at Envy. "Would you like that, Your Highness? Seeing her come for me?"

Camilla's attention drifted past the goddess, coming to rest on the prince.

Envy's expression was hard now, his chest barely rising. He was no longer lounging across his throne, his hands gripped the arms of it, knuckles white.

Like he was trying not to launch himself off it.

"Do you think he'll stroke himself?" Vittoria asked, shooting him a dark look. "Make himself come all over that pretty throne? Or do you think he'll envy me as I make you writhe?"

She moved a step closer. Camilla didn't retreat.

"What is it about you?" Vittoria muttered. "Your very presence seems to incite passion."

That was an effect of Camilla's true nature. And the goddess was entirely too observant. Or maybe Camilla was tired of chaining herself, dimming her light as Wolf had accused.

Perhaps she should seduce the goddess in front of Envy, give him a taste of his own game.

Envy suddenly rose from his throne, all demon. He took one fierce step at a time, closing the distance between them in an excruciatingly slow procession.

Camilla held his stare the whole time.

This battle of wills was one she could not lose; it would give him too much power, alter their dynamic in a way she'd never regain ground from. Camilla was an equal here, not a pet.

It was high time he realized that.

The prince stopped close enough for her to feel the heat of him, so close she had to tilt back her chin to hold that glittering, dangerous stare. Sometimes she forgot how large he was, how tall and commanding. He used every bit of his size now, crowding her space.

Camilla's chin notched a degree higher; she was not cowed.

He moved so fast she didn't register what had happened until her cloak hit the floor.

"You smell like Unseelie, Camilla."

Vittoria laughed quietly. He tensed.

"Alexei. See the goddess out. We're through."

"No, we're not," Vittoria challenged. "Things are just getting fun."

Jealousy had Camilla feeling downright murderous. No matter if the goddess ruled over Death, Camilla would find a way to end her if she touched Envy before Camilla did.

"Alexei." Envy was pushed to his limit too. "Now."

Camilla hadn't known the vampire was there, she'd kept her attention only on Envy. But now he swooped in, ushering Vittoria out with a bitter curse and a foreboding thud of the throne room doors. Camilla heard a bolt sliding home, locking them in.

Envy was still.

It was the stillness of a predator. Of a being who wasn't human and never had been. The sort of stillness that unnerved.

And it would have, if Camilla hadn't been as still, mind whirling as the puzzle slowly came together.

All at once, she understood. She thought Envy had been reacting to *her* jealousy, his sin surging, being stoked by her strong emotion, but the stillness, the tension…

He was jealous. Of more than the goddess's taunts. Those had been a mere distraction, a way for him to try to get his true envy under control.

And he'd failed to do so.

Wolf had touched her cloak.

Her locket.

He'd danced with her across the snow.

He'd hugged her, run those big hands along her spine, attempting a mortal's embrace. And Camilla had sunk into it, allowing Wolf to envelop her for a moment, brief though it had been.

But Envy wasn't human, his senses weren't dulled.

From the second she walked in, he would have scented Wolf all over her. Had probably assumed that the Fae had sought her out once Envy went to meet the goddess.

And there was only one thing Wolf was legendary for.

A puzzle that wouldn't have taken Envy long to solve.

Camilla imagined that Envy was vividly picturing all the things the Fae had done to her, the same way she'd just pictured what Envy was doing here. On the throne. With the *goddess*.

Camilla wasn't jealous of Vittoria; she was envious that *he'd* dare to touch another the way she wanted him to touch *her*. Only her.

"I spoke with Wolf," she said.

"I know."

His sin chilled the chamber, frost lightly coating the walls. If she'd possessed that ability, Camilla would have iced over the chamber with her envy too.

Finally, his gaze flicked down to her locket. Or maybe he was staring at her breasts. An eternity passed in a handful of moments before he looked up, face impassive.

"Did you fuck him?"

His voice was low, but his words carried a punch.

If he expected Camilla to flinch, she refused to do so. Clarity came without warning. This wasn't about her. Or whether she'd allowed Wolf into her bed again.

It wasn't even about Envy's sin, about his inability to be satisfied, like his brothers all thought. His one-night rule was about Envy punishing *himself*. Repeatedly.

Brick by brick he'd built a wall around his heart. His refusal to spend more than one night with a lover meant he never had to risk that wall crumbling. Never had to risk getting hurt, or falling in love, never had to risk losing. Because he *had* been hurt before, he'd played the game of romance and had lost; the scar ran deep, the fracture never quite mending.

And he blamed himself for a choice that was never his to make.

His mortal had gone to the Wild Court of her own free will. What had happened was tragic, but he was not to blame.

"Once." Camilla gave him the truth, knowing he'd sense a lie. Knowing, too, she wanted to offer an olive branch. "A long time ago."

His gaze traveled to her lips.

"Was he the male in your memory?"

"Yes."

"How long." His voice held no trace of anger. It wasn't a question, either. "A year? A decade?"

Camilla's throat tightened. He was asking so much more than he appeared to be.

"Two mortal years."

There was a flicker of understanding in his face. Perhaps relief. Even if he didn't know *what* she was, it was an admission that Camilla wasn't human.

Moonlight streamed in from high-set windows, pooling around them. For the first time, Camilla noticed how the light bathed him in silver, giving him a celestial glow; a star fallen to grace mortals with its splendor. As if he needed any heavenly assistance to make him more alluring. Looking at him now, Camilla wondered how she'd ever believed he was human.

"Is that why you wear the locket?" he asked. "A charm to ward him off? Or is it an enchantment to hide your true nature?"

"Did you love her?"

Camilla didn't clarify who she meant, and he didn't ask. They both knew she was asking about the mortal, not the goddess.

He'd gone still again; this time a storm was quietly brewing behind his gaze as it turned inward.

"Infatuation. Intrigue. Deep admiration. But never love."

He bared his teeth, like he expected her to think him monstrous for that admission of truth and played the role to own it. Masks upon masks.

Deception would be their undoing.

When she didn't react, he filled the silence.

"I brought her to the Wild Court. Introduced her to her death. Made a selfish mistake that has impacted my entire court. That responsibility weighs."

And then she'd wager his one-night rule was born.

Camilla knew what it was like to make a single mistake that continued to ravage. Some mistakes grew fangs and claws, always hungry for more wickedness, more regret. She wanted to ask what he'd done but sensed that was a door he'd keep firmly closed for now. She'd just walked the halls of his House, knew his mistake had grown more than proverbial fangs.

"Your turn," he said. "Tell me about the locket."

She expelled a breath.

"It was a gift from my mother. It wards against Unseelie males."

It did more, but that was all she'd reveal now.

His gaze sharpened on her admission, the wheels of his mind spinning. She saw the exact moment he'd added all his clues together. "You're Seelie. How old are you truthfully?"

Far older than twenty-eight human years. "We left Faerie when I was six."

Envy blinked, calculating. Time in Faerie was much different. But Fae children aged slowly there even by those standards. She'd been born more than a century before.

Camilla hadn't truly started to age until she'd left her realm and come to Waverly Green, where human time had quickly ushered her to full adulthood.

It was one of the many reasons she'd refused to marry. Camilla wouldn't age another day in her life, would have to leave Waverly Green eventually, before anyone grew suspicious. She wondered sometimes if that had been one of the reasons her mother had left.

"Were you going to bed the goddess?" she countered.

He considered her question.

"That was the plan, if it came down to it."

This time Camilla did flinch. Truth was more hurtful than a blade. But he'd given it to her as she'd done for him, and for that she was grateful.

Envy moved in, like a shark scenting blood in the water.

"You see, Miss Antonius, the truth is, I've fucked for less. I've fucked for more." He nodded to the doors, the moonlight shifting into shadow on his face. "I would sooner stick my blade in that goddess than my cock. But if that was her price, I was willing to pay it."

He was no better than a scorpion, striking out when cornered.

Camilla drew herself up, unwilling to become anyone's pincushion. Being hurt and regretful was one thing, being an ass and lashing out was another.

"By all means. Go after her. I'm only here because I deciphered the last clue—the 'dearly twin' is a carved pillar, not a person. *That* is why I sought Wolf out. All for your stupid game. Though he did offer to make me his mate. Perhaps I'll allow him the chance to convince me. He was *quite* talented with his tongue."

Envy looked stricken, but then realization dawned. "The Twin Pillars of Faerie."

"Perhaps you ought to take your goddess there. Stab or fuck to your heart's content, Your Highness. Maybe a blood sacrifice unlocks your next riddle."

A beat later, his eyes narrowed. Like he'd just deciphered what else she'd said.

"He wanted *what*?"

"Oh, please," she said. "As if you truly mind."

"Swans mate for life. I've heard the Fae are similar. Do you really think I don't care if another male *mates* with you? Do you know what other creatures mate for life?"

Camilla almost drew up short. Wolves. The very creatures Envy had chosen to symbolize his House of Sin. It was just one more twist in their game. And she'd had enough.

"You only want *one* night. Am I supposed to simply swear off all other lovers for eternity? I assure you I'll carry on living my life long after you and your magical erection are gone from it."

Camilla turned, furious. He could keep his damn wall up for eternity. When—and if—he ever grew up, he could seek her then.

"A curious thing happened." Envy didn't chase her, but something in his tone made her pause. "My cock—diligent soldier that it normally is—refused to cooperate with Vittoria."

Of all the asinine things to say...

"Is that supposed to *console* me?" Camilla spun. It seemed his cock had more sense than his brain. "Perhaps you ought to speak to a royal physician, Your Highness. I'm sure there are herbs for that problem."

He advanced on her then. For every step he took forward, she matched it stepping back, until she found herself pressed against a column and could go no farther.

Her heart pounded, a tiny thrill racing down her spine as he closed in.

The smooth stone cooled her flushed skin through her clothing. Her whole body suddenly warmed, her senses heightened. Her breasts chafed against the fabric of her gown, aching to be freed, yearning for the cool air to kiss her flesh.

Damn it all. She couldn't *possibly* be aroused.

Envy pressed one hand to the stone next to her, the other snaking around her waist, holding her firmly against him. The scent of bourbon and berries mixed with something unmistakably masculine surrounded her, intoxicatingly dark and sinful—just like him.

Camilla could get drunk on that scent alone.

His hips ground against her. The hard ridge of him sliding against that most sensitive area, even through their clothes, stole her breath.

"Does it *feel* like I have a problem, Miss Antonius?"

He moved again, hitting that same place with unerring precision. A responding throb of pleasure pulsed between her legs. It felt like *she* had a problem.

The problem was that she wanted him to do that again.

His gaze captured hers, penetrating and deep. *He knew.* He'd sensed her desire, her want.

Camilla didn't try to pretend otherwise; didn't demand he retreat.

Her traitorous hands roamed over the backs of his defined arms, the muscles flexing beneath her caress, encouraging her to explore his back, his waist, before rising again to tangle in his soft hair.

"You didn't answer me." His voice was a hoarse whisper now.

Another sinfully decadent stroke had her parting her thighs on instinct, inviting him closer, deeper. She should push him away, protect her heart. This was destined to end in a few short hours.

Instead, she touched him everywhere, committing each curve, each ridge, each line to memory to paint later. The bones of his cheeks, his nose, those seductive lips... she wanted to map the road of his body and travel it again and again in her dreams.

"My only problem," he said, gently nipping at her fingertips, "is that I want you."

His confession was nothing but a raw whisper near her ear, a blade of truth so sharp it carved him open on the way out. Maybe she would regret it tomorrow, maybe they would both break into a million pieces after, but right now all she wanted was to soothe the ache in his voice, the responding ache in her soul.

One night.

It would be enough. Envy now knew she wasn't human. Knew she was an equal, that neither one of them had to hold back or worry about breaking the other.

They could be as wild as they desired.

A ragged breath escaped her; perhaps it was a moan, or a wordless plea for more. Whatever language she spoke, he understood. He moved against her again. And again.

Heat bolted through her with each torturous thrust.

"I want you so fucking much," he murmured. "I should be focused on the next clue."

Hips met hers again, harder.

"I *should* be on my way to the pillars." Another punishing, delicious thrust. "My court stands in the balance. Yet I'm here."

His fingers tightened on her hips, branding, possessive. Her body grew slicker.

"Plotting everything I'm going to do to you. I want you shouting my name when you come, every time you come. On my tongue. My fingers. My cock. You've destroyed me, Camilla. I want to return the favor."

This time, she met his thrust, grinding against him.

A low growl rumbled in his chest. "Tell me you want me."

Camilla clasped on to him, fists bunched in his shirt, holding him against her. It was the only answer she'd give him, the only one that mattered now.

More.

His face dropped to her neck, hips grinding again. And again. His breath was hot on her skin, a bit ragged, too. God, she wanted him.

His grip tightened again, like he was holding himself back from a terrible fall and failing, his control slipping. He was coming undone right along with her.

Lips ghosted across her skin, the sensation haunting her senses. Maybe this was what it was like to die from pleasure, to exist outside a physical form, to only know boundless ecstasy.

And he wasn't inside her yet.

"Camilla."

Her name was a curse, a plea. *You've destroyed me.*

He'd done the same to her. Tearing down her walls, her happy little human life. False though it had been, it had been safety. Being near him, back in this realm, wasn't safe at all.

It was dangerous and alluring and tempting and made her recall who she truly was.

He'd been right when he said she didn't want Prince Charming.

She wanted the demon.

The ruthless lover who'd demand and command and force her body to submit to pleasure.

Camilla wasn't sure how to go back to Waverly Green. How to shove herself neatly into that restrictive box again, simpering and pretending. Hiding her passion and lust for life and art and each dark game she liked to play. Pretending she did not desire as men there did.

Closing the distance now would send them hurtling over the edge. She moved so their lips brushed, breath panting in unison. His mouth hovered against hers.

"Camilla, *fuck*."

The last tangled threads of their control were slipping, unknotting, releasing them from their restraints. She wondered who would move first, damn them both.

Knew it would be her.

"Destroy me." Her voice didn't sound like hers. It was rougher, lower, filled with sensual promises. "Kiss me."

Envy lowered his head, closing the last breath of space between them, his lips the sweetest poison Camilla had ever tasted. If this was all they'd have, she'd make it count.

His erection strained against his trousers; it was cruel to keep it caged. She broke away from their kiss, working the laces on his trousers loose, needing to see and feel him without anything between them at last.

He drew back, gaze searching.

"You know my rule."

Camilla nodded.

"You're sure?"

"Yes."

He dropped to one knee, propping her foot on his raised leg, fingering the hem of her gown. In the matter of seconds, he magicked her stockings away.

A devilish smile curved his mouth as she shuddered at the first brush of his hands on her skin. He'd only touched her ankle, yet the bolt of awareness that shot through her tingled everywhere.

She leaned against the large column, eyes trained on the prince kneeling before her, head bent over her as if in prayer.

Camilla reached down, running her fingers through his dark locks, tracing the curve of his jaw, then drawing his attention back to hers as she tilted his face up.

From his position, it might look like Envy had surrendered, was bowing to his princess, but Camilla knew that was nowhere near the truth. On the contrary, he was about to conquer.

And she'd gladly allow him to win this round, knowing she'd be the ultimate victor.

"Brace yourself, pet," he growled. "I'm going to fucking devour you."

FIFTY-TWO

CAMILLA DID AS he'd commanded, holding on to the column behind her as Envy slowly pushed her velvet skirts up, trailing openmouthed kisses as he traveled higher. His hands wrapped around her thighs, moving in slow, wonderful strokes, his thumbs getting closer to the apex of her body with each pass, revealing more and more of her tantalizing skin.

Desire pulsed through her and directly into him. He grew harder at the thought of finally coming with her, of bringing their flirtation to that aching finish line.

The payoff they'd both feel would be unmatched.

He thought about taking her to his bedchamber but couldn't resist the way she looked so prim and proper with her back pressed against the marble column, foot balanced on his thigh. It was her gaze, though, that promised she was a sinner in the sheets.

Because she chose to be. Just like him.

Envy's teeth grazed her skin, little goose bumps rising in his wake.

His own desire sparked low in his belly, his cock so hard it pressed against his stomach. He swore he could come just from tasting her. But he needed to delay that gratification. He pressed a chaste kiss just inside her thigh, right above her knee.

Camilla squirmed against the column, growing impatient.

He pushed her skirts to her waist, and she took them from him, watching as his hungry attention roved over her. Thighs, hips, the throbbing apex of her body, he wished to taste every delicacy she had on display and couldn't decide where to start. She was wet, glistening. Aroused by the sight of him kneeling before her.

He flashed a knowing grin. "Sweet deviant. You like me bowing before you?"

She bit her lip, nodding, grip tightening involuntarily on her skirts.

"Good. Praying at the altar of your body is one of the only ways to get a sinner like me on my knees. I promise I'm going to worship every inch of you. Starting with this incredible, wet pussy."

Her silver gaze shimmered with lust. He'd noticed it before but was now certain she loved it when he used dirty language. It turned her on. The proof was there in the way she squeezed her thighs together, her breath coming in short bursts.

Lucky for them both, Envy could be a filthy fucking bastard.

He pressed another kiss above her knee, then higher up the inside of her thigh.

Chaste, sweet brushes of his lips that he sensed made her hunger for more. His hands caressed everywhere his lips had touched, then began their own independent exploration, sending shivers of pleasure through her.

Envy's gaze darkened when he finally reached the slick folds of her sex.

The first stroke wrenched a foul curse from her, her back arching off the column as if she'd been struck by a lightning bolt even though it was soft, languorous. Like slowly licking cream off a dessert. The second stroke was firmer, parting her folds as his tongue dipped inside.

She tangled her hands in his hair, holding him right where she wanted him.

He rewarded her with another slow swirl.

"You taste like sin, Camilla."

His thumb followed the path his tongue had just taken, pressing against a bundle of nerves that made her push herself onto him, needing him deeper.

She was drenched and he'd only just begun.

"I absolutely fucking love it." He lowered his mouth to her again, alternating between letting her ride his fingers and replacing them with his tongue.

Envy opened his senses so he knew exactly what she needed, and when.

"Oh...," she moaned, eyes rolling back.

He traced the seam of her body, following every drop of wetness, growling his own need against her sex.

"Oh, God," she panted. "Don't stop."

He was not God, but he would damn well make her think he was *a* god before the night was over.

He hummed against her, noting that the vibration of his voice, the depth of it, pushed her toward that edge. Her breath turned short, ragged—her orgasm was close. He repeated the sound, then slid two fingers inside, stretching her.

Envy rocked back on his heels, watching as she began to pant.

Riveted, he slowed to massage her gently, sliding his fingers across her slick folds, hitting that secret bundle, then drawing back before she climaxed.

"No more playing," Camilla warned.

He grinned as she took over, rolling her hips, seeking release.

Still thrusting deep with his fingers, he began kissing her legs, her stomach, nipping and sucking, the friction so glorious neither one of them seemed capable of catching their breath.

"I'm close," she panted. So was he.

When he lowered his mouth to her sex, her orgasm crashed through her.

Camilla gripped his hair, holding him against her, her body spasming with each wave of pleasure that broke.

His strokes slowed, lapping up each drop of her desire until her breathing evened and she floated back into her body.

Envy pressed one last kiss to her, then flicked his attention to hers.

"That was..." She bit her lower lip, seemingly without words. Except one. Written clearly across her face. *More.* "I need you inside me."

He needed to be inside her, too.

He'd murder anyone who interrupted them now.

She gently tugged his hair, beckoning him to stand. As he came to his feet, his body sparked with energy, with power. He was charged in ways he couldn't recall ever feeling before, her orgasm still fresh on his tongue, inciting him to crave more.

Camilla dragged his shirt up and over his head, then went at the laces on his trousers again, this time undeterred from her mission.

He gave her a lazy smile when she pulled his cock free. She inhaled sharply, then gave him an almost shy look as he kicked his trousers off.

"You're magnificent."

Huge. Was what she didn't say, but Envy was well aware of other lovers' reactions to it. Her expression shifted to concern, then determination. Even if he hadn't been reading her emotions, he'd know exactly what she was thinking. She had no idea how it would fit. Nervous or not, she was very willing to try.

"Lie down," she commanded him.

Gods' bones. He adored it when she ordered him around.

Envy led her back toward his throne, then stretched his long body out on the hunter-green runner at the bottom of the dais, arms folded behind his head, lips quirked. It wasn't the most comfortable place to take a lover, but neither one of them seemed concerned by the hard floor.

Camilla gently knelt, spreading her skirts around her, and then reached over, tracing his length with a graceful finger.

"Nervous?" he asked, grinning wider.

"Not at all."

He released a low chuckle, sensing her dishonesty.

She moved to straddle him, just below his knees, studying his erection. The blunt head twitched each time she touched it, forcing him to bite his own lip.

Gods' fucking blood. With a small smile, Camilla boldly wrapped her hand around his thick shaft, which pulsed harder than steel. He all but passed out.

A bead of liquid glimmered on the tip, proof of how aroused Envy was too. She swirled the liquid with a fingertip, circling the ridge, and he let loose a curse.

"Mm." Her eyes darkened.

Without warning, she suddenly lowered her mouth, following the same path with her tongue. His body coiled from the sensation of her gentle sucking.

She drew back, licking her lips. "You taste like sin too. My favorite kind."

"Camilla."

His hands pressed into the marble floor, his breathing turning shallow. She had him by the balls, quite literally.

She drew more of him into her mouth, her grip on his shaft just shy of painful while she swirled her tongue across the tip.

He jerked inside the heat of her mouth, but she took him deeper, pumping her fist up and down as she licked. She couldn't seem to help herself; she moaned, and the vibration sent little sparks of pleasure up his spine. Fuck, Camilla missed nothing. She swallowed him down more, then groaned as if sucking his cock turned her on as much as it turned him on.

He propped himself up on one elbow, watching with half-lidded eyes as she played with him, licking in slow, lazy, tantalizing strokes.

"Fuck."

He threaded his fingers through her shimmering hair. Her head bobbed up and down, her rhythm getting faster, her suction harder. She wanted him to come. The muscles in his abdomen tightened with each flick of her tongue. He was close.

He wanted her. All of her. Desperately.

She paused and looked up the length of his body, over his strong hips and his muscled stomach, his tattoos dancing across his gleaming chest, drinking him in.

Camilla had tamed the beast. The uncivilized demon pacing below the surface of his princely veneer bowed to her, a loyal servant to its master.

He saw the exact moment she realized that.

A slow, wicked smile crossed his face.

He knew, too. Maybe he'd known longer than she had that one day this silver-haired, sharp-eyed, clever woman would bring him to his knees, and he'd be all too willing to go.

Envy suddenly pulled her up, onto his chest, her velvet dress caressing his flesh, his knees bent behind her in support. His cock twitched against her bare backside.

His gaze turned molten.

"Take off your dress."

His command, his low growl...it appealed to her. He felt the truth of that by how much more aroused she became. She *liked* when he ordered her around in the bedroom.

Camilla arched a brow, bracing her hands on his shoulders. "What happened to *you* destroying *me*?"

He skimmed his hands up her sides, along her collarbones, across her chest, and then ripped her dress down the middle, from collar to hem, savagely tossing the pieces aside.

She had on a beautiful scrap of lacy lingerie that he admired for all of one beat before he shredded that, too.

If she wanted him to be wicked, he would make all her dark fantasies come true tonight.

FIFTY-THREE

"Devastating." His roughened fingertips traced the curve of Camilla's breast, thumb rolling across her tender nipple. She felt the corresponding twitch of his arousal against her backside, spread her thighs a bit wider as she rubbed herself against him.

Camilla brushed his dark hair from his brow, pausing to admire the beauty of him.

He was all bronze skin and sharp shadows now, the light of the moon revealing only slices of the chiseled angles of his face. She couldn't help but drink in the deep hunter green of the runner on the throne room's checkered floors as they spread behind him.

She imagined painting him like an angel, unfurling in the darkness of this room. She tentatively traced the bridge of his nose, as strong and powerful as the rest of him.

"Camilla." His voice was as tender as his touch when he pulled her closer. "I have one request. I want you to say my true name when you come."

She pulled back, searching his eyes. It was no small request.

"I thought demons closely guarded their true names."

"Which is why I only wish for you to say it tonight."

She considered this, knowing it couldn't be a normal request. Otherwise, half the realm would likely know his true name. But maybe he needed to feel less alone just this once. After walking through his empty corridors, she thought she understood why. If anyone knew what it was like to want to chase away loneliness, it was Camilla.

She nodded. "All right. Tell me."

"Leviaethan."

It was beautiful; the way he'd whispered it rolled off the tongue. Levi-aethan. He'd spoken like it was two words, two names. She imagined them as the wolves of his House symbol: Levi and Aethan.

Camilla leaned forward, kissing him softly, then nipping at his lush bottom lip, giving him a secretive grin. The time for talking was through. He'd promised to be a demon and right now he was being far too charming.

She lifted herself up a few inches, then angled her body before lowering onto him, only taking the first inch or so. Testing.

"Fuck." His breath came out in a harsh burst.

In another wondrously fast movement, he had her on her back. Her legs spread wide as he pressed closer, lowering his weight, supporting himself on two strong arms on either side of her head. His powerful mass was an erotic sensation on top of her.

She inhaled as deeply as she could, his scent filling the space around her. All she could see was him, all she could feel. And she loved it. Wanted more.

Envy kissed her. Slow at first, his tongue reminding her of all the sensual things it had just done to her. She clawed him closer, her body already throbbing as his cock twitched at her entrance.

He smiled against her neck, pausing his torturous exploration as she attempted to seat him inside her from their current position. His low laugh sent a dark thrill through her, the pulse shooting straight to that juncture between her legs.

"Patience, Camilla, darling. I promise I'll fuck you as hard and fast as you like, soon."

Before she could argue, his mouth had closed over her breast. His tongue did that glorious thing—a combination of tantalizing strokes and slight scrapes of teeth that made her throb everywhere.

Her hands tangled in his hair again, her body arching up to meet his. They'd played this game long enough; she needed him. Needed that release.

"Please."

Envy glanced up, his hungry expression matching hers.

He positioned himself at her entrance, rubbing his tip back and forth across her folds, ensuring that she was slick and ready even though he knew damn well she was.

He pushed in slowly, allowing her time to adjust to his size, her walls clenching around his intrusion.

Envy brushed his lips across hers, the kiss quickly becoming a tangle of tongues and teeth, then pushed in deeper, her breath catching against his.

Camilla realized the kissing was a distraction, to help her body relax, to welcome his impressive length. They repeated the motions, him slowly thrusting in, inch by inch, pausing to kiss and tease, bringing Camilla to the brink of pleasure, then pulling out. Each time he plunged in farther, stretching her, but she still feared he'd never completely fit.

With a final, powerful thrust, he was seated fully inside her.

He propped himself up on his forearms, searching her face.

"You're all right?"

"Yes." Camilla's voice was breathless. *All right* was an understatement. His size filled her beyond what she'd imagined she could take. She felt every twitch of him, every throb of herself responding to that silent call. She'd never felt more alive.

Tentatively, she gripped his elbows and shifted her hips, sliding across the marble to take him impossibly deeper. He pulled out with a hiss and then thrust back in. God, he was *enormous,* taking up every trembling inch of her, owning her flesh with each stroke.

He hadn't lied. He would ruin her.

Camilla wasn't sure how anyone else would ever compare.

She caught the sharpness in his gaze moments before snowflakes began to fall across her skin. He must have sensed she'd thought of others. The territorial, beautiful beast.

"*No one* will." He pulled out, leaving only the tip inside before slamming back home, earning a moan from her.

"What?" She was nearly incoherent from pleasure, waves of it crashing through her with each expert roll of his hips. But he needed to say it, confirm her thoughts.

"Touch you again," he said. "I'd kill them."

His mouth claimed hers, branded her. When they broke away from the kiss, his look said it all: *mine.* Something primal in her *liked* that. Wanted to claim him in return.

He must have read the look on her face. If he'd been holding back, he stopped.

Envy set a punishing pace, one hand now gripping her hip, anchoring her as each thrust went deeper, faster, moving her body with its force.

Camilla gripped his shoulders, nails viciously digging into his flesh, branding him.

Hers.

She matched his pace with her own, meeting each of his strokes, slamming their bodies together until they were both swearing out loud.

Sweat dripped down his chest, mixing with hers. Their limbs slid together everywhere, the sensation erotic. The sounds of their bodies slapping together, the musky scent of their union—it was heady. Wonderful. So beautifully wicked it made her pulse pound.

"Harder," she commanded.

"Fuck, Camilla."

His voice was raw, his grip on her tightening. They were both going to be scratched and bruised by the end of the night.

If he was going to ruin her, she wanted to ruin him, too.

Let him remember this night of passion, think of her hips crashing against his, their bodies shattering long before their stubborn wills ever would. She wanted him to shout *her* name, his orgasm ripped from the deepest depths of his soul.

"More," she said, pulling him closer, tasting every inch of his salty skin she could.

She tugged his hair harder, his mouth crashing against hers before falling over her neck, her chest, her breasts. He licked and kissed and nipped until she thought she'd go mad.

He slipped a hand between them, playing with her sensitive clit, his cock still pistoning in and out. She was drenched, her body holding on to him tightly, needing him deeper.

He was branding her, forever imprinting himself in her body and worse, her heart. She reached down, gripping his length too. Her hands slick with their passion.

"Camilla." He swore, fucking her so hard the chandeliers began to sway above them.

She hoped they'd bring his throne room crashing down around them. Still making love in the debris. Powerful. That was what she wanted to feel right now. She wanted him to remember this night the same way she would never forget it.

"Wait."

He stopped instantly, his breath ragged. He was still buried deep inside her, cock throbbing with his heightened pulse. It was almost enough to make her forget her request. Thc way it hit that spot deep inside her…he was her god in that moment.

Though she'd never admit it.

She pushed at his chest. "I want to fuck you on your throne."

He looked her over carefully, his expression inscrutable. Then he grinned.

"Lovely little deviant."

His smile was radiant, warmer than any summer's day, his eyes just as bright. It was an expression she'd never seen on him before, an expression that made her breath catch.

For a male whose displeasure chilled the air around them so often, she really shouldn't have been surprised that his joy could rival the sun with its warmth.

In a flash, he was seated on the throne with Camilla on his lap, facing away from him.

She steadied herself by gazing out at the chamber. From where they sat now, with the tall arched windows directly behind them, they were both bathed in an otherworldly glow.

Camilla ran her fingers across the arms of the throne, admiring the silver filigree she hadn't noticed from afar. Hunter-green velvet cushions softened the back and seat, with two covered sections on the arms. It was a beautiful throne. Powerful and sleek. Like the male who ruled from it.

Emeralds glittered in the metal, the gemstone meant to inspire envy. Across from them, towering canvases hung along the walls. Winged beings, florals, scenes of war and glory.

This, too, was a battle. One she'd not fought before.

Envy leaned back, legs spread wide, allowing her to do with him as she pleased. She shifted forward, flattening her palms on his thighs for better leverage.

Envy positioned himself against her entrance, waiting for her to make her move. His other hand stroked up her spine, encouraging, tender.

He misunderstood her hesitation. Camilla hadn't paused out of nerves, she was allowing him to drink her in from behind, freezing the moment so it would imprint on him in some way. She knew he'd have a wonderful view of her backside, knew it would drive him wild. The idea of him being turned on, losing control, made her so wet it ought to be a crime.

She wanted him to picture her there, poised to take him. Right there on the seat of his power. Camilla wanted Envy never to forget that he might rule over his sinful court, but she'd ruled his body for one blissful moment in time. Just as he'd owned hers.

He expected her to take him inch by inch again, and she earned a surprised huff as she sank onto him in one hard motion. They both swore, their panting a mixture of pleasure and pain. He filled her so incredibly much, from this position, he went deeper.

Camilla slowly lifted herself up, all the way up his shaft, then dropped again, this time circling her hips. He swore. His mouth finding her shoulder, his teeth grazing her skin.

Envy gripped her hips, kneading her flesh as he allowed her to set the pace.

She rolled her hips, her movements slow and purposeful. Until she leaned forward, hitting a spot that made her moan, and fire seared through her veins.

After that, their game didn't matter. Only their pleasure. Soon his thrusts matched hers, his hands moving her up and down as she bounced on his length.

Her muscles ached from the movement, tightened. She didn't care.

Envy kissed along her spine, his fingers digging into her sides. His cock swelled inside her the same moment the most intense bolt of heat raced through her.

They both swore, fucking harder, knowing the end was upon them. She was no longer sure whether he was making love to her or she was making love to him. They were frantic, feral, pounding against each other as if their very lives depended on it.

Right before she came, his fingers slid across her slick folds, teasing her clit until she lost herself in the sensations, her orgasm roaring through her. Wave after wave of sparking pleasure hit her, tugging her under, over, and she yelled his true name.

"Leviaethan!"

Warmth spurted inside her as his release found him, and Camilla plummeted over the edge again, riding the last waves of pleasure until she turned boneless and fell back against Envy's chest, breath heaving.

His arms circled her, drawing little shapes along her stomach, under her ribs, along the curve of her breasts with his own quivering muscles.

"Fucking hell." His breath was warm on her neck, her skin pebbling pleasantly. He'd softened a little but remained inside her. "You kiss like a saint but fuck like a deviant."

"I wanted our one night to count."

"Fucking hell," he said again, quieter this time.

Perhaps she *had* ruined him.

Her lips twitched upward before the smile faded.

Dawn wasn't far off, and they needed to get the next clue. Their time was over.

The moment she stood, she knew she'd be leaving this fantasy behind.

To his credit, Envy didn't seem to be in a rush to leave their little bubble behind either. She knew he must be thinking of the game again too. Of what it meant to his court.

Yet he stayed right there. With her. Like he didn't wish to be anywhere else.

His hands moved to her arms, lightly tracing them.

Their breathing had long since evened out, and the silence hung heavy between them.

The slow, light touches moved along her silhouette, her waist, the curve of her hip, then meandered below her navel, sliding closer to where their bodies were still joined.

Her breath hitched as his hand dipped lower. He was hard again.

"What about the game?" she asked, hating that she had.

"Do you want me to stop?"

She shook her head. "Not at all."

"Thank fuck."

He shifted so that Camilla was fully seated on him but he was in a more commanding position. While she was still facing away, her back to his chest, he was the one in control, lifting her up along his shaft, teasing her with the ridge as he slowly pumped in and out, making love to her like he'd never let go. There wasn't anything hard and fast about his movements.

Now that he was back in control, he focused solely on wringing as much pleasure from her body as he could. The ridge of him hit a spot inside her that stole her thoughts.

He pulled out, then thrust in again, hitting that same glorious place.

She leaned against him, hands curled back around his neck, playing with his hair. He reached around, cupping her breasts as he moved, allowing himself room to thrust.

"See that mirror over there?" he asked, pointing to a gilded mirror she hadn't noticed across the room.

"Yes."

"Watch." He widened his legs, forcing hers to follow his lead, exposing her glistening sex. If his court had been here, they would have had quite the show. *She* had quite the show.

Envy's fingers swirled over her clit, pressing against it while he slowly thrust up.

Camilla practically panted from the sight.

"Watch how hard I make you come."

Camilla bit her lip, already feeling her body's response to his wicked demand.

His gaze remained locked on where their bodies were joined, drinking in the sight like a starving man who'd come upon a feast. He drew his fingers to his mouth, attention locked on hers in the mirror as he licked her arousal off.

"So fucking sweet."

When he touched her again, with his erection nestled deep inside, it was almost too much.

He pressed tender kisses to her neck, his fingers continuing to slowly torture her. He thrust once in a while, just to add to the overwhelming sensations vying for her attention.

His legs widened farther, baring her more. Soon, much too soon, her breath turned uneven. Her climax was close.

Her eyes drifted shut.

Envy slapped her clit, sending a wave of sensation through her. "Eyes open."

"Beast."

"You fucking adore it."

That she did.

Camilla kept her attention fixed on their show, feeling and watching his skill as a lover; he was drawing pleasure the same way she could draw realms. And he was every bit as talented.

"Come for me, love."

His teeth were on her neck, his thrusts coming faster now. Still slow, still punishingly wonderful. But he was close again too, waiting to join her the moment she tumbled over the edge. Camilla tried to hold off, tried to prolong this moment. But her body responded to his quiet demands, finally giving in to the overwhelming pleasure.

"Leviaethan!" She came with his name on her lips again.

This time, when he shouted her name, then held her in his arms, she felt like he was already long gone. Like a star shooting across the night sky, there was nothing left but the memory of how beautifully bright it had once shined.

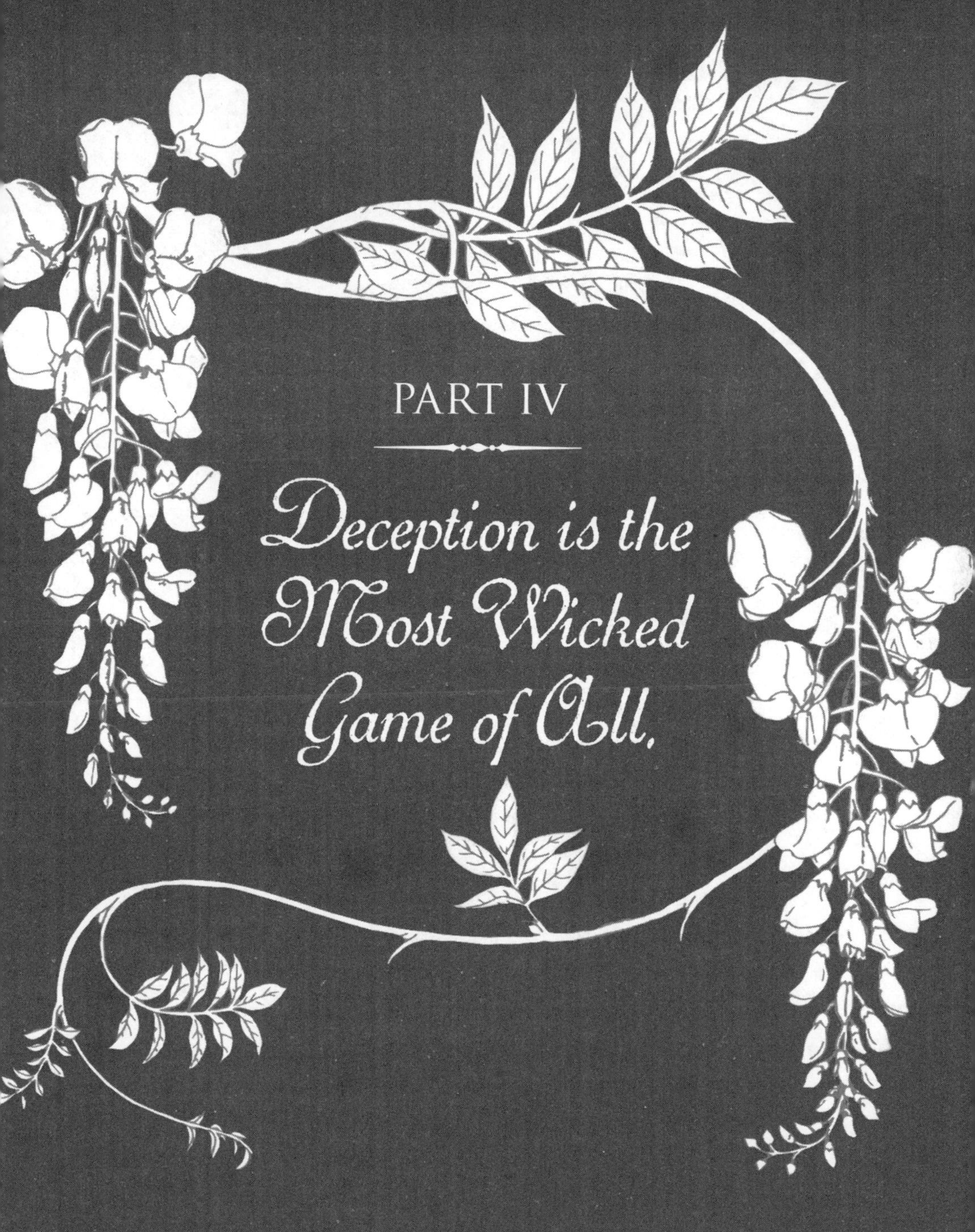

PART IV

Deception is the Most Wicked Game of All.

FIFTY-FOUR

SURPRISINGLY, ENVY WASN'T the one who ended their night.

Camilla rode him two more times on his throne, calling his true name every time she came. Backward and forward, her appetite insatiable.

Each time she said his true name, something inside him wound tighter. He should have felt the tension easing after the first time they made love. It didn't abate as he imagined it would.

He'd bent her over the damn throne, stroking and teasing and worshipping every inch of her body until she snapped at him to fuck her again.

Still...the want, the *need,* persisted.

They'd gone to his bedroom suite—so he could monitor what she saw in his House while his court was unpredictable, and so he could devour her on his mattress one more time.

One more time led to three more times. Her coming on his tongue, him on hers.

They were currently sprawled on top of his sheets, her legs tangled up with his, his fingers stroking the length of her arms, as he considered what had gone wrong.

Late-morning sunlight slanted into the room, signaling that their night had been over hours before. It was well past the time he'd normally feel sated.

Camilla pressed a kiss to his palm, then rolled to face him.

"It's morning."

His attention flicked to hers, amusement lacing his tone. "I do comprehend what the sun indicates, pet."

Her gaze narrowed. "We need to get out of bed."

He pulled her on top of him, nuzzling her neck.

"Soon."

Camilla kissed him, softly at first, then succumbed to the gentle tease of his tongue against the seam of her lips. He was hard again, ready. They could definitely spare another hour before they left. He'd clearly deprived himself of carnal pleasures for too long. It was the most reasonable explanation for his thirst for her.

She pushed herself up, bracing against his torso.

"It's time to get up, Envy. We need to go to the Twin Pillars."

He gave her an annoyed look. "It's Envy again, is it?"

"Why wouldn't it be?" she challenged. "Did you expect something else?"

He raked a hand over his face. "No."

"Lie."

He looked her over. "Fae cannot sense lies like demons can."

"Perhaps not, but I can read your face well enough by now." She scrutinized him much too closely. "You're not satisfied."

"Incorrect. I am much too satisfied. Hence the issue."

Camilla didn't speak for a long moment, the tension growing uncomfortably thick as she stared down at him. It would have been less irksome if his cock hadn't been twitching against her body every time her gaze flicked over him.

"We agreed to one night," she finally said. "Is that something you want to renegotiate?"

"Of course not." Envy sat up, carefully lifting her and setting her down on the bed. "I'll never break my rule, Miss Antonius. Don't confuse my arousal for romance. I simply enjoy your tight, wet cunt."

She sucked in a sharp breath, her eyes flaring with challenge.

He knew he'd gone too far.

"We'll see, then, won't we." Her smile was pure malice. "I'm sure you'll be completely unaffected if I should run into Wolf again. Perhaps I'll allow him to enjoy my *tight, wet cunt* for the rest of our long, immortal lives. At least he doesn't act like one."

His jealousy ignited in a blaze.

Before he could call her back, apologize, Camilla stormed into his bathing chamber, grabbing the new dress he'd magicked for her on the way.

She slammed the door hard enough to rattle the portrait on his ceiling. The one she'd eyed with mirth instead of lust earlier.

Envy fell back onto the bed, cursing. He was a miserable prick.

It had been hours since Envy had been inside Camilla, an hour since their fight, and the craving *still* hadn't abated. If anything, it had worsened. Especially after he relived each of their encounters, his mind pausing when she'd suggested they move to his throne.

He knew *exactly* what that had been about, and she'd been correct. Envy would never sit on it again without picturing her round little bottom bouncing with each thrust, silver hair gleaming like the dagger it was, aimed straight to his heart.

She'd skewered him with her cunning. She'd owned him on his damn throne.

And he *liked* it.

Camilla was dangerous. She made Envy want things he shouldn't.

After she'd left him hard and wanting in bed, all but calling him the cunt he'd been, he reminded himself of the game. His goal.

His court.

And the mistake he'd made that continued to punish him.

He needed to move on from their night. Focus.

Perhaps Camilla was the ultimate test.

If Envy didn't win, he would no longer *have* a court.

And that would be exactly the sort of thing Lennox would want. To first see the vampire court in chaos, quickly followed by Envy's circle falling.

No matter what conflicted feelings he felt at the moment, Envy wouldn't lose sight of his goal now.

Which was why they were now standing in the antechamber of a throne room that didn't belong to him, awaiting entry.

He slanted a look in Camilla's direction. She stood beside him, spine straight, keeping her attention on the double doors, probably admiring the carvings. She'd worn Envy's House colors without argument, even after the frustrating end to their night.

The gown he'd magicked was deep hunter-green silk bordering on black. It showed more skin than the styles she was used to in the mortal realm, but she never seemed put off by that.

Modesty was coveted by humans, but she shed that easily, adapting to her surroundings and true Fae nature.

In fact, the longer she remained in the Seven Circles, the less the societal restraints of Waverly Green seemed to hold her prisoner. She would thrive in his world, should she choose to stay and stop pretending she was something less than. But Envy wasn't sure how well *he'd* react, knowing she was close by, likely falling for someone else. It was selfish, given that he would never invite her to his bed again. Still…

Camilla looked like a royal standing there, shoulders back, gaze bordering on cruel. He'd told her briefly how they should act, the role they needed to play in rival courts.

He sensed her excitement, though she gave no outward indication of her emotions.

She wore the emerald-and-diamond ring he'd given her back in Waverly Green. Neither one of them commented on it. He'd offered her an emerald necklace, too, but she'd declined, choosing her silver locket instead.

The royal announcer stepped into the chamber.

"His Majesty and the queen will see you."

Envy adopted his cold, royal expression. A new game was about to begin. The game of posturing and court politics, of provoking and winning.

Without looking at Camilla, he followed the announcer into his brother's gleaming chamber, Gothic and elegant, made to seduce and intimidate. Camilla's steps were steady and sure beside him, and he wished he could see her face as she took in the throne room.

He did a subtle sweep, trying to view it as she might.

Black marble floors with pale gold veining, a towering arched ceiling, columns in even intervals, carved from a deep gray stone; stained-glass windows allowed light to trickle in, casting muted colors along the chamber.

Massive black gemstone chandeliers hung like watchful demons, hovering thirty feet above them. Gold weapons decorated the walls, while fierce serpent sconces spit fire.

A dark burgundy runner spanned the length of the room, a trail of blood leading to the dais and the demon king sitting there with his queen.

That dais was carved from opaque gemstone that looked like frozen smoke; the very same stone was found in the void between realms.

Two matching thrones sat at the top, intimidating champagne bronze serpents curved around black leather, thorny vines twined around the serpents' bodies.

A nod to both regents' power.

Envy fought the urge to glance at Camilla, wondering what she thought of his war-loving brother. Wrath radiated subtle menace, his power rumbling even while under control.

Envy *supposed* his brother might also be wound up because Envy winked suggestively at his wife.

Emilia shook her head, lips twitching. She knew exactly what Envy had done, knew he'd needled Wrath for the thrill of it. What she didn't realize was that Envy *needed* to stoke his jealousy. He needed to pull as much power to himself as possible; his court was spiraling, and he was extending too much energy keeping them together.

He hadn't fully restored himself since the vampire battle, and he'd need to do so before they left here. Otherwise, he wouldn't be helpful to Camilla or his court.

Camilla stiffened beside him, and he silently cursed himself for not mentioning that this was Vittoria's twin.

"Lady Emilia," he said, smiling so that his dimples showed. Wrath looked ready to launch himself out of the throne. But Camilla relaxed. "You received my gift?"

The queen blushed. "I cannot believe you sent *that*."

"Fear not. The original still hangs above my bed. I had it replicated for you. Just in case you grow tired of your husband and want a little excitement."

Envy turned to Camilla, his expression mischievous.

"You've seen the life-sized portrait above my bed. A few months ago, Lady Emilia was given leave to use it as a stimulating visual when she was fighting with my brother. He's envious that my cock is so legendary."

Wrath sat forward, eyeing their exchange with interest. "You spent the night together."

Envy's teeth ground together audibly. "Yes."

Wrath and Emilia glanced at each other, a silent conversation playing out. Envy practically saw them plotting right there in front of him. Some people clearly needed to stick their noses in other people's business to have any form of excitement in their lives.

Camilla looked Envy over coldly, then said, "Perhaps I should offer the king a portrait of his own. It only seems fair."

Envy stared at her. She'd gone and stoked his sin. Then he realized why. Even though Camilla knew this wasn't Vittoria, she was still unhappy with his gift.

He opened his senses, and Camilla's envy hit him hard. He silently cursed.

"I've never fucked Emilia, or tried to," he said. "Else she'd be *my* princess."

He couldn't resist adding that last part; his brother's fury and envy exploded.

Envy drew it in, filling his power to the brim. Even if Wrath punched him, it would be worth it for the massive envy he'd sent out into the chamber.

Wrath's glittering, night-colored wings—once wrenched away from him by magic—shot out, the span of them meant to intimidate. Once upon a time they'd been silver-tipped white flame—a weapon he'd wielded in battle time and again.

Camilla still wore the cold, cruel expression she had earlier. Barely sparing Wrath and his wings a second glance. This time, however, there was an edge in her tone.

She was well and truly pissed off at Envy.

"Do you always share nude images with other women?" she asked.

For a moment, Envy had nothing to say.

"I *like* her, dear brother." Emilia laughed, breaking the tension. "You must be Miss Camilla Antonius. I'm so happy to meet you. It's about time someone gave Envy a bit of hell."

"A pleasure, Your Majesty. Please call me Camilla."

"How are you liking the Seven Circles?" Emilia asked.

Some of the tension in Camilla's stance loosened. She gave Emilia a tentative smile. "Aside from meeting your twin last night, it's been interesting."

"I can imagine."

"So." Envy clapped once, drawing everyone's attention back. "Now that we've established that Emilia hasn't had the pleasure of riding my massive cock, I do have a request."

"Whatever it is, my answer is no." Wrath was not amused.

His wings beat softly in warning. Their inky color nearly faded into the background of the chamber. Shadows upon shadows. It was odd to see them without the flames.

Envy knew how much Wrath had loved them, how they'd been part of his very being. It was a testament to how much he loved his wife that the wings were now ebony. Through the careful sleuthing of his spies, Envy knew it was a price Wrath had paid so Emilia didn't have to.

A twinge of jealousy twisted through Envy. His wings had also been taken, along with the rest of their brothers'. Until his court was settled and returned to its full glory, Envy didn't have the power to summon his. They were there for the taking, but to unleash them for the first time...the magic involved would take too much from his battle to keep his court intact. With the ward, holding his court's minds...he had no power to spare for his wings.

"I need access to the Twin Pillars."

Wrath stared at him hard. "No."

"The game leads there."

"My answer stands."

Envy and Wrath stared each other down. A slow rumble shook the floor. Wrath's anger was manifesting. Envy's own sin growled a low warning in return.

"I'm asking nicely"—Envy's voice was quiet—"but I'll get there one way or another. You cannot bar me from them."

"As they sit below *my* House of Sin, that's exactly what I can—and will—do."

Envy took a step toward the dais; Camilla's hand came down on his arm, forestalling him. It would not be good for the realm if either of them unleashed themselves.

Emilia cleared her throat.

"Where are the Pillars?" the queen asked.

Wrath looked inclined to keep his mouth shut, but never resisted his wife. "The entry is in the Crescent Shallows."

Her brows rose.

Interesting that she hadn't known that. Envy kept silent. Emilia was the living embodiment of fury, and he didn't need to use his senses to see that Wrath had stoked *her* sin.

"What other surprises do we house here?" Her voice was low with warning.

Wrath shot his brother a look that promised vengeance. "Nothing."

Envy snorted, holding his hands up when Emilia glared.

"What do you know?" she demanded.

Envy considered his next move carefully.

"You recall the afternoon in the garden?"

That afternoon he'd stolen her magic after she'd stolen a book of spells he'd left for her.

Emilia's puzzled expression smoothed out. She shuddered. "That terrible, keening howl. You told me not to be curious."

He nodded. "You still shouldn't be, *especially* now. Abyssus guards the path to the Twin Pillars. Abyssus feasts on goddess blood; placing him there was a means to keep unwanted deities away from the Fae."

"Why don't I know about this?" Emilia's gaze was on her husband. "From... before."

Wrath looked ready to shove his fist down Envy's throat.

Envy would love to see his brother *try.*

Camilla's grip on Envy's arm tightened in warning. Wrath could be intimidating when he wished to be. But he didn't think she was staying his movements because of that.

Envy cut a cruel smirk his brother's way but didn't advance on him. "Keeping secrets from a vengeance goddess isn't a wise idea."

Wrath blew out a slow breath, trying to wrangle his temper. "It's not something anyone outside my court is supposed to know."

Envy's spies were well worth the gold and sin he supplied them with.

"I don't need to enter the tunnel from your House," Envy said. "We'll use the entrance in the fountain."

"No." Wrath's tone was harder than his look. "I don't want you anywhere near the Well of Memory."

Envy's frustration had him taking a threatening step closer. A move his brother did not miss. "I will swear a blood vow to leave your precious well untouched. I just need access to the Twin Pillars. That's all."

"Your issue, not mine, Levi."

"It's the most direct path there."

"But not the *only* one," Wrath said, mouth set into a firm, unyielding line.

Envy's pulse roared, but he kept his face free from the strain. Wrath would not budge on this. Envy turned to Emilia, playing his last hand.

"Do I still have the queen's favor?"

After her coronation, they'd spoken about her potentially being in his debt. He didn't really mean it then, but he'd call in a favor now. Even if it meant burning one more bridge, destroying the friendship before it had a chance to truly begin.

Emilia, for her part, seemed amused.

Envy realized she was all too pleased to annoy her husband—his anger would be taken out in the bedroom, where they both could enjoy it. He only hoped they waited until after Envy and Camilla left their circle.

"I do recall saying it sounded ominous," Emilia said. "But I cannot give you my favor just yet. My husband and I will discuss the matter and send for you once we reach an agreement."

Wrath's nostrils flared with his sin. He did not want to permit Envy to use the tunnel, but Emilia was not a submissive partner. They could be arguing for hours. And the bastard would enjoy every glorious second of it.

"There's a bedroom suite set up with refreshments for you," Wrath said.

With a jerk of his chin, the king of demons dismissed them.

Hours later, with still no word from his gods-damned brother, Envy was practically crawling up the walls. Camilla sat perched on the end of a settee, sipping tea, lips curved in obvious delight.

Envy shot her an exasperated look.

"Am I amusing, Miss Antonius?"

"Wildly so."

"Glad to be a diversion," he muttered, feeling downright ornery.

"I can think of more stimulating ways to pass the time."

Envy drew up short, breath catching.

One look at Camilla confirmed she was playing with him, testing the truth of his one-night rule. He paced around the perimeter of the room, jaw locked.

Now that she'd said it, he couldn't stop thinking about all the stimulating ways they'd distracted each other last night and a few hours ago this morning.

His frustration grew. He damn well should not be considering touching her again. Ever.

"You are twisted, pet."

"What can I say?" Amusement laced her tone. "You bring out the very best in me."

He expelled a breath, part huff, part laughter. The problem wasn't his one-night rule, the issue was that Envy liked Camilla. Far beyond her body. Her clever mind, her wit...she challenged him in ways that stimulated his need to solve riddles, to strategize. To win.

And now she was using those same tactics to toy with him.

"Fuck."

Envy caught his reflection in a mirror hanging between two towering shelves of weapons. His eyes were bright, cheeks flushed, and his hair was a complete and utter mess. He'd raked his hand through it so many times he looked on the verge of madness.

Or maybe he looked feverish.

"That *was* the suggestion," Camilla mocked, her tone silky.

His eyes squeezed shut. He wondered what he'd done to deserve such sweet and vicious punishment. This new game Camilla was playing was downright dirty.

John Lyly, a mortal author of the 1500s, once wrote, "The rules of fair play do not apply in love and war," making Envy believe he must have battled Camilla at one time.

The poor bastard never stood a chance.

Finally, a sharp knock came at the door.

Envy almost wrenched the door from its hinges as he tugged it open.

Instead of a royal guard or servant, Emilia stood there, brow arched high.

"Are you all right?" she asked, dropping her voice to a whisper.

"Do I still have your favor or not, Emilia? Time is one thing I cannot steal more of."

She pressed her lips together, rose-gold eyes studying him carefully. He knew she was concerned, that she'd sensed there was more happening below the surface. His sister-in-law always seemed to see through some of his masks. But not all.

He kept his expression impassive, waiting. Camilla came to stand beside him, and he fought the urge to reach for her hand. Emilia's gaze fixed on him before she nodded.

"Yes. You still have my favor."

Her rose-gold gaze shifted to Camilla. Something soft flashed in her expression, something that looked like hope. Or perhaps happiness.

"I grant permission for you to seek out the Pillars."

"You've always been my favorite sister-in-law."

"I'm your only sister-in-law." She rolled her eyes. "But...Wrath had one condition that wasn't negotiable."

Envy's smile froze on his face. He knew, before she twisted the knife, what his meddling, gods-damned brother would have demanded.

"You must use the path that cuts through the Crescent Shallows."

Envy silently called his brother every cursed, foul name he could think of. In every language he spoke. Twice. The Crescent Shallows were precisely what he'd wanted to avoid.

The water was magical—it forced whomever entered it to speak only the truth.

Nothing made could enter the water without causing death. Which included clothing. Envy would need to wade into the magical water nude with Camilla. And if she asked any question, he'd be compelled to offer truth.

As if this journey weren't hard enough.

Emilia clasped Envy's hands in hers, squeezing gently.

"Don't be an ass to your lady. Or there will be no more cannoli in your future."

He scoffed but didn't remark. They *had* been delicious. And he couldn't deny liking that Camilla was seen as his. Even if it was fleeting, or untrue.

Emilia smiled warmly at Camilla.

"I hope to see you again, Camilla. Next time we'll leave the demons to brood and battle on their own."

"That sounds wonderful; I look forward to it."

Envy kept his mouth shut. After the game ended, Camilla would return to Waverly Green. There was no point ruining the moment with the truth, though, so he silently watched Emilia and Camilla make plans, knowing it would never be.

Emilia turned to him, then pulled a vial from saints only knew where.

"Here. You'll need this."

He looked it over, then smiled at the goddess. She'd given him a gift for Abyssus.

"You really are my favorite."

"Go. Before my husband levels a mountain. Again."

A guard escorted Envy and Camilla down to the cavern far below House Wrath.

It would have been much faster and more efficient if Envy could have magicked them there, but Wrath's generosity had been pushed to its limit.

Once they reached the tunnel, the guard stopped and stepped aside. "You may go the rest of the way on your own. Orders of the king."

"How magnanimous," Envy muttered, tone dripping with sarcasm.

Camilla strode ahead of him, silent since they'd left the suite. He didn't note any lingering jealousy, nor did he sense any anger. Her emotions were tightly wound, flickering too quickly for him to get a solid understanding of what she was feeling.

Perhaps she was just taking everything in, cataloguing each aspect to use as inspiration.

A moment later the tunnel opened to the cavernous lagoon.

Black sand glittered, and pale blue water lapped lazily at the shore. Mist hung low, inviting and unassuming. Its entire appearance was designed to entice, then entrap.

The phases of the moon were painted along the far wall, indicating the next tunnel hidden behind a large stalactite.

"It's so beautiful. The water sounds... it's fizzing."

Envy grabbed Camilla's hand, tugging her back before she stepped into the water.

"I wouldn't do that."

"Why?"

He nodded toward the bones she'd missed, jutting up farther down the sand.

"Nothing made can enter the water."

"Nothing made?" she repeated, brows knitted. "You mean..."

"We need to disrobe to cross it. And remove anything else that isn't natural. Like your jewelry."

"Oh?" Camilla asked, slowly raking her attention over him.

His hands fisted at his side as he drew up an image of his court, of the bodies. Shame burned through him, more potent than any temptation or desire. No matter that he was a being fueled by and created for sin, he wouldn't allow the Shallows to tempt him.

Or Camilla.

He decided against sharing the fact that the lagoon's waters compelled anyone who entered—and survived—to tell only the truth.

Demon princes weren't exempt from the magical properties of the Crescent Shallows. It was magic that existed outside them.

"What happens when we emerge on the other side?" Camilla asked, looking back at the water. "We'll have to travel nude the rest of the way?"

Her tone was more curious than nervous. If anything, she sounded *intrigued* by the thought, a little breathless. His Fae artist wanted to travel naked. Devil curse him.

He could lie and claim they'd need to remain naked, admiring the masterpiece that was Camilla's unclothed form as they wound deeper into the underground labyrinth.

"I'll magic our clothing to the next tunnel."

Camilla faced him, expression inscrutable, then kicked off her shoes.

She slipped her gown off her shoulders, gracefully stepping out of it, the silk pooling at her feet. She had nothing on underneath.

He swallowed hard, caught by surprise. Not by her nakedness, but by the knowing gleam in her gaze. Camilla was definitely playing another game of her own, making rules up as she went.

Long silver hair glimmered in the dim lighting of the Shallows, covering her breasts. She looked like a nymph who'd sprung from the magical lake, tempting and wicked.

He would know. She was tempting him, and he was feeling especially wicked.

Envy motioned to her hand and body, his voice rough.

"Take your ring and necklace off too."

"Very well."

She turned around, lifting her hair and glancing over her shoulder, knowing exactly what she was doing. He tried—and failed—to ignore her taut backside.

"Unclasp my necklace?"

Envy drew in a ragged breath, swearing.

Her lips curved.

He moved to her, fighting the urge to run his knuckles along her spine.

He *wanted* to kiss her. But their time had passed. He had her necklace off in less than a second, then stepped back.

Camilla said nothing of his hasty retreat, though amusement flickered in her eyes.

She pulled the ring off, slowly bent over in front of him, laid it carefully on top of her gown, taking far too long to complete the task before straightening up again. Her gaze locked with his, daring him to hold it, daring him to look away from her.

Envy had been wrong when he thought the Sin Corridor had tortured him.

This was *much* worse.

And it shouldn't be.

He shucked his clothes off, trying to focus on the task in front of them. He refused to get hard now. No matter how difficult avoiding that currently was.

"Come on."

Camilla grabbed his hand and tugged him toward the water.

He followed, barely noticing the slight fizz of warm water against his skin, then stopped.

Camilla fearlessly strode out to her waist, then dove under, emerging several feet away. She flipped her wet hair back, laughing. Her eyes shone moon-bright, reflecting in the lagoon.

"This feels incredible!" She treaded water. "Come join me, Your Highness."

Envy considered the lagoon. Water lapped at his calves, tempting, fizzing—a million tiny bubbles bursting over his skin. They had no choice but to wade across it to reach the tunnel that led to Abyssus. Magic was forbidden until the waters had gotten their taste.

He took another step, the water encircling his knees.

He hadn't gone more than a few feet before he paused, sensing he was in trouble.

"Do you want to swim with me?" Camilla asked.

He was compelled to give her the truth.

"Yes."

Her smile was dazzling, bright enough to rival the most brilliant star in the night sky.

"After last night," she said, swimming closer, "do you still crave me?"

His throat closed, his teeth clamping together. Envy glanced back at the shore, wanting to plunge himself back to the safety of the sand. It was no use.

"Yes." His mind raced; he needed to get to the other side of the damn lagoon. He flashed Camilla a wolfish grin. "Do you still crave me, Miss Antonius?"

Camilla dragged her teeth across her lower lip, brows knitting. It looked like she was trying to force a lie out and suddenly realized she couldn't.

She waded back, glowering. "Yes."

He swam out deeper, fortifying his will. Repeating his rule in his head.

He would not touch her again. Would not kiss her.

But he liked that she still craved him. That he wasn't alone in his cursed desire.

He swam closer, gaze locked on her as he circled her.

"Do you like me, Camilla?" he asked softly. "Do you enjoy my company?"

She splashed water at him, her mouth puckering before she released the truth.

"Yes. And yes." She splashed him once more for good measure. "And I also hate you."

She drifted away from him, then fired off a question of her own. "Is your court in peril? Is that why you're playing the game?"

He inhaled sharply, realizing he was near the center of the lagoon now. Warm fizzing water lapped at his shoulders, the magical compulsion too strong for him to bear.

"Yes. To both."

Camilla was much too clever. He dove toward the other side of the lagoon.

They would swim across to the other side, put their clothes on, and be on their way.

Camilla was suddenly before him, reaching out. Stopping before they touched.

She looked him over, gaze searching. Gone was any hint of teasing. No more cunning game or strategic moves.

"Do you believe you'll win?"

He swallowed a sudden lump his throat. His feelings were conflicted, the truth not easily accessible. He wanted to win. Would fight with all he had, give everything he had to win. But whether that mattered, he wasn't sure. He pushed a hand through his wet hair.

"I don't know."

"Do you want to touch me?" she asked, softly. And he had an uncanny sense that she'd known he needed her to distract him. "Right now."

He inhaled slowly, then exhaled.

"Yes."

Before she could drag any more truth from him, she held her arms open, a half smile playing across her lips.

"What—"

"Follow my lead, Your Highness."

Camilla surprised him by waltzing them around the water, dancing in the bath-warm lagoon like it was their own private ballroom. She held his hand tightly, laughing as they twirled, sending droplets of water flying against each other.

"See?" she asked, grinning. "You're touching me."

It wasn't at all what he'd meant, and she knew it. Still, he couldn't help but return her smile. Camilla had played her hand beautifully. He'd admitted to far more than what she'd truly been asking—she'd worded her question with Fae cunning.

A trait that made him like her all the more.

For a few brief moments, there was no game. No court in trouble. No rules to break.

There were only Envy and Camilla, pretending this was what life would always be. Dancing in magical lagoons, naked, and wild and free.

They danced with only the sound of the splashes and droplets as their music, their laughter and the echoes softly bouncing back to them.

Much too soon, Envy stepped back, pressed a kiss to her palm, then led them to the other shore. Daydreams were not real. And a nightmare still lay ahead.

"Dress quickly." Envy summoned their clothing, then turned to give Camilla privacy.

"I sense Abyssus waiting for us."

FIFTY-FIVE

Camilla stared down at her clothing, shaking her head.

Envy had magicked more than what she'd been wearing, improving upon her clothes for their next destination. He really thought of everything.

A long-sleeved dress, a delicate slip, undergarments, thick stockings, and a velvet cloak were folded neatly at her feet.

Silken slippers had also been replaced by sturdy boots. Supple leather, butter-soft, and finely crafted. Her ring and necklace sparkled in the strange glow of the Shallows.

She pulled her clothes on, stealing looks at the prince as she did so. He stood fully clothed with his back to her, ramrod-straight, muscles taut, tension radiating around him.

Gone was the male who'd surprised her by accepting her dance in the magical water, holding her close and humming softly. The cold, remote Prince of Hell had returned.

Focused, ruthless. Attention fixed only on his game.

Camilla wondered whether Envy even realized he'd been humming a tune for them to dance to. For a few precious moments, he'd seemed completely at ease. It was the first time she'd ever seen him so relaxed.

He'd been even more tightly wound after their night had come to an end. Like he was fighting some invisible foe Camilla couldn't see. But in the Shallows, in a place where they clearly couldn't lie, he'd been free.

No scheming or plotting, no hiding behind cool arrogance or indifference.

She'd only meant to start their dance as a game. But he'd pulled her closer, like it was the one moment he'd permit himself to take what he wanted. To show a softness he'd never let anyone see. He'd cradled her against his body simply because he wished to hold her.

It would have been far easier if he'd tried to kiss or seduce her.

Even with his insistence about his one-night rule, Camilla would understand his admitting to wanting to take her hard and fast in the water, unleashing his carnal nature, setting a punishing pace for breaking his rule.

Passion and lust were simple, animalistic urges. Completely natural. Uncomplicated.

His softness was much more dangerous than those sharp edges.

Camilla could snuggle into that tenderness, let her guard drop, realizing too late that she'd been carved open far deeper. She'd bleed out before she knew she'd been cut.

They both needed to realize that one night was all they'd get. Because as much as he seemed to fear another night for his own reasons, Camilla needed to protect her heart.

She would regain her stolen talent from the game master, then return to Waverly Green. She'd cuddle Bunny and give her extra treats and warm cream to make up for leaving her. Envy would restore his court, then continue with his games here.

Sometimes two people weren't meant to be more than one moment. Wondrous and unforgettable though it might be, not all good things were meant to last.

"Ready?" he asked, still facing forward.

As if they weren't far beyond modesty with each other.

As if they hadn't been inside each other's skin.

Each time he tried so hard to put up a wall between them, it made her want to batter into it, remind him that they did share more than a casual encounter. Even if it wasn't for more than a few hours, it was still something worth appreciating.

"Almost."

Camilla tugged her boots on, then finished with her ring and necklace. She wasn't sure what had made her take the ring earlier—it was only meant to be used in Waverly Green, to convince society they were betrothed. It certainly didn't symbolize that here.

They'd slept together. And while it was an incredible night of passion, that was in the past now. It would never happen again. He'd made it clear his rule still stood. And Camilla was all right with that, more than all right. She wanted uncomplicated, and Envy was anything but.

Yet the ring...Camilla liked it. That was all. When their time together ended, she'd give it back.

Fully dressed, she strode to where he waited, leaving their moment of tenderness behind with the Crescent Shallows.

He looked her over. "Stay behind me. If Abyssus takes an interest, you're to return to the Shallows immediately. Do not let it touch you."

Camilla opened her mouth to respond, then shut it.

"Touching is half the fun, Prince."

Envy hadn't been the one to speak.

The male voice was not nightmarish. It didn't sound demonic. Or rough. There weren't many layers screeching together, no clicking of tongues or smacking of teeth.

No growls or roars.

It spoke in a silken purr, a low murmur that curled around your senses, rubbed against them like a house cat seeking affection. And was far more dangerous for it.

Envy pressed her behind him.

"I have a gift from the queen," he said, holding up the vial.

"What care do I have for kings or queens?" Abyssus asked. "Perhaps I seek company. Conversation. A taste of emotion, a kiss of skin. Perhaps I crave oblivion."

Camilla did not like any of those options, least especially the last few.

If Envy responded, she would never know.

The world suddenly vanished as if it had never been there at all. There was no cave, no ground or walls or ceiling, no tunnel. No Envy. No ancient, sweet-voiced creature.

Camilla was alone. Completely. It was solitude in a way she'd never experienced—there was always some form of life. Whether it was grass or clouds or sky. Birds chirping, bugs buzzing, wind blowing softly through leaves. She'd never realized how much life there was all around her, always.

Here was . . . empty.

No earth. No stone. Nothing. Vast, unending, *nothingness,* stretching in every direction, swallowing *everything.* Worse than the void outside realms, this was heavy and oppressive.

"Hello?" she called, voice echoing into nothing.

Nothing responded. She wasn't sure whether she was relieved or more frightened at that.

She took a step forward, hands outstretched, searching. It was like walking through space, except there were no stars lighting the sky. No form beneath her feet.

Her heart pounded.

She could be falling or standing still, nothing registered.

Once, when her father had passed away and her mother was long gone, she'd thought she was all alone. Then Wolf came and reminded her there was another path, another choice laid out for her to take. Before that, there'd been a time she'd wished for solitude. A way to escape from the world. Had she ever truly grasped what that could be?

This place was fear. Infinite. Solitude beyond what any creature should have to know.

"This isn't real," she whispered. "I'm in a cavern. Below House Wrath."

Camilla squeezed her eyes shut, knowing it had to be an illusion.

Some powerful magic or glamour. Closing her eyes or keeping them open made no difference, everything remained the same, unchanged, endless dark.

"This isn't real," she whispered again, hating the tremble in her voice.

"What is reality? If it feels real, looks real, is it not so?"

Abyssus suddenly was there, holding a ball of glowing light in his palm. She squinted at the blazing light, eyes stinging. Once she adjusted to the glow, she could see the being in all his glory. He certainly didn't look like a monster. His skin was golden, his hair the same luminous shade as his skin. He wore a white toga, showing a powerful, sculpted body.

Abyssus looked like a sun god, bound to the Underworld. Wholly out of place.

Except for his eyes. They were fully black, fathomless, and hungry.

Camilla's gaze darted around, searching for Envy.

He was nowhere to be seen.

"Do you not feel the darkness?" Abyssus asked. "Is it not real? The same as sky and earth and blood are real?"

Camilla began to shake her head, then stopped. She *could* feel the darkness. A feat that should not be possible, even with magic. It was many things—soft, cold, warm, terror and protection. Each essence flickered over her wildly, until she could scarcely draw breath.

"This isn't real," she repeated.

Fragments of emotions mixed with physical and mental truths. Breaking and shattering and melding together until she couldn't breathe.

"Make it stop," she gritted out.

Abyssus smiled faintly, amusement flickering in his dark eyes.

Just as quickly as the world had been stripped away, it was back. Envy was barking orders, like only a moment had passed for him. It felt like hours for Camilla.

"Don't look him in the eye, Miss Antonius."

Abyssus flicked his attention to Camilla again, a secret smile curving his lips.

She was immediately ensnared by those ancient, terrible eyes. They held her prisoner, drew her in, made her forget life and happiness and light. It was different from the first darkness he'd shown her; this suffocated, corrupted the soul. Made her wish for death.

Darkness. Cold, endless darkness swept in, chilling her.

There had never been any light, never anything except this endless dark. This—

"Enough."

A voice shattered the hold over Camilla.

Abyssus lurched forward, and Envy shoved her back toward the lagoon.

"Run!"

Camilla didn't hesitate. She turned, darted two steps, then halted.

A shadow peeled away from the cavern wall, chuckling darkly. At first, she thought Abyssus had managed to get past Envy; then the shadow spoke.

"Hello, Camilla, darling. You look like you've seen a ghost."

Crimson eyes glowed like dying embers in a fire as the vampire fully stepped out from where he'd been hiding. She could not believe it. Maybe he *had* made a deal with the devil. He certainly seemed to cheat death as much as he'd cheated half of Waverly Green's elite.

"Vexley. *How?*"

His head canted to the side, more animal than human in movement.

"Foolish woman. You had no idea how much venom was running through my veins."

He flashed his teeth. The incisors were gleaming, sharp instruments of death.

"It hurt like hell. The change. Took a while for me to come to. I wanted to find you, thank you personally. Repay the honor."

Horror filled Camilla. She'd turned Vexley into an even worse demon.

He took a step closer, attention fixed to her neck.

"We were interrupted before, Camilla. Procreating might be...difficult. But we can certainly try. I still need an heir. Why not make an immortal legacy? Let me turn you."

Envy was suddenly there, eyes glittering and dangerous. Camilla glanced around, feeling the walls closing in. She wanted to ask what had happened to Abyssus but kept silent. Envy must have a plan. He *always* had a plan.

Vexley drifted closer, gaze darkening with thirst. He hadn't noticed the demon yet.

"Don't." Envy's dagger glowed softly. "She's *mine*."

"Lord Synton." Vexley laughed, shaking free from his thirst. "I've heard many interesting tales about you. Too bad we're both playing the game. I might have liked you, *Your Highness*."

Camilla felt trapped between mountain and stone, between supernatural predators. And the deadly lagoon. The tunnel was much too narrow for all of them. If they couldn't get past Vexley, they'd need to retreat toward Abyssus. Worse and worse.

Envy stalked closer. Fear in a handsome, male form. Camilla could suddenly breathe again.

"My brother gets a little touchy when creatures cross his wards."

Envy pressed the queen's vial into her palm, nudging her back in the other direction. She clutched it to her chest, taking a step back.

"How did you cross them?"

She suddenly understood what he was doing—he was distracting Vexley, catering to his vanity.

Vexley all but preened at Envy's appeal to his ego. The idiot.

"Connections. Perhaps you don't know the right creatures."

Envy smiled faintly.

Between one breath and the next, Vexley attacked. His fangs scraped across her throat, liquid heat dripping down her neck. But his move had been sloppy, wild, a feral animal too mad to be strategic. Immediately he was tossed across the tunnel, the demon's rage nearly ripping his arms off. Vexley crumpled, and Envy turned back toward Camilla.

Envy didn't see him coming, didn't think he'd get up. The demon was focused on Camilla, his gaze locked onto her blood.

She screamed, but nothing came out. Vexley leapt, his hands transforming into talons, his fangs lengthening. He was no longer a simple vampire; he looked like a werewolf. A beast. Some demonic being that could only be spawned in the Underworld.

He opened his fanged mouth, a roar bouncing off the tunnel walls, and he ripped Envy's head clean from his shoulders in one brutal swipe of his teeth.

She dropped to her knees, retching. Over and over.

Vexley had killed Envy.

She couldn't....

She heaved, emptying the contents of her stomach, tears streaming down her face.

"CAMILLA."

A voice bellowed behind her. She couldn't focus. All she could do was stare at the headless body of the prince, heaving. Vexley was gone. Like he'd never been there.

It was so shocking, so unexpected, it wrenched her from her tears.

Camilla glanced around, confused. Why would he kill Envy and not take her?

She crawled to Envy's lifeless body, shaking him.

"Get up!" she screamed. "Please. Get up."

"CAMILLA!"

Her name was a command, issued by one she could not ignore.

She turned.

And the world flipped upside down once more.

Envy was standing there, shouting her name, over and over. His expression furious, terrified.

Camilla glanced back. There was no headless body. No vampire.

There never had been.

For the first time she noticed the pile of bones. The darkened earth. Walls splattered with entrails and God only knew what over the millennia. A circle of shimmering gemstones was embedded deep in the earth. She'd crossed them.

She looked back at Envy.

He was on the other side, pounding his fist against a wall she couldn't see.

Hot breath caressed her neck. A tongue darted out.

She realized with growing horror that the blood had been real.

"Little deceiver, you may only pass once the tithe has been paid," Abyssus crooned softly. "Should we take it from the prince?"

"No."

"Mm." Abyssus canted his head. "*No*. I do not enjoy that word."

She rushed forward, nearly tripping over her feet as she tried to cross the line. It sizzled over her skin, hissing and tossed her back. She scrambled on her backside, crawling away from the ancient being who now stood over her, surveying her with growing intrigue.

He crouched in front of her, golden skin glowing.

"Did you truly believe you wouldn't be tested?" he purred. "That you would simply walk back, be given all that you seek? We both know that's not the way of kings. Most especially dark ones."

Camilla froze, her mouth dry.

Abyssus had removed all their surroundings again, set them hovering in a suspended state of nothing. Darkness devoured her hands, tendrils curling over her where she remained sprawled on the ground. Or what had once been the ground.

"It's when we're trapped in complete darkness that our true selves are revealed."

His otherworldly glow winked out.

"Who are you when the world fades away? What are you made of? How strong is your mind, your will, your capacity to fight? When there is nothing, who do you become?"

He was pressing her, taunting her, all the while the darkness shadowed all. Blackness was a color she knew; it had form, variation. This was the absence of all. No color. No matter. Her eyes were open—closing them didn't make any shift in the endless void she was trapped in.

"What do you fear above all, little Fae?"

"I don't know!"

"Mm. Look deeper."

Then even his presence was gone.

There was truly nothing.

No spark. No life. No joy or pain. No past or present, no future she could ever hope for or dream of. No way out of this endless abyss that had swallowed the world.

But there was fear.

Camilla felt it pressing into her chest, stealing what little air remained. The darkness learned her, carved her open, tasted what her soul was made of. Decided to play.

It sipped from her fear, drank down her cries, indulged in the sorrow that threatened to trap her mind forever.

Time lost all meaning. There were no seconds or minutes or hours. They were constructs that belonged to civilizations, and Camilla was so far removed from anyone else, was so *alone.*

"There." Abyssus's voice drifted over her on a dark wind. "We have found your test."

Just as suddenly as the abyss appeared, it was gone.

Camilla was on her hands and knees, panting. She glanced up at the cave, the walls dancing with shadows, the dirt packed hard beneath her. Tears streamed down her face.

She swiped at her nose, then sat back.

Abyssus was gone, the circle of gemstones falling below the surface, freeing her.

Camilla drew in a deep breath, then hauled herself to her feet. She gave herself another moment to collect her emotions, then turned.

Envy was nowhere to be seen.

"Envy?" she called out, voice echoing softly.

There was no response, no sound aside from her own voice.

"Abyssus?"

She felt him stir in the space around her, incorporeal.

"Where is the prince?"

Silence stretched between them.

"Go to the Twin Pillars," he whispered. "You'll find your answer there. If it's not too late."

A different sort of fear gripped Camilla. "How long have I been gone?"

"To some... it might feel like decades. Or months. But it has only been a few days according to the laws of this realm, little deceiver. Run. The last clue awaits, but the king left this message for you."

Days. She'd lost days to the abyss. Critical time as the game grew closer to the end.

Had Envy left her and solved the next clue, or had something darker happened to him?

Camilla took the folded parchment from Abyssus, stomach twisting.

"Solve the final clue before the sun sets. Or lose your talent forever."

Camilla swore. They were underground; she had no idea what time it was.

"Abyssus! How long before sun sets tonight?"

"Thirty mortal minutes, maybe less."

Without wasting another moment, Camilla plunged down the tunnel, and ran as hard and fast as her feet would carry her.

FIFTY-SIX

ENVY SLUMPED AGAINST the column on the edge of the underground site of the Twin Pillars, his eyes drifting shut from the latest wave of pain. The magical chains that bound his wrists and ankles burned his flesh, searing it nearly to the bone.

Days had passed since he'd been imprisoned in the underground cathedral by Abyssus.

As far as prisons went, Envy supposed it could be worse.

The cavern was a beautiful mix of natural rock formation and demon-made ingenuity. The soaring walls were hewn from the natural rock found that far underground, while the floor had been laid with black marble tiles. The ceiling was reinforced with gold arches, the metal forming a Gothic architectural element that made one stop and admire it.

Even when one was magically shackled and beaten.

The moment they had passed over the ward Abyssus set up, Envy had been spit out at the Twin Pillars, chained and bound by magic across from them. It was the worst sort of fate—to be in the place where his next clue was and to be wholly unable to get there and solve it.

Then Vexley appeared.

And he'd changed.

The gleaming fangs and crimson eyes were badges of honor for the fool.

He now wore his sadism proudly instead of hiding behind his mortal veneer of debauchery. Envy hated him either way.

The newly turned vampire kicked him in the side. Bones snapped. He felt a fragment of broken rib pierce his lung, his breath wheezing out from the impact.

Envy spit blood onto the marble floor, running his tongue over his teeth, tasting the fragrant ichor that ran through his veins.

"You missed a rib."

Vexley hauled off and kicked him with his newfound strength.

Pain seized Envy, but he gritted his teeth, defiant.

"Surely you can do better than *that*."

"Are you out of your damned mind?" Vexley said, lunging forward. "I am a god now."

A god of idiocy.

Envy yanked his chain taut at the last second and slumped out of the way, the vampire's fist coming down on the link instead of his head. The chain heaved but didn't break. Envy dragged himself back to a sitting position, breath shallow.

If he could get Vexley to damage the chain, even a link of it, he'd stand a chance at breaking free. He had no idea what had happened to Camilla and was determined to find a way back to search for her. If Abyssus had her and was playing one of his illusion games...

"You failed Lennox's game. It's a bit pathetic to keep showing up."

"*That* game doesn't matter anymore. I have almost everything I want." Vexley shot him a haughty look. "Perhaps I seek a different prize now."

There was no mistaking what the prick meant.

"Camilla has made her feelings clear on the matter, what with the murder and all."

"She set me free." The vampire shrugged. "Now she belongs to me until I say she doesn't. Death agreed, or I wouldn't be standing here, close to all I'd wanted anyway."

Vexley paced in front of him, ticking off reasons like Envy gave any sort of shit.

Black spots gathered at the edge of his vision, growing in density. Envy was worse off than he let on. Much worse. It was getting hard for him to maintain enough power to sustain his court, keep the ward up around his circle, *and* not lose consciousness.

If Envy didn't stay alert, it would be almost impossible for him to hold himself together much longer.

Still upholding his court, and regrowing his heart, he couldn't risk using any more power to heal himself. Eventually his wounds would repair themselves on their own, but that could take hours in his weakened state.

He was lucky if he had minutes.

"First, I was playing for immortality," Vexley said, drawing Envy back to his monologue. "I now have that."

And an unquenchable thirst for blood, thus preventing the idiot from returning to Waverly Green until he got that minor little inconvenience under control.

"I will be even more legendary in Ironwood Kingdom now."

Envy doubted that the satire sheets would indulge Vexley's antics when he started slaying half the nobility. Maybe they'd all get lucky and someone would behead him.

Envy's eyes drifted shut. He leaned his head against the stone column near the edge of the ancient site, his breathing labored. He was certain his skull had cracked at some point, if the pounding, monstrous pain was any indication. It was a testament to his will and power that he hadn't fallen yet.

"Next, I want Camilla's talent," Vexley said. "We'll make enough money to do whatever we please for as long as we please. I assume she's not human, after her display of magic. Which means we can lie, cheat, and steal for eternity."

"Except that Camilla said *no*."

"Once I take her as my wife, it won't matter much what she wants. I know what's best."

Envy's entire body screamed in protest, but he slowly got to his feet, bracing himself against the column. Half dead or not, he was going to break free of these chains, and then he was going to snap the vampire's neck.

Envy would be sent to the True Death before he'd let Vexley touch her.

"Women are *not* possessions. She belongs to herself, you arrogant halfwit."

Vexley's fist connected with his jaw, the crack echoing in the cathedral-like chamber.

Envy's head smashed into the stone, the fracture in his skull knocking him out for a beat before he regained his footing. He went down to his knees, the bones cracking against marble.

Vexley towered over him, fangs gleaming in the strange half-light that filtered in from who knew where.

"There are no rules about teaming up with other players. Did you know that?"

Envy's vision teetered between blurry and spinning.

He should have killed the mortal back in Waverly Green when he had the chance. His instincts about rotten souls were never wrong. Vexley had been a foul man and was a worse vampire. No one ought to suffer this fool for eternity.

"Arrogant demon fuck." The vampire jabbed him twice in the gut, the air whooshing out as Envy doubled over. He was going to be sick. "You should have focused on eliminating your competition. Instead, you assumed they'd just fail."

Envy hadn't thought that at all. He'd decided that moving forward to solve his clues and riddles as quickly as possible was the best tactic.

He didn't respond. And only partly because he had nothing to say. The pain was beginning to overwhelm his senses. Soon, he'd pass out.

His eyes slitted open, barely allowing him to make out the shadow creeping along the far wall, getting closer. He didn't know whether it was really there or he was imagining it. Couldn't tell if the glint of silver rising was a blade or a beautiful, violent dream.

Didn't know whether Vexley sensed or saw it too. If he did, the vampire didn't let on, leading Envy to believe that the shadowy figure wasn't there.

Envy's head jerked forward, then back, his fight to remain alert slipping. Vexley chuckled darkly, enjoying every moment of pain Envy suffered.

The magic in the chains sizzled, the fire going bone-deep.

A huff of pain escaped him, and the vampire closed in.

"Perhaps we'll play a new game too." Vexley crouched before him, crimson eyes sparkling. "The 'drain you dry' game." He leaned forward, as if to whisper a delicious secret. "The rules are simple. I drain you dry. You slowly revive. Then we repeat for eternity. How long do you think you'll last before madness creeps in?"

He yanked Envy's arm out of its socket, the pain a hot sear that lashed down his spine, wrenching another groan from him.

"One, two…five hundred years?" Vexley asked, tugging Envy's arm up to his mouth. "I'm willing to wager if you are."

His fangs pierced Envy's wrist, the venom causing an extra jolt of pain.

Darkness rippled behind Envy's eyes. He could feel the venom colliding painfully with the ichor in his veins. He blinked once, twice, and in between Vexley was dead.

What?

Envy tried to open his eyes again. Vexley's head had rolled next to Envy's foot. Or had *he* fallen over? Envy's cheek was pressed to the marble, the cool stone slick with blood.

Envy stared unblinking at the severed head. It looked back with the same dull expression, the same lack of life.

"Get up."

The voice was sweet. Even if the command was less than appreciated.

Envy's eyes closed. He wanted only to sleep, to dream of that voice.

"Envy."

"Ah," he said, eyes still closed. "A dream. A lovely, wonderful dream."

Hands were on him now, soft, gentle. Searching. She hissed as if his wounds had hurt her, too. Then she rattled the chains.

"No. Don't." He attempted to pull them out of reach, the movement too much. "They'll burn you, too."

Featherlight fingers brushed across his brow, soothing again.

"Leviaethan." The sweet voice held a twinge of panic. "You *must* get up."

FIFTY-SEVEN

Camilla glanced around the underground chamber, her pulse pounding a frantic beat. She'd raced here the second Abyssus's ward had disappeared but was still too late.

Envy was severely injured. He *should* have started healing, and she wasn't sure why he hadn't but suspected it had to do with his dwindling power.

He hadn't admitted so out loud, but she'd seen his court. Knew things were grim. And he would ruin himself to save his demons. *Was* ruining himself.

"How can I break these chains?" she asked, gently pressing a hand to his forehead.

His skin was cold, clammy. She suddenly wanted to drag him into her arms and away from this place.

"We need to hurry," she said. "Please. Help me."

His eyes fluttered but didn't open.

Vexley must haven been torturing him for however long she'd been trapped in the abyss. And even someone immortal couldn't withstand days or weeks of being beaten without healing. The magical chains were a nasty trick, ones she suspected were Abyssus's doing. The constant pulse of pain seeping through them into Envy's skin was clearly wearing him down.

How Lord Vexley had gotten involved she neither knew nor cared—she'd thought it was just a vision when she'd seen him attack Envy in Abyssus's tunnel. But he must have really been here, in this place, beating the prince. It was one of the hardest things she'd ever done, but Camilla had waited in the shadows until Vexley had been overcome by blood lust, needing him to be distracted. Then she'd struck hard and fast.

Camilla squeezed her eyes shut, forcing the image of beheading Vexley from her mind.

She hadn't known she could do something like that until a savage, wild rage had descended when she saw how hurt Envy was. Something dark had awakened in her, the threat Vexley posed igniting her long-dormant instincts. He was trying to take what was *hers*.

And she'd snapped.

Camilla had used the dagger Blade had gifted her, crafted of sharp, immortal steel, but it had been *her* strength, her inner power, the Fae part of her locked deep inside, that had emerged.

Ruthless, feral.

She'd struck at the connective tissue in Vexley's neck, sawing through the tiny bones of his spine in one, brutal, ragged slash. If time hadn't been running against them, Camilla would have fallen upon Vexley's undead corpse, tearing him apart, bit by bit.

She'd caught Vexley by surprise, getting lucky.

Camilla needed to focus, remain calm, plot how to get them out of this predicament immediately. She darted a look at the entrance several yards away on the other side of the ancient site. She hadn't spared more than a cursory glance at the Twin Pillars.

She'd spotted Vexley and Envy and had circled them, gaze split between the floor and the vampire, doing her best not to make a sound as she slowly approached.

Vexley's headless corpse was gruesome.

And, most unfortunately, in the way.

She grabbed him by the ankles and dragged him off to the side, the procession slow and painful, his weight and size ensuring that she worked hard to rid herself of him.

Once he was far enough away, she squeezed her eyes shut and grabbed his head, holding it gingerly by the hair, trying not to gag as she deposited it next to his unmoving form.

That dark deed done, she rushed to Envy again.

Camilla rattled the chains once more, the magic burning her skin. She wasn't sure how Envy had survived so long with them wrapped around his wrists and ankles. The pain was overwhelming in her brief contact with them.

She braced herself and picked up the length of chain again, turning it over in her hands, attention searching. There had to be some way to break them. A clue. A riddle.

Camilla thought of the game master, of what twisted way he'd devise for them to be unlocked. Then she saw it, faintly etched onto the links. A riddle.

She looked closer, spying a series of letters that could be moved around the lock to form an answer. The space made it clear she was looking for one word. Five letters.

For some plants, mortals, and all animals, too,
this begins but has no end
and ends all that begins.
Answer me correctly at the start, or after three tries I'll
permanently stop his heart.

She expelled a long breath, staring at the last warning. She had three chances to answer the riddle correctly, or somehow Envy would die.

She covered her face, fighting the urge to scream. Pressure built behind her eyes, in her chest, stealing the breath from her lungs as she tried to puzzle out the riddle without thinking about the clock ticking. Without worrying about a wrong guess.

"*For some plants, mortals, and all animals, too,*" she said aloud, hoping it would spark some connection. "Stems, limbs, teeth..."

She swore roundly. Nothing made sense for all of them.

Perhaps if it hadn't felt as if a dagger were being held to her throat, she'd have been calm enough to *think*. Why couldn't this be a riddle based on art? On something she knew without question?

"Breath, souls, heart..." Could plants have hearts? Camilla had never really paid much attention but knew there were plants that had *heart* in the name. Bleeding hearts. It was certainly morbid and threatening enough, but was it correct? The riddle didn't say *all* plants, just some. Mortals and all animals had hearts.

For some plants, mortals, and all animals, too,
this begins but has no end
and ends all that begins.

It didn't fully connect with the second part of the riddle, though. But maybe it did, and she just couldn't see that part clearly now.

Her fingers trembled as she reached for the chain again.

"Please be correct."

Camilla had three chances. If this failed, she still had two more tries.

She rolled the first letter into place.

H

Then the second.

E

The third.

A

Fourth.

R

And hesitated on the fifth. She read over the riddle again, this time with growing suspicion. It didn't mention any consequence for a wrong response, but she didn't trust the game master.

For some plants, mortals, and all animals, too,
this begins but has no end
and ends all that begins.

Envy's chest barely rose, his breathing labored. Even if they didn't have to hurry to solve the next clue after this, they were running out of time.

Camilla sent up a quick prayer to whomever might be listening and twisted that final letter into place.

T

Envy's body jolted as if struck by lightning, a howl of pain tearing free, echoing through the chamber, a symphony of agony. The magical chains flared with a light so brightly intense, Camilla had to blink several times before the little spots disappeared.

"Envy!" She went to pull the chains away from his skin, then screeched. The chains pulsed with power now, ratcheting up in intensity. *"Shit."*

He slumped back to the ground, groaning. He was still unconscious. The chains radiated a menacing buzz now, indicating that each wrong response would intensify the magic running through them until it grew so powerful it could end an immortal life.

Camilla jumped to her feet, pacing. She could *not* get the next one wrong.

For some plants, mortals, and all animals, too,
this begins but has no end
and ends all that begins.

What? What connected them all? It had to be simple.

Camilla felt tears threatening. She was frustrated and scared and downright furious with the game master. His game was bad enough without subjecting them to mental and physical torture. She stopped pacing, using her surging emotions to center herself.

The game master knew they were close to finishing the game. Which meant she'd see him soon. Camilla focused on that, allowed it to fuel her. She and Envy had not come this far to be thwarted by the Unseelie King in the final moments of their game.

When she walked into that wretched court, not *if*, she would do so as a victor.

Starting with this cursed riddle.

Camilla repeated it out loud, determination running through her in waves. The game master thought himself clever, but she was too. She knew the answer. Knew it was simple. Fear had shut down her logic, but she would not allow it to overtake her now.

For some plants, mortals, and all animals, too,
this begins but has no end
and ends all that begins.

Some plants. Mortals. And all animals, too. *Think,* she commanded herself. What do they have in common? The careful phrasing. *Some* plants. *All* animals. And simply *mortals*.

They were all living things. But that didn't connect them. *Some* plants. Camilla paced away, her thoughts focused inward. Some plants...all plants were alive. But some plants...

"All right," she said. "If I were in House Sloth, plants would be broken down into categories. Flowering, fruits, trees, bushes...and annuals and perennials."

Her pulse thrashed. That *felt* right. Some plants were annuals; they needed to be replanted each year. Some plants were perennials. They came back each year on their own.

Suddenly, she knew what the answer was.

Chills raced down Camilla's body.

"Death."

Some plants died. Mortals and all animals died too. Death ended all that began. And once it began, there was no undoing it. *Death* also had five letters. It fit.

It *had* to be the correct answer.

Still, as she knelt next to Envy, seeing the sickly pallor of his normally healthy, bronze skin, she hesitated. One more wrong answer and she didn't want to consider the torture he'd experience. At her own hand.

She couldn't waste any more time debating.

Camilla hissed through her teeth as she clasped the chain again, finding the link with the letters. She twisted them into place quickly this time, pausing for only a beat on the final letter.

DEATH

She hoped she wasn't dooming Envy to his. The *H* clicked into place and an eternity passed in a second; then the glow intensified, and Camilla internally damned—

The chains shattered in a flash of fire, freeing the prince.

Camilla sobbed and then gently pulled him onto her lap, stroking his head.

"Please. Please get up."

She had read enough fairy tales as a young girl to know that the prince was supposed to wake the love of his life with a kiss. But Envy was a demon, and Camilla was no damsel in distress. She pressed her lips to his forehead.

He didn't magically stir. But his skin was starting to regain some color now that the chains weren't constantly attacking him.

Camilla rocked him gently for a few more seconds, still painfully aware of the clock Abyssus said was counting down their time to solve the final clue. They were so close. They were in the site. If they lost, her talent would be stolen forever.

She could leave Envy, find the next clue on her own...

Awareness suddenly prickled against her skin. She glanced down, startled to find Envy's emerald gaze locked onto her.

"Did we lose?" he asked, his tone void of emotion.

"Not yet."

"You could have left me."

She could have. There was a question in his eyes. One she did not have an answer for.

Camilla carefully maneuvered him off her lap and stood, brushing down the front of her dress, then glanced around. "Abyssus said we have until sunset to solve the last clue. We're almost out of time."

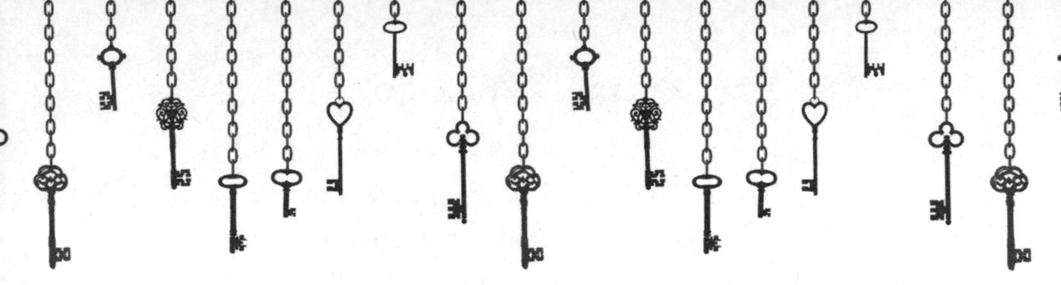

FIFTY-EIGHT

ENVY TOOK QUICK stock of his injuries as he sat up. On the surface, he didn't appear too bad. But looks could be deceiving. The worst of his aches and pains were still there.

He pushed himself up to his feet, head pounding from the strain.

Camilla, thankfully, had already turned her attention to the Pillars. The fear he'd seen in her, the tenderness, both were gone, replaced by a brutal determination. If he hadn't seen her, hadn't experienced that hellish torture, she'd have given no outward indication that they'd battled a dark force. He wanted to ask about Abyssus, if she was all right, but she clearly was.

She was a woman on a mission. And he was glad of her help.

Unable to move just yet, Envy watched Camilla take in the pillars, a look of awe and reverence on her face.

He understood her fascination. Even in a world full of magic and riches, they were truly something to behold.

The pillars stood twenty-two feet tall and were each carved from a solid piece of shadowstone, a gemstone found only in the Seven Circles that was like a smoky moonstone. Each massive column was adorned with images ranging from flora to fauna to astrological.

Many had speculated on what the symbols meant, but no one could be certain that their theory was correct. Only the oldest of the Fae knew what the Pillars had fully been capable of.

She was looking at them with appreciation, but he also saw the way she methodically scanned them, running her hands over each image, her mind hard at work to solve the mystery of why they'd been sent there and how it related to the game.

He looked them over from where he stood, slowly regaining his strength.

In the mortal world, there were a few ancient sites that were similar, but nothing compared to these pillars. Some believed supernatural beings had created the ones across the mortal world, but if they saw what had been made by the Fae, they'd understand the differences.

These columns glowed with an inner moonlight, the art casting shadows. And that was while they were buried below ground, far from the sun and moon, which legend claimed they'd been created to celebrate.

Envy had seen the Pillars once before: when Wrath had each of the seven ruling Princes of Hell come together to nullify the Fae magic, in a sense leashing the Pillars.

What they knew of the Twin Pillars was that they were an access point, like a mortal train station of sorts, where both the light and dark Fae could travel to different realms.

When the portal was open, they could go to the mortal world whenever they pleased, bypassing the Gates of Hell and any royal request they'd need to make.

That had been their ultimate downfall.

The Unseelie liked playing with mortals. Liked taking human pets. Changelings were also amusements. They left Fae children in human homes, watching them wreak havoc on the unsuspecting parents.

Both courts had been warned that such games were not to be played in the mortal world. The Seelie took their pleasures elsewhere, never as intrigued by humans as the Unseelie were.

Lennox and Prim Róis weren't as easily tamed. Since they were embodiments of Chaos and Discord, it wasn't unexpected. Until the portal was sealed, they continued to freely send their court to meddle. Wrath had issued two warnings. The first a courtesy, the second a royal decree.

Lennox had sent even more of his court to spite the king of the Underworld.

The Pillars were buried below the earth and bound shortly after.

Now, as they stood in the ancient place, once teeming with magic, an odd sense of muted power thrummed from the inert columns.

Envy had never felt that before, wondered if the game was responsible. He made his way to them, the ache in his body dulling considerably.

Camilla walked to them like a person possessed, touching and marveling at each carving.

"The reproductions at House Sloth...they pale in comparison. The carvings are different, too. At least on this one."

Envy snorted. "Please tell my brother that. He'll be furious."

She traced the art, slowly circling the columns. He wished they could remain there for as long as she liked, coming up with their own theories. But that wasn't meant to be. She'd said Abyssus had mentioned sunset; he'd wager that was less than a quarter of an hour away.

He left the artist to her quiet contemplation and strode around the perimeter, looking for any clue or hint of what they were meant to do next.

The cavern had no other unique attributes aside from the Fae relics. He studied the shadows cast on the ground, wondering if they were meant to spark an idea.

Camilla expelled a breath, the sound breaking the stillness of the chamber. He turned to face her; she'd been watching him. As closely as she'd been just examining the pillars.

"What's wrong with your court?" she asked. "Before we go any further, I need to know. I know that's what's driving you. I want to know what happened."

His brows rose. That was the last question he'd expected her to ask him.

"The butler, your guards, the blood..." She narrowed her eyes, as if she could see through the wall he'd erected. "I've been going over my interactions at House Envy, and I can't make sense of them."

"What interactions?"

"Your butler didn't remember where he was or who you were. Your guards could only repeat the same phrase continually. It's like..." She nibbled on her lower lip. "It's like they're all losing their memories. And the blood..."

She glanced back at the pillars, brow crinkled.

"That's it, isn't it? Your court is losing their memories. And in the wreckage, somehow tearing each other apart."

She wasn't looking at him. Like she knew if she did it would be too hard for him to respond.

He remained still, silent. Waiting for her to piece more together. After a moment, she continued.

"The artifact you're after, somehow that will stop the memory loss and whatever is making them attack one another. That's why you need to win the game. Your court is falling apart, literally ripping itself apart in the process."

Envy ran a hand through his hair, pacing away.

"I wouldn't say falling apart. *Fuck*."

That was exactly what was happening.

He walked away, shaking his head. Camilla watched him silently, allowing him time to speak without prompting.

Envy had been holding on to this secret for so long, he didn't know how to let it go.

He stopped pacing.

"Like all demons in each House of Sin, my court isn't immortal like me and my brothers, but even being long-lived is not without its complications."

Camilla gave him a wry smile. "Mm."

"To sum it up succinctly. Yes. My court is failing. Every few hundred years or so they need to purge memories in order to make new ones. A problem mortals wouldn't understand. There are…complications when they aren't able to purge. Namely, they begin forgetting. Overloaded, they confuse delusion with reality. Friend becomes foe. Everyone poses a danger."

Understanding flickered in her gaze.

"If they can't remember or make new memories, they cannot fuel their sin of choice, either."

He gave her a bittersweet smile. She was much too clever indeed.

"Which in turn cannot fuel *my* power," he added softly, for the first time confessing the full scope of what he'd been facing.

The chalice was the missing piece. Envy had inadvertently given it up more than two centuries before, and every year since, they'd been slowly losing power.

Then the game had begun, and things had gotten worse.

Camilla did not gasp or pity him. She was suddenly beside him, grabbing his arm, squeezing it firmly.

Silver eyes flashed like lightning, her words just as striking.

"You're *going* to win."

His mouth curved into a faint smile. "I never should have lost to begin with."

"Don't blame yourself."

"It *was* my fault. I gave up the Chalice of Memoria, setting everything in motion."

He wished he could take that action back. It was one of the few regrets he'd ever had.

"It's a long story," he added, noting her continued look. "We don't have time for it now."

"We absolutely do," she said. "I think I solved the clue. But I need to know what you're really after before I hand over whatever prize you're seeking."

He knew she wasn't lying, so he finally gave in and told her the whole story.

"Without the Chalice of Memoria to offload memories, eventually my court will weaken to extinction, my rule will weaken, and my circle will be susceptible to being absorbed by another more powerful circle or sin. The chaos of a circle falling...let's just say it would give the Unseelie King an opening to create more discord in our realm."

He exhaled.

"There are two objects needed to set things to rights. The Chalice of Memoria, and the Aether Scrolls."

Camilla remained silent, listening.

"I loaned the Chalice of Memoria to the mortal I was involved with. It was a silly request—she wished to drink from it on her birthday, be the envy of her friends."

"She knew your sin."

He nodded.

"It was only supposed to be gone for a few hours, so I didn't see the harm. I should have. I knew what losing it would mean to my court. Instead of a small gathering with her mortal friends, she brought it to Faerie that night. When she died, Lennox found it and discovered its value."

"She sounds like she was selfish."

He lifted a shoulder. "Aren't we all sometimes?"

Camilla pursed her lips, looking like she had a lot more to say on the matter but wouldn't.

His sin ignited, flaring with her burst of jealousy. It fueled him, healing some of his wounds. Camilla misunderstood his defense.

Envy did not care for the mortal; he refused to even speak her name. He simply didn't view her selfishness as her worst sin.

"What do the scrolls do?" Camilla asked.

"It helps to fully understand the chalice first. The Chalice of Memoria is carved with symbols and runes. So it not only siphons memories, but when activated properly can grant immortality, strike an enemy down, or give someone infinite wealth. Or anything else they desire. It is an object of immense and terrible power that predates even the oldest demons in the realm. The Aether Scrolls contain the spells needed to activate the chalice."

"All the players were after the same prize, then."

Envy lifted a shoulder. "The Chalice of Memoria can become anything for anyone, making it unique to any individual. I imagine that's why Lennox used it."

"Why can't you give your court memory stones to help?"

"That would be rather convenient, wouldn't it?" He gave her a wistful smile. "Memory stones only work when the person purging the memory recalls what they'd like to forget with clarity. Since the memory fog started, my court cannot recall in enough detail. Even though it's been a slow descent into madness, when it first started, we weren't prepared. The fog only lasted for a few moments, easily passed off as tiredness. It wasn't until things got much worse that I understood. Then it was too late to offload any memories to the memory stones."

Camilla seemed as frustrated by that as he had been.

"Who has the scrolls?"

He hesitated. This was information even his second-in-command didn't know.

"I do. But…I can't access them now."

"Why not?"

"Because I cannot summon my wings."

"Expand on 'cannot summon' them, please."

"My wings are still there, under my skin, waiting. Sometimes the need to summon them…is uncomfortable. But I can't risk it. Yet. I do not have enough power to hold my court together at the same time. Especially when seeing Lennox is inevitable. I cannot waste an ounce of reserves before I fight him."

"And how do your wings relate to the scrolls?"

He thought of the single emerald feather Lennox had sent him, the mockery of the gesture. "After the chalice was stolen, I had the scrolls fused with my wings to keep them out of enemy hands. Think of them like invisible tattoos, I suppose. It's an ancient demon trick."

Camilla stared, stunned. "You've had access to them this whole time?"

"Not truly. As my court weakens, so does my power. And they mean nothing without the chalice."

"But you fought those beasts and the vampire prince," she argued. "How is your power that diminished?"

"Brute force, darling. Not magic."

"What about the Hexed Throne?"

"I stabbed it with my House dagger, no magic needed."

Envy clasped her chin, drawing her gaze to his.

His tone hardened. "*This* look is exactly why I haven't told anyone. I am not yet defeated, Camilla. Do not pity me."

She bared her teeth, a lovely little feral animal hiding behind her pretty, cultured smile.

"I don't pity you. I'm simply trying to make sense of your story."

"Truth for truth." His attention sharpened on her. "Time for you to share with me, Miss Antonius."

Camilla pointed to the carvings.

"I believe the scales here represent Libra. These circles are the sun and moon. The sun sits on one scale and the moon on the other. They're equal in size, but the moon is lower, heavier."

She dropped her finger to an intriguing creature.

"At first, I thought this was simply a stylized satyr, but look closely. The legs and horns of a goat are likely a depiction of Pan." She dragged her finger across a series of dots and lines. "This half-goat, half-fish also symbolizes the sea goat."

"And a sea goat relates how?"

"Simply put, this geometric design is the constellation Capricornus. Pan standing beside it is the biggest indication."

She followed the carvings up—past what looked like crude depictions of evergreen branches to the top, where a sword dripped blood, a crescent moon shadowed on its blade.

"This is basically a carved set of instructions on how to activate the pillar."

A chill caressed his spine. "Camilla . . . you're brilliant."

He went to prick his finger, but she stopped him.

"Not your blood. Mine." She nodded at the pillar. "The symbols all indicate a date. The evergreens, the constellations, the moon. Everything represents the winter solstice. The longest night."

"What does that have to do with you?"

Something flickered in her expression. "It's my birthday."

He sensed a partial lie. "The date can vary for mortals—"

"We're not in the mortal realm."

"But the Pillars were carved thousands of years ago. By your own admission you weren't born then."

"Envy . . ."

Something in her tone made the skin along Envy's spine prickle.

"There's something I—"

A deep rumble shook the ground, splintering the marble floor. They were almost out of time. Envy flashed a grim smile. "Now, Miss Antonius. Whatever you have to say—let it wait."

A war raged behind her gaze. "It shouldn't be delayed. You really ought to—"

Another crack split the floor near the mouth of the cavern. She flinched.

"We don't have the luxury of time, Camilla. Activate the Pillars, quickly, now."

She looked torn, but finally heeded out of necessity.

Once they made it through the next several hours, Envy might consider the possibility of breaking the rules he'd set for himself so long ago. Because he knew where they were headed next: the Wild Court.

Maybe if he could face his own demons there, he could pursue Camilla after all.

Because, truth for truth, Envy would have to admit: one night hadn't nearly been enough.

He was starting to want much more.

Not *starting*. He wanted more before she'd ever left his side.

And with the game nearly won, perhaps he could have it all.

"When you're ready," he said, handing her his House dagger, hilt first. "Let's end this."

FIFTY-NINE

CAMILLA'S NERVES TWISTED into intricate knots as she took his dagger, wondering how they'd gotten here, stuck in this tangled web of deceit. She went over the events of the last several weeks, searching for a different choice she could have made.

Why hadn't she tried talking to him then?

She knew. Of course. Fear.

Her father had told her repeatedly that fear was the one force that drove all darkness in the world. Love, on the other hand, was the greatest source of power. Love strengthened the weakest, gave them a ferocity that fear never offered. Mothers defended their children. Partners, friends, good people stared down evil, becoming something to *be* feared.

Because of love.

Yet love wasn't the path Camilla had chosen. She'd succumbed to that same mortal trap.

Change was terrifying. The unknown always was. It was the very essence of its *being* unknown that made it so. The familiar was comforting even when it wasn't necessarily good.

She recognized instantly what she'd seen in the prince's face.

Knew it intimately herself.

Fear flashed in Envy's eyes. It hadn't been from the strange rumble of warning cracking the ground under their feet. His fear had meant something else. A look so unsettling she realized she'd never seen it on his face before. And Camilla wondered if he knew. Even if he hadn't admitted it to himself.

Maybe he was afraid of being right. Of what it would mean. Perhaps this was one last game he was playing with her, the game of denial. To acknowledge the truth meant accepting change. Neither one of them seemed ready for it.

Change was terrifying but necessary. Especially now.

She wished she could save him from any hurt she'd unintentionally caused. She hadn't known what he would come to mean to her. Not really.

Somehow, along the way, she'd grown attached to the game-playing deviant. And she saw, through all his bluster and lies of omission, that he felt the same for her. Camilla hadn't believed it was real. She should have. It was there in his actions all along.

Against all odds, despite his rules, Envy *liked* her.

Not her body. But her mind, her passions. He liked her ruthless, savage side as much as her soft, artistic side. He'd seen her kill a man and he'd seen her walk before a king. There wasn't anything she could do to shock or disgust him.

But that wasn't quite true, was it?

Taking a deep breath, she slashed her palm with the blade, ignoring its greedy glow to place her palm on the pillar. Delaying the inevitable only made it worse.

And things were about to become worse enough as it was.

Her attention moved to the Pillars, to the glittering sheet of light that had burst between them, giving off a soft, otherworldly hum. Jasmine, gardenia, wisteria, and musk. Night and its many pleasures. The scents of the Wild Court.

Once they walked through that portal, everything would change.

Envy hadn't looked at the portal, still wouldn't.

He'd been watching *her.*

His expression was carefully blank. But he was no fool. He solved impossible puzzles, and it looked like he'd finally pieced the mystery of her together.

She wondered if this was the one riddle he'd never wanted to solve.

But it was too late.

Before she lost her nerve, Camilla grabbed Envy's hand and stepped through the portal, emerging directly into the Unseelie King's stronghold.

They'd won the game, but Camilla couldn't help but fear she'd just lost so much more.

SIXTY

The Wild Court was a tangle of flora and limbs, not unlike the last time Envy had visited this court. He drew in a deep breath, forcing his mind to think of the game, not of hunting down the bastard king and pushing his demon blade through Lennox's rotten heart.

The portal had spit them out at the back of the king's garden room, a long rectangular outdoor terrace directly off his throne room where the dark Fae enjoyed dancing and making love under the moon.

Wide paved stones covered in moss were still used for the dance floor.

Trees lining the perimeter twisted toward the night sky, sheer panels hanging between their branches to act as partitions for Fae games.

Flowering ivy crawled up trellises, the walls living and seductive.

Thick, wide trunks carved from the most ancient of trees had been sanded down, used as raw-edged tables to line the dance floor, holding glittering bottles of Fae wine and liquor and overripe fruits. From all outward appearances, it was an enchanted world. An ode to the night and its many wonders.

Envy glanced at Camilla. For a moment, she looked so small and afraid, her gaze locked on the far end of the space. Then she noticed his attention and her expression shuttered. He wanted to grab hold of her hand again but refused to give Lennox any more reason to hurt her.

Camilla took a small step toward the dais at the opposite end of the outdoor chamber, but Envy stopped her.

"Wait."

Around them, Fae writhed against each other, dancing or fighting or fucking to dark, pulsating music. Behind them, two giant pillars knifed upward, slicing into the night sky like unsheathed swords. The transverse of the Twin Pillars, still sizzling from their arrival.

That dark music, discordant and loud, started pounding like an unsteady heartbeat. Vibrating across the paved stone floor, up the makeshift walls, setting his teeth on edge.

Night-blooming vines twisted around tables and upturned chairs, while Fae rolled around the earth, tangled in each other, completely unaware of their newest guests.

Until all at once they *weren't* oblivious anymore.

Envy counted how many Unseelie surrounded them, strategizing the best plan to keep Camilla from harm should they desire to stir up discord.

The dark Fae stared at them, some snickering, some sharing knowing looks.

Against his better judgment, Envy grabbed Camilla's hand, an unspoken promise that he would not leave her side. No matter what.

Camilla raised her chin, ignoring the growing whispers.

To be Seelie in this place was not ideal.

Envy was proud of her defiance. Of her unwillingness to be cowed.

The Unseelie were midnight creatures, born of moonlight and wickedness. And they were all suddenly still, staring as Camilla dropped Envy's hand.

She started walking toward the Shadow Storm throne.

"Camilla," he whispered, charging after her.

No matter what Lennox wanted with her, no matter how their courts felt, it was dangerous for her to march toward him, almost in challenge. Light against dark. The night battling the day.

Envy's hand twitched toward his dagger. He couldn't use it before he'd collected his prize.

He prayed Camilla had a plan. That she wouldn't forget that he still had much at stake.

She stepped nimbly over broken branches and shattered glass, her attention fastened on the Fae male who'd put this cursed game into play. Her expression was as cold as his was.

Lennox, the Unseelie King, had stopped speaking midsentence, watching her approach. Silver-and-white hair cascaded down to his shoulders, his skin a deep bronze. Elegant pointed ears poked from beneath that sheet of ethereal hair.

He was ageless. Beautiful. And utterly without conscience.

It was easy to see why so many mortals thought him a god. He was cold, untouchable. Forbidden. He had no concept of morality. Lennox did as he pleased whenever he pleased. And if someone died? It was their fault for being fragile. Some believed he'd inspired mortal gods, had actually been the great Zeus.

Envy knew he was no mere god, he was a Titan. The beings who birthed the gods for their amusement. But mortals had it wrong in their legends—the Titans weren't bested by their offspring. They thrived in the chaos.

The way he looked at Camilla... Envy's sin threatened to ice over the entire court. But finally, Lennox's gaze, midnight black with glittering stars winking in and out, shifted to Envy.

A cruel smile lifted his full lips.

"Prince Envy."

While Lennox might have tried to orchestrate the outcome of the game, it had played out differently than he'd anticipated. It was written all over his cold, arrogant face. Something dark paced in his gaze, amused.

In a life that spanned eons, anything that produced a thrill was welcome. Whether stirring up discord, crafting war, or meddling with mortals, Lennox lived for the Wild Hunt he'd once created.

A hunt the Seelie had forbade him from continuing, as once per year, he'd unleashed the most ruthless hunters of their kind. Their prey was human and Fae alike.

Envy's attention cut to Camilla. Was that why Lennox wanted her? To somehow barter or—more likely—threaten the Seelie with giving him back the Hunt?

"Well. This is unexpectedly pleasant."

His voice was a dark rumble, more elemental in nature than any human sound. It could raise tides, summon constellations, make the moon itself fall at his feet.

Only to be crushed if it amused him.

Envy paused beside Camilla, slanting a look in her direction. She'd completely shielded her emotions from him.

Her attention had shifted to the male Lennox had been speaking with. A golden-skinned, dark-haired Fae with dark eyes. He wore a deep crimson tailcoat, looking like a ringmaster.

"Ayden." Camilla's voice was cold.

Envy glanced between them, brows knitted. That she would know another Fae wasn't surprising. But that one…He knew who Ayden was by name. Knew he was an Unseelie prince. And her tone. He swore his heart started to thud painfully against his chest.

"Last I heard, you were terrorizing mortals with your carnival tricks. What was it? The midnight circus?" she asked, her tone mocking.

Envy had gone very still beside her.

The Fae gave her a once-over, annoyance clear in the pressing of his mouth.

"The Moonlight Carnival."

Lennox chuckled, dark and ominous.

"Still boasting about your midnight bargains?" Camilla needled. "Who was the unfortunate lady this time? I assume she didn't succumb to your seduction, or else she'd be here."

The Unseelie Prince tugged at his white gloves. Envy noticed moons stitched across the knuckles, the ode to his court.

"Still pretending to be a mortal artist?" the Unseelie Prince shot back.

"Better than a two-bit magician."

Envy's gaze bored into her, like two hot pokers at the back of her head. He knew she sensed it, saw the slight stiffening of her shoulders.

A horrible, startling realization clicked into place.

Envy forced his feet to stay planted on the ground, not to let the betrayal show.

Lennox had been watching very closely, so Envy knew the moment he'd decided to have his own fun. He leaned forward, steepling his fingers.

"Children," he all but purred. "*Enough.*"

His gaze was fixed on Envy. The flicker of victory unmistakable.

Envy's hands curled into fists. His expression as icy as the coldness rushing through his soul. Camilla had been keeping many secrets, it seemed.

Camilla was not Seelie.

She was an Unseelie princess.

Daughter of the male who'd ruined his court. His worst enemy.

A flash crossed his mind of when she'd nearly fainted on Vexley's roof. Of course. The metal roof had been iron. No wonder she'd gotten so ill.

She finally dared a glance in his direction, but Envy refused to acknowledge her.

Envy might be a ruthless bastard, but Camilla had far outplayed him.

How foolish he must have seemed to her, speaking of his hatred for Unseelie royalty.

While fucking her on his throne. He thought of that night in a new light now, of her mockery. She'd owned Envy on his seat of power, knowing damn well her father had royally fucked his court. It was really quite impressive, how alike she was to Lennox.

To think he'd even briefly fantasized about breaking his rule for her.

Screwing Envy *and* his throne. It sure as hell would be the last time an Unseelie royal ever played him.

"The game is over," Envy said, definitely feeling the first slow beats of his heart. Of course it would fucking regenerate now. Right when it was poised to break. "Where's my prize?"

SIXTY-ONE

Camilla imagined Envy hated her beyond anything, had probably jumped to all the wrong conclusions the moment Lennox confirmed their familial connection, because she hadn't confided the truth. She wanted to comfort him, to explain, to beg forgiveness, but weakness in the Wild Court would never stand. If her true father saw how much she cared for the prince...

She gave her father, the Unseelie King, a ruthless smile her mother had taught her.

"He won the game, but I want my talent back. Now."

She finally flicked a glance over her shoulder, scanning the demon. Envy stared back at her, hard. If looks could kill, Camilla would be lying dead at his feet this moment.

"Give him his prize and be done with it," she said, bored.

The Unseelie King sat back, studying her far too closely.

"You speak for him?" Lennox asked, his voice low with warning. "Why."

It wasn't a question.

"You sent him to my realm. Had him require *my* assistance for your pathetic game. Then you had the Hexed Throne steal my talent."

"And?" Lennox asked, his voice a silken, dangerous purr.

"It was obviously a way to force me here. You knew I would only come for my talent. Since sending Wolf to fetch me years ago didn't work so well. Mother said you do not understand the concept of being denied."

Camilla was almost certain Envy still hadn't drawn a breath.

"Please. I want to restore my magic and go back home. To Waverly Green."

She saw her father's gaze narrow. Felt his displeasure a moment before violence erupted.

The Unseelie King was in front of her a moment later, eyes bright and flashing like starlight. His hair had changed too; gone were the silver-and-white locks, replaced by inky strands. Night was light and dark, moonlight and the absence of it.

The Unseelie King's eyes and hair changed with his mood.

"*What* did you say?" he asked, his voice low and terrible. Unseelie chattered excitedly in the background. "I'm sure no child of *mine* deigned to plead."

Camilla internally cursed. Mortals so often said "please," she'd forgotten what an insult that was to Unseelie royalty. How she'd just proved herself no better than a human pet.

"You want to be restored, daughter?"

She held his stare, jaw locked. "Yes."

His fingers turned to talons; in a move that was all preternatural speed, he reached behind her, then slashed those talons across the back of her head. Hot blood spilled down her neck, dripped to the floor. Where he clawed, her skin burned.

She bit down on her scream, refusing to give him the satisfaction of seeing her in pain.

Envy flinched beside her, his hand drifting to his blade. She didn't dare look at him.

"I wouldn't do that." Lennox hadn't missed the demon's reaction either.

Camilla gritted her teeth, knowing exactly what Lennox had done. Magic sparked over her skin, revealing all she'd kept hidden from the world.

Her ears lengthened to elegant points; her limbs regained their immortal strength. The wound on her hand healed instantly, along with the cuts her father had just made. Her talent came whooshing in next, filling her, that hollow void brimming with power. The return of her essence was a balm, but the soothing victory was short-lived.

Gone was her glamour. The mask she'd hidden behind for most of her life.

Lennox had destroyed the symbol tattooed under her hairline, revealing the truth of what she was. What she'd *always* been. Unseelie. An Unseelie royal—the beings Envy despised above all others. She couldn't bring herself to look at him again, couldn't see the disgust.

After his story of why he hated the Unseelie court, guilt had eaten away at her. Camilla was everything he loathed, symbolized the near destruction of his people.

She hated the king. Hated this court. Hated herself for being too weak and afraid to tell Envy. But he'd kept secrets from her, too. Had initially even lied about his name.

Instead, Camilla glared coolly at Lennox.

"Are we through? I need a bath."

"Camilla...you don't..." His laughter was dark and sinister. He glanced at Envy, giving him a conspiratorial look. "Changelings. They do delight. Full Fae, but with human sentiments."

His gaze was hard when it turned to her.

"There is no Waverly Green for you anymore. Welcome home, Princess. We'll burn the mortal blight out of you."

Camilla lost some of her false bravado.

Lennox meant that more literally than figuratively. He would torture her until she became as cruel and twisted as her elder sister and brother. They'd not been given over to the mortal world—they'd been trained to lead their courts. That they weren't here now indicated they were playing twisted games with their own Fae.

Her younger brother surprised her by stepping forward.

"I'll bring her to my court."

Ayden stared their father down, his expression a practiced snarl.

"Two brilliant little fools. More mortal than Fae in spirit." Lennox nodded. "What trouble might this stir? Leading your courts...or will they lead you? Chaos."

He considered Ayden's offer. Then he looked at Envy again.

A slow, saccharine smile curved his mouth.

"My daughter will stay here. With me. The Wild Court could use fresh royal blood. Give me her locket."

He motioned to a male standing near the dais, one of his personal guards, with a piece of iron piercing his nose. A sign of strength. Of his power. And his penchant for enjoying pain.

Camilla clasped her mother's locket in her hand, backing away. "This belongs to me."

Lennox gave her a dark smile.

"Your mother stole it from my coffers before she stole you, too. The locket is mine. And I've gone to a lot of trouble to get it back."

Camilla inhaled sharply, still holding on to the locket as the guard approached. He held a hand out, eyes glittering with challenge. She didn't hand it over. But he didn't seem to care.

He sliced the metal from her neck, then brought the prize to his king. Lennox closed his fingers around it, a strange, silver light emanating from his closed fist. Camilla hadn't known the locket held that kind of power, had been told it repelled Unseelie males.

It worked against Wolf, but the king was different, she supposed.

Had that truly been what Lennox was after all this time—not Camilla, but her locket?

Lennox glanced up, as if he'd forgotten he had an audience. He waved a hand dismissively. "Get the demon's prize. Send him on his way."

Lennox flicked his hand toward another member of the court.

Wolf stepped out from behind a tangle of Unseelies, his pale yellow eyes gleaming.

"Claim your prize, Wolf."

Wolf looked Camilla over, his perusal long and lingering. "With pleasure."

Unseelie chittered and laughed, delighted by the charged look Wolf gave her.

She kept her reaction perfectly bland.

Once upon a time, he'd been sent to Waverly Green with an invitation for her to return to the Wild Court. She'd refused, of course, but their night together had changed everything.

His expression was as rakish as ever as he slowly dragged his attention over Camilla again. Wolf would never cross any unforgivable lines, but he'd play the part the court expected in public. She knew this was only an act. But Envy didn't know that.

She sensed him beside her, a storm of barely leashed jealousy whipping below the surface. Envy hated her, might never wish to speak to her again, but his sin was still provoked.

Wolf didn't appear to notice he was needling him. The Fae strolled down the dais, gaze locked on her. "Let's get you naked and wet, Princess."

"I'll bathe on my own," she said, knowing what he'd meant.

Wolf *did* notice Envy's coiled violence. Was continuing to provoke him.

Camilla recalled the way Envy had fought at the vampire court, knew it wouldn't end well for anyone if he finally snapped. One glance at Lennox and she realized that was exactly what he was hoping for, had set into motion. Chaos and discord were his happiest melodies.

And he'd played them all.

He wanted Wolf to bait Envy. Wanted an excuse to delay giving the demon his prize.

"Congratulations on your win, Prince Envy," Lennox said, tone far too innocent. "Unless you'd like to stay and watch our little show, get out."

The iron-pierced Fae went to usher Envy out, and the demon exploded.

In a movement that was almost too fast to see, the guard flew across the room, landing at the Unseelie King's feet, his arm and leg bent in the wrong direction.

"You broke my commander," Lennox said, no emotion in his voice.

An inhuman growl sounded from Envy's throat. "*Don't* push me, Lennox."

Wolf didn't retreat, but he stopped walking toward Camilla.

The king eyed Envy speculatively, then shrugged. "You appear more road-weary than I thought. Allow me to make amends. A guest suite will be prepared if you'd prefer to stay and watch the fun."

With a flick of his wrist, Lennox dismissed them all, the party and chaos once again taking over the night.

Camilla looked at Envy, but the demon turned on his heel and strode after another guard.

She knew no tears or pleading would make a difference.

She was the daughter of his greatest enemy. And Envy would never forgive her for that.

This game had been about getting Camilla back to Faerie from its inception, and Envy's court had paid a steep price for that.

If there had been any flicker of hope of his forgiving her, that ember had died.

SIXTY-TWO

Envy's rage balanced on a knife's edge, one step away from razing the whole Wild Court. A vast dichotomy split inside him, separating two warring halves directly down the middle.

One side was betrayal made flesh. Cold, unyielding.

An ancient hurt that knew no beginning and no ending. It was a snarling, two-headed beast that wanted to strike out, inflict pain. Tear and gorge and decimate. Like the wolves inked onto his skin, the monsters he kept on a tight leash wanted retribution.

Camilla had played the ultimate game, and he'd had no idea.

The other side was worried. Protective. Champing at the bit to see Camilla, to wrench her free of this court of nightmares. Her true home. With her true family.

That side worried him the most. It was cold but in a different way. The icy precision of calculation. Of plotting. And for once, it had nothing to do with game strategy.

The Chalice of Memoria would be delivered soon; then he was expected to leave the Wild Court.

He *should* leave.

He should never look back, never spare another moment of his existence thinking of the deceitful Fae. This had been the worst game of all. He'd fallen for the lie.

But Camilla...it wasn't as easy as it should be to walk away from her.

How much she'd known, how deeply she'd been involved in the game remained to be seen. Envy wanted to jump to conclusions, toss her in with the rest of her deplorable family. But he hadn't sensed any duplicity in her. She hadn't wanted to paint the Hexed Throne.

Had refused him time and again. All part of her strategy, or genuine?

"Gods' blood."

This was what happened when someone mixed pleasure with what should only be business. Envy couldn't tell if his sentimentality, his cursed *fondness* for the artist, colored his perception. Made him seek good when there wasn't any.

Camilla was Unseelie. Daughter of the king and queen of dark Fae. Even with her magic bound, she possessed the ability to paint new worlds. There was no telling how powerful she was now that Lennox had obliterated the glamour mark and she'd regained her full magic.

Envy snorted. No wonder she'd been so confident the night she'd tempted him to massage her. She knew he wouldn't find a glamour mark under her hairline.

Had regaining her true form been her ultimate goal? Had she finally agreed to help Envy so she could be restored to her full power? It would be tempting and understandable.

Perhaps he'd been a means to an end for her. A passing fancy.

That thought rankled. For centuries he'd been the one to leave lovers wanting more. Now those tables had not just been turned but had been upended on him.

But…her lust, her passion, that hadn't been fake. He sensed how much she wanted him, knew it had nothing to do with any sort of revenge for her family. That was real.

It was also part of her true nature.

"Fuck." He ran a hand through his hair.

He wasn't sure whether she was his enemy or not.

Her *father*, though…

Envy put his fist through the wall, then yanked it out, watching the wound bleed before slowly stitching itself together.

Lennox was a master at chaos, feeding off it and the passion it stirred in those who devolved into the lowest common denominator when provoked.

Envy refused to spiral. He would not fuel that prick's magic here.

He sat on the edge of the bed, forcing his mind to still, to think clearly. This was just another puzzle to solve. And he already had a good portion of the pieces. If he removed all emotion from it, he should be able to put everything together accurately.

"Facts," he reminded himself. "List the facts."

Lennox was Camilla's biological father. But she had not called him that. He'd seen the love she had for Pierre when she spoke of him, the pride in his studio and its secret passages and entries. Saw the hurt when she'd recalled his death. He had not sensed any lies.

Envy was starting to think that Lennox's inclusion of her had less to do with taunting Envy than with Lennox's luring Camilla back to the Wild Court. She was one of the four Unseelie heirs; maybe her father wanted her to rule over one of the smaller courts. Or maybe he was just pissed off that her mother had stolen his trinket and wanted it back.

"Not my court. Not my problem," Envy muttered to himself.

Lying to himself.

Camilla must have known. Must have figured out what her father was truly after. Yet she'd continued to help Envy, had come all the way to the Fae realm, knowing what lay in store for her, knowing how much Envy hated Unseelie royalty.

Though that wasn't out of the goodness of her heart, as he'd just found out. The Hexed Throne had stolen her talent, driving her to follow the game until it ended. A detail Camilla *hadn't* shared. One more Unseelie royal playing him for a fool.

Devil below. He'd fucked an Unseelie princess on his throne.

A sworn enemy, hated beyond anything, *owned* him in *his* court.

And Envy liked it. That was what needled him the most. He couldn't even pretend that he hadn't considered giving everything up, damning his whole circle, because he'd gone and gotten addicted to the clever, wonderful female who'd stood up to him time and again.

No wonder her passion was endless. It was her nature, seeking emotions that were large, feeding her own power.

That didn't quite sit truthfully, though.

Logic told him that what they'd shared was real. The hurt he felt... that was also real.

A soft knock had him yanking the door open, ready to either kiss or kill—

"Wolf."

The Fae's eyes glittered darkly. "Expecting someone else?"

"Get the fuck out."

Wolf folded his arms across his chest, staring down his nose at Envy.

The look was pure Fae arrogance.

Envy thought about punching it off his face, feeling the satisfying crunch of bone.

"I don't like you," Wolf said simply. Envy gave him a dark look. "I do like Camilla. I like her heart. Her creativity. And I love that sound she makes right before she comes."

Envy's jaw locked, his hand curling at his side. If he struck Wolf, Lennox might hold off on delivering his prize.

His court. He had to think only of saving his court now.

"Get to the point, Wolf."

"I want her. I go after what I want. With gusto." Wolf's gaze flared. "But she seems to want you. Personally, I think she'll get over it. Once upon a time, she liked me, too. When you're gone, I'll still be here. Comforting her."

Envy silently counted backward. Focusing on his failing demons. On the monstrosity of his court. On the way it would feel to have Wolf's blood spilling across his fist.

"And when she wants me to, I'll be right back in her bed. Pleasuring her."

Envy went to slam the door in the Fae prick's face, but Wolf shoved his boot over the threshold, blocking him from doing so. There *was* a satisfying crunch, though.

"Would you like me to set up a parade?" Envy asked.

"When you walk out of this court," Wolf said, "I want you to think about what you're leaving behind. Who. And then I want you to remember that there are others who are far less foolish, who won't simply walk away when things get hard and aren't a perfect fairy tale anymore."

"Any other words of wisdom?"

"If you hurt my princess," Wolf quietly growled, "I'll hunt you down, demon."

"*Your* princess?" Envy's sin ignited. "Camilla will never be your anything, Fae."

"Ah, but I'll always be her first." Wolf's expression turned mocking. "And now her father wants us together again. Who am I to deny the king? He suggested I escort her down to court, then take her in front of them. Remind her what fun we used to have."

A thin sheet of ice shot around the room, coating the furniture, the ceiling, the walls. Envy's internal meter was turning away from betrayal and landing solidly in the section of wanting to destroy anyone who threatened Camilla.

"What do you think of that, Your Highness? Should I remind her what it was like? Should I stamp out any traces of your demon taint upon her skin?"

Wolf cocked his head, eyes narrowing.

"Do you think that now that she's unbound she'll fuck more ferociously?" He whistled. "Two Unseelies going at it... you cannot begin to imagine the intensity. Passion feeds in a mirroring loop. I cannot wait for her pretty mouth to be filled with my come again."

Wolf was goading him. Envy knew it. And he didn't give a shit.

Envy took a step toward the Unseelie, allowing every dark thing that made him a Prince of Hell to roll off him.

"Camilla belongs with *me*."

Wolf smiled.

"Then I suggest you pull your head out of your ass and go after her. Lennox will send for her soon. If I were you, I'd come up with a plan before then. The king is not kind to mortals—and Camilla is far more human in behavior than Fae."

All amusement vanished from Wolf's face.

"And my original message stands, demon. Hurt her, and I'll make you regret it." He stepped back into the hallway. "Now come, Your Highness. I'll take you to her."

Indecision warred inside Envy.

He didn't want anything to happen to Camilla, but he wasn't ready to see her. Envy had never been someone's hero. Didn't know how to be.

Wolf looked him over, a sneer forming on his face.

"You don't deserve her."

"Never said I did."

Wolf was silent a moment, then said, "I might have forgotten to mention...Lennox has summoned you. He expects you in court in exactly thirty minutes."

Without looking back, the Unseelie walked away, shaking his head.

SIXTY-THREE

Camilla stared at her reflection in the mirror, at once foreign and familiar.

Her face was mostly unchanged. If anything, her eyes were a bit more metallic, the silver polished to a gleam. Her hair shimmered with a brightness it hadn't had before, like moonlight on a cold winter's night.

Her ears...there was no denying what she was, no hiding. Any notion she might have harbored about returning to Waverly Green was gone now.

Not that she wanted to return anymore. After experiencing the Seven Circles and even the terrors of Malice Isle, Camilla had seen the breadth of the world. The idea of returning to Waverly Green without her family, without...anyone...no longer appealed.

But she wanted Bunny. Needed to go back and retrieve her sweet cat. Say a proper goodbye to Kitty, too.

She touched the soft tips of her elongated ears, now foreign to her.

The choice to be glamoured hadn't been Camilla's.

Not much in her life had been, in fact. She was a child when everything familiar was suddenly wrenched away. Her home, her family, her realm. One night she was a high princess of the Wild Court, the next she was a mortal child without magic in Waverly Green.

Her mother, Prim Róis Fleur, had kidnapped her from the Wild Court for reasons she would probably never fully understand. Ever since, Lennox had been trying to tempt her back. Wanting her to take her throne.

To Camilla, it had been one of the worst games her parents had ever played.

But one piece still didn't fit: Why had Prim Róis stolen the locket, and then left it with Camilla? And why had Lennox gone through so much to get it back?

More puzzles, more riddles, more deception. Such was the way of her family.

Not all had been a lie, though. Her mother had become fond of Pierre. Had even used her true middle name, offering him some honesty.

It hadn't taken much magic for her mother to convince Pierre that the young child had been his—she'd given him false memories, of her being pregnant, of the first few years of Camilla's life. Of him teaching Camilla how to hold a paintbrush nimbly between her fingers.

All lies, pretty little magical glamours.

But Camilla had truly loved him. Staying in Waverly Green, running Pierre's gallery—that had finally been Camilla's choice. With her human father, Camilla had learned how powerful love was. How fear could never hope to compete.

Camilla wondered, though, if her mortal father had known. If there had been a piece of him that could see through Prim Róis and her Fae magic. She feared that that was what ultimately drove him to his obsession and madness.

But perhaps it was also what led Pierre to fill her head with fairy tales. He'd been the one to warn her of the Fae and their bargains. He'd taught her about the vampire prince. And the seven ruling Princes of Hell.

Camilla did not believe in coincidences.

Her fingers brushed the soft curve of her ears again.

Would her mortal father hate this form?

No. He'd love her anyway. Pierre's love was unconditional, without games or strings.

She dropped her hands into her lap.

Envy was not Pierre. He would not care for her now that her truth was revealed.

"Princess?" Wolf called from outside her door. "You indecent?"

His tone held a note of teasing, and maybe a little hope. He would wait for her.

He'd told her as much when he'd walked her to her bedroom suite. And that ought to comfort her, knowing she wouldn't be alone. Envy was only ever going to be hers for one night. That was truer now than it had been before her deception was revealed.

"Princess? You're making me think thoughts that are downright filthy."

Camilla finally managed a smile, the first since she'd arrived here.

"Come in."

He slipped into her chambers and gave her an appreciative once-over. "Bold."

"I tried."

She knew he didn't mean the cut of the gown, which plunged to form a deep V to her navel in both the front and the back.

Camilla had chosen the deepest shade of green in the wardrobe she'd found in her suite. It might not matter, but even if Envy wasn't there to see it, she wanted the Wild Court to know it hadn't all been a lie.

Her father, however, would not be pleased.

She assumed he'd hate the emerald-and-diamond ring she'd strung on a necklace, to rest over her heart, even more.

Wolf's gaze paused on the emerald. "He's an ass."

"He's hurt," Camilla said. "I should have told him who I was."

Wolf snorted. "I'm sure he was nothing but honest with you."

"I'm not responsible for anyone's actions but my own." Camilla exhaled. "My human father taught me better. I was afraid. I let fear of losing my talent forever rule my actions first. Then as I grew...closer to Envy, I feared how he'd react to my truth. He hates Unseelie royals."

"I repeat, he's an ass."

"I imagine you aren't here to discuss my love life," she said, smiling weakly. "Has the king summoned me?"

Wolf nodded slowly, his gaze drifting around her private suite.

Windows took up three of the four walls, and the ceiling was also made of glass, allowing the moonlight to cascade in like a silver waterfall.

When his attention came back to her, he seemed uncertain.

"Play your father's game, Camilla. Or things will go very badly tonight."

She'd already played enough of Lennox's games, but she nodded to keep from speaking the lie aloud.

Wolf looked her over, a frown tugging at his lips, then escorted her to court.

"Good." Lennox glanced at Camilla, his gaze narrowing on her gown. He didn't miss the subtle *to hell with your court and games* of her color choice. "You're right on schedule." He motioned to the guards flanking him. "Bring her here. I'm ready to begin."

All but the new head guard descended on her. He hung back, holding an object under a velvet cloth, surely something nasty to threaten her with if she didn't do as her father said.

She felt Wolf stiffen beside her, didn't dare to look in his direction. Her father was watching her every move, the cunning gleam speaking volumes. She hadn't failed to notice that no one else was present in the Crescent Court now. An oddity. When she was a child, the room, shaped like a crescent moon, was always filled with Fae.

Now it was still. Silent, save for the handful of guards, Camilla, Wolf, and the Unseelie King. Perhaps they were all still indulging outside on the terrace. That didn't feel right…

She glanced around again, her unease growing.

The silver floor had been designed to reflect the moonlight streaming in through the glass ceiling, but for some reason her father had had the roof covered.

Another ominous, foreboding sense of worry gnawed at her.

The Wild Court worshipped the moon, bathed in its light, celebrated it. That her father had covered its magic…didn't bode well for her.

She allowed the guards to usher her to her father's throne. An easel and a small wooden table had been set up near the foot of the dais, holding a strange assortment of art supplies.

A paintbrush, charcoal, silver paint. Black, gold, and iridescent Fae colors not available in the mortal world. The Fae colors drew her eye, made her drift closer despite the prickle of trepidation she felt.

"You will paint the key and locket together."

Lennox held the portal key up in one hand, and the silver locket swung in his other fist.

Camilla's heart raced. Pierre had become obsessed with that portal key. It looked so much like a regular skeleton key, with an emerald set in its base, but to her it had become so much more. She wanted to steal it back, hold it to her chest, and promise her mortal father that she'd never let it out of her sight again.

"Camilla." Lennox's voice was laced with disapproval. "I thought the mortal adoration was an act earlier. Tell me you don't actually harbor feelings for that pet your mother played with?"

Wolf's warning fluttered through her mind. *Play your father's game.* Camilla bit the inside of her cheek, stopping herself from snapping at the king.

Instead, she stared at the portal key and the locket, trying to puzzle out why he'd want them painted together. What nefarious plot had he hatched now? Asking him outright would only enrage him—the Unseelie King's orders were to be met with obedience.

Still...

"How are they meant to be painted together?" she asked, the question innocent enough.

Lennox's hair shifted from silver to white to black, his mood rapidly changing.

"A chain, a rope, a ribbon of silk," he said, shrugging. "Your talent will guide you. All that matters is that the two are bound."

Camilla knew exactly what she wouldn't paint, then. But her defiance...

She swallowed hard, then picked up the paintbrush, her gaze once again drifting to the shimmering, ethereal Fae colors. One—lavender, blue, silver, undulating in iridescent waves—was magic in liquid form. She dipped the tip of her brush in it, then accepted the portal key and her locket, laying them both on the little wooden table, on top of each other, her pulse suddenly racing.

"Oh, one more thing."

Lennox's voice was a dagger dipped in poison, pinning her in place.

"Should you not do as I say, I'll destroy this."

He motioned to his head guard, who unveiled what he'd been holding. It was meant to torture her, all right. Except it wouldn't simply hurt her. It would destroy Envy's court.

There, clasped in the guard's hands, was what had to be the Chalice of Memoria. The cup was etched over with runes, the magic dulled but waiting.

Camilla swallowed the sudden lump in her throat. Her father hadn't let Envy leave yet. Hadn't yet ended the game. No matter that she didn't want to bind the portal key and the locket together, she couldn't harm Envy or his court again.

Lennox watched her closely, the corner of his mouth tipped up. He loved it when his plan unfolded perfectly, had bet she'd fall into line.

And worst of all, he was correct.

Outmaneuvered, cornered, and without choice, Camilla dove into that well of magic, the talent that came from other worlds, just like her.

She closed her eyes, allowing her muse to take over, to show her how the object wished to be bound. Thin Fae-colored chains spiderwebbed around the key and the locket.

Giving herself fully to her talent, Camilla painted each thread in the magical color, going so far as to add little droplets, like dew on a spider's web. The stem of the portal key slowly fused with the locket, the silver liquefying and seeping until the two objects melded into one.

It wasn't a painting, but a new tangible object.

A shocking, horrible truth broke free, tossing Camilla backward in a magical blast. Her body flew several feet across the throne room before she crashed and fell into a heap, her head smashing against metal bars.

She could scarcely see the here and now; she was still half lost to that strange power. Last time, Envy had been there, shaking her back to reality. Now she was on her own.

And what she'd seen...

"Hexed object." It was all she could manage to whisper. On their own they'd been just a portal key and her locket. Bound, they became something more, something other.

Camilla commanded herself to focus, to find her reality.

Cool metal pressed against her palms.

No. *She* was sprawled on a metal floor. The Crescent Court's floor wasn't metal.

She blinked, trying to force herself into the here and now.

A clang rang out, drawing her attention up.

"No." Her voice shook. He'd caged her. And hung her far above the throne room, where her cage swayed dangerously with each of her movements.

It was a fine prison. A mockery of a cell.

"Let me out."

Lennox didn't bother to look at her; he strode down to where she'd left the bound key, plucking it up and turning it over.

"Do you have any idea what this is now capable of?" he asked.

Nothing good, clearly.

Camilla's hands wrapped around the metal bars, burning from the iron. She wrenched them back, then tried again, shaking the door. For doing as he'd commanded, her father had imprisoned her in iron. It was unfathomable.

"You cannot cage me."

Lennox gave her a pitying look. "I just did."

"Why?" she asked, uncaring that she wasn't meant to question the king. "I did as you asked!"

His hair turned black and his eyes gleamed white.

"Is that what I did...*ask* you? Like a nice mortal friend. A loving, human father. Or did your *king* give you an order? One you would have refused had I not given you a *reason* not to?"

He advanced on her, his gaze steely and void of any pretense of civility.

"You mistake your place in my court, daughter. You were invited to come home. *Twice*. First with a friend I sent for you, in case you needed one of our kind. Next, I sent Wolf. In case you required a mate. You chose to stay in that mortal cesspool, lowering yourself. Pretending you were a human."

Anger unleashed her tongue. "*I* didn't choose to leave in the first place. Or have you forgotten your little game with Mother? You made me a changeling. Then you condemn me for choosing to stay where I'd been just another game piece. I never would have left the Wild Court."

"The queen stole you," Lennox snapped. "You should have proven your loyalty to our court when I summoned you the first time."

"My loyalty? It seems like I am simply your little pawn, moving around your game board based on your whims."

His smile was crafted of nightmares. He held the key up. "This is the Silverthorne Key, little pawn. Do you know what it does?"

Camilla felt as if she'd taken a hit. She slowly shook her head, an awful realization emerging. Puzzle pieces clicked into place. Pierre's obsession with the portal key, with keeping it in Waverly Green. The locket her mother told her never to let go.

Silverthorne Lane. The dark market in Waverly Green. The place where Unseelie solitary and exiled Fae bargained with mortals.

Somehow, some way, the key and the dark market were connected. And if Camilla's growing fear was correct, she had likely created a direct link from the mortal world to this court.

"No."

Lennox's gaze turned ebony again, his hair shifting back to its godlike silver-white curtain.

"I see you understand perfectly well. Silverthorne Lane *is* a realm line. This key? It unlocks that doorway and leads it straight to..."

He walked to a silver mirror leaning against the wall, oversized, wide. Large enough for even the tallest human to pass through.

"Here."

Lennox stuck the key directly in the center of the mirror, the glass rippling like liquid as he twisted the hexed object. Camilla stared, trapped in her cage, as the mirror flickered. Shadow and light, light and shadow. Images played across it, too fast to see clearly; then came sounds. Birds, people, carriages...the sounds of Waverly Green's bustling streets.

"No," Camilla said, again, rattling her cage. The iron burned, the pain a wild ache in her bones. "Please. Leave them."

Lennox glanced over his shoulder, his expression one of egregious delight.

"One by one, little pawn, I'll lure everyone from that city here. We're in need of fresh fun in the Wild Court. And once Waverly Green falls, we'll move on to the next. Now be silent."

He cocked his head, then ran a hand over his clothing, magicking a new suit before her eyes. If Camilla hadn't known how dark and twisted he was, Lennox would have looked like a fairy-tale prince. Except this prince was a diabolical king and this cruel king wasn't interested in stealing hearts at all—he wanted to break souls. Beaming with false kindness, he turned back to the mirror as the first few mortals stumbled through, bright-eyed and dreamy.

Widow Janelle, the Lords Harrington and Walters, and several other regulars from Vexley's circle stepped into the throne room.

Camilla pressed her hand to her mouth, biting back a scream. She knew these humans. Had attended parties and gatherings with them.

And they did not deserve the fate that awaited them here.

Their gazes swept around the chamber, then paused on her, on her Fae ears.

Camilla looked at them and screamed, "*Run!*"

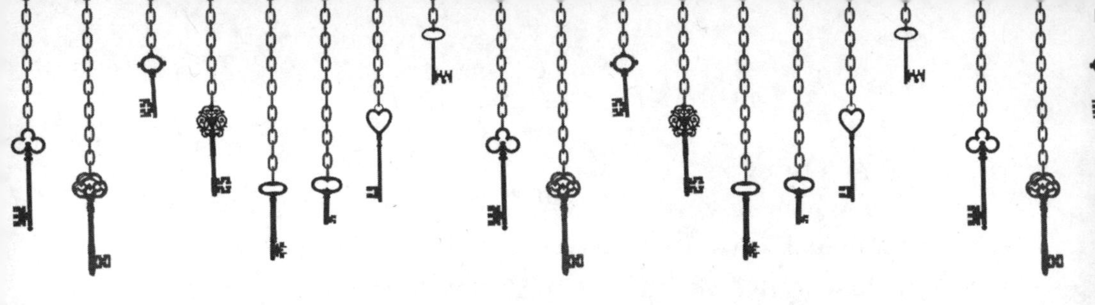

SIXTY-FOUR

THINGS HAD CHANGED inside the Wild Court since the last time Envy had attended a soirée there, more than a century before.

And not for the better.

Unseelie gatherings used to be sinful, delicious events. Where wine flowed freely, lovers paired off for a night of fun, and the king and queen ruled over all with dark glee. Art and passion were celebrated above all. When the moon was full, even better.

The entire Unseelie court had been crafted as an ode to the moon, the chambers all designed to mirror its shifting phases. Most of the castle roof was made of glass, allowing the moonlight to bathe everyone strolling along the floors below. All the furnishings were in silvers and midnight blues and plush black velvets. Little fairy orbs floated in the chambers and corridors, to make guests feel like they were walking among the stars.

It was ethereal, grand, otherworldly in a way that both seduced and relaxed. All the senses were fed by its beauty, and the wine...it was transportive. Addictive. The flavors rich and decadent and made to be savored. Spicy, sweet, sour, and robust.

Demonberry wine came close, but nothing tasted the way Faerie wine did. It found every fun, passionate part of a person and magnified it, giving them confidence to dance and sing and fuck and create whatever their innermost passions called for. As long as guests were consenting adults, the Wild Court became the individual's fantasy.

Everyone wanted an invitation to the Wild Court back then. From Princes of Hell to witches and the normally stoic shifters. Lust even envied the dark Fae for their full-moon indulgences, honoring the heavens from which they drew their power.

That was not the Wild Court Envy saw now.

He walked into the Crescent Court, which had once been the most beautiful of all the chambers. Now it was dark, and not just because the ceiling had been painted black. Torches burned around the room, the fire heavily licking the air.

High above, guests had been penned in cages, like cattle awaiting slaughter. Horned Fae took turns taunting them, setting pokers into a nearby fire until the metal glowed crimson, then screamed along with the humans, whose flesh sizzled and scarred.

The sickly-sweet scent of burnt flesh wafted through the castle, the smoke prickling Envy's eyes. That wasn't the worst of the horrors or depravity on display.

Humans already chosen from their pens were tied to tables, their meat being carved from their bones while they still lived. Even for a Prince of Hell, it was horrific. Then Envy stopped short, recognizing Lord Harrington.

He was screaming as they peeled his flesh away strip by strip.

Bile seared up Envy's throat, burning as much as the rage he choked back down.

Lennox had been a mischievous king, rejoicing in his wickedness, but this was beyond depraved. Beyond cruel.

Wolf sidled up to Envy, a dark cocktail lightly smoking in one hand.

Envy would pay a serious amount of coin to send the damn male on his way.

"Welcome to the new Wild Court." Wolf sipped his drink, attention straying to a nearby fairy whose wings had been set on fire. "Home to the female you refuse to claim."

Wolf tossed back the rest of his cocktail, then threw the glass against the wall, smiling as a courtier cursed him.

"If you think Lennox will treat her any differently just because he wanted her back, you really are a dumb fuck." He twisted, dropping a mockery of a bow. "Your Highness."

"She's Fae."

"Do you think he cares?" Wolf asked quietly. "Lennox wanted the necklace first. Camilla second. And only because Prim Róis kidnapped her. Do you think he'll be kind to the daughter who refused to come home? Look around, Your Highness, does it seem like Lennox likes mortals? Like he would appreciate one of his heirs defying him for them? You were in Waverly Green for a time... notice anything familiar?"

A sick feeling gripped Envy. Lennox had targeted the city Camilla loved.

"How long." Envy didn't ask so much as demand.

"The mortals?" Wolf paused. "I thought you would have pieced it together."

"I've had a lot on my mind," Envy snapped. He still hadn't fully healed from his torture. His power needed to be replenished and he needed to get the fuck out of this court to save his demons before he *couldn't* get out. "Is he only taking from Waverly Green?"

Wolf glanced around, lowering his voice.

"For now."

"And how is he doing it?"

"Now that he's brought Camilla back, he's somehow been able to open a new portal. By uniting her locket with a key."

"The portal key."

Envy's mind spun. The game had never been about him at all.

"What does the portal do?"

Wolf waved at the scene around them. "It lets Lennox come and go in the mortal realm whenever he pleases. Specifically, from the dark market. All these humans?" He scanned the room again. "They're only the beginning of Lennox's new nightmare court. This is what he brought tonight, a lesson for Camilla. Imagine a week from now, a month. We are outside the Seven Circles here. Our wards legendary. Even your king cannot breach this territory if Lennox doesn't will him to."

"It needs to stop. My brothers won't let it stand."

"But you will?" Wolf studied him for a long moment. "Better not keep the king waiting."

A fight broke out behind Wolf, and Envy saw his mask return. With a look of puckish delight, he howled and flung himself into the fray, biting and snarling and punching his way through the growing madness.

Envy watched impassively, the brawlers giving him a wide berth. Even the most rabid Unseelie sensed the menace radiating from him.

The Wild Court wasn't Envy's problem to solve. He had his own court to mend. And yet…these weren't all strangers. They were humans he'd come to know, even briefly, while he'd been in Waverly Green. They'd come to his estate, danced at his ball.

And this torture was beyond any Fae amusement.

He could not imagine what Camilla would feel when she saw it. Hoped she was somewhere far away.

Envy pushed through the fight that had grown to two dozen Fae, heading toward the throne. Wolf was correct about one thing: Camilla was in many ways more mortal than Fae.

Surely the king would not subject his own daughter to this?

Envy hadn't even posed the question to himself before he knew the answer.

His steps faltered as he took in the horrific sight next to the throne.

There, dressed in Envy's colors, hung proof of what Wolf had said about the Unseelie King. Lennox would make Camilla pay for denying him.

Was making her pay.

Envy's freshly regenerated heart thudded painfully, his need to protect urging him forward. But he had to plot his next move carefully.

This scene might have been designed to prey on Envy's reaction to seeing Camilla trapped in a cage a dozen feet off the ground.

Or it might just be a punishment the Unseelie King doled out to a defiant child. Maybe this was his way of breaking Camilla's will.

Nothing would surprise Envy when it came to Lennox and his

manipulations. He took in her prison, noting with horror that it was much worse than he'd thought at first glance.

The birdcage was strung up over a fire, the flames licking greedily at the metal floor, heating it to an angry, orange-red hue. Inside, Camilla had been chained by iron handcuffs to the cage's center pole.

Envy stared at the welts forming on her skin, at the smoke curling around her shoes. The metal floor must be unbearably hot, but Camilla stared out defiantly, silver eyes blazing star-bright, jaw locked. Like she refused to allow one tear to fall, to show one ounce of pain, to spite her father.

Envy went still, the full scope of what Lennox had done sinking in.

Unlike a human who would eventually succumb to the torture, Camilla's immortality wouldn't let her die. She would be tortured nightly, over and over until the king eventually tired and found a new game to play.

How many of the friends and acquaintances she'd made over the years would he parade past her during that time? All because she'd chosen a life for herself.

Envy now stood before the throne.

"Lennox."

The Unseelie King's head swiveled, his dark eyes glassy and unfocused. The chaos and fighting were fueling his power so much he was drunk on it.

"Shame you didn't bring any other mortals," the king slurred. "That last one amused. Greatly. The things she liked to do with her mouth...well, I'm sure you remember."

Envy kept his attention on Lennox, made sure he didn't glance in Camilla's direction. His mask would slip if he did.

"Give me the chalice."

Lennox sat forward. "That's not all you want, though, is it? You want my daughter."

Lennox was prying, testing. Envy threw a wall up around his emotions.

"Already had her. I don't do repeats."

One side of Lennox's mouth curled up. "Interesting."

He flicked his attention to where Camilla was trapped in the cage; Lennox was trying to force Envy to follow his gaze. He didn't.

Lennox eyed him again, looking bored. Envy was no longer the most amusing creature in this room.

"Perhaps you and I are more alike than previously thought. I, too, believe in rules. A win is a win. Here's your prize."

They were not alike at all.

The king held up the Chalice of Memoria. The gold glinted in the moonlight, the runes stark as tattoos. Magic hummed from it, like sound from a struck tuning fork, almost lost in the cacophony behind them.

Lennox didn't move from where he sat on his throne, forcing Envy to take the two steps up to him.

He felt Camilla's gaze on him, would know the feel of it anywhere.

He did not succumb to the temptation to drive his House dagger through the Fae. At least not yet.

Envy gently wrapped his fingers around the chalice, the magic flaring when it recognized its owner. It had taken centuries, but he'd finally be able to save his court. Envy's grip on it tightened, and the Unseelie King let it go, that mocking smirk still fixed to his face.

"Congratulations, Your Highness." Lennox's voice was silken, low. "I'll give my daughter your regards. Well, after the show."

Envy couldn't help it; he glanced over at Camilla. Her expression was a mask of regret and pain. She held Envy's gaze, as if silently saying a final goodbye. She knew what he'd been after.

And now he couldn't linger.

"My little dove needs to be reminded what happens when she flies the proverbial coop. Her mother played a dangerous game, stealing her away. All because I was...how did she put it? *Losing myself to depravity.* As if Prim Róis ever felt an ounce of anything else herself."

Envy's heartbeat tripled, his mind racing. When he spoke, his tone was bored.

"You never sent her away."

"Of course I didn't. She's far too valuable. Why else do you think that bitch queen kidnapped her?" Lennox stood, eyes and hair rippling darker. "Time to celebrate your princess!" he called out to his court. "Who wants to play with her in the cage?"

The Unseelie behind them erupted. In their excitement they were tearing one another apart, limbs and wings and talons flying. They wanted to hurt their princess. Watch her burn.

Later, he'd blame the influence of the wicked court, fueling his magic. He'd claim the chalice had restored him. He'd say that his hatred for Lennox made him snap. He'd lie.

When the first Fae climbed up to claw into that cage, ripping Camilla's dress with its talons, Envy became the demon he was.

He thought of Camilla being trapped in that cage for eternity, thought of the Fae mocking her, hurting her. And the magic he'd resisted wielding to free his wings, the power he didn't have to spare...shattered against the full might of his sin releasing.

He felt the ward around his circle break. Felt the minds of his demons slipping from his grasp. He knew he had only a few minutes, which he needed to make count.

Then he needed to be gone.

Dark, glittering emerald wings shot out from between his shoulder blades, his feathers razor-sharp, slicing through the Fae gathered near him like daggers.

Blood splattered across the silver floor.

It wasn't nearly enough. It wasn't Lennox's blood.

His wings pulsed with unspoken power, the spells from the Aether Scrolls tattooed across each feather, inert for decades, searing to life. They called to him, begged him to use them. They offered a cruel spell for a crueler king. But they offered him something else first.

He plucked one of his feathers and flung it swiftly at the cage, its magically razored edge blasting the door open, freeing Camilla.

Lennox let loose a howl of rage.

Envy turned to the king, a vicious smile curving his mouth. He held his House dagger in one hand now, aiming it straight at the Unseelie King's heart.

"Get in the cage, Lennox."

Envy knew the king wouldn't submit easily.

He sneered. "You first, demon."

Lennox unleashed his moonbeam magic, blanketing them all in a complete whiteout that temporarily stole all sense of sight and sound. Like a blizzard crafted of moonlight.

Envy realized this wasn't the end. A new game had just begun.

And this one would end in death.

SIXTY-FIVE

THE BIRDCAGE PRISON blasted open, the impact of the spelled feather nearly knocking Camilla off her feet.

Silver-white light fell upon her, like celestial snow, before she'd regained her footing. Her father's moon magic.

Camilla blinked against the blinding light, knowing he'd call forth his shadow magic next. The moon was light and dark, and so was Lennox's power. Now a sea of unending black rolled through the chamber.

It was the darkness of killers, of nefarious deeds.

But after a second, it blasted back to brightest moonlight. Lennox alternated between the two contrasts, a rapid strobe from light to dark and back that made it difficult to see anyone approaching until they were right on top of you. He was Chaos, and all now felt it.

Lennox's power was meant to disorient his victims, and it worked beautifully.

Though most were fleeing, tripping over themselves and others as they shoved and darted toward the exits at each corner.

Envy had been standing entirely too close to Lennox when he'd let his cloak of night drop. Camilla saw that he was still reeling.

Camilla had recovered faster, nimbly climbing out of the cage and stealing across the throne room. A large male Fae barreled into her, knocking her into a table where a human had been tied.

Please, the woman mouthed. *Help.*

Camilla cursed, unable to turn away.

She worked the ropes tied at the human's wrists, her fingers slipping in the blood. She was trembling, trying to hurry while still glancing back to where Lennox and Envy were slowly circling each other below the throne.

Even without his senses fully intact, Envy was a predator who would not easily be taken down.

Camilla moved to the woman's ankles and stopped short.

The moonlight and shadows flickered violently, but she saw enough to know that the woman wouldn't be walking out of this room. Her legs had been carved to the bone, her feet missing.

Bile rose up swiftly, but she swallowed it, trying to keep the fear and horror from her face.

She turned back to the woman, ready to lift her and carry her to safety, but the woman's eyes were glazed, lifeless, fixed on a point hopefully far better than here.

Camilla was frozen with grief for a moment, glancing around at the chaos.

This was her father's court. His nightmare.

Fae crashed into each other as they panicked, trying to flee. No one wanted to be around Lennox when he lost his temper and let his magic out to play.

Mortals who'd been tied and savaged either fainted or screamed.

Camilla wanted to help each of them back through the Silverthorne Lane portal, back to Waverly Green. Then she'd smash the damn hexed key.

A flash of emerald caught her attention.

Envy's wings were spread wide, striking out like weapons. Silver white, black, and emerald. The colors of the two males battling blurred as their powers clashed and clawed.

Something else caught her eye...gold ichor. Envy had been injured.

"No." She stared as her father changed the flicker of his power, stretching the time between the light and the dark so he could move without being seen.

Envy must not have fully recovered from Vexley's attack...

"His wings."

He'd told Camilla he didn't have enough magic to call forth his wings, hold the ward around his circle, and help his court.

"Oh, God."

Camilla's blood turned to ice. He'd used his final store of power.

To save her.

No matter that he was furious about her secrets. No matter that she was the flesh and blood of his enemy.

Envy had risked everything he'd fought for to ensure that she was safe.

She could not let him ruin his court for her.

Lennox struck another devastating blow, slashing his Fae blade low, tearing through the demon's shirt. Even in the strobing light, Camilla saw Envy wince.

Camilla searched for a weapon, something, *anything* she could use against the king.

She hadn't come armed to their meeting. And even if she had, Lennox would have taken anything from her when she'd been imprisoned.

Think...

She wasn't physically strong enough to overpower the king. She couldn't hold him back while Envy ran him through. She couldn't bind his power or use hers to stun him.

There had to be—a sense of calmness dropped over her.

Camilla was dangerous with or without a weapon.

Because she could create one. All she needed to do was get to the paint and the brush. Then she'd summon a weapon deadly enough to kill an immortal king.

Two large hands grabbed her by the waist and tugged her back.

She thrashed, calling forth the magic that had killed Vexley.

"Easy, now." Wolf's mouth pressed against her ear. "You're getting entirely too close to my favorite appendage."

"Put me down."

He did but didn't unhand her.

"Wolf," she warned.

Wolf dropped his hands but remained close.

She didn't have time to waste. With Wolf following closely on her heels, she picked her way around the chaos and snatched the brush from the floor. Understanding what she was attempting, Wolf grabbed an unbroken jar of paint, thrusting it toward her, then jerked his chin toward the alcove behind the throne. She spared him one long look. Wolf was committing treason. If they failed, Lennox would torture him. Slowly.

Go on, Princess, he mouthed.

She nodded, then took one final look at the raging fight.

Envy and Lennox were locked in battle, their blades flashing across the dark and light like lightning strikes of gods.

Camilla pushed their fight from her mind, rushed to the alcove, and dropped to her knees, forcing herself to dive deep, deep into that well of power, summoning an image of what she needed most. At first there was only glittering darkness, no shapes or images to be found.

Then, like moonlight rippling across a lake, she saw it.

A bold, curved sword forged its way into her mind. The blade was graceful, violent. And the weapon was made of Fae killing iron.

With the image of the curved sword in her mind, Camilla began painting it across the silver floor, her brush flying back and forth, the strokes heavy and light, bold and thin. She hoped she was working quickly, that she wasn't transported to some other realm.

That she was *in* Faerie gave her hope that only a few moments had passed.

When the sword practically gleamed, she reached into the floor, yanking the weapon free from where it had slumbered in the ether. She hissed as the very real iron burned her palms, searing the shape of the hilt into her flesh like a brand.

Wolf jerked back as she pushed to her feet, gritting her teeth to keep from screaming. Not that anyone would hear her cries with Lennox's power surging as strong as ever.

A series of moonbeam blasts drew her attention to the dais. Envy was on the floor, her father towering over him. She gasped, but then the demon prince's wings shot out, knocking the king down.

They grappled on the floor. Blood splattered everywhere.

Camilla took one excruciating step at a time, hand clamped around the sword, refusing to drop it. Even as her flesh sizzled and the sickly-sweet scent wafted through the room, she forced herself to where her father battled.

Lennox was drawing his arm back, sword dripping with Envy's ichor, ready to end the fight.

Camilla didn't think. She acted.

She swung the curved blade as hard and fast as she could, aiming for the back of Lennox's knee. She felt the metal bite through his flesh.

With a roar that broke through the oppressive power of Unseelie magic, her father spun on his good leg, eyes flickering between black and white. A vicious sneer lifted his lips.

He advanced on her, sword swinging.

Camilla held her ground, striking again. This time the iron seared across his chest, carving a gaping wound.

Over Lennox's shoulder, she saw Envy rise. He towered anew, his wings fully unfurled, and when Lennox lifted his sword to strike his daughter down, the demon prince drove his blade straight through the Unseelie King's chest.

Immediately the flickering, strobing light stopped.

Sound returned, crashing down like a rain of glass.

Lennox went down to one knee, glittering blood smearing across his teeth as he coughed. Holding a hand to his collapsing chest, he spit the blood out near Camilla's feet.

Instead of snarling at her, her father smiled. It frightened her more than if he'd screamed.

"You are my child, through and through."

Camilla's eyes burned as she dropped her weapon, shaking her head, holding up her charred palms.

Of all the things she'd imagined him saying…

Envy dragged his demon blade across Lennox's throat, silencing her father forever.

She stared as the Unseelie King slumped to the ground, unmoving.

A terrible war took place inside her. She hadn't dealt the killing blow, but she'd ensured that he didn't win the fight. Her own father.

Fingers wrapped around her wrist, squeezing gently.

"Envy, I'm so—" She turned, then closed her mouth.

The prince hadn't taken her hand.

Wolf gave her a sad smile. "I'm sorry, Princess. He left."

A fist clutched her heart, squeezing until she felt dizzy. It couldn't be true. Not after what they'd just done. Her gaze darted around, searching. There were no emerald wings towering above the chaos. No gleaming demon dagger shining like its own bloody star.

Wolf was correct. Envy was gone.

He'd left her.

Tears pricked her eyes, but she blinked them away.

Sometimes actions spoke far louder than any words.

The demon prince had not forgiven her, after all. Now that he'd won the game and killed his greatest enemy, he'd gone home. It shouldn't hurt so much that he'd done exactly what he'd always said he would. But hearts weren't always logical, and Camilla's ached at the loss.

"Your Highness?" Wolf asked, voice quiet. "What will you have me do?"

Camilla pulled the broken pieces of herself together, then glanced around the chamber.

No living creatures remained, all fled or crumpled to the ground. The beauty of the Crescent Court was buried in blood and smoke. But against the wall, the portal still gleamed, and she knew what to do.

"We find all the mortals and escort them safely to Waverly Green."

"Then?"

"I'll close the portal and destroy the Silverthorne Key," she said.

Wolf winced.

"What?"

"Princess...the key is gone."

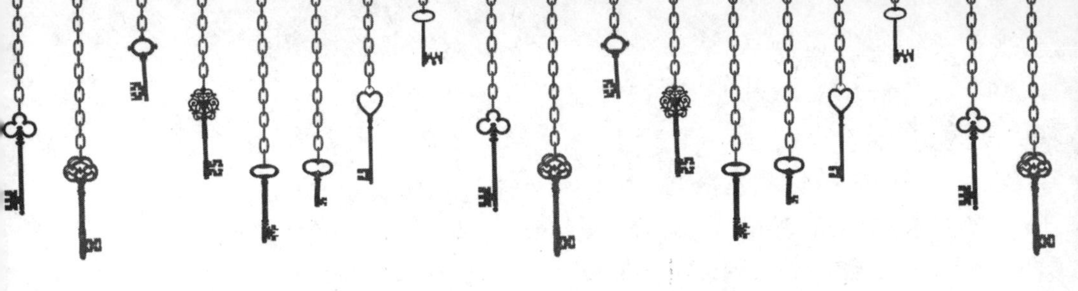

SIXTY-SIX

"Is it working?" Alexei asked, pacing around the stark room they'd set up to restore Envy's court in the farthest wing of House Envy.

They'd emptied the chamber of everything except for the oversized wool rug, a high-backed chair, two stools, and a small table to set the chalice on. And chains.

"Too soon to tell." Envy lifted a shoulder, forcing casualness he didn't feel. His gaze slid between the demon strapped in the chair—his unfocused eyes feral with fear—to the clock. For the hundredth time in a second. Thus far, there was no discernible change. The demon seemed as terrified and as lost to that terrible fog as ever.

"Now?" Alexei pressed.

"Does he look restored?" Envy snapped as the demon struggled against his restraints. Envy blew out a breath, bringing his emotions back under control. "We'll know when it works. He'll recognize us."

It had begun when Envy had picked up the Chalice of Memoria, the activation runes glimmering hunter green. It looked like it used to. Envy had cast the same spell he'd always used before, then offered the chalice to Lord Alden.

The demon had knocked the first attempt out of Envy's hands.

Then Alexei had come in, held him down.

When that didn't work, they'd strapped the demon to the chair and forced the chalice to his lips, tipping his head back to pour the spelled drink down his throat.

Forty-seven excruciating seconds passed. The fog didn't dissipate from behind the demon's eyes. Frustration built in Envy's chest.

Winning the game was supposed to save his court.

To think it had been one more false hope...

"Fuck!" Envy paced around the room, mind whirling.

He could seek the Crone again—the creator of the Underworld itself. The Crone was to goddesses what Titans were to mortal gods. If anyone could help, it would be her. But he'd been desperate once before, had asked her years back.

She'd laughed in his face and vowed to do worse next time.

He supposed he could kidnap her daughters, force her hand.

But that wouldn't end well for any of them.

Envy walked to the arched window on the far side of the room, gazing out at the grounds. It was twilight, a soft blanket of snow falling, the flakes tumbling and swirling as they danced down to the winter grass.

"Your Highness?"

There was an odd edge in Alexei's tone.

Envy twisted, gaze snapping to Lord Alden. The demon blinked slowly, then squeezed his eyes shut. His head moved from side to side, as if shaking some internal nightmare away.

Envy moved closer, hope igniting once again.

He paused a few feet away, his breath lodged deep in his chest.

Another thirty seconds ticked by.

A minute.

Come on, he silently urged. *Open your eyes, recognize where you are, remember* who *you are.*

Lord Alden's hands fisted, his wrists twisting, testing the restraints on the arms of the chair. Envy and Alexei both leaned forward, neither daring to speak. Lord Alden opened his eyes, squinting at first, then glanced down at his bound arms.

He looked back up, brows knitted as his focus moved from Alexei to Envy.

"Is this some new kink, Your Highness?" he asked, sounding annoyed. "I despise chains."

Air whooshed out of Envy. He wanted to grab the demon by the lapels and plant a kiss on him but refrained. Lord Alden was properly aggravated. A personality trait he'd had for the last six centuries.

"How do you feel?" Envy asked instead.

Lord Alden's gaze flattened. "Like House Wrath is looking appealing, Your Highness. Unless I'm being held for treason, untie me."

Alexei snorted. "Same old prick."

It had worked. Envy expelled another breath, relief barreling through him. The Chalice of Memoria would stop the memory blight. After years of turmoil, that dark, unending descent... the nightmare was finally ending. Part of him couldn't believe it.

Alexei began untying Alden, then directed him to the Gallery of Dreamscapes, where Envy had set up refreshments in hopes the newly saved demons would need a safe space to wait until they'd restored everyone's memories.

Once Alexei returned with the next demon, they started all over again. After the second successful restoration, they brought in more chairs and restraints.

Days passed, Envy staying right there with his court, even though plenty of volunteers had come together from the healed, helping their fellow demons.

Once it was clear the tide had turned, days later, Alexei cleared his throat.

"You haven't said a word about her."

Envy stiffened, then carried on as if he had no idea what the vampire meant. Alexei gave him a look that said he knew better.

"There is nothing to say. She's Unseelie royalty."

"You don't honestly give a shit about that," Alexei said. Envy's attention snapped to his second. The vampire's smile was all fang. "Your Highness."

Envy assisted the next demon in line, then strode to the other end of the room, swiping an icy glass of water from a tray. His cursed second trailed after him.

"Everything is under control here. You can go back to the Wild Court. Talk."

Envy's jaw strained. "Talk. Yes, open and honest communication worked so well for us before. There is nothing left for us to say."

"You knew she had secrets. You're just angry that she outplayed you. I didn't take you to have so much...pride."

Alexei was pushing Envy too far. Envy's eyes flashed and Alexei held his hands up, slowly backing away.

"You like her. Enough to consider breaking your rule. Don't let another sin get in the way. Do you think Wolf is sitting back? If you're all right with him taking her to his bed, his cock pounding all memories of you out, then fine. Leave her to it. She'll be better off."

Envy stood in one of his favorite galleries—where a statue of a fallen angel was proudly displayed. All the years his wings had been trapped, he'd come here, sipping a drink as he was doing now, plotting. With his court almost fully restored, his power was growing stronger, hour by hour. He summoned his wings now, allowing them to spread wide.

It felt good. The muscles between his shoulders straining as he moved them, testing the weight. His thoughts turned to Lennox, to the final battle.

Camilla hadn't been the one to deal the killing blow, Envy had made sure of that. He'd seen something in her face just before he drove his dagger through the Unseelie King. She did not like her father, but it would have cost something precious for her to murder him.

Camilla was good. Lennox had seen it. Hated it.

He tucked his wings in close, then leaned against the wall, his Dark and Sinful going down easy. A detail flickered across his memory. In the cavern where the Twin Pillars were, Camilla had been about to confess something to him.

Envy sipped his cocktail, turning that conversation over in his mind. Looking back, it was easy to see she'd been about to tell him who she really was. She'd known, the moment they entered the Wild Court, that he'd figure it out.

He had, though. Already known.

He scratched the back of his neck.

Truth be told, Envy had started suspecting much earlier. It was easier for him to blame her for betraying him; otherwise, he'd have to consider facing the truth. He'd recently been able to lie to others, but Envy had been lying to himself far longer.

Did his one-night rule truly protect his court, or did it prevent him from ever feeling heartbreak?

He finished his drink, staring into the glass. Camilla might not want to see him. She might be perfectly happy in the Wild Court. With Wolf.

That meddling prick Alexei, now Envy couldn't unsee Camilla and Wolf rekindling their flame.

Envy squeezed his eyes shut. That gods-damned Fae had truly gotten under his skin too. He knew the Unseelie would be attempting to win Camilla back. Maybe he already had.

Perhaps Wolf was holding her right now.

Jealousy froze the glass in his hand, until it began to crack, drops of bourbon leaking into his palm.

Envy glared at the physical proof of his displeasure.

"Gods' blood."

Miss Camilla Elise Antonius, lover, betrayer, Unseelie princess, drove him absolutely fucking mad, even here, realms away from Faerie.

The question now was, what Envy was going to do about it.

He sensed one of his spies a moment before he materialized, partially corporeal.

"I have news from the Wild Court, Your Highness."

His tone made Envy's skin crawl. "And?"

The spy handed him a folded piece of parchment.

Envy scanned the report, then crumpled it in his fist. "Fucking hell."

SIXTY-SEVEN

"ARE YOU READY?" Wolf's voice carried through Camilla's bedchamber.

She stepped out from behind the ornate dressing screen, her silk floor-length gown a beautiful lavender gray.

Camilla looked every inch an Unseelie princess as she situated a flower crown on her head. She twisted to the side, admiring the silver cuff she wore on one of her elongated ears. Little moons and stars were carved along the metal, an ode to her heritage.

She'd stopped wearing hunter green days ago, when the Prince of Envy made no attempt to contact her. When he'd left without uttering a single word, not even a curse.

She'd been foolishly hopeful. Those first few nights. Thinking he'd returned to his court, save them, then he'd be back.

Fighting with her.

Kissing her.

Playing games they both loved.

Surely he had something to say after... everything they'd been through. Camilla thought his freeing her from her father's cruel games meant he'd forgiven her. Or would at least allow her the chance to explain. To admit how terrible she'd felt, keeping this secret.

But she'd been so afraid. Scared that he'd react exactly this way.

His silence spoke loud and clear. The Prince of Envy was never coming back. And Camilla needed to move on with her life, help her brother

Ayden establish his temporary rule, then return home, to Wisteria Way. She missed her gallery, her cat, and Kitty.

Wolf gave her a long once-over, momentarily snapping his mouth shut.

The gown was indecent by Waverly Green standards—clinging to every curve like a dream. In the Wild Court it was rather tame. But she was not interested in playing courtly games. At least not here. Things might have been different if her mother had never kidnapped her, bound most of her magic, and made her grow up human. Maybe if she'd grown up in Faerie she'd be as abominable as her older brother and sister.

Wolf's gaze slid back up, his yellow eyes darkening. He'd made his intentions clear.

The blessed reprieve lasted only a moment. Then Wolf started in again.

"Ayden cannot rule in your father's place forever," he said. "We don't even know if he's capable. He might disappear one night and play carnival again."

"Well, until our mother decides to return, there's not much choice, is there?" Camilla said, her tone as gentle as she could manage.

"Your mother might not ever return, Princess."

They'd had this same disagreement for the last week, and it was growing tedious. Camilla wanted to return to Waverly Green. Had no interest in staying to help rule the Wild Court. She had no interest in ruling the court she was supposed to see to, either. It had been running as a principality for decades and was doing just fine.

"You know I have no wish to stay here," she said. "My brother will marry soon and have an heir. In a few decades the issue will resolve itself. His heir will rule over his court until—and if—our mother returns."

Over the past week, Wolf had helped her glamour the minds of all who'd been tortured by the king, a necessary evil, a choice Camilla did not make easily before sending them home again.

It was one of what would be many difficult decisions in the wake of Lennox's death.

Wolf wanted Camilla to take hold of the Wild Court before her debauched elder brother or sister scented opportunity. She'd immediately suggested Ayden step in. He had his faults, but he'd spent time among humans too.

"And you'll simply live alone in Waverly Green, glamoured for the rest of eternity? You know that doesn't suit you anymore. You have friends here, family. Me."

He'd struck the one chord that always hurt. Camilla did not want to be alone.

"We could mate for life," Wolf suggested. "I would help you acclimate again. You might not love me now, but love grows."

"Except for that bothersome little fact that I do not wish to stay here."

"Faerie?" he pressed. "Or the Underworld as a whole?"

Wolf was fishing. He wanted to ask what she thought about Prince Envy.

And that was much too complicated. Part of her wanted to pen him letters of apology, part of her wanted to paint his head onto an oversized donkey, pointing out that he was obviously an ass. But the longer they went without speaking, the more unsure she became.

Maybe it was for the best, giving up. Letting go.

Then Camilla wouldn't have to worry about him leaving again one day.

A knock sounded at the door, followed by a mewl.

Camilla rushed past Wolf to open the door, smiling for only the second time since she'd set foot in this court.

"Kitty! Bunny."

Her friend swept in, setting her cat on the floor, and hugged Camilla close. Then she stepped back to look Wolf over.

"Did I interrupt?" Lady Katherine asked, ever hopeful.

Camilla snorted. "Hardly."

"That tone is most unappreciated, ladies." Wolf shook his head. "Has no one in the mortal realm heard my legends recently? I might have to rectify that."

"How are you here?" Camilla asked, ignoring Wolf. "You didn't have to leave Waverly Green, Kitty."

"I did, actually. When your glamour broke, mine did too. Most inconveniently." Lady Katherine pulled her hair back, revealing her elongated ears. "It took some time for me to explain things to William, but he's coping surprisingly well. You're all right?"

Camilla lifted a shoulder, then dropped it.

Kitty had originally been tasked with asking Camilla to return to the Wild Court, a decade before, when Prim Róis had finally left her side. Then, when Camilla refused, Lennox had commanded Kitty to stay, to keep an eye on Camilla.

Little had he expected the two to unite as friends. And after her first refusal to return to the Wild Court, their true identities were a secret they never discussed.

Now, with her standing here, in all her Unseelie glory, Camilla knew Kitty had never forgotten her home.

"Bunny threw a fit that rivaled William's. Think she's tired of her glamour too."

Camilla smiled. The cat had transformed into her true being. A lovely little gray-and-white Fae lioness.

"You could have talked to me," Kitty said, her voice unusually soft. "About everything. We were close, weren't we?"

Camilla expelled a breath, nodding.

"Of course."

She wasn't sure how to say it. Part of her had worried that Kitty preferred being blissfully unaware, freed of Unseelie chaos. And the other part had worried that Kitty remained a tool for her parents. Someone sent to spy and report back. Lennox and his games were never-ending.

Instead of admitting that, Camilla said, "Vexley's a vampire now."

Kitty looked at her for a solid minute before bursting into laughter.

"How?"

Camilla told her. "I... I was the one to kill him, though."

"You beheaded him and set him on fire?" Kitty's eyes were round, a mixture of impressed and horrified.

"Not exactly. But I did behead him."

Wolf looked pained. "Unless you set him on fire and watched his ashes scatter, he likely isn't dead. A vampire isn't easy to kill."

Camilla felt oddly relieved. Vexley was a nightmare, but it was one less death on her hands.

Kitty remained far too amused. "Fitting. A mortal driven by his thirst for lust is now driven by his thirst."

"When he was a human at the vampire court he was...still Vexley."

Kitty laughed, delighted. "Please tell me he bedded a succubus."

"He held her tail and..." Camilla shuddered. "I'm sure you can imagine. Blood lust at the vampire court is a sight."

"Speaking of lust," Kitty said, far too casually, "I heard the most *interesting* rumor. It seems your Lord Synton is the Prince of Envy. Please"—she grabbed Camilla's hands—"please tell me you had wild demon sex with him."

Camilla's thoughts went immediately to the throne room.

"You did!" Kitty jumped. "Oh! I think I'm experiencing envy at the thought. How was it? I've heard his cock is huge. Is it?"

"Please, *don't* answer that," Wolf muttered.

"Oh!" Kitty practically bounced. "Please, please tell me it was as legendary as they say. There are rumors a portrait hangs above his bed, a kind of...visual stimulant. Would you sell your soul for another taste?"

Camilla sank her teeth into her lower lip. The portrait did hang above his bed, but nothing compared to the reality of the demon. She couldn't very well admit it aloud.

"I—"

"I'm curious too, Camilla, darling," a low voice drawled from the doorway. "Would you? Sell your soul?"

At the sound of *his* voice Camilla spun around, a hand pressed to her heart.

Envy stood in the doorway, his enormous glittering wings tucked close to his body.

Blood dripped from the feathers onto the floor.

For a horrifying second, she couldn't tell if the blood was his.

Envy stepped fully into the room, scanning Wolf, then Kitty. He gave no indication of surprise when he took in Kitty's true form. He did pause on the lioness, though, and she could have sworn amusement flickered before he banished it.

His attention settled on Camilla. Cold. Merciless.

She glanced again at the blood dripping off his wings. It wasn't ichor; it was Fae.

"What have you done?" Her voice was barely a whisper.

His gaze remained locked on hers when he said, "I'd like some privacy with the princess."

Kitty came up to Camilla's side. "No."

Envy arched a brow, waiting. His expression said *You owe me that much.*

Despite the dangerous glint in his eyes, Camilla silently agreed.

"Go," Camilla said. "It will be fine."

Kitty's jaw tightened. She looked to Wolf, who stared Envy down.

"We'll be close," he promised, gaze on the prince. It was a warning.

Wolf escorted her friend out, leaving Camilla alone to face the very angry demon prince.

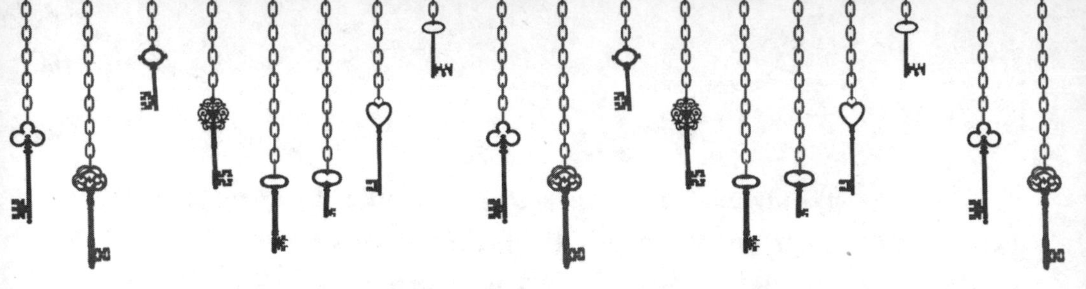

SIXTY-EIGHT

ENVY TOOK A perverse bit of pleasure at seeing the shock flicker over Camilla's features. She hadn't heard his approach, hadn't expected him to be standing there.

She certainly hadn't expected to see his wings.

Truth be told, *he* hadn't expected to be there either. And he likely wouldn't have been if Alexei hadn't taunted him.

A wild, snarling, territorial beast had risen inside him. He'd almost leashed the monster inside; then his spies brought news of an assassination attempt, sealing Camilla's fate.

He knew right then it was time to challenge the Fae.

Seeing the Wild Court as it had been after Lennox had opened the portal...

Envy would not leave her to the plotting of her wretched siblings.

If he had to throw her over his shoulder and magic her to his court, so be it. He didn't know the first thing about being a hero, but he excelled at being the villain.

Now that they were alone together, Envy looked Camilla over and swallowed thickly. His gaze snagged on the necklace she'd made of his ring, then hardened. If her cursed siblings had gotten to her first, they would have ripped it from her throat.

Camilla must have mistaken who had angered him.

"I'm sorry," she said, reaching up to undo the necklace. "I wanted to give this back to you..." She dropped her hands, looked at them. "I wanted to tell you the truth. I should have."

But he'd given her every reason not to.

When he'd told her how much he hated Unseelie royalty, she'd flinched.

Thinking back on that conversation now, when Envy had admitted what had happened to make him despise the king so much, he saw her reactions in a new light.

She'd paled when he told her the role her father had played. A tear had slipped down the curve of her cheek. She'd also apologized.

Envy thought it was that foolish mortal reaction of accepting blame for others' actions.

Now he knew. Camilla had been apologizing on behalf of her family.

Apologizing was no small thing for a Fae. It was something they rarely did.

And she'd just done so again.

Fresh anger iced the chamber.

"Do you know whose blood that is?" Envy pointed to the floor.

She swallowed hard, the column of her throat moving with the action.

"Some is Onyx's," Envy said. "The rest is from his guards."

Her gaze sharpened on him. "My brother?"

"Yes."

"You killed him? Are you mad?" she hissed. She looked around, as if searching for any spies. "You probably just started a war."

He gave her an amused look that seemed to rankle her more.

"Whose side will you choose, pet?"

She glared at him, notching her chin up.

Envy wasn't sure how he'd ever mistaken her for anything but royal.

"My own."

Devil, grant me sin. That tone, that haughty, defiant look.

He was inconveniently aroused.

"Your brother isn't dead. He's...caged."

Envy's smile was all teeth as he thought of Onyx. He'd thrown the scheming Unseelie Prince into the birdcage Lennox had crafted to torture Camilla. A clever ward would keep him from hearing or speaking to anyone outside his cage. There would be no plotting or escape.

Onyx would have a good long while to reflect on his sins.

"I spelled the bars, trapping him for eternity. Unless of course your other brother decides to grant him a pardon. Though I wouldn't count on that. Ayden will make a fine king. He seemed to have everything under control. Your doing, I imagine."

"I helped, yes." A tiny crease formed between her brows. "Why did you strike at Onyx?"

Without thinking, he reached over to smooth the crease away.

She flinched, and he dropped his hand.

"He plotted to kill you. My spies reported back."

If she was surprised by this revelation, she didn't appear so. If anything, she seemed to exhale relief. She'd known it was only a matter of time before her older brother or sister made a move.

"My mother will hear of this and fight—"

"Your mother hasn't been seen at court since she left you." Envy hesitated. "My spies have been looking for her for years. No one knows where she went."

Several emotions flickered across Camilla's face before she schooled her features into forced indifference. He understood how complicated their relationship must be. Understood that it wasn't easy to walk away from the ones who'd hurt us the most.

"She's been traveling. But she will eventually hear of this and return. This court means everything to her."

Envy wouldn't mind if the queen burned in the deepest, hottest pit of sorrow he could find, but he hated the worry in Camilla's voice.

"Don't," he warned quietly. "Don't romanticize her. For all we know, she is playing another game and couldn't be bothered."

He glanced around the suite. He could feel more and more of his court being restored and needed to get back.

"Do you want to take anything from here?"

"What?"

He knew she'd heard him. He also knew she was trying to figure out his plan.

Envy kept his smile to himself, walking around the room. He fingered some of the clothing. It was pretty. His tailors were better.

"If there's anything of sentimental value, grab it now."

If he listened quietly, he was almost certain he could hear her heart pounding.

He pivoted and stood before her, holding out his hand. She looked at it like it was a snake ready to strike.

"What are you doing?" she asked.

"Grabbing what has sentimental value to *me*."

He took her hand, braided their fingers together.

She didn't remove it.

"We're leaving. Unless you wish to stay here."

Her thumb stroked his, hesitating.

His heart raced.

A small eternity passed.

"Your rule..."

"Fuck the rules," he growled. "You're *mine*."

Her excitement hit him a second before her desire did.

Thank fuck. In all the stories, the damsel didn't get aroused by the villain threatening to steal her away.

But this was *their* twisted fairy tale.

"You can come back, of course, as you need," he said more softly.

Camilla gave a small nod. "This has never been my true home anyway. But wait—I can't leave without Kitty and Bunny."

A few moments later, after being ushered back in, Kitty promised to travel to House Envy on her own. She had family in the Wild Court she hadn't seen in years. Wolf gave Envy a hard look but hugged Camilla close. Promising he'd also visit soon.

Bunny gave Envy a long, lingering look of her own, then sauntered over. The unusually colored little lioness hopped into Camilla's arms, nestling in.

Envy dragged Camilla and her lion closer, wrapped his other arm around her waist, then magicked them all to his House of Sin.

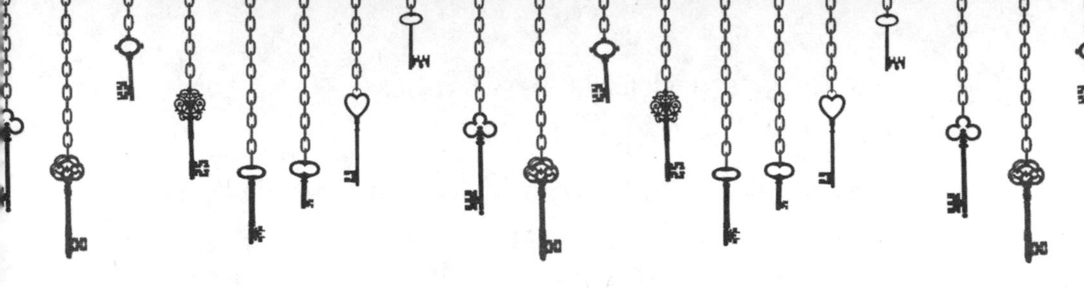

SIXTY-NINE

"WHAT DID I tell you?" Gluttony grinned, rubbing his hands together. "Pay up, brothers."

"You don't know that for a fact," Lust shot back sourly.

"The invitations said, and I quote, 'We would be honored to celebrate our betrothal with you,'" Gluttony said in falsetto. "Facts are facts, brother. You lost. Again."

Envy ignored the petty argument, his attention straying to the silver-haired beauty holding court with the Queen of the Wicked Emilia, her friend Lady Fauna, Lady Katherine, and—much to his *constant* annoyance—Wolf. The gods-damned silver-tongued Unseelie.

Though Envy supposed it was beneficial to his court to have him around; Camilla gently but playfully provoked his sin just to get a rise out of him.

And rise he did. Camilla's passion ignited his constantly.

They'd barely slept since they returned to his House of Sin. Once the last of his court had drunk from the chalice, chasing off the madness of no new memories, they'd focused on one another. Healing old hurts, forging a bond stronger than steel.

He was relieved to show her how spectacular his demons were. And spectacular they were tonight. They wore their best gowns and suits, their finest jewels. Their eyes as clear and cunning as ever as they flitted around the party, mingling with the other demons, showing off their riches. Attempting to inspire jealousy by sharing stories and discussing new art.

Envy had never been happier, seeing his court as it should be.

And Camilla...she was worth facing his fears.

Envy had never imagined the strength he'd feel the moment he became vulnerable.

His Unseelie princess had been a tireless lover, demanding he make love to her in every room, every floor of his sprawling House of Sin.

Harder, faster, gentler, *deeper.* Camilla loved ordering him around.

And Envy must be mad, because it made him hard as steel every time.

But he could only take orders for so long.

He'd push her down, spread her thighs wide, devouring *her* in the kitchens, on the dining room table, in their bedchamber, in the gallery. She'd arch up from the table, shouting his name, cursing him, praising him, bucking as he suckled every bit of her arousal, then flipped her over and fucked her until she came again. And again.

His court would hurry by, averting their gazes, though he knew they secretly adored Envy's infatuation. They wanted their prince as happy as possible, wanted him to enjoy all he'd fought for. And Camilla enjoyed stoking envy in everyone who knew she was the one to make him break his rule.

They'd made love on the throne every night: fingers, tongue, cock. And he wanted *more*. Forever. And since she wasn't human, they had all that time and more.

For the first time in his long existence, he wanted to experience *everything* with another.

More laughter, more quiet moments, more midnight snacks, strawberries dipped in chocolate, the two of them sprawled in front of the fire, talking of art.

More games and bringing out each other's human aspects that hadn't existed before.

More walking the hallways of House Envy, rearranging paintings and sculptures based on what she preferred. When they could manage not to tear each other's clothes off, they moved some of her art from Waverly Green, combining their collections.

It wasn't enough. Envy wanted more still.

More running his fingers through her soft hair, watching her drift off to sleep, her face peaceful. Those full lips parted in dreamy contentment.

More games to play—and he was delighted he didn't even know what they'd be yet.

Envy would remake worlds for her. Would break every rule to make her smile. He'd—

"Are you even listening?" Gluttony waved a hand in front of his face, shaking his head in disgust. "Witches' tits. You're worse than he is. He jabbed his thumb in Wrath's direction. And he's abhorrently in love. Look at him. He's making doe-eyes at Emilia right here."

The demon of war bared his teeth, his smile feral, so at odds with his finely made suit.

"One day you're going to gorge yourself on those words, brother." Wrath's voice was laced with dark promise.

Gluttony snorted, the sound filled with derision.

The reporter he was feuding with hadn't responded to the invitation Envy had sent, and he was *sure* Gluttony's foul mood had nothing to do with that.

"Don't count on it," Gluttony said. "I bet Lust will be next."

"Not a fucking chance in any of the realms combined. Where's Sloth?" Lust asked. "Maybe he'll make a chart and line up all the variables for me. I cannot fathom how you're all content to bed the same person for the rest of your days."

He shivered.

"Sloth went to find Pride," Wrath said, gaze landing back on his wife. "I saw a book in his jacket, though."

"Of fucking course." Lust groaned. "I'll see where he's hiding. If he doesn't start acting like a gods-damned demon, we're all going to get bad reputations." He jabbed a finger into Wrath's chest. "You need to lay down a law or something."

Wrath's gold eyes glittered. "First rule? Don't touch me again."

"Don't kill each other in this room," Envy said. "I just had the floors waxed."

He'd had the entire House scrubbed of any evidence of how close the court had come to falling. Looking at it now, no one would ever suspect they'd been on the brink of collapse.

Gluttony glanced around, brows knitted. "Where's Greed?"

"There was an issue at his gaming hell," Envy said. "He sent his regrets."

Gluttony snorted. "I'm sure he did. Prick."

Wrath and Gluttony began debating about boxing, and Envy took that as his cue to leave.

He strode down the corridor, walking to where Pride lounged in a chair he'd pilfered, his crown tilted to one side. His shirtsleeves were rolled to his elbows, showing corded muscle, his shirt half untucked from his trousers.

His head was tilted all the way back, his eyes closed. An empty glass hung from his fingers. Pride played the role of debauched prince so well, Envy wondered if he'd finally become that.

He stood over his brother, then kicked Pride's boot, drawing his gaze.

It was slow, unfocused.

"Party over, Levi?"

Envy noticed the rest of the empty bottles, the broken wineglasses. They'd been shoved into the alcove beside him.

This time Pride wasn't pretending to be the drunken royal.

"What happened?" Envy demanded.

Pride lifted a shoulder, dropping it as if he couldn't be bothered to respond or care.

Envy kicked him harder. "Answer the damn question, Luc."

"Sursea won't tell me anything."

The First Witch, Pride's consort's mother, had cursed them all when Pride and Lucia wed and then refused to dissolve their relationship. Witches and demons were sworn enemies, but that didn't stop Pride from falling in love with the one witch he shouldn't have. Lucia was strictly off-limits, but they chose each other, despite all the reasons they shouldn't have.

One day, Lucia left House Pride without a word. Pride didn't know if she'd been taken against her will, imprisoned somewhere, or given a True Death. He'd been searching ever since, even when the First Witch cursed them all, keeping them trapped in the Seven Circles for years. She'd done something worse to Pride before that, though, something he refused to speak of. Envy knew it had been the true root of the miscommunication between Pride and Lucia.

None of the demons felt anything but hatred for Sursea and her quest for vengeance.

"How convincing were you?" Envy asked.

Pride gave him a withering glare. "She knows where my wife is. Knows what happened. Do you think I showed any mercy?"

Envy thought Pride would never be as ruthless as he could be. He might hate the First Witch, but he loved Lucia and wouldn't hurt her mother.

"She's contained?" he asked.

Pride nodded. "Until I know what happened to Lucia, she stays at my House."

"I'm going to ask you something; you're not going to like it, but I don't particularly care. Understand?"

Pride narrowed his eyes but nodded again.

"Do you want Vittoria?"

"That's a bullshit question and you know it."

"Then answer it."

Pride's hand tightened on his glass.

"Are you keeping something from me?"

Envy smiled. "I've heard rumors. Courtiers are so interesting when they're drunk and think no one is listening."

"Get to the point, Levi."

Envy leaned down, lowering his voice. "I know you never fucked the goddess."

Pride had gone perfectly still.

"I don't know what your game is, why you let your court and wife think otherwise. I assume you have a reason. And that reason has to do with Sursea's meddling and magic."

He stared at his brother. Pride's expression was carved of stone. He'd locked his emotions down entirely, not giving away any secret.

Admittedly, Envy *hadn't* heard that rumor; it was a guess.

One that might prove to be true, given the way his brother had stopped breathing. If Pride hadn't been distracted and drunk, he would have sensed the lie.

"*If* Lucia is alive, if she's found happiness elsewhere, would you destroy that?"

Pride's teeth grinded together. "Would you hurt Camilla?"

He'd sooner rip out his heart. Again.

Envy pulled the folded parchment from inside his coat, handing it to his brother. Before he let it go, he said, "Don't screw this up."

Pride yanked the note from his hands, then read it over.

Envy watched as the drunkenness was quickly replaced by sharpness. Pride sat straighter, body tensed, reading the note again.

"How?" His voice was barely a whisper.

"My spies have been hard at work." Envy gave him a cold look. "Then Emilia's 'grandmother' whispered a secret in my ear a few months ago." Two, actually. That his House would soon fall, and the one he'd share now. "Lucia doesn't remember. Any of it."

"You saw her?"

Envy thought about the young woman he'd had kidnapped for a brief time to break the wards on Emilia's family home, then used to force Emilia to do his bidding. Even now, his thoughts of her were muddled, like he couldn't quite recall her face, even after their memory curse had been broken. Envy hadn't known it was Lucia and that bothered him.

Sursea was far too powerful for his liking.

He decided to leave out the part about him sedating her with magic, no need to enrage his brother. Desperate times had called for extreme measures. "Yes, I believe so. I think she might have a glamour, though. I didn't immediately recognize her when our paths crossed."

Something suspiciously close to hope lighted in Pride's gaze. "But she lives."

Envy nodded slowly.

"Make sure you know what you want before you seek her. If it's just your pride..."

Envy didn't finish the thought. Pride knew.

Pride uncoiled from his chair, note clutched tightly in his fist. He ran a hand through his hair, seeming unsure of what to do next.

"Well?" Envy pressed.

"Looks like I'll be traveling to the Shifting Isles soon."

"You likely only have one chance."

Pride gave him a genuine smile. "It's more than I had this morning."

He took off down the hall, disappearing around the corner.

Lust stepped from the shadows, his expression contemplative. "My money's on the goddess."

"Not a chance." Envy snorted. "Pride will choose Lucia. It's *always* been Lucia."

Mischief flared in Lust's charcoal gaze. "Shall we place a wager?"

"*Now* you want to bet?" Envy looked his brother over. "What was your bet with Gluttony, again?"

"I bet you'd be a stubborn prick. You lived by that gods-damned rule for centuries. It seemed like a sure win."

"Looks like my coffers will be as legendary as my cock." Envy grinned as his brother scowled. "I accept your wager. Pride wins back Lucia. Vittoria ends up with the werewolf."

"Or the new vampire prince."

Envy scoffed. "Blade doesn't consort with death goddesses. And he's already said he's choosing a vampire bride."

Lust tossed an arm around him, walking back toward the reception. "Not what I've heard. Our friend secretly enjoys dancing with true death."

"House Vengeance and Malice Isle as a united front." Envy shuddered at the thought. "Work your charm before we all live to regret it. If you're not amenable, maybe we can convince Wolf to seduce her. Hell, maybe she'll even keep the shifter, Fae, and vampire."

"Look at you, scheming already." Lust snorted. "*This* is why you're my favorite brother."

Camilla stepped into the hall, took one look at the brothers, and shook her head.

"Whatever you're plotting, stop." She leveled a cold look at Envy and his gods-damned desire for her flared. "I mean it. No games tonight."

Envy's mouth curved wickedly.

Oh, there would be games.

Tonight, however, he'd keep them in the bedroom.

Right where his cunning little fiancée liked them.

Envy and Lust entered the throne room behind Camilla, the party well underway. Emerald-encrusted trays towering with Dark and Sinfuls made the rounds, while a central fountain of demonberry wine cascaded in a dark, glittering wave down a tower and into hundreds of coupe glasses. House Envy twirled across the checkered dance floor.

Lust went to flirt with a demon near the shellfish table, where platters were laden with pearl-like delicacies and other oceanic marvels.

Envy stood in the shadows a moment after waving his brother off.

He chuckled when he saw Bunny, rubbing around Wrath's legs. The General of War glanced around quickly before scrubbing behind Bunny's ears, earning an amused look from Emilia at her husband's new friend.

Envy caught a flash of silver, winding its way around the crowd, heading toward the dais. His heart stuttered a beat as Camilla climbed the steps and slowly twisted, her gaze finding his across the room. Her mouth curved as she sat on his throne, her expression a wonderful, taunting promise of what was to come.

Later, after the last guest had gone, once the last drink had been drunk, Envy would take her in his arms, dancing her around the throne room.

Then he'd make all her fantasies come true.

SEVENTY

CAMILLA CLUTCHED ENVY'S arm, a thrill racing through her as he guided her down another corridor, blindfold snugly fitted over her eyes.

During breakfast, he'd casually mentioned he had a surprise, then sipped his coffee. Like he hadn't just ignited her curiosity, set her mind whirling in a hundred directions.

When she'd pressed him for more information, he'd just given her a roguish wink.

Once their meal was finished, he pulled out the blindfold. Camilla's thoughts turned to the night he'd used her robe's sash to cover her eyes, then kissed her *everywhere*.

Her husband-to-be knew how to drive her mad in the best ways.

The hard muscles of his arm flexed as he steered her down another corridor, their pace unhurried, unlike her heartbeat.

At first, she'd tried to mentally follow their path, mapping out what section of House Envy he'd taken her to. But she quickly gave up when it seemed like they'd doubled back in some places and ventured down hallways she hadn't explored yet.

"Are we close?" she asked, excitement lacing her tone.

She felt the smile in his voice when he answered.

"Almost."

He was as excited as she was.

Envy had surprised her. In the weeks following the truth of who she was, a tender, romantic side emerged when they were alone together.

Her fiancé wooed her often and with reckless abandon, as if he were making up for years of never permitting himself to have a soft side. Or maybe what he'd said was true—that Camilla made him want to do those things.

Gifts, walks in the garden, around the circle, all over the House, conversations about everything and nothing, lovemaking... Envy wanted to know her mind, body, and soul.

He still had his wicked side, which she loved equally. That side stirred her passions, fed her Fae nature unlike any other. Envy's gaze still glittered dangerously, still owned all her senses. They fucked as often as they made love and their appetites for each other were relentless.

She wondered whether he was part Unseelie or simply insatiable. Whenever she desired him, he was ready for her, ready to do everything she wanted and more. And their games, those were as tempting and gloriously sinful as ever.

They finally stopped. Camilla strained to hear any sounds that would indicate where they were. After the court had regained their memories, the castle was usually filled with pleasant noise.

Silence stretched. Though, distantly, Camilla almost swore she heard a sound like faint, tinkling bells.

Envy's lips brushed her ear and she shivered from the pleasant sensation.

"Ready?"

She bit her lip, then nodded.

Anticipation thickened the air, made her pulse pound harder. The damn demon was teasing the moment out, knowing she'd grow taut from the unknown.

Was he about to make love to her here? Was there a new gown? A new painting? A—

The blindfold fell away.

An enormous, arched silver door gleamed in front of them. Their reflections were distorted by the number of carvings on it. Runes.

Camilla's gaze swept over the door, above and around it; wisteria vines had been carved, so lifelike she would have thought they were real if it hadn't been for the silver.

Her attention snagged on the one part that wasn't solid silver—an emerald lock, shaped like a heart. She stepped forward, brushing her hand along the door.

The humming, bell-like sound intensified.

"It's gorgeous," she said. "Where does it go?"

When Envy didn't respond, she turned to him.

He held a gold key, also heart-shaped, with a tiny emerald that matched the lock. Her breath caught. It was her father's key. The Silverthorne Key.

"You took it," she whispered.

"I wanted to keep it away from the Wild Court," he said. "But I wanted to hold on to it in case you wished to use it."

She blinked the stinging from her eyes. He'd planned this before he knew she'd agree to come with him. Had hoped she would.

Envy pulled her into his arms and kissed the top of her head, holding her while she cried. When she quieted, he pressed one last kiss to her head, then stepped back, holding the key up for her to take.

"Feeling adventurous, pet?"

She stuck the key in the lock and twisted. The silver melted, revealing a long, narrow corridor. Camilla knew exactly where this led. It wasn't Silverthorne Lane. It was much better.

She grabbed Envy's hand and hurried into the tunnel, wondering how he'd managed such a thing. They emerged in her father's studio.

She heaved a contented sigh. Everything was just as she'd left it. Only a month or two had passed since she'd been there, but it felt like everything had changed inside her.

She donned a glamour, not as good as her mother's but one that allowed her to pass as human, and went to her home.

After speaking with her house staff and assuring them that all was well, Camilla pulled Envy into her bedchamber, then wrapped her arms around him, kissing him deeply until they were both breathless.

"Thank you," she murmured against his lips. "This is the best gift in the world."

Envy traced the curve of her face, tucked a strand of silver hair behind her ears, then kissed her nose.

"Your gallery, your memories of your mortal father—I know how important this city is to you. I don't want you to sacrifice anything to stay at House Envy."

He glanced around, his gaze pausing on the bed, then the door to the bathing chamber.

"Now we can spend the day here and come home at night."

"You're going to come back to Waverly Green too?"

He smiled. "As often as I can."

"What if I'd like to spend the night here?" she asked, tugging at his lapels.

Envy allowed her to lead him to the bed.

In a move too swift for a human to detect, he had her pinned beneath him, his body hard and ready.

"I'm sure we can find something tempting about that."

She smiled, unlacing his trousers. "I'm sure we can."

When he pushed inside and began those deep, rhythmic thrusts that made her body lose all control, Camilla felt as if they'd truly won it all.

SEVENTY-ONE

"There's one more surprise I might have forgotten to mention yesterday."

Envy stood beside the studio doors, giving Camilla the chance to enter first.

"This studio is yours whenever you'd like to create here," he said. "I know you've got your father's studio and the gallery in Waverly Green, but I want you to feel at home here, in House Envy, too."

Her attention traveled along the candlelit room, pausing on the unrolled canvas lying on the floor, a second sprawled across the mattress he'd had brought in.

The far wall was entirely comprised of windows—he'd had the iron grates replaced with silver, keeping the curling filigree design.

A wooden bookshelf soared the twenty feet to the ceiling and was stocked with rolls of canvases, paintbrushes, pencils, chalks, watercolors, charcoals, sketchbooks, clay, knives, and every possible object she could dream up to use, to create and mold to her heart's content.

There were gilded mirrors and fruits and other objects if she wished to paint a still life. Chairs and easels and stools. Frames in a thousand different sizes and shapes lay stacked neatly.

"It's perfect."

Flowers—gardenias and jasmine and wisteria—spilled out of urns and vases, the scents meant to invoke the good parts of her family's court.

Envy knew she had a fondness for wisteria, knew she didn't want to turn her back on her court entirely.

Though she'd made it abundantly clear she didn't wish to rule. Yet.

There was no telling what the future held—unless they were the divining Seven Sisters with their threads of fate, or the Triple Moon Mirror with its ability to see the past, present, and future, they would need to wait and see what tomorrow brought.

Ayden sent letters weekly, trying to convince her she was needed to balance the five-point star court. With their mother missing and father dead, two courts were without leaders. Three, technically, since Onyx was captive.

Camilla did not want to take up that royal mantle.

Envy would support her in any decision. But now wasn't the time for worrying about the future. This evening was about them.

Paint buckets in every shade of silver, purple, blue, yellow, white, and green lined the perimeter. Their colors, and the colors found within her favorite flowers.

Candles flickered everywhere.

"Tonight, I have a very special painting planned."

Camilla's silver gaze snapped to his, intrigue igniting in her eyes.

"Oh?" she asked, tone innocent.

As if she hadn't already figured out exactly what he'd planned. He watched her roll the buttons on her bodice between her fingers, waiting for him to order her around. But only in this setting. Camilla would have his balls if he ever tried that outside their bedroom games.

His mouth curved. "Take off your dress."

The silky gown pooled at her feet.

He admired her nude form, all tantalizing golden skin, hard nipples, and soft curves. She'd taken to wearing lingerie only sometimes now, keeping him constantly guessing what was beneath her clothes. Skin or lace. He liked it all.

Envy jerked his chin toward the mattress and Camilla stepped back, stopping when the backs of her legs brushed against it.

He dipped a finger into the silver paint, then traced the swell of her breast, curled around her peaked nipple, then drew a line down to her navel.

Camilla's skin pebbled from the cool liquid paint, her breathing turning erratic.

He swirled another finger into a lighter silver paint, then drew his hands up the sides of her thighs. Camilla watched him with a hungry, silent stare. She wanted him to use her body as a canvas. Had wanted it for quite some time. Tonight, they'd both get their wish.

He considered the green paint, then dipped both hands into the one that matched his eyes best. His palms dripped with it, and Camilla let out a little gasp when he clapped both hands to her plush bottom, leaving his mark right where he wanted.

"Sit down, love."

Camilla's gaze sparkled. She did as he asked, making sure to slide her body across the canvas he'd laid out on the bed.

He stripped, enjoying the way her pulse ticked faster with each layer he slowly removed. When he kicked his trousers off and his length sprang free, she wet her lips.

She sat up, like she was about to lick him from tip to root, then stuck her hands deep into the silver paint. She tossed a handful of liquid silver at him, laughing as it dripped down his chest, splattering his erection.

"That, my love," Envy purred, "means war."

He unleashed his wings, knowing how much she liked them.

Camilla traced the emerald plumage, her touch gentle, stimulating. He almost forgot his plan. Just as his brilliant wife-to-be had plotted. He grabbed a bucket and tossed its contents at her, loving the squeal of delight as she shrieked and jumped back.

She tossed a bucket of hunter-green paint at him, laughing as he swore.

Soon they were both covered in paint, panting and rolling across the canvas. His wings became a mess of wild color.

"Fuck me, now," she demanded at last, breathless.

"With pleasure."

He slammed inside her, and they both cursed.

Camilla's walls clenched around him, milking him as he thrust in and out, the paint erotic as it glided over their skin, their love creating its own masterpiece. Camilla's nails dug into his shoulders, right between his wings.

She tugged him closer, wrapped her legs around him.

He fucked her hard, their bodies smearing the paint all over in wild strokes.

He slipped a hand between them, playing with her clit until she panted.

They both roared as they came, bucking until each last ounce of pleasure had rocked through them. He knew, without a doubt, that the work below them would be the most prized painting in his collection.

They lay entwined for several long minutes; then Camilla climbed on top of him.

"More."

He admired her as she rolled her hips, taking him slow and deep as she set the pace. Then he flipped her over, shot them out through the window, then flew up until they were soaring and made love to her among the stars.

At some point, they returned to the studio, rolled around in the paint some more. Camilla demanded he climb on top of her, extend his wings so she could hoist her legs up over them. He did as his princess commanded. Holding her legs straight up, bracing them first against his shoulders, pumping into her hard and fast, their skin clapping in pleasure.

Later, once they'd finally managed to drag themselves away from their art, he had the piece framed. He grinned at Camilla, splattered from head to toe and every delicious crevice in between in a rainbow of colors.

"Where should we hang this?"

She pretended to think for all of one moment.

"I know just the place, Your Highness."

She led him to their bedchamber, then glanced up at the ceiling, brows raised expectantly.

He tossed his head back and laughed.

Apparently, his legendary art was being retired.

Envy couldn't imagine a more perfect replacement.

Before he could offer any sort of retort, Camilla drew his mouth to hers and kissed him.

"I love you," she whispered as she moved back, gaze searching.

He stared at her, heart pounding. Truth slammed into him.

And for once, he didn't lie in return.

"I love you, too."

Soon, they were tangled up in his sheets—dried paint flaking off onto the hunter-green silk—and Envy found he didn't care about anything but the female he'd happily break all his rules for, from now until forever fucking more.

ACKNOWLEDGMENTS

First, a huge thank-you to my readers. (Both old and new alike!)

Thank you for coming along on this journey as my work shifted into the adult realm. From the very beginning of the Kingdom of the Wicked series, I'd hoped I would one day get to share each prince's story—and maybe even a goddess or werewolf or vampire prince, too—so this has been an absolute dream come true. I love your enthusiasm and how deeply you've come to care for the Seven Circles and all these wicked, sinful characters.

On the publishing side of things, I am infinitely grateful to my agent, Barbara Poelle, who championed these books while they were still mere dreams. My team at Irene Goodman, Heather Baror-Shapiro at Baror Intl, Sean Berarad at Grand View.

Helen O'Hare, editor goddess and amazing partner in publishing crime, I cannot thank you enough. I am so thrilled that we get to keep working together. I think we're having more fun than each of the demon prince's stories we're working on next. This book is the book of my dreams because of your edits.

To my whole Little, Brown team, I am so lucky to work with each of you. Thank you for all that you do behind the scenes to help usher these books into the world. Your excitement, your enthusiasm, your hard work and creativity is appreciated beyond measure. Gabrielle Leporati, Danielle Finnegan, Gianella Rojas, Linda Arends, Liv Ryan, Mary Tondorf-Dick, Bruce Nichols, Craig Young, Sabrina Callahan, Judy

Clain, Gregg Kulick, Taylor Navis, Elece Green, Meg Miguelino, Martha Bucci, Cyanne Stonesmith, Sharon Huerta, Suzanne Marx, Raylan Davis, Claire Gamble, Karen Torres, copyeditor Barbara Perris, and audiobook narrators Steve West and Marisa Cain.

To my lovely UK team at Hodderscape, you are all absolutely brilliant and I could not be more grateful for everything you do. Your support is as legendary as Envy's art collection. Molly Powell, editor extraordinaire, thank you for your wickedly delightful notes and early support of Envy as a romantic lead. Kate Keehan, our messages always brighten my day, and I am SO happy we have two more princes of sin to go wild over. Natasha Qureshi, Sophie Judge, Laura Bartholomew, Aaron Munday, Claudette Morris, Carrie Hutchinson and the whole team, thank you a million times over for all that you do.

Mom, Dad, Kelli, Ben—love you all beyond words. Dogwood Lane Boutique—AKA my sister's store and my favorite retail therapy, huge thank-you for keeping me and my home as stylish as the Houses of Sin.

Stephanie Garber, I say it all the time, but I am so grateful for our friendship. Anissa de Gomery, I adore you to pieces and love our chats. Thank you for being such an amazing friend. Isabel Ibañez and J. Elle, you are the best.

Book sellers, librarians, and every single reader who shares a post online, tells their friends about this series, and spreads so much joy and positivity, thank-you will never seem big enough of a word. You are more magical than you know. I cannot wait for our next adventure.

I am also infinitely grateful for Ayman Chaudhary (@Aymansbooks) and Pauline (@thebooksiveloved) for their early support of the Kingdom of the Wicked world on TikTok, and to everyone on BookTok who has come together for the love of books. You are absolute treasures. I hope all the good you put out into the world comes back to you in a million wonderful ways and that your next books are all five-star reads.

ABOUT THE AUTHOR

Kerri Maniscalco grew up in a semi-haunted house outside NYC, where her fascination with Gothic settings began. In her spare time she reads everything she can get her hands on, cooks all kinds of food with her family and friends, and drinks entirely too much tea while discussing life's finer points with her cats. She is the #1 *New York Times* bestselling author of the Stalking Jack the Ripper series and the Kingdom of the Wicked series. *Throne of the Fallen* is her adult debut.